Burn, Missouri, Burn

"*Burn, Missouri, Burn* is a fine novel, and it should launch a long and successful career as a historical novelist for Randal L. Greenwood. Writing with passion and power, Greenwood tells the story of the Civil War in the western states of Missouri, Kansas, and Arkansas. His characters are compelling and his research impeccable. I'm already looking forward to his next novel."

—James Reasoner, author of *Rivers of Gold* and *The Healer's Road*

BURN, MISSOURI, BURN

RANDAL L. GREENWOOD

A TOM DOHERTY ASSOCIATES BOOK
NEW YORK

This is a work of fiction. All the characters and events portrayed in this book are products of the author's imagination or used fictitiously.

BURN, MISSOURI, BURN

Copyright © 1995 by Randal L. Greenwood

Cover art by Charles Keegan

A Forge Book
Published by Tom Doherty Associates, Inc.
175 Fifth Avenue
New York, N.Y. 10010

Forge® is a registered trademark of Tom Doherty Associates, Inc.

ISBN: 0-812-53455-7

First edition: December 1995

Printed in the United States of America

0 9 8 7 6 5 4 3 2 1

Lovingly dedicated to my Aunt Evelyn Prather, who has been like a second mother to me. Her encouragement helped guide me through periods of countless self-doubts. She made sure I had the money to attend the writer's conferences that were a necessary element in making this dream come true.

Acknowledgments

I want to thank Robert Gleason, formerly of Tor Books, for believing in my book, *Burn, Missouri, Burn*, despite its enormous size for a first-time novelist. He had the foresight to see my novel as a series and, for that, I am grateful. He has helped make my dream come true. I would also like to thank Harriet McDougal, Nadya Birnholz, and the staff for completing the job Bob Gleason began. My special thanks to my agent Nancy Yost of the Lowenstein Agency in New York for negotiating my contract and soothing a rookie's nerves and concerns. Thanks to Linda Quinton, Larry Yoder, and the sales staff of Tor/Forge Books for getting out there and selling my book. You make it work.

A special thanks to Lois Harvey, Cynthia Coker, and Kenneth and Midge Greenwood for proofreading my manuscript and catching most of my mistakes. Thanks to Mom and Dad and Aunt Evelyn for their encouragement and for keeping me motivated. They eagerly awaited each new chapter as I wrote it, and their interest helped me see it through.

Thanks to my wife, Rebecca, for seeing to it I had the time to write and for helping keep a roof over our heads and food on the table. To my children—Evan, Amber, and Ciara—who understood when I had to take time away from them in order to write.

Special thanks to novelist Johnny Quarles and his wife Wendy Quarles for taking the time to read my book and for giving me their honest opinion and encouragement. They have gone out of their way to help a complete stranger and fellow writer when others probably wouldn't have. They did all they could to assist me in finding an agent and a publisher and I can't thank them enough. Their friendship is deeply appreciated.

I wish to thank Wilson Powell of Batesville, Arkansas, for his historical information and description of the area. A special thank you to Stephen Burgess (and his brother) of Fayetteville, Arkansas, who gave me a personal guided tour of the Cane Hill, Arkansas, battlefield and shared his insights.

Last, but not least, I want to thank a man I have never met but who unknowingly shaped my life, Harold Kieth. Harold Kieth wrote a book called *Rifles for Watie*, published in 1957, and it won the Newbery Award for "most distinguished contribution to children's literature." I loved his book and it is still one of the best I have ever read. He instilled in me a love for the American Civil War and an interest in the war west of the Mississippi that has been with me all my life. I can offer no greater tribute than to say he gave me a lifelong love for books and a desire to write a novel set during the Civil War. I have fulfilled the dream Harold Kieth planted so long ago in one little boy's heart. Thank you, Harold.

I used these books and sources for authentic information about Jo Shelby's cavalry and the guerrilla war in the Trans-Mississippi Region: *Shelby and His Men, or the War in the West*, by John Newman Edwards, published in 1867; *General Jo Shelby, Undefeated Rebel*, by Daniel O'Flaherty, published in 1954; *William Clarke Quantrill, His Life and Times*, by Albert Castel, published in 1962; *Gray Ghosts of the Confederacy*, by Richard S. Brownlee, published in 1958; and *Quantrill and the Border Wars*, by William Elsey Connelley, published in 1909.

CONTENTS

Foreword

This book is a historical novel based on actual Civil War events. General Jo Shelby and his Iron Brigade really existed, and all the campaigns and battles in this book actually took place. Although the rest of my characters are fictitious, and are not made to represent anyone living or dead, their parts were actually played by various real persons. The Kimbrough, Bartok, Cahill, Stryker, Farnsworth, Covington, Lightfoot, Burkes, Mayes, Farley, and Thomas families and all the slaves are fictional. There wasn't a Third Kansas Cavalry during the war; all the men assigned to it are therefore fictional, including General Kessington and Major Kenton Doyle.

Colonel Shelby's and other real people's conversations with my fictional characters are made up, but within the scope and personality of Jo Shelby and other historical persons. Briarwood and all the plantations are fictional places, but the events that happened there really occurred on plantations in Missouri and Arkansas and throughout the South. It is my hope to give an impression of the effects the war had on people in Missouri and Arkansas—why they fought and died, and what life was like for those that lived it. The Trans-Mississippi region, located west of the Mississippi River, has largely been ignored by history books and writers in general. The bloody border battle between Missouri and Kansas escalated into a fiery, full-fledged war unequaled in the history of the United States. The Union ordered entire counties emptied of Southern people; their homes and properties were stolen or destroyed. Neighbor fought neighbor; homes and towns, burned. There were roving bands of guerrillas, bushwackers, and freebooters working for both sides, and some just stole for themselves. Through all this, there were men of honor and courage that fought in regular army units, both Union and Confederate. Both sides fought for what they believed in. Quantrill and the other guerrillas are largely condemned, but I think it is important to understand why they acted as they did. It is time the Jayhawkers and the Kansas Red Legs are recognized as just as evil if not worse than the bushwackers. It is my hope that history will come alive to the reader, and that a greater sympathy for the Southern people will be gained.

Hugoton, Kansas   Randal L. Greenwood
    July 28, 1993

1

Moonlight Skirmish Among the Dead

He felt it first as a gentle nudge, easy to ignore. Then a stiff poke, followed by a rough shake. Sounds drifted into his sleep-fogged mind. "Ross, wake up! There's cavalry comin'."

Sergeant Ross Kimbrough jerked upright into a sitting position, instantly searching behind his neck for the butt of the sawed-off, double-barreled shotgun he carried on his back in a special holster. He felt a firm hand grab his wrist, stopping him from drawing his weapon.

"Easy, Ross. It's me, Jonas."

Through eyes still glazed with the mist of sleep, he struggled to focus on the face before him. The low, dancing light cast by the dying embers of the campfire formed grotesque shadows across the face of wiry Jonas Starke. "What, Jonas?"

"Cavalry comin' down the road from the north, Sergeant. From the sounds of it, there's a passel of 'em."

Ross quickly rolled out from between his blankets and rose to his feet. A lingering soreness stabbed at him, a painful reminder of the rough day's march.

Captain Jo Shelby had assigned him to picket duty for the night. As sergeant in command of the camp guards, he stood his watch first, then took his turn at sleep. Captain Shelby's company, the Lafayette County Cavalry, now dismounted, was assigned to cover the retreat of General Beauregard's Confederate army moving south from Corinth, Mississippi, to their new base of operations at Tupelo.

For two days the Southerners had been moving slowly south. Yankee cavalry made occasional probes along the road hoping to locate the rear of the Confederate army, but so far they had not pressed the attack.

Ross turned to Terrill Fletcher, who had been sleeping beside him. Terrill was awake and heard the exchange between Ross and Jonas. Ross gave his order. "Fletch, wake the men and get them ready. Tell Captain Shelby we might be under attack, and be quick about it!" Seconds later, Terrill began rousing the soldiers from their slumber.

Ross hurriedly gathered his cast-off equipment. He reached for his musket, still leaning against the tree where he had left it earlier, and turned to follow Jonas toward the men standing guard on the perimeter. The full moon cast eerie, forbidding shadows from behind the trees lining the hard, packed road along which the two men moved.

Ross felt glad to be in open country and away from the low, marshy ground around Corinth, Mississippi. The Rebel army suffered horribly while stationed there. Bad drinking water, exposure, and disease decimated the ranks, causing a steady stream of the sick to be shipped south from the city. The dead, mounting in numbers, quickly filled local cemeteries. The Southerners finally abandoned the city, defeated not by Union guns, but by unhealthy conditions. The Confederate evacuation of Corinth at first went unnoticed by the soldiers of Union General Halleck. The Union troops were slow to pursue.

Ross reassured himself the sawed-off shotgun was still in the custom-made holster on his back. He felt the cool, carved pistol grip jutting from the holster's top. The weapon had been his constant companion since the days when he had ridden with Jo Shelby against the Free-Staters of Kansas. When the Southern War of Independence began, Ross was already an experienced fighter trained in the harsh arena of border war. He had personally sent many a Jayhawker bandit to an early and permanent rest.

Ross affectionately called his sawed-off shotgun "Double Twelve," because it was twelve inches long, twelve gauge, and double barreled. Loaded with double-ought buck it was an awesome, room-clearing weapon at close range.

Ross and Jonas moved with speed over the crest of the hill and through the somber gravestones of the cemetery that lay beside the road they were ordered to hold. The wind whispered through the lonesome monuments glowing white in the moonlight, which gave mute testimony to those whose days of trial were ended.

Jonas's eyes bulged wide in fear. "It's bad enough we camped beside a graveyard, now the damn blue-bellies gonna jump us too!"

Ross laughed and felt the surge of adrenalin pumping through his veins. Danger is a powerful drug, and Ross loved it.

They neared the stone fence bordering the north end of the cemetery, then turned for the west corner, the one closest to the road. Rebels from the picket line stood ready, muskets pointing down the hill toward the bridge below.

Ross approached a familiar figure standing at the wall. "What's out there, Rube?"

The veteran in his ragged slouch hat leaned over and spat a stream of tobacco juice over the stone wall. "I don't know, Ross. We haven't seen 'em yet, but we can darn sure hear 'em. Definitely a cavalry column coming this way. I'm guessing there's at least a company of 'em and they're takin' their time."

Sergeant Ross Kimbrough whispered down the line, "Everyone keep quiet and stay low. Don't shoot till I give the yell. It might be some of our boys."

Ross leaned his musket against the wall. He quietly pulled Double Twelve from its holster as he knelt behind the wall and waited. He felt with his thumb, making sure the percussion caps were still in place over the nipples and under the hammers of his shotgun. Using the same thumb, he cocked both hammers and heard the reassuring click as they locked into position. Ross strained his eyes, looking for any movement on the dark road. A full moon behind and above their backs illuminated the panorama, casting deep shadows of their bodies and painting the scene with a ghastly glow. The road led downhill to a bridge spanning a small creek, up a slight incline, then turned right where it disappeared from view behind a wall of trees.

The cavalry remained hidden from view, but the sound was unmistakable. The rhythmic beat of the horses' hooves on the hard road, the jingle and slap of sabers and carbines against the soldiers' and horses' sides, combined with the creaking of leather, all gave familiar signals to those who lay in wait. Finally, two riders appeared and moved at a slow walk down the small hill. They crossed the bridge. They started up the hill where the Rebels lay in wait. As the two riders reached the end of the bridge, a column of troopers appeared, riding four abreast behind them.

Ross knew they couldn't wait for the column to reach their ambush. Long before the two point riders reached their position, one of them would surely notice soldiers waiting behind the wall. Through observation, Ross realized the point riders were inexperienced. The nearest man kept his eyes on his companion while he listened to a joke. Both men paid little attention to the cemetery.

Ross wondered why this column didn't have scouts further out front, especially in enemy country. Only inexperienced or poorly led green troops would make such a drastic mistake. Men would die for such carelessness.

"Rube," whispered Ross, "I'm going after the closest point guard. Cover his buddy. If he'll surrender we'll take him; if he tries anything, shoot him!"

Rube Anderson nodded, and tightened the grip on his Mississippi rifle. As the Yankees approached the low rock wall of the cemetery, the point riders laughed loudly. The head of the cavalry column cleared the bridge and headed up the hill.

The point riders neared Ross, with only the wall separating them. A great commotion stirred behind Ross, as the rest of Shelby's command rushed forward through the cemetery to reinforce the picket line. The Union point riders reined in their horses, frightened by the sudden sound of Shelby's Rebels moving through the cemetery toward them.

Taking advantage of the distraction, Ross jumped up on the wall and brought the shotgun crashing down on the head of the closest rider. Simultaneously, he gave a rebel yell, "Yaaaah Hooooo!" The Yankee slumped in his saddle and slid to the ground.

The horse ridden by the other point rider skittered sideways, then reared up, dumping the trooper on the ground. Ross ran over and stuck Double Twelve into the stunned man's chest. "Over the wall, Yank, and be damn quick about it!"

At the sound of Ross's rebel yell, six Confederate muskets lit the night, hurling their deadly messengers at the advancing column. Two riders were hit. One sprawled on the ground, the other slumped in his saddle. The surprised column halted, milling around in confusion. A Union officer brandished his sword over his head and charged toward the cemetery. Encouraged by his actions his soldiers followed.

In the confusion, Rube and Ross got the two Yank prisoners behind the wall. They delegated a guard for the prisoners and sent them back toward camp.

Shelby's company reached the low stone wall and stood, rifled muskets at the ready. Captain Shelby, now at the wall, gave his orders. "Cut 'em down, boys. Fire!"

At his command eighty muskets lit up the pre-dawn night, rattling like a string of firecrackers. The Union troopers were nearly upon them and most of the first two ranks of cavalry went down from the musket fire. Men tumbled and rolled from their horses. Screams and whinnying from dying and wounded chargers pierced the moonlit night. The cavalrymen in the second rank over-ran those troopers in front, still scattered in heaps on the ground, and more went down. Horses stumbled in the confusion. The survivors picked their way through the mayhem and continued the charge. Miraculously, the gallant lieutenant still led his men.

The night filled with the din and flash of battle as the Rebels began loading and firing as fast as they could. The Yankees began a sputtering return fire from a few carbines, but most carried drawn swords and few of them came close enough to use them.

The magnificent Union officer rode his black stallion directly to the wall. His swinging sword bit deep into human flesh as a Rebel soldier screamed in pain and fell backward, yanking the sword free of the officer's hand. The officer drew a revolver from his holster as his horse pawed the air.

Ross admired the Union officer's cool courage, but it was clear he intended to shoot Captain Shelby who, unaware of danger, was busy directing his troops.

Ross tightened his trigger finger and Double Twelve belched forth fire and buckshot at near point-blank range. The blast caught the gallant officer full in the chest, flipping him from his horse and spilling him rudely onto the road. When the Yankee lieutenant went down, the rest of the Union line wavered, slowed, then broke in disordered retreat for the bridge and rode out of sight.

The road and the area alongside of it from the bridge to the wall lay littered everywhere with horses and men stilled by death. Among the dead, here and there, a wounded soldier cried for help. Soldiers with minor wounds tried valiantly to crawl or walk away from the battlesite. The Rebels held their ground and let the wounded escape.

For Ross, the sight of injured horses struggling to gain their feet, or limping away on shattered limbs, ripped at his guts. He had seen it time and time again, but he never got used to it. The soldiers were here by choice and took on the sheer butchery of war willingly. For the horses it was another matter. Ross had always loved horses and it was not the brutality of man against man that struck a chord in him. It was man's habit of inflicting his barbarity on poor, helpless animals that touched his heart. The horses were nothing more than innocents forced into harm's way.

Captain Jo Shelby walked along the line of his soldiers. "Steady men, hold your positions and be ready. The blue-bellies might try again!"

Ross glanced at the still form of the Yankee officer, sprawling like a broken doll in the middle of the road. There was not a single sign of life, and Ross felt a tinge of remorse. "Took a load of guts to lead that charge up here," Ross thought. "Death makes few distinctions between the brave and the coward, claiming both equally. When you're dead, you're all one and the same."

Within the hour it was clear the Yanks had all they wanted and would satisfy themselves with the knowledge of the location of the end of the Rebel column. Captain Shelby issued orders to round up the Yankee wounded that were capable of walking. The dead and seriously wounded would be left for the Federals sure to follow. Wounded were a luxury the Rebels could ill afford and would only slow the retreat. Shelby knew better than to deplete precious medical supplies desperately needed by his command. As the first rays of the morning light streaked the sky, the cleanup was well under way.

Confederate casualties were very light with only one killed, one seriously wounded, and a couple of soldiers with minor wounds. The dead Confederate soldier, Bobby Jo Canton, was wrapped in a blanket and laid to rest in the graveyard. A few simple words were hurriedly said as his friends gathered around him. Ross had hardly known the lad. He was just another young Missouri boy taken before his time.

Weapons and equipment were collected and water given to the Yankee wounded left on the field. Within two hours the Southern column was under way once more, unmolested and unchallenged.

Three days later the Confederates camped near the peaceful town of Tupelo, Mississippi. Ross received word Captain Shelby wanted to see him. He reported immediately.

"Sergeant Kimbrough, by God it's good to see you." Captain Shelby smiled as he shook hands. "I wanted to let you know how pleased I am with the way you handled your responsibilities on the way down here. Your quick response might very well have saved our company and definitely protected our retreating column. I just wanted to thank you in person for a job well done."

Ross drew himself to full attention. "Thank you, sir. We were only following orders."

"You handled yourself well Sergeant, as you have in the past. Please, stand at ease." Jo Shelby walked behind his field table and took a seat while Ross relaxed. "I received some good news today I think you'll want to hear. I've a commission from the Secretary of War to return to Missouri and recruit a cavalry brigade." Ross could see the twinkle in Captain Shelby's eyes as he continued. "They're letting me take the remainder of the Lafayette County Cavalry with me."

The news lifted Ross's spirits. "That's great news, Captain." He paused for a moment as he studied his commander's face. "I was never meant to be in the infantry and I have to admit I'm damn tired of walking everywhere we go. We all remember how good it was to be cavalry before they dismounted us. I can't wait to get a good horse underneath me again."

"I know it's been hard on the men. After all, they signed on to be cavalry troopers, but orders are orders." Shelby sighed deeply as he shifted in his chair and leaned forward. "Some damned general sitting behind a desk somewhere felt it would be difficult to get the horses across the Mississippi. In truth, I feel it was just an excuse to dismount our cavalry. Time and time again I've heard generals leading infantry brigades say how it's infantry that wins the war." He dropped his clenched fist on the desk for emphasis. "I disagree."

Jo Shelby stood and leaned forward on his field desk. "Cavalry, I believe, if used properly, can do more toward winning the war than infantry ever will." Captain Shelby, fired with enthusiasm for his topic, began to pace around the tent as he talked, gesturing for emphasis. "I believe a fast moving cavalry troop can tie up more enemy units and be much more effective in combat. Missouri is a different field of operation than most of the Confederacy, but I believe my tactics would work anywhere if properly implemented."

Intrigued, Ross asked, "What sort of tactics are you talking about, Captain?"

Shelby stopped and clasped his hands behind him as he studied Ross. An odd twinkle came into his eyes. "It's right there in front of you, Sergeant, and yet, like so many others, you just don't see it. Let me explain. We started out as cavalry and later, when we crossed the Mississippi, we were changed to infantry. We've been forced to learn and adapt to infantry tactics." He paused for a moment as if to build drama. "What would happen if we were to take these same strategies and combine them with cavalry tactics?"

Ross hadn't taken time to consider such tactics, but now, when Captain Shelby mentioned them, he wondered why it hadn't occurred to him. "I can see where it might prove useful."

"Think of the implications, Sergeant. The cavalry offers superior mobility. We have the power to move our men great distances and to do it swiftly. Once there, dismount the men and fight them like infantry. It not only makes sense to make a lesser target of the men, but it saves the loss of our horses as well."

Shelby sat on the edge of the table as he warmed to his subject. "I've noticed again and again the effectiveness of artillery. At a critical moment in battle, it can sway the action in your favor. I intend to have fully mounted artillery attached to our brigade once we have it formed. Where we go, they will follow."

Shelby's eyes were as enthusiastic as a new teacher's, eager to teach his first students all he knows. "The most important thing I have learned from being in the cavalry is the weakness of the cavalry sword in battle. A sword is a mean weapon in close, but you never get close enough for them to be effective in most battles. I believe pistols have much more to offer. Outfit each trooper with two or more revolvers and we can command more firepower and concentrate it quicker at short range than any unit we face." A sly smile crossed

Shelby's face. "I think we can give the Yankees a lot more than they bargained for when we get back to Missouri."

"Captain, I believe in what you're saying, and you know I'd follow you to hell itself if you ordered me to go, but I don't understand why you've explained all this to me. Pardon me for saying so, sir, but I'm just a sergeant."

Shelby looked at Ross as if it all should be apparent to him. "Sergeant Kimbrough, you've been with me for a long time. I have seen few men that can ride, shoot, or scout better than you. I'm telling you all this because I want you to be chief of my scouts." He paused as he let his words sink in. "It's important now, but it will be even more significant when we raise our command back in Missouri. Will you accept the assignment?"

Ross, stunned by the news, eased himself into a chair. "It would be an honor, Captain, but I hope you'll let me pick my men."

"Of course, Sergeant. How many do you think you'll need?"

"Well, I think four will do for a start. I'd like Jonas Starke, Terrill Fletcher, Rube Anderson, and Bill Corbin."

"You've got 'em." Captain Shelby walked around the desk and sat down again in his chair. "Here is the plan. Tomorrow morning we'll board the train here at Tupelo and take it to Meridian. We'll march from there on foot to the Mississippi River, and it will be your responsibility to find a way to get the company across the river. That could prove to be difficult, but I think you can handle it. The Yanks have control of the river, and gunboats regularly patrol the area. I would like to cross in the vicinity of Helena, Arkansas."

"If it can be done I'll find a way, Captain. I'll gather my men and get them ready to go." Ross pulled himself to attention and saluted.

Captain Jo Shelby returned his salute. "See to your men, Sergeant. We leave at dawn."

The next morning, the dismounted Lafayette County Cavalry boarded the train at Tupelo and began the slow rail trip to Meridian. Already the effects of war had taken their toll on the rail-line. The tracks and rolling stock were in a deplorable state. The train had to inch its way slowly over the worst sections. There were no passenger cars available, so men were loaded on flat cars and in box cars. Ross rode most of the way perched on top of a box car.

The soot and ash from the old steam engine made his eyes burn and his flesh itch, but it sure beat walking. The men were in excellent spirits, for they all knew they were headed home and it had been a long time since they had seen their families and their loved ones.

When they arrived in Meridian, they marched on foot. The summer heat and the rising dust from their marching feet churned up clouds of dust that settled upon the veteran troops. Still, they were happy and marched with order and pride.

When they reached the mighty Mississippi River, Shelby led his men to a camp in a large grove of cypress trees draped in Spanish moss. There they fell out of formation and scattered into the woods to catch a few hour's rest before night fall.

Three hours later, after a short nap, Ross crept to the edge of the river with his scouts to see what perils lay in their path. As he gazed out on the rolling expanse of the wide river, his eyes fell on the ominous sight of two grim-looking Federal ironclads.

The first was tied to a Helena wharf; the other lay at anchor a half-mile up the river. Helena, once a quiet little river-port city, had been turned into a stern looking fortress bristling with cannon emplacements, breastworks, and walls of sharpened stakes and wooden spikes that formed rows of abatis. Helena, Arkansas, presented a formidable barrier—with the ironclads present, crossing was out of the question.

The scouts took shifts watching. Ross was on duty around sunset when one of the ironclads slipped its moorings at the Helena dock and floated downriver. As the brilliant sunset lit the western sky and reflected its gold and reds in the waters of the Mississippi, the chugging sounds of the steam engine on the mighty ironclad filled their ears. She drifted down-river with the current and away from them.

The other ironclad, which lay further up the river, was also making preparations to move. She fired two brilliant rockets and one of her cannons to the leeward side to signal the other ship, then glided toward the soldiers. Ross could see the Union lookouts posted on the ship and he prayed the Federals hadn't discovered the Rebel camp in the cypress grove.

The ominous ironclad nosed toward the East bank, spreading ripples from the bow in the shallow waters along their shore. As the sun faded into twilight the waters turned a deeper blue. The lookouts apparently saw nothing to arouse their suspicions, and the gunboats slid past them and out of sight.

Ross, knowing they must find some means of crossing the river, sent out some of his scouts. Soon word arrived that Rube and Fletch had found a small skiff up river that would serve to cross a small party to the opposite shore.

Ross ordered his scouts into the boat, but Jonas Starke seemed reluctant to board the skiff and lingered on the bank.

Ross, disturbed by the delay, yelled, "Jonas, hurry up! We need to cross before the Yankees come back with their iron-clads."

"If'n it's all the same with you, Sarge, I'll just wait here till you get back."

"Jonas, I haven't got time to sit here and argue with you. Get in."

Jonas's eyes were as wide and scared as they had been the night of the skirmish in the cemetery. "I ain't good in water, Sarge. I didn't sign up to be in no navy."

Ross could sense his friend's fear, yet his compassion was tempered by the need to cross quickly. "I know you don't like water and you can't swim. Most of us are frightened by something and there isn't any shame in it, but I'd like you to remember one thing—one way or another, you've got to cross this river to get back to Missouri."

Jonas shifted his eyes to the menacing river lapping at the bank near him. He nervously shifted his weight from one foot to the other as he considered the truth of the situation. Then he glanced up at Ross. "Sarge, can I stay on the other side when we get across?"

"Yes, if there's any way possible I won't make you cross twice. Now would you please get in the boat?"

Eyes wide with fright, the little, wiry soldier climbed into the skiff and sat in the stern of the small boat. His knuckles turned white as he grasped the edge of the seat tightly.

The scouts wrapped shirts around the oars to muffle the sound and, covered by the darkness of night, they began their perilous passage. As they neared the far shore, the moon began to rise; with each stroke, the oars shed droplets that sparkled like diamonds in the moonlight.

Ross could feel the tension building in his men and himself as they neared the far shore. Out here in the middle of the Mississippi there was no place to hide. Ross prayed they would make the other side without being spotted. The men struggled against the current, fighting to keep the skiff from drifting down to where the fortifications surrounded Helena. There would be no hope for them if the ironclads should return. Ross released a big sigh of relief when the skiff beached in the mud on the far shore.

After a brief search in the direction of the city, a flat-bottom boat was found at a nearby ferry. Ross fully expected pickets and patrols on duty to guard the ferry boat, but when they rushed the shack they found only two civilians sleeping inside.

Upon questioning their prisoners, the scouts learned the Yankees didn't think Southerners would be bold enough to try an assault on Helena's fearsome defenses. The small guard detail usually stationed at the ferry had been withdrawn to support and protect a Yankee supply train. The ferry operators insisted the soldiers should be back soon. In fact, the soldiers were long overdue. Ross wasn't surprised when Jonas Starke volunteered to stay and guard one prisoner. The other returned with the scouts to ferry the Lafayette County Cavalry. By three in the morning, Shelby's command was safely across the barrier of the mighty Mississippi and stood again on Arkansas soil.

Shelby's men hacked holes in the ferry's hull and watched her slide beneath the muddy waters, where it settled in the river bottom. The Rebels moved out quickly once their task was finished. Ross Kimbrough guided them to a plantation, not far from the outskirts of Helena, for breakfast.

There, almost under the noses of the Yankee garrison at Helena, Shelby's little command was treated like returning heroes. Served by the lovely belles of the plantation, the men dined on ham, biscuits, fried fish, and scrambled eggs. They drank goblets filled with champagne, poured for them by the servants. It was the best meal Ross and his fellow soldiers had enjoyed for many months, but Ross knew Shelby would not let them rest for long. By now, Yankee patrols must know of the crossing and would be searching for them.

Their journey lay before them, but the great barrier had been breached. Nothing nearly as formidable as the Mississippi River stood between them and their homes in Missouri. If only they could avoid capture by the Union army, Ross knew nothing could stop them.

2

Briarwood Plantation
June 1862

Glen Kimbrough stood in the portico of Briarwood Plantation, studying his land. A short distance to the north the estate bordered the rolling waters of the wide Missouri River. The smell of freshly mown, early summer hay floated toward him, carried by a soft breeze. To the south, east, and west lay the gentle, rolling green hills of his beloved Briarwood.

Most of the plantations in this region raised crops of cotton, corn, or hemp for rope making. Indeed, hemp was becoming the main cash crop locally. Nearby, on the Shelby Plantation, there stood a rope walk used for the manufacture of hemp into rope. Briarwood, unlike the others, bred thoroughbred horses.

The Kimbroughs kept a few families of slaves. Glen was proud of how well they were treated in comparison to other slave holders he knew. In his estimation, any plantation owner would be a fool not to care properly for such an expensive investment.

The slaves helped raise and harvest the small crops of

corn, hay, and oats used to feed the thoroughbreds. They also took care of the feeding and training of the livestock.

Glen, lost in thought, was startled when his oldest daughter Cassandra Marie Kimbrough touched his arm. "Father, dinner is ready and Mamma wants you to gather the boys."

Glen turned to his eighteen-year-old daughter. Her long blond hair cascaded over her slender shoulders and flowed down her back. Her fair complexion complemented her fine, beautiful features and blue eyes.

"Cassie, tell your sister to fetch Calvin from the breeding barn. He's working with the new mare we just got in from Kentucky."

"Elizabeth is up in her room, but I'll go. I need the walk. And besides, I want to see if Sultan has taken to the new mare. I'll tell Calvin," replied Cassandra.

Glen glared with impatience. "How often have I said the breeding barn is no place for a lady? A stallion can be dangerous when he gets excited."

"Those mares are ladies, Father, or Sultan wouldn't be bred to them," Cassandra teased.

"You know what I meant, young lady. I swear, the older you get the more you delight in teasing me." One look at his daughter told him he might as well be talking to a post. This daughter always had a mind of her own despite his wishes otherwise. Reluctantly he said, "Okay, you may go, but be careful. Just tell Calvin dinner is ready and get right back here." Glen paused. "Does she know Jessie is out overseeing the haying?"

"Yes, Fanny fixed Jessie and the field hands lunches this morning."

The tinkling sound of dinner plates and silverware drifted through the doorway. "I hear Fanny setting the dining table. Sometimes I think our housekeeper has more pull around here than I do." Glen turned toward the door and limped inside with the help of his cane.

Cassandra's gaze followed him through the entrance. She turned to go, but her thoughts were of her gentle, strong father. He had struggled to adjust to his recent disability, caused by being pinned against the wall in the stable by a frightened horse. He suffered broken ribs, a broken hip, and damage to his knee. His injuries were healed now, but the hip and the knee would never be the same. Glen found it hard to accept. He had always been the strong, guiding force of Briarwood; a man used to taking an active role in running his affairs. Depending on help from others galled him.

Ross, the oldest son, was away serving with Shelby's command, so Calvin and Jessie had stayed on to help run the plantation. Now that Glen was healed his sons were eager to return to other activities. Jessie dreamed of going to war, while Calvin wished to return to college.

Cassandra knew Glen Kimbrough was a man firmly set against the war—he felt nothing could be gained from it. He tried to take a neutral stance. She had heard him say the war could destroy everything he had worked for over the years.

Despite his misgivings, there was unmistakable pride whenever Glen talked of his son, Ross, serving with the Confederate army. It was something Ross had wanted and despite Glen's best efforts to talk him out of it, the boy couldn't be denied. Ross was always the son who looked for adventure and different worlds to conquer. Cassandra secretly envied his ability to do those things.

Cassandra's eyes strained to adjust to the darkness of the barn. Calvin, having noticed her entry, walked to meet her.

"Dinner is ready, Cal. You'd better hurry as fast as you can. You know how Mamma hates to keep Fanny waiting."

"We've just finished introducing Sultan to the new mare—I think she likes him. We'll try putting them together after dinner. I'll walk back to the house with you." Calvin smiled. "Jethro," he said over his shoulder, "get something to eat and we'll finish later."

"Yessuh, you and Miss Cassie go on. I'll be comin' along directly. Fanny promised me some good vittles. Lawdy, that woman can cook!" responded the tall, powerfully built, dark-skinned man with his wide, kindly smile. Jethro, born at Briarwood, was loyal to the family after years of service. Lately it had become evident to the family that he was getting sweet on Fanny, the family cook and head housekeeper.

Cassandra eyed her sandy-haired brother as they rounded the barn and headed for the house. His six-foot-three-inch body was slender and lean. Although pale blue eyes twinkled with life in his lightly freckled face, Cal was beginning to grow restless and distant. He was often lost in thought, with the look of a person searching for new directions.

Overcome with curiosity, Cassandra asked, "What are your plans, Calvin? Have you decided what you're going to do, now that Father is getting better? Will you go back to the college?"

Calvin shook his head. "Things are different at the university. From what I have heard, many of the boys have left to join the armies. There is even talk of shutting down the school until the war is over. Most of the professors have left to take up arms." He kicked at a small stone in their path, sending it skittering away. "School is out for the summer, anyway. I have a few months to think it over." His voice sounded more hopeful. "Maybe the war will end."

"I don't see it ending soon," said Cassandra. "I hate the way the President has ordered in troops to occupy our county and state. Many of the boys want to drive them out."

They approached the great house of Briarwood, but as they turned to enter, sounds of many riders pounding up the lane toward the house reached their ears. Calvin turned to look at the column. "Cassie, get Father! Looks like Yankee troops!"

Calvin stood on the portico and leaned against the railing. He studied the large Union patrol and the officer leading them. As the hot and dusty column approached, they fanned out into double rows and halted in front of the house.

"Column, halt! Troop, dis-mount!" The officer giving the command, a man of average height and stocky build, looked to be in his thirties. He swung stiffly out of his saddle, handed his reins to an orderly standing nearby, and walked up to the front steps.

"Good afternoon. I'm Major Benton Bartok. I'm here on

official government business. Are you the owner of this plantation?"

"No, sir, my name is Calvin Kimbrough. My father owns Briarwood. He should be out shortly."

"Thank you, Master Kimbrough. May my men rest and water their horses?"

"Of course, Major. There's plenty of fresh water. They may help themselves."

The major issued orders and the troopers broke ranks. Glen Kimbrough walked onto the portico followed by his wife, Ellen, and his daughters, Cassandra and Elizabeth. As Glen approached, he eyed the Union officer. The major's face was dominated by a prominent hawk-billed nose. His eyes looked dark and dangerous.

"Welcome to Briarwood. I'm Glen Kimbrough, owner of this plantation. How might I be of service to you, sir?"

The Major carefully pulled his long leather gauntlets from his hands and slapped the dust out of them against his leg before responding. "I'm Major Benton Bartok, commander of this district." He paused, letting the importance of his position sink in. "I've heard of the fine horses bred at Briarwood and I've come to purchase mounts for government service. Judging from the horse flesh we saw as we rode in, I'm sure we can do business."

"I'll be glad to discuss sales with you, Major, but my family and I were preparing for dinner. Would you join us?"

"Thank you. I would be happy to accept."

Fanny, the black housekeeper, stood in the doorway with her chubby arms crossed beneath her robust chest. Never one to conceal her true feelings, Fanny grimaced in disgust as she turned her portly body toward the dining room to set an extra place. As she left, her mutterings were quite audible to the family standing on the portico. "Invited some ole, dusty, blue-belly cavalryman into my clean dining room. Didn't even ask to see if we got enough for extras."

Fortunately, her comments did not reach the ears of their guest. Cassandra and Calvin grinned at each other, then followed Ellen in the procession to the dining room.

The spacious dining room held a dark mahogany table with twelve matching chairs, brought up river from New Orleans by steamboat. Large windows along two walls filled the room with light. Above the table hung a massive crystal chandelier. Glen took his place at the head of the table and motioned for the major to sit on his left. Ellen sat beside her husband, the rest found their places.

Glen broke the silence. "I'm sorry we can't feed your men, Major."

"My men have their field rations. I didn't expect you to feed them. I was wondering how many horses you can spare."

"It depends on the price you are willing to pay."

"As the commander of this district I have the power to requisition and forage for anything I feel my command requires. My only obligation is to offer you the going price. You must submit claims for payment to the Government and, in due course, if you are a loyal citizen you will be paid." Bartok eyed Glen. "However, if you are a secessionist and in rebellion to our government, then we simply condemn and confiscate your property." Bartok leaned back in his chair, a smug expression on his face. He enjoyed intimidation and reveled in it.

Bartok's gaze sought Cassandra's. He found her beauty captivating and felt a warm surge of lust and a twitch in his loins. He decided to use his position and power to take advantage of her. "Such beauty should be enjoyed," he thought.

Just then, a young man burst through the door. He stood tall, had brown, wavy hair and piercing gray eyes. Bartok guessed his age to be about seventeen.

"Father, I saw riders approaching the house and figured I'd better get here."

Glen Kimbrough turned to his guest. "Pardon the interruption, Major. I'd like to introduce my youngest son, Jessie Adam Kimbrough." Glen looked at his son. "Jessie this is Major Benton Bartok, our district commander."

Major Bartok shook hands with Jessie. "Pleased to meet you, Jessie. A strapping young man like yourself would be a welcome addition to our local militia."

"No thanks, Major, Father still needs my help here."

Anxious to change the subject, Ellen Kimbrough interrupted. "Gentlemen, I must insist we stop talking business until after dinner. It's been delayed enough and it's getting cold. After dining there will be plenty of time to discuss business without ladies present."

Fanny started serving the meal and conversation slackened. An undercurrent of tension pervaded the room as the Kimbroughs studied their unwanted guest. The strain kept the conversation soft and subdued. All the while, Cassandra felt the Major's presumptuous, lustful stare burning into her, undressing her with his eyes. Unable to stand his leering stare she averted her gaze. She knew she could never be comfortable with a man of his type. Yet she knew he would not be easily dismissed.

After dinner, the men retired to the library to discuss business and enjoy brandy and fine cigars. Bartok took a whiff of his brandy snifter, smiled, and seated himself in a comfortable chair, "How many horses do you have ready for service, Mister Kimbrough?"

"I've got fifteen fine thoroughbreds saddle broke and ready to ride. I have others in training that will be ready in a few days."

"Pardon my bluntness, Mister Kimbrough, but fifteen mounts is a small amount for a horse breeding operation of this size. I've taken time to make inquiries about you and your family." Benton deliberately paused, set his glass down, and bit the end off a cigar he fished from his pocket. "I know you have a son in the Confederate service. It occurs to me you might be saving horses for the Rebels."

Glen's anger began to rise, but he knew if he lost control the outburst could prove fatal. He forced himself to remain calm as he sat down. He leaned forward in his chair. "My son is twenty-four and he makes his own choices. I'm opposed to this war, and so is the remainder of my family. We want no part of it. It is my wish to remain neutral and let those who are more inclined fight their war."

Bartok rolled his cigar in his fingers, then lifted the cigar to his mouth and clamped it firmly in his teeth. He took a long draw and blew a cloud of smoke slowly in Glen's direction. Bartok's glare was intended to intimidate the gentleman from Briarwood.

Bartok spoke in a stern voice. "We will no longer tolerate those who try to sit the fence. You can't declare yourself neutral and just let others fight your war for you, sir. You are either with us or against us." The major stood, walked to the fireplace, and took another puff of his cigar.

"Perhaps you are unaware of a new directive recently issued from Governor Gamble. It states all men between the ages of eighteen and forty-five must enroll for militia duty. All who fail to enroll their names and show up for duty will be considered spies and traitors and will be treated as such." He used the cigar to punctuate his point. "If you fail to demonstrate your loyalty to the Union, then you will be presumed guilty. Do I make myself clear, sir?" Smiling wickedly, he leaned back against the fireplace mantle, letting his words settle like heavy lead on the mind of each Kimbrough.

Glen, glancing at his sons, fought to regain control of his emotions. He needed time to think about these new developments. He knew he couldn't take up arms against his friends and the South. He must play along. "You have us at a disadvantage, sir. We hadn't heard the governor's decree, so it is news to us. Of course we want to cooperate and support the Union. How long do we have to enroll?"

The statement rang flat and hollow and Bartok didn't buy a word of it. The father was ill at ease, and he could sense the anger of his two sons.

Savoring the moment, Major Bartok replied, "You have until the end of summer to enroll. I must trust in your loyalty after such wonderful hospitality. I'm sure we can work this out. It would be such a shame if you failed to do your duty." Bartok smiled broadly. "Why, I would have to confiscate your livestock and seize your property. I would have to arrest you and your sons and free your slaves if we prove you're in rebellion against the United States."

These threats forced Glen to respond. "As a loyal citizen of

Missouri, I know the governor of this state and the Federal government protects my rights to own slaves, sir! Slaves can only be freed in states actively in rebellion against the United States. Has anything changed?"

"That's the way it stands for now," mocked Bartok. "I don't think you'd be fit for militia duty because of your obvious disability. However, your sons should be proud to serve. We need assistance against these vicious guerrilla intrusions into the area. The militia will aid in resisting any troop movements by the misguided Rebels."

"The decision will belong to my sons. I'm sure they will make the proper decision, given time."

Jessie had sat quietly through the pompous major's threats. Like his brother, Calvin, he knew better than to interfere with his father's business. However, he found his anger swelling to the bursting point. He stood and headed for the door, moving in quick strides.

Bartok shouted at Jessie, "Where you going, boy?"

Jessie turned to him and yelled, "Don't call me 'boy'! I'm seventeen and I'm not one of your soldiers. I've got haying to attend to and I don't have time for idle talk." Jessie left the room.

Bartok felt his cheeks flush with crimson. "He'll pay for his insolence," he thought.

Glen tried to cover for his son's impetuous behavior. "Forgive my son's rashness. We've been working him hard lately. I'm afraid he hasn't been getting enough rest."

"No reason to apologize," Bartok lied. "Perhaps, now, you could have your people gather the horses and we can complete our business."

"Yes, of course. Calvin, take Jethro and a couple of the hands down to the pasture and round up the horses for the major. You know which ones are ready."

Calvin also had listened quietly and carefully to the conversation, but unlike his hotheaded brother he tried to analyze his position. He realized his family was on a collision course with the events swirling around them, and that it was necessary to use caution with people like Major Bartok. The family needed to face some tough decisions. He decided to buy needed time.

"Yes, Father. I'll get the ones fit and ready to ride. I'll pick out a special mount for the major, one befitting his rank for his personal use."

"Thank you, Calvin. I'll finish the paperwork with your father. Tell Sergeant O'Leary to pick a squad to give you a hand."

After completing the necessary forms, Bartok excused himself from his host and walked out onto the wide veranda. From his vantage point, he spied Cassandra and Elizabeth in the rose garden behind the house. He moved down the steps and strolled in their direction. The girls gathered roses as he approached them. Once again he found himself transfixed by Cassandra's alluring beauty.

She wore a snug-fitting day dress that clung tightly to her body until it reached her hips. From there the dress flared to a full-length skirt. The wind blew the skirt inward to show the curve of her hips and legs. As he watched her bend over he imagined how it would be to come up behind her like this if she were naked. The thought made him swallow hard.

This was a different dress than the one she had worn at dinner, less frilly and more suited for garden work. He wanted to stare longer at her figure, but he tried to lock his eyes on hers, not wanting to be too obvious in his desires. "Miss Kimbrough, I must say you look lovely."

Cassandra wished she had noticed his approach so she could have avoided him. Now she was forced to acknowledge his presence. "Good afternoon, Major Bartok. Have you completed your business with Father?"

"Yes, we talked and we've struck a deal. Please, I would prefer it if you would call me Benton."

"If you wish it, Major. Oh, excuse me, Benton." She displayed no evidence or spark of interest in her face or manner.

Benton looked into Cassandra's captivating eyes, as blue as the sky on a clear sunny day. The outside edge of her iris was a tinge of deeper, more vivid blue, as if someone had outlined them with color pencil for a special accent. Men would willingly fight and die for a woman such as this one. As if on cue, the wind gently lifted her long blonde hair and framed her face.

Bartok said, "I understand there will be a ball in Waverly on Saturday. I would be delighted if you'd allow me to escort you to the dance, Miss Kimbrough."

"No thank you, Benton. I don't plan to attend."

His manner changed. His jaws tightened. "Don't be so quick to dismiss my request, Cassandra. Perhaps you don't understand my authority. As commander of this district I can make things go smoothly for your family, or I can make things difficult."

Cassandra turned to her sister. In a voice low and edged with steel she said, "Elizabeth, take these roses to Fanny. I wish to talk privately with the Major."

Elizabeth, being the younger, was intrigued by this visitor. "Can't I take them in later?" she pleaded. Cassandra shot her a stern look, and Elizabeth reluctantly followed her sister's instructions.

When Elizabeth was out of earshot, Cassandra whirled to face the major. Anger burned in her eyes as she waved a finger in his face. "Don't you ever threaten me! I have made other plans for Saturday night and I don't have to explain them to you. Besides, I wouldn't waste my time in the company of a man so many years my senior."

She turned to go. Bartok reached out and grabbed her arm roughly, forcing her to look at him. His face was red and twisted. "If I were you I'd reconsider, Miss Kimbrough. No one insults me or keeps me from getting what I want." A nervous tick appeared under his left eye. He said slowly, and with great emphasis, "There will be another place and time. You *will* see me—one way or another."

Cassandra tore herself free of his grasp. "Believe me, Major. Seeing you would never be by my choice." She gathered her skirt in her hands and ran swiftly to the house, too scared to look back. She knew she had not seen the last of Major Benton Bartok.

Bartok, still angry, walked around the landscaped rose garden. Even the brilliant colors of the roses couldn't distract him. She was one hell of a woman—and spirited. She was going to be a challenge, but well worth the effort. He would have her, by heaven, or destroy her family and bring this place crashing down around her ears. "Before I'm finished," he said aloud, "she'll come to me begging for forgiveness. It'll amuse me to make the bitch grant my every wish. I only hope she is as spirited in bed."

Major Bartok became distracted by the approach of his men on horses. Sergeant O'Leary joined him to make his report.

"Sir, we have the mounts. If'n it pleases the Major, sir, we should ride out. It's still a long way to Waverly."

"Of course, Sergeant. Give the orders. I want to reach Waverly before dark."

"If I might say so, sir, the horses are of the finest quality. The Major might want to take a wee bit of time to pick himself out a new mount." The sergeant spoke in a lilting Irish brogue.

Bartok picked out a fine chestnut-colored, two-year-old mare. He ordered his men to switch the saddle and accoutrements from his old horse to the new one. The other horses from the Kimbrough estate, plus his old mount, were led by halters behind the mounted troopers. Bartok issued his orders and the cavalry pulled out in columns of two.

Calvin stood with his father and watched the column as they rode away. "Father, I have a feeling the major isn't going to be put off so easily. What will we do?"

"I don't know, Son. I can't bear arms against the South, but it appears the Union won't let us stay neutral. I'll delay my decision as long as I can. I think we'll have until the end of the summer, anyway." Glen let loose a deep sigh. "Maybe events will change. With luck the war will find a more pressing need for the major and his command somewhere else. Somewhere far away, I hope. For now, let's keep our wits about us and take each day as it comes."

Calvin nodded in agreement, and then he followed his father into the house.

3

Bushwackers

Ross Kimbrough squinted as he looked toward the rising sun, climbing above vapor clouds of mist. Today would be a scorcher and the air already hung heavy and damp. He knew today's march would soon take the starch out of them, but they had to keep moving. Helena was swarming with Union troops, and if they caught Shelby's tiny command, they could expect to spend the rest of the war in some Yankee prison camp.

Terrill Fletcher, Rube Anderson, and Bill Corbin were sent ahead to scout the way on this first day of the march, while Ross and Jonas Starke would march with the company. Ross took his place near the head of the column, marching with Shelby's staff. As he waited for the order to move out, he thought about the briefing Captain Shelby had given him last night.

Today would be the first leg of a journey that would take them to Little Rock. Once there, the captain hoped he could secure cavalry mounts for his company. Until then, they would have to travel on foot. The first objective was Clarendon, nestled along the White River. At Clarendon they would try to find passage on a steamboat to Duvall's Bluff. From Duvall's Bluff they could travel by train to Little Rock. If everything went as planned, their travels afoot would be limited.

As Captain Shelby gave the command to move out, Ross studied his commander. Shelby was a smart-looking officer, the kind who demanded respect from all who saw him. Although he never attended West Point or had any other formal training, he was a born leader.

Ross felt deep admiration and affection for Jo Shelby. Cool under fire, he reacted swiftly in battle, always instinctively knowing what was needed. Ross thought the captain looked especially dignified today as he marched near him.

Shelby wore a black felt hat over chestnut-colored hair, its front brim pinned back, cavalry style, with a gold buckle. The collar of his uniform carried the bars of a captain sewed over solid gold braid. Shelby kept the collar buttoned tight, even in this sticky, warm weather. The gold braid gleamed.

His russet-colored beard was full and luxuriant, and hung in curly waves. His mustachios hung down with long, tendril-like tips that looked as if, left alone, they could grow to the point where they could be tied together. Black leather officer cavalry boots that rose just above the knee completed the picture. Jo Shelby was a young man of thirty-one, but he was battle-tough and lean as hickory wood.

Indeed, Shelby cut such a dashing image that other commanders paled in comparison. Shelby was a spit-and-polish officer, when he could enforce such a regimen, and now that he was in command of his own men, his influence was already apparent. From the very first day in command he had seen to the care of his men. They were armed with the best weapons he could obtain, as well as the finest government-issued Confederate uniforms, unlike the majority of the Confederate commands in this region. In fact, Ross knew many Confederate commands lacked uniforms. These uniforms, now adorning Shelby's men, had originally been ordered for General Pike's Indian Brigade. Last February, before the battle of Elkhorn Tavern (or, as the Yankees called it, Pea Ridge), the uniforms arrived in camp, shipped all the way from the Confederate capitol—Richmond, Virginia.

When Shelby heard they were planning to give the new uniforms to the Indians, he ordered his men to take the Confederate uniforms at gun point and outfit his own company. Ross smiled as he recalled Jo Shelby's comment. "I'll be damned if any bunch of Indians are going to be better uniformed than my men!"

General Pike had been enraged at the audacity of a mere captain, confiscating the uniforms he had garnered with careful diplomatic craftsmanship in Richmond. He had convinced his superiors that the Indians would make good fighters for the Confederacy, if the South would show good faith by outfitting them in regulation uniforms and good weapons. Pike failed to consider how the other troops in their rags would react to taking a backseat to the Indians.

When the general realized his Indians had been robbed of their uniforms even before they received them, he filed formal charges against Captain Shelby. Fortunately for the captain, the battle at Elkhorn Tavern delayed any calling of a special court martial. After the battle, Pike's Indians were disorganized and scattered and the rest of the army was ordered across the Mississippi to fight. The argument over who should be wearing the uniforms would have to wait until another time if, indeed, the theft would ever be dealt with at all.

Ross's thoughts returned to the present as Shelby's command proudly stepped-off on route march. As the day wore on, the discomforts of their surroundings began to weigh heavily upon them. It was hot—the kind of oppressive, sweat-dripping heat only felt in the South during the summertime. The road they were traveling passed through bayou country, muddy, swampy land, more fit for alligators and snakes than for men. Mosquitos, flies, and other insects attacked them in swarms. If the men were not being covered with mud, or being drenched from wading through river water, they were being covered by a fine coat of dust caused by the steady tramping of the men before them.

Ross could feel the wet, sweaty weight of his uniform. He was sore from the chafing of the wool as it rubbed between his legs. As the day wore on, his legs and shoulders ached under the burden of his rifle, blanket roll, canteen, haversack, and other accoutrements. The dust caked his throat and clogged his nostrils. When they made river crossings, his boots filled with water and sometimes with mud, adding to his discomfort. His feet, like the feet of many others, began to blister and sting. How he hated the life of the infantry!

Giving up their mounts had been difficult, though they didn't march much while they were in Mississippi. Once there, they had fought in the fortifications protecting Corinth. Their first real marching had not come until the withdrawal to Tupelo.

Ross forced himself to stay in stride. He had his pride, and he knew he could match any man in the command if he set his mind to it. "Close your mind to the pain, one foot before the other, over and over again," he told himself. Still, the march became monotonous and he found himself staring at the back of the man directly in front of him, all the while keeping his pace and rhythm. The men became so uncomfortable, all joking and banter ceased. They just marched, sweated, and marched some more. Finally, the day ended and the men were ordered to fall out and set up camp for the night. Ross and Jonas were weary and foot-sore when they received the bad news—it was their time to take the lead as scouts; they would get little rest.

Ross was so tired he didn't try to cook supper. He just ate a couple of apples and a piece of dry bread from his knapsack. He was thankful he had brought them along from the plantation near Helena. In the middle of eating, Ross fell into a deep sleep.

The next day was more of the same, except this time he and Jonas were ahead of the others, scouting the way. At least the dust wasn't so bad in front of the company. Marching became more difficult for the men as their feet developed blisters, which then broke. The pace slowed in the oppressive heat. Rest breaks became more frequent to allow those who were straggling to catch up with the company. Shelby could ill afford to lose any more in his tiny command of less than a hundred men.

The third day found Ross out front with all the scouts. As they neared a hill in the road, Bill Corbin signaled them to take cover.

Ross inched forward to Corbin's position. "What do you have, Bill?"

"There's a log cabin just over the hill and around the next curve. It's located about thirty yards to the right from the road. I've spotted heavily armed men and horses. I count maybe five of 'em."

"Did you get a look at them, Bill?"

"Yeah, Sarge, they ain't soldiers. Looks like bushwackers to me. I saw a young boy fetchin' water from a well for their horses, and I heard a woman scream from inside the cabin. I counted their horses, but only saw two standing outside."

"Where is the well?"

"It's behind the house. The guards stay pretty much to the front of the cabin." Corbin added, "The outhouse is out back, too."

"Tell Captain Shelby what to expect. I'll take Rube and go behind the cabin, while you bring the others along the road. Take your time and move quietly. Let's check these boys out."

Using the woods as cover, Ross and Rube reached the back of the cabin. Rube hid behind the woodpile, while Ross hid behind the outhouse. It wasn't long before a guard came around the cabin and approached where Ross was hiding. He shuffled along quickly, as if he had delayed a little too long. He had his pants already half-unbuttoned by the time he reached the outhouse door. He leaned his shotgun against the wall, opened the door, and walked in, leaving the door hanging open. Standing with his back to the entrance, he relieved himself. The guard muttered softly under his breath, "Damn, that gal was fine. Ain't had such fun in a long while. Be worth gettin' in line for again."

Ross pulled a Bowie knife from his scabbard. Creeping

with caution around the outhouse, he entered from behind the preoccupied stranger. Before the man knew he had company, Ross had the Bowie knife at the guard's throat and a hand over his mouth.

"Friend, if you don't want me to slice your throat like I'm slaughtering hogs, you had best do what I tell you. Do you understand?" Ross whispered. The man, frozen in fear, nodded quickly. "Put it back in your pants and maybe I'll let you keep it." He slackened his pressure slightly, giving the stranger a minute to compose himself. "Now, put your hands against the wall." The stranger did as he was told.

"How many men are in there?" Ross asked in a low voice.

The stranger whispered, "Three inside with the woman, and her kids. Rufus is outside. Take it easy, mister!" the man pleaded.

Ross leaned out and motioned Rube to move to the back of the cabin. When he was in position he ordered the stranger to entice the other guard back to the outhouse. "I warn you," Ross snarled, "Make one move to alert the others, or tip him off, and I'll kill you."

The stranger yelled out, "Hey, Rufus! Come here; look what I found. The woman has some money stashed in the outhouse."

"Good move, mister." Ross reached behind his neck and drew out Double Twelve. He brought the shotgun crashing down on the head of his prisoner. The bearded man slumped forward, unconscious. Ross lowered him down until the man's face rested in the seat's open hole.

Ross turned to look through the crack between the door and the hinges and saw the other guard rushing toward the outhouse, closely pursued by Rube. Rube cracked the butt of his rifle on the back of the man's skull, and the stranger crumpled into a heap and lay still.

"Stay here, Rube, and keep an eye on these two. I'll go get the others."

"Sarge, wait for our men to come up?"

"The others might notice these two are missing and come

looking for them. Besides, I don't think this party is the woman's idea. I want to put a stop to it."

"Careful, Ross, and don't worry about these two—they ain't goin' nowhere."

Ross moved along the cabin using all the methods of silent movement he had learned from the Indians while Shelby's company was serving with Pike's Indian Brigade in '61 and '62—before Shelby had stolen the uniforms.

He slipped the Bowie knife into the back of his belt and checked the primer caps under the hammer of Double Twelve. Then he removed the musket, slung over his shoulder, and leaned it against the outside wall of the cabin. Every nerve was alive, every sense on razor edge. The old feeling was back—the thrill of living in danger and taking chances. Ross felt every heartbeat, his breath coming faster and more shallow. He felt the surge of pure adrenalin rushing through his veins.

He neared the open door and peered inside. The deep shadows in the room made it difficult for Ross to see. He could hear the laughter of the men and their taunts directed at the woman. He heard her crying hysterically. As his eyes adjusted, he saw a man with his pants around his ankles, lying on top of the woman, his white hips humping away. Another man stood at the head of the bed pinning her arms, watching and laughing. "Hurry up, Tom, I want my turn before you wear her out."

Through the crack in the door between the hinges, he spotted a third man sitting in a chair at the table, watching the action and smiling. Ross heard the sounds of small children crying in the adjoining room. Ross stepped through the door. "Good afternoon, gentlemen."

The men were stunned to see Ross appear seemingly out of nowhere. The man at the head of the bed stared, his mouth gaping open in surprise. For a split second everything froze.

Then the stranger's smile at the table faded, and he grabbed for his pistol lying on the table just inches from his hand. Ross swung Double Twelve off the man at the bed and in the blink of an eye, aimed it at the man in the chair. As the man's hand closed on the butt of his pistol. Fire belched forth from the first barrel of Double Twelve and Ross felt the reassuring buck of the gun in his hands. The ragged-looking man took the blast in his chest, throwing him and the chair over backward, spilling him onto the floor.

As the gun recoiled in his hands, Ross swung the barrels of Double Twelve toward the brute at the head of the bed. The man reached for his gun, but before he could lift it up from the nearby chair, Ross leveled the gun's barrels inches from the man's forehead. Their eyes locked on one another as the stranger's eyes widened in horror. Again Double Twelve roared to life. The stranger was lifted off his feet and slammed into the wall behind him, sliding to the floor. From his nose up he was nothing but a bloody, grisly pulp. Smoke curled up lazily from smoldering hair caused by the closeness of the muzzle blast and burning shot wadding. Blood and the remains of the top of the man's head stained the cabin wall.

The third man, slithered in terror on the floor, his legs tangled in his pants. He pleaded for his life. "Please mister, don't kill me! We was just havin' fun."

The woman still lay on the bed, naked and bruised. Ross turned his attention to the stranger trying to rise to his feet, while attempting to pull up his pants. Ross kicked the man in the groin, hard. The rapist, with his pants still at haft mast, went down groaning and clutching himself. Ross stuffed the still-smoking shotgun into the scabbard behind his neck, then pulled out his Bowie knife. Through the open doorway, Ross heard a loud commotion as men rushed the house. Relief flooded through him when he realized it was his men who had rushed ahead at the first sound of gunfire.

Ross nearly jumped out of his skin as a piercing scream came from the woman behind him. He turned to face the man looking up at him from the floor just in time to see the naked woman plunge a butcher knife into the man's back. The surprised rapist's eyes opened wide in shocked disbelief as she slashed the knife home again and again. Sergeant Kimbrough stepped forward, grasped her tightly by the wrist, and twisted until she dropped the knife. The woman, her anger partially spent, wilted to the floor.

From the next room two children came running to their mother, a boy about seven and a girl about four. The mother pulled her babies to her. They stayed there, clinging to one another, crying. Ross saw the terror in their eyes and felt sick to his stomach. He couldn't help but silently curse the scum who moved around in armed bands, taking advantage of those left helpless and alone. They were nothing more than a pack of scavengers, circling for the kill. He pulled the blanket from the bed and wrapped it around the young woman and her children.

Ross guessed she was no more than twenty-four or twenty-five. Her hair was long and dark, now twisted and tangled by the men. Blood, from the murdered rapist, bright and crimson, tinted her hands. Splattered droplets dotted her chest. He tried not to notice her firm, full breasts, as he moved to cover her, but he couldn't help himself. Nor could he completely wipe out the memory of the beauty and feminine curve of her legs which was locked into memory. A fleeting glance had burned the portrait into his mind, as if a photographer had set off a pan of flash powder used to illuminate a pose.

All those long moments of terror and anguish she had survived made him feel ashamed of himself. It had been a long time since he had been with a woman. He was now urgently aware of his buried desire, and he found it disturbing that no matter the intended nobility of the heart, he was still subject to this need.

She wasn't exceptionally pretty and the rough handling she had taken at the hands of the freebooters had left her face bruised and streaked with tears. Even so, Ross had to admit she was attractive. "Are you okay, madam?" he asked, already feeling stupid for asking such a question.

She clung to her children and rocked back and forth, sobbing. Her only reply was the positive nod of her head.

Captain Shelby entered the cabin and studied the scene, a worried expression on his face. He eyed Ross. "Sergeant, are you all right?"

Ross turned and saluted. "Yes, sir. I'm sorry I've made such a mess in here. Rube has a couple of prisoners out back."

"Yes, it's bloodier in here than a butcher's shop. What happened?"

"These men were raping and robbing this woman when we happened along, sir."

"I see. Who are they?"

"I don't know, sir, maybe we can find out." In the next two hours, the two remaining prisoners were questioned and identified by the woman. Rube extracted the information they sought by threatening to turn them over to her. They saw the bloody body of their friend and heard how she killed him. Their fear of facing her alone with their hands bound scared them more than facing the Rebels. They decided to talk.

They were simply freebooter rabble, owing no allegiance to any army. They tried to stay one jump ahead of the draft committees, the armies, and the law. When a country is ripped asunder by total war, with the families' protectors gone off to war, many become vulnerable. The freebooters hunted for the helpless women and children left behind, taking what they wanted.

Graves were dug for the three men who had died in the house. Shelby's soldiers helped to clean up the bloody mess and to repair the damage done to the dwelling.

Lieutenant John Edwards approached Captain Shelby. "What do you want done with the prisoners, Captain?"

"Shoot them. Use a firing squad, Edwards."

"But, sir, shouldn't we turn them over to local authorities or give them a trial?"

"Lieutenant, these men are nothing but criminal scum. They have been identified by men of my command and that poor woman over there as the guilty parties. Don't you understand? There are no local authorities left, except whatever local army is in control for the time being around here. These men don't deserve mercy, and I'll not allow them to be turned loose to do this again. By heaven, I have found them guilty and I sentence them to die! Now carry out my orders."

The condemned men were forced to dig their own graves, and the command was formed in line to witness the execution. Seven men, muskets in hand, came forward. On command from Sergeant Kimbrough, the soldiers lined up before the outlaws. The condemned men faced the firing squad. "Do you have any last words?" Ross asked.

The man called Rufus answered with a grimace, "Let's get on with it. I'm just sorry I didn't have time to get a second chance at her before you all came along. I'll save you all a spot in hell." He finished by spitting a stream of tobacco juice and stood glaring defiantly at the firing squad.

The other man, trembling and sobbing, fell to his knees crying, "Please, don't kill me! We didn't mean nothin'. I'm sorry! Please . . . I don't want to die."

Rufus kicked at him, catching him squarely in the ribs. "Shut up, you yellow bastard! Crying ain't gonna save you. Get up off your ass and die like a man. Hell, I'd kill you myself if I could."

Soldiers moved forward and separated them. Then the condemned men stood before their graves. Rufus held his head high and stared into the heavens. The other man slumped down on his knees, his head down, crying. The orders were given and the volley fired. Rufus collapsed on the pile of dirt dug from his grave, his shattered body still convulsing. The cowardly man buckled and fell on his face. The two men were shoved roughly into the open graves.

The money taken from the freebooters before the execution was given to the woman. They also provided her with a pistol and shotgun. As the soldiers prepared to fill the graves, she came forward to eye the dead bodies. She cursed them, spit upon their corpses, then returned to her cabin. Captain Shelby ordered his men to camp for the night.

In the morning before they left, the woman came to see Ross. "Sergeant, my name is Dee Ann Farley. The last I heard, my husband Robert was off servin' the Rebel army with General Beauregard in Mississippi." She paused, tears filling her eyes. "I want to thank you, Sergeant Kimbrough, for what you done. If you hadn't come along they might've killed me and my kids. I just want you to know I'm real grateful. If'n I can ever repay your kindness, Sergeant, it would make me proud. You just remember you and yours will always find shelter and a friend here if you need one." Dee Ann leaned forward and kissed Ross on the cheek. She quickly returned to her cabin.

The kiss caught Ross by surprise. He stood with a smile upon his lips for several minutes after she was gone. The memory of the tender warmth of her kiss on his cheek lingered long in his mind, even days after the command had moved on.

The march continued. At least the company now had five horses from the freebooters. Ross and Jonas were provided mounts and sent ahead of the company to find sanctuary in Clarendon and to arrange passage on a river steamer. The way Captain Shelby figured it, the company still had a three-day march by foot. The horses should give them at least a day-and-a-half head start to make arrangements.

They rode at a steady, but cautious, pace. At any moment, Ross and Jonas expected to run into enemy patrols or troops. Friendly local citizens along the way informed them they were now beyond the range of the Helena garrison. The Yankees, expecting an attack by Beauregard's army on the fortress of Helena at any moment, kept their armies close at hand. They slipped through without incident.

4

Southern Belle

Near Clarendon, they entered the gates of a fine and noble plantation owned by a Colonel Lightfoot, who served with the Confederate army. The butler informed Ross that the colonel was at home, convalescing from wounds received at the battle of Elkhorn Tavern.

The butler took Ross and Jonas to the colonel.

"Good afternoon, Colonel Lightfoot," Ross said as he snapped a salute. "Permit me, sir, to introduce myself. I'm Sergeant Ross Kimbrough and this is Private Jonas Starke. We are scouts attached to Captain Jo Shelby's Lafayette County Cavalry. Our command is en route to Little Rock and then north to Missouri. Captain Shelby has been authorized to return to Missouri to recruit a new cavalry brigade."

"I'm pleased to meet you, Sergeant, at ease. Please make yourself comfortable. Is your command nearby?"

"No, sir, I would guess them to be at least a day and a half away. We have been sent ahead to locate food and camp sites for the command and to find passage on a riverboat for the company." Just then, Ross noticed a young officer in Confederate uniform sitting in a chair near the fireplace.

He was a handsome man with dark brown hair and eyes. He had a thick brown mustache that curled up slightly at the ends. The rest of his face was clean shaven. The young man had a strong jaw line with a dimple in his chin and one in each cheek. His was a face that always seemed on the verge of breaking into a smile.

"Sergeant, I would be honored if your company would stay with us here on our plantation as our guests. We shall endeavor to make them feel comfortable. But first, if you will allow me," continued the colonel, "I'd like to introduce you to Lieutenant Evan Stryker of the Sixth Texas Cavalry."

"Pleased to meet you, Lieutenant Stryker."

"The pleasure is all mine, Sergeant. Is your Captain Shelby the same one that fought at Elkhorn Tavern?"

"Yes, sir, he is. Were you there, sir?"

"Yes, I was. I caught a minie ball in the shoulder as my company helped cover the retreat of our army from the field. As I was loaded into a field ambulance, I had the good fortune to be placed in with Colonel Lightfoot. The good colonel was kind enough to invite me to rest with him here at his plantation until my shoulder was healed."

"I'm afraid I haven't been as fortunate as the lieutenant," stated the colonel. "I lost the use of my knee . . . I fear it's not going to heal." He looked down at his leg and stroked his wounded knee. "I, too, have heard of Jo Shelby's cavalry company. It is a good outfit with a fine reputation. I deem it a privilege to share my home with them. Sergeant, if you'd like to stay here, I'll help you find a steamboat tomorrow."

"Thank you, sir, I would appreciate your help. If I might borrow a fresh horse for Jonas here. I will send him back to inform Captain Shelby and to guide our company back here."

"Of course we have a horse the private can use—and we can get him a good bath and a meal before he leaves."

"Thank you, sir. I will see to Private Starke and then return to discuss business with you later, if that's all right?"

"Sergeant, why don't you get something to eat and enjoy a hot bath first. I'll have a servant wash your clothes."

"Thank you, Colonel."

The necessary arrangements were made. Jonas bathed first, though he did so only on orders from Ross. Jonas ate, then rode to find Shelby. Ross also cleaned up and joined his host three hours later. He felt much better after having a hot bath and changing into the fresh clothes loaned to him by the colonel. He met Colonel Lightfoot as he reached the bottom of the stairs.

"Good to see you again, Sergeant, are the clothes comfortable?"

"Yes, they feel good, sir, but I must admit it feels strange to be out of uniform."

"Don't worry, Sergeant, we will have your clothes clean and in top shape before your company arrives tomorrow. I believe dinner is ready, so why don't we go into the dining room? We have another guest for dinner tonight I think you will enjoy meeting."

Ross followed the Colonel. Upon entering the dining room, his immediate attention turned to Lieutenant Stryker, busily engaged in conversation with two ladies. They turned to greet him as he entered. "Ladies, I'd like to introduce you to Sergeant Ross Kimbrough of the Lafayette County Cavalry of Missouri. You'll have to pardon him tonight, for being out of uniform, but his clothes are being laundered."

Ross smiled.

"Ross, I'd like to introduce you to the colonel's daughter. This is Sarah Ann Lightfoot, and this is her charming friend, Valissa Covington of Batesville, Arkansas."

Ross was spellbound. He could not look away from Valissa. She was one of the most beautiful women he had ever seen. Ross had always been comfortable and at ease with women. He always charmed them, but seldom could a lady hold his interest for very long. He would become bored with them and move on, eager to enjoy the excitement of a new chase. Never before had a woman so stunned him that he found it difficult to speak.

He looked into eyes of the deepest green color, with just a hint of blue, the color of new bluegrass in the spring. Her eyelashes were long and curled, her hair—a deep, rich auburn—caressed her shoulders in thick, soft curls. Her complexion was without a hint of freckles or blemishes. She had a smallish nose and high cheek bones. Her lips were full, sensual; and when she smiled, dimples showed.

If she had any flaw at all, it was her eyebrows, which were rather wide near her nose, but they arched prettily over her eyes and tapered to a fine point. She stood five-foot, five-inches tall. Her green satin gown, accented with black lace, belled out with full hoops that hung to the floor. Her breasts were full and made her already tiny waist seem even smaller.

"I am pleased to meet you, Va-Valissa," Ross finally stammered, as he reached for her offered hand and kissed it, never looking away from her eyes.

There was a pause when Sarah Lightfoot leaned over and offered her hand. Ross had to force himself to turn his attention away from Valissa and to greet the daughter of his affable host. If she had not been in the company of Valissa, he was sure the perky brunette would have attracted his undivided attention. Sarah was of obvious good breeding—refined and attractive.

"I am very pleased to meet you, Sarah. I want to thank your family for their generosity."

"You are welcome, Sergeant Kimbrough. Now, Evan, would you see me to the table?" Sarah wrapped her hands around the arm of Lieutenant Stryker, and they turned to be seated.

Colonel Lightfoot, obviously amused, had been enjoying Valissa's quick conquest of Ross. He turned to them both and said, "Ross, I'd like you to meet my wife, Debra Lightfoot."

Ross beheld a woman small of stature but of regal bearing. She was still attractive despite her years. He knew the dark-eyed woman must have had legions of beaus in her day. "I'm pleased to meet you, madam. You have a lovely home."

"Thank you, Mister Kimbrough. I hope you will enjoy your stay."

"I am sure I will. You have all made me feel most welcome."

"Now that everyone has been properly introduced, let us enjoy our supper." They took their seats.

Ross was at his very best behavior during supper, fearful he might embarrass himself before Valissa's eyes. During the meal, Stryker asked many questions about Shelby's command and their plans, and Ross dutifully answered them. In truth, he silently resented anyone that tried to compete with his attention for, or tried to distract him from, Valissa.

She smiled shyly and laughed softly whenever it was apparent he wasn't paying attention to Evan's conversation. After supper was completed, he caught her alone. "I must admit, Valissa, that I am extremely pleased I had the good fortune to meet you. Had fate not brought me here, I am sad to say I might have missed meeting one of the world's great beauties." He had rehearsed this opening statement in his mind several times during dinner. He hoped she wouldn't think him insincere.

"Thank you, Ross, you are most kind, though I don't feel worthy of the honor you have bestowed on me. I am glad I stopped by to see Sarah." She smiled.

"Are you originally from Clarendon, Valissa?"

"No, my home has always been in Batesville, Arkansas, farther up the White River valley."

"How do you happen to know Sarah and her family?"

"My father runs a cotton plantation and has been a long-time friend of Colonel Lightfoot. Ever since we were very young, Sarah and I have been friends. Several times a year our families get together for social events, and we take turns visiting each other. It has been fairly easy for us to travel back and forth on the river by taking passage on steamboats. My father often has to travel past this plantation on the way to sell our cotton and to buy supplies.

"Sarah told me your company should arrive tomorrow. I know the Lightfoots are anxious to meet your captain." The conversation continued, but the evening ended much too quickly for Ross. Still, he had the anticipation of seeing Valissa again.

In the morning, after enjoying a hearty breakfast, the colonel and Ross left to make inquiries for a riverboat to Duvall's Bluff. After asking some questions at the river wharfs, they managed to arrange passage for the company on a little river steamer called the *Charm*. Ross was anxious to return to the Lightfoot Plantation, and he was happy when his task was completed.

On arriving at the plantation, he was met by members of his company. Captain Shelby, led by Jonas, had arrived with the men. They were now camped on the front lawn. Ross had mixed feelings. He was glad to see his friends, but he had hoped to spend more time with Valissa. He knew Shelby would not want to be delayed long.

That evening, a splendid banquet was prepared for the company. All the best people of Clarendon had been invited to the feast. Heliotrope and roses smothered the room in scent. The table gleamed with fine linen and was lined with smoked meats. Good food, wine, and drink were plentiful. Shelby ordered the command to line up in formation after the meal. Mrs. Lightfoot and her daughter, Sarah, presented the company with a handmade silken flag of the first Confederate stars and bars. Captain Shelby was obviously touched and proudly accepted the flag. From that moment on, the flag was to be Captain Shelby's personal headquarters' flag. His staff would proudly carry the flag at the head of his column and into every battle and skirmish.

Following the presentation, a local band began to play and a grand ball was held behind the great house. Ross, early on in the festivities, asked Valissa to be his partner, and she happily complied with his request. She danced lightly, her effervescent smile carrying him away from all worry. The evening came to a close much too quickly, and long before he was ready to quit the dance ended.

Ross asked Valissa to walk with him. They followed the winding path through the flower gardens and along the gentle flowing waters of the White River. She looked so beautiful illuminated by the moonlight. He loved the way she walked close to him.

They paused at the water's edge and looked deep into each other's eyes. Ross hesitated, not wishing her to think he was being forward, then leaned to kiss her. To his surprise her lips eagerly sought his in return, and they locked in embrace. He pulled her closer and felt the warmth of her. The smell of light jasmine filled his senses. It felt so good to be with her he wished he could slow down time. If there were some way, he thought, to capture this moment and relive it whenever he was lonely, how happy he would be. When it became late they walked reluctantly toward the house, holding hands.

"I must see you again, Valissa. Will you write me?"

"Yes, of course I will." She put her hand in her small handbag and handed him a calling card that held her address. He carefully placed it in his uniform pocket. They lingered and kissed once more before parting, neither wanting their time together to end, but knowing it must. Ross moved to the foot of the lawn and joined the scouts in their camp.

When Shelby's command had arrived, there were no longer enough rooms for a mere sergeant to have one of his own. It was hard for Ross to give up the feather bed and a room in the plantation great house and return to sleeping on the ground with his men. Ah, for the privilege of rank!

By River, Road, and Rail

The next morning, the command marched on to Clarendon and loaded aboard the *Charm*. The horses were led into the bow, their bridles tied to hawser mounts on the deck. Ross was surprised to see Lieutenant Evan Stryker accompanying Captain Shelby. When he got the chance to visit with Evan he found that the Texan, his wound healed, had asked to be transferred to Shelby's command.

To Lieutenant Stryker the choice was simple for four reasons. First, his command, the Sixth Texas Cavalry, had been ordered to fight east of the Mississippi. He never wanted to fight that far from home. Like most of the men of Shelby's command, he wanted to help protect the Confederacy to the west of the great river. This was their homeland and through it lay the doorway for invasion to Texas. This war was much more personal to Stryker than the shadowy, distant war far to the east.

The second reason was just as important to him. The Sixth Texas Cavalry was dismounted, as was Shelby's cavalry, when they crossed over to Mississippi. Stryker had signed on to be an officer in the cavalry, not the infantry. A gentleman rides to war on a gallant charger, and from the part of Texas Evan came from, a man without a horse was worthless.

Third, while he was from San Marcos, Texas, most of his command were from Austin and Dallas. He had little personal identification with his old command. Fourth, Evan already was aware of Shelby's reputation and knew his chances for advancement would be good when the brigade was formed. Like most people, he was greatly impressed by the personal aura of Jo Shelby. When Stryker asked, Colonel Lightfoot signed the necessary order of transfer, fully understanding Evan's feelings on the matter.

The company had its first taste of river navigation on the crooked, but deep, White River. The *Charm* chugged softly along, clouds of white smoke billowing from her stacks. The boughs of the trees interlaced overhead, making a beautiful green arch above the river. The trip was a welcome departure for soldiers weary of marching on foot.

The Captain of the *Charm* quickly assured Shelby he was personally acquainted with Colonel Nelson who was in command of some of McCulloch's Texans defending the fortifications at Duvall's Bluff, but Colonel Nelson was not aware he was receiving visitors, and when darkness fell all river craft looked and sounded much the same to him.

Shelby's men spread out to sleep on the decks. A breeze blew off the river and across the rails of the steamer, cooling them on this warm summer night. Suddenly, they were aroused from sleep by the familiar sound of the drums of infantry beating out the long roll. As they approached Duvall's Bluff, men were preparing for battle, thinking the riverboat might be carrying Yankees to the attack. They could see in the moonlight a great earth-work loom above the pines with the ominous snouts of three huge, ugly cannons pointing their bores in their direction. Long lines of infantry were forming on the crest of the hill behind the fort. Two field batteries were unlimbered and brought to bear on the vessel. Just as orders were about to be given to open fire on the innocent little *Charm* and her passengers, her furnace doors flew open quite by accident, illuminating her deck, and the Confederates on shore recognized she was not a Yankee gunboat. Seconds more and the little craft would have been reduced to a smoking, shattered hulk drifting on the river. Still, the colonel was not totally convinced that this was not a Yankee trick, so he sent a guard aboard to secure the boat until morning—apparently, the captain of the *Charm* was not as well known as he had claimed to be. After a brief conference between Shelby and the colonel the next day, the confusion was straightened out.

A few weeks later, Shelby heard reports that the captain of the *Charm* had been caught spying for both sides of the war. He was arrested, tried, and found guilty of treason in Little Rock. The sentence of hanging was quickly administered by the military court.

Colonel Nelson had reason to believe the Yankees meant to attack Duvall's Bluff with a fleet of ironclads and riverboats. The Union fleet was moored at the mouth of the White River, where it joined the Mississippi River. While stationed there, a letter came in the mail from the Clarendon area. It was addressed to Ross, from Valissa Covington.

Within its contents Ross was given valuable information. Valissa had invited the Lightfoots to accompany her to her home at Batesville. The Lightfoots and the colonel, still not well enough to return to duty, were forced to accept her kind offer. The offer was timely, for the Union army soon occupied Clarendon with three thousand troops, supported by a fleet of Yankee tinclads and gunboats. Ross gave the information to the officers in charge—the Yankees were near.

The attack failed to materialize, but rumors were rampant and in a mistake of judgment by Colonel Nelson, Duvall's Bluff was abandoned. The Confederate army fell back to the Little Rock area, using the Little Rock railroad. Shelby arranged for the transportation of the five horses as well. For the time being, the White River was open to Duvall's Bluff for the Yankee invaders, and the terminus of the little railroad also would fall. With the railhead in Union hands, the railroad would be of little use to the Confederacy.

Nelson was soon removed from command and replaced. Meanwhile, Shelby's company camped near Van Buren, Arkansas, at Frog Bayou. There Shelby found his old commander, General Rains, now wearing a Brigadier's uniform. Shelby received the happy news that Colonel Vard Cockrell was ordered to Missouri to recruit, and that Shelby could join him when his command was properly equipped.

The company was ecstatic with the news. They were going home to raise a new cavalry brigade, with Jo Shelby to be promoted to colonel and in command of the men he recruited.

Shelby and his staff were disappointed by the meager supplies provided by the quartermaster. What remained was the dregs of the Arkansas supply barrel. Horses and mules of every size, variety, and condition were used. Saddles, sheepskins, and blankets were all used for seats; bark bridles and rope halters were forced to make do. Despite the quality of their mounts and horse equipment, however, the men were well armed.

They carried their Mississippi muskets and one hundred forty rounds of ammunition per man. Many of them still carried their cavalry weapons as well. The company was very light on swords and sabers, but it mattered little. Shelby preferred pistols for close combat, anyway. Most of the men carried at least one pistol and some carried more. The company was well equipped with large Bowie knives of every conceivable description.

Before they were to leave, Shelby asked the men to dismount and line up in formation. Shelby then gave a speech that Ross and the rest of the company would never forget.

"Men, we are about to embark on a perilous journey back to Missouri and our homes. When we arrive we will recruit a brigade of cavalry to serve the Confederacy. On the way, we will take what we need from the enemy. I want no man with me that is not up to the task. I therefore ask every man to enlist in Confederate service for the duration of the war. This command will swear to fight for the South until she is free. We will fight for twenty years if necessary, or until there is no one left alive to carry on the fight.

"I have here in my hands a commission that reads, 'If Captain Jo Shelby can recruit a brigade of Missouri soldiers for regular Confederate service, he shall be promoted to Colonel to lead this command.' This order is signed by General Beauregard and General Hindman. Gentlemen, I fully intend to do just that! My command will make every attempt to punish the armies of the Union that have invaded our state and even now are destroying the homes and property of our citizens. Missouri and the Confederacy have the right to decide their destiny. They joined the United States of their own free will and they have the right to abandon that union whenever the government for the people, by the people, becomes unjust.

"Lincoln and his black Republicans have forced war upon us and have ordered all the states to raise armies to invade the South and force her to remain in the Union against her will. We fight to defend our state, our rights, our homes, and our honor. They march upon our cities and towns. They destroy our property and take from us whatever they please, and they order us to obey. If there is any man here that is not capable of making this commitment, to fight this fight, I do not want him in my command. You may step forward now and be discharged with no dishonor to you. Those that stay will take the oath of service to the Confederacy until the end of the war."

A silent hush fell over the company. Not one man stepped forward. After a minute, Shelby, proud tears in his eyes, swore the Lafayette County Cavalry into regular Confederate service. No longer would they be a Missouri State Home guard unit, but regular Confederate troops. The absurdly mounted troops formed in columns; the bugles blew and they were on their way back home to Missouri.

6

The Invitation

Smoke still curled from the barrel of Jessie Kimbrough's thirty-six caliber Colt revolver as the echoes of the gun reverberated off nearby Mount Rucker. A smile creased Jessie's face as he eyed the broken bottles scattered in the grass, near the Missouri River.

"Good shootin', Jess, you got all but one," shouted Calvin. "Of course, they weren't shootin' back."

"I should have hit them all, but I'm satisfied," Jessie replied.

"Never be too easily satisfied with your shooting," Calvin remonstrated. "It can get you killed. Time to work on hitting a moving target. Jethro, take this old frying pan and hang it on the rope there on the tree."

"Yessuh," replied Jethro, with a gleam in his eye.

Jethro knew what was coming next. In these uncertain times knowing how to shoot well was more than a luxury, it could mean survival. Jethro knew Calvin was an excellent shot—maybe as good as any man remaining in the county.

The broad-shouldered slave reached the tree and attached

the frying pan to the rope. He extended the rope and pan in a straight line and released it. The pan swung in a large arch, like a pendulum.

Calvin waited until Jethro moved safely out of the way. He glanced at his little brother, then quickly drew the Colt revolver from his belt and fired. The round pistol-ball struck the pan. Calvin carefully tracked the swinging pan, hitting it twice more in the same pass. As the pan began its backswing, Calvin squeezed his fourth shot. Nothing happened. Cal tracked the pan on its return trip and fired shots five and six, both striking the target.

"Nice shooting, Calvin!" Jessie yelled proudly.

"I'd have hit the pan all six if my fourth shot hadn't misfired. The cap snapped, but the powder didn't ignite."

Calvin stepped over to a crude bench and, with a small pick, soon reamed out the nipple. He placed a new cap on the nipple, cocked the hammer, and bounced another lead ball off the still-swinging pan. "Nipple was fouled; she's shooting fine now."

Calvin began the tedious job of reloading the Navy Colt. First, he rammed an oily patch down the barrel and removed it, cleaning out powder residue. He poured a measured portion of powder into each chamber, then set a round, greased felt patch over the first chamber. Using his free hand he gently inserted a round, thirty-six caliber ball in the middle of the patch and firmly pressed down. He pulled the hammer to half-cock, so the cylinder rotated freely into position under the loading rod. He applied pressure on the loading lever forcing the rod down until it touched the lead ball and drove it firmly against the powder charge. This left a small ring of lead on the lip of the chamber cut from the ball, which he brushed away with his finger so it wouldn't cause a cylinder jam. The patch would reduce the chance of a cross fire caused by sparks from one chamber igniting the others around it. He repeated the procedure for each chamber. Cal pointed the barrel down and slipped pistol caps over the six nipples of each chamber on the revolver, completing the loading procedure.

Calvin lifted his head at the sound of an approaching rider arriving from Briarwood. Calvin eased the hammer down and slipped the revolver back in his belt. The rider slid his thoroughbred mount to a halt before them. Leon Pepper, the main exercise rider and jockey at Briarwood, sat astride a beautiful sorrel mare. "Massa Calvin, Massa Jessie—Massa Kimbrough wants y'all to come to the house," the little man said.

"What does he want, Leon? Do you know?"

"Massa Calvin, he don't say. I was given Red Roses a run and he flagged me down, an' asked me to tell ya."

"Thanks, Leon, would you tell Father we'll be there in a few minutes?"

"Yessuh, Massa Calvin. I'll tell him." Leon turned the big mare around and galloped toward the plantation.

"Well, Cal, I guess we'd better go to the house. I can't outshoot you, but you still haven't seen the day when you can beat me at fencing."

Calvin smiled at his brother. "Don't worry, Jessie, you're showing big improvement. All you have to do is lead the target a little and keep your swing smooth. I noticed you halt your motion as you pull the trigger."

"Sure, give me advice on shooting, but I noticed you totally ignored my comment on fencing," replied Jessie.

"Don't get cocky, Jess. I know you're good with a sword, and you can handle a rapier with the best. Never forget, a sword doesn't do you any good unless you can get close enough to use it. Up against a good man with a gun, you're just dead meat rotting in the sun." The men swung into their saddles and rode toward Briarwood, with Jethro bringing up the rear.

Cassandra entered the family room with a look of worry on her face. She found Glen and Ellen seated near the fireplace, talking quietly.

"Father, is it true? Are we really going to the Thomas plantation?"

Glen glanced away from his wife and smiled at his daughter. "Yes, dear, Harlan Thomas has invited us to Dover for the

Fourth of July weekend. He wants us to bring a few of our best thoroughbreds for the races. Harlan will run his best horses, and there will be other horses entered as well."

"Will there be very many people?" she asked excitedly. "It's been such a long time since we've been to a party. I can't wait to see everyone."

"Looks like Harlan is planning a grand jubilee to celebrate the Fourth. I would bet half the county will be there." Glen smiled mischievously. "I hear they are planning a grand ball and that Gilbert will be there."

"So what if he is, Papa. I don't care." Cassandra shrugged her shoulders. "Besides, he's not as old as I am."

"He's only a couple of months younger than you and he comes from a fine family. There are very few eligible men around here because of the war."

Fanny dusted as she listened to the conversation. Unable to restrain herself, she said, "Now, Massa Kimbrough, don't you be tryin' to match off this child. She got plenty of time to find her a good man. Why, they'll be standin' in line just to see if they can talk to her." She held the dust rag clenched tightly in one fist, while both fists rested on her wide waist.

"Fanny! I can talk for myself, thank you!"

"Yes, Miss Cassie, but I got to speak my mind." Fanny turned and left the room with a flourish.

Glen Kimbrough, trying hard to suppress his laughter, glanced at his oldest daughter. Her face looked perturbed as small squint lines showed her anger, but soon she broke into a smile and, finally, into chuckles. She couldn't help herself, watching her father's shoulders shake with laughter. "Father, what are you laughing at?"

"Cassandra, she loves you like you were her own. She's taken care of you kids since you were babies and I find it amusing the way she protects you like a big ole bear defending one of her cubs. You know she would do anything for you."

"I know, and I love her, too, but is it right to let a slave talk like that? It doesn't show proper respect."

Glen's smile quickly faded as his face turned stern. "She

might have been a slave when she came to this plantation, but she has become part of this family. As far as I'm concerned, she is a vital part of this household, and as long as I am head of this house she will have the right to speak her mind. Don't ever forget, even though she is a slave, she is a human being with feelings." He sat upright in his chair. "She may lack formal education, but she has a great sense of judgment. And more often than not, she is usually right."

Ellen Kimbrough spoke up, "I agree with your father, Cassie. Loyalty is precious and she does so much for all of us."

"If you feel so strongly about it, then why don't you free our slaves?"

"Cassandra Marie!" snapped Ellen. "Don't be insolent!"

"It's all right, Ellen. It's a fair question and deserves an answer." Glen leaned back in the chair. "I've been thinking about it lately. More and more slaves in this area are lured into running away by the Abolitionists of Kansas and the Federal troops occupying our state. Have you ever wondered why our slaves have stayed?"

"No," Cassandra said as she thought about it. "I guess it's because we take good care of them and treat them well?"

"Slavery can be a mean, awful business. Your grandpa taught me how to keep slaves working yet happy. The trick is to keep them together as families. If you break up their family and cause them to be separated, you breed only hate and disloyalty." He stood up and began to pace around the room as he talked. "You must supply their basic needs. Feed them well, give them decent housing and clothing, and they will serve you loyally. They know what can and does happen to other negras on other plantations and they appreciate the way we treat them." He stopped and looked into Cassandra's eyes. "I expect them to work hard, and when they do they earn our respect and respect for themselves. We take care of our slaves just as we would our thoroughbreds."

"I know you have always said you judge a man by how well he treats and cares for his property," Cassandra answered thoughtfully.

Glen clasped his hands behind his back as he walked toward his chair. "They know at Briarwood they will be cared for. If they run away they won't have nice cabins, good food, and clothes provided." He stopped and rested his hand on his chair. "Never forget the need for freedom is powerful, but the fear of suffering and death is stronger. Away from here they worry where they'll find their next meal, that they must hunt for some squalid protection from the elements while being tracked down like animals. Fear keeps them from running away. If you treat them fairly and fulfill their needs, the rest takes care of itself."

"Do you think they would stay if they weren't slaves?"

"I don't know." Glen paused. "I know freedom is something important to all living men. I have thought it might be possible to pay them by giving them a portion of the crop for their work and by letting them buy their cabins. Let them work as share croppers on our land. I think they would stay if we are fair to them. It could be cheaper than it is right now." He sat heavily in the chair. "This war is going to take the decision right out of our hands if the Confederacy doesn't win."

"It makes me so angry, Father, when those Northerners try to act so superior! They put men to work in dimly lit, nonheated factories for up to eighteen hours a day, seven days a week. They don't pay their workers enough so they can provide for their families. If they get sick or too old to work, they just fire them. I can't see how that makes them any better than us. Southerners take care of everything for their slaves, even those too old to work."

"There are evil men everywhere, Cassandra. Some will always take advantage of others and use their positions to inflict harm upon those under them. I have seen men treat their slaves worse than cattle, neglecting them and beating them. They show no appreciation for property or know how to win their devotion. I have no respect for people like that."

The door swung open and Jessie and Calvin entered the room, fresh from their target practice. "What's going on, Father?" asked Calvin.

"I have just aired my opinions on slavery. I am afraid it's nothing you boys haven't heard before."

"Leon rode down and told us you needed us, so here we are," said Jessie.

"Yes, of course, I have some news. We are invited to the Thomas plantation at Dover for the Fourth of July celebration. They have planned a day of horse racing and a grand ball."

"Sound like fun. Which horses are you planning to take?" asked Calvin.

"I want to race Sultan and Red Roses for sure. If Sultan can whip the local stallions again, we'll have the pick of good mares brought to him for breeding. We can certainly use the stud fees." Fanny served the Kimbroughs fresh lemonade while the men continued to talk.

"Sultan is the best, but it's going to be hard to find someone stupid enough to bet against him in these parts."

"Cal is right, but maybe some of those Yankees from out of state won't know better," Jessie teased.

"Father, how about running Star's Pride in the races? He's showing great potential for a young two-year-old. I think he takes after his father Sultan."

"Good idea. I've wanted to see how he would do against good horses. His mother Bright Star has been a good brood mare for years, and he's the best prospect we have had out of Sultan."

"In the morning I'll tell Leon to get them ready to run for the Fourth." Calvin glanced at Fanny. "Now, what's for supper? I'm so hungry I was ready to eat my horse on the way in!"

"I ain't servin' no horse, but what I got gonna taste a whole lot better," Fanny replied with a smile.

"Let's eat, gentlemen," Ellen said, leading the way to the dining room.

7

Riverview Plantation
July 4, 1862

Listen, Harlan, I think Red Roses can whip your horse, and I'm willing to make a side bet for fifty dollars, Federal money. You got the gumption to take it?" challenged Glen Kimbrough.

"You must be some kinda fool if you think any mare in these parts can beat my Belle of the Ball! If you are foolish enough to waste your money, I'm not above taking it. You've got a bet."

"You're on!" shouted Glen Kimbrough. Glen walked over to his sons. "I got Harlan to bet another fifty dollars on the race," Glen stated proudly.

"Father, you're betting a pile of money on this race. You know Belle of the Ball is a good mare. No mare has ever beaten her in a race," chided Jessie.

"She's not the only good mare," said Calvin. "I think the Redd family's mare, Last Flight, is going to be tough to beat."

"Well, none of 'em have run against Red Roses. She is a slow breaker from the start, but she finishes strong. With

Leon in the saddle, we can win." Glen turned toward the tiny, coffee-colored jockey. Leon stood rubbing and petting Red Roses' nose.

Glen started giving him his race instructions. "Leon, you know she likes to break slow. Just try to keep her in the pack until you round the last hedge and you are in the stretch to the finish line—then let her go."

"Don't worry, Massa. Red Roses, she's strong. She's gotta lot a heart and a great finishin' kick to bring her home," said Leon Pepper.

"Horses to the line! Horse to the line! Race starts in five minutes," yelled Harlan Thomas.

Calvin helped boost Leon into the saddle. Leon slid into the stirrups and Jessie handed him his riding crop, then Calvin led Red Roses to the starting line.

The race course started at the entrance road to Riverview Plantation. A rope stretching across the lane served as a starting line. The lane, lined with mighty oaks and maple trees stretched over a distance of half a mile. As the lane approached the great house of Riverview, it turned in a large, gentle circle until it rejoined the entrance road. Where the drive neared the mansion and began its half-circle, the hedge-row started and ran as a border on the inside of the circular drive. The spectators were scattered alongside the boundary ropes running from the porch of the plantation's great house and down both sides of the lane from start to finish. Some spectators stood, others sat on blankets, and still more were in carriages and wagons. Many brought chairs to sit near the boundary along the lane.

On the line, seven horses stamped and jostled for position. The jockeys fought to keep the horses alert, eyes pointing down the lane.

No one awaited the start of the race more eagerly than Cassandra. She stood just a hundred yards down the lane from the starting line. From there she could observe the start and the finish of the race. Seated next to her were Gilbert and Katlin Thomas, the two children of Harlan Thomas, Riverview's owner.

Gilbert asked, "Cassandra, if Belle of the Ball beats your horse, will you let me escort you to the dance tonight?"

Cassandra wrinkled her nose mischievously. "Shame on you, Gil. You know there will be many beaus at the ball tonight. Surely you don't expect me to limit myself to just one, do you?"

"What's the matter, Cassie, don't you think Red Roses can win?" teased Katlin.

"Of course I think she can win! I just want to know what Gil has to wager."

Gilbert said excitedly, "I'll bet you a bottle of our finest champagne and a candlelight steak dinner."

At that moment, the rope dropped and the horses exploded off the line. Cassandra shouted over the crowd noise, "I accept the wager, Gil. I just hope the champagne is a good vintage."

Little Princess broke away from the line first and had the early lead, followed two lengths back by Belle of the Ball. Last Flight followed closely. Back another four lengths came Red Roses, followed by the remainder of the field. The clatter of hooves sounded like hail pounding on a tin roof as they charged by Cassandra's position.

"Go Leon! Go Roses!" Cassandra screamed. "You can do it!"

Leon had the big mare into a good rhythm. She broke slow, which was normal for her, but now she was finding her stride. She began to close the gap. As they neared the great house, Leon eased Red Roses inside the black mare, Last Flight. Into the turn they roared.

The jockey on Last Flight tried to cut off Red Roses by pulling to the hedgerow. When the horses slammed together hard, Red Roses was momentarily thrown off stride. Leon felt the hedgerow tearing at his legs and, for a moment, he thought about swinging his crop at the other rider. The black mare bounced away and stumbled slightly, and Red Roses surged ahead.

It was a close call, nearly a disaster, but Leon and Red Roses were still in the race. As they cleared the turn and sped into the straightaway leading to the finish line, only one horse stood in the way. In the confusion, somehow, Little Princess had fallen back. Only Belle of the Ball remained in front of Red Roses. Leon hugged the saddle as they chased the flying Belle. Leon began to use the whip, urging on Red Roses. As they closed on Belle, her jockey applied his whip. With every stride Red Roses closed the gap until she slowly pulled alongside Belle. Leon had Roses just a neck back now as she gained precious inches with each stride. Buster, the jockey aboard Belle, eyed Leon closing and struck Red Roses hard, swinging his riding crop into her throat. She shied away and pulled up slightly from the blow. It was just enough as they crossed the line to give Belle of the Ball the win. Red Roses finished a close second.

"Did you see that, Dad?" hollered Calvin. "He hit Red Roses! Harlan's jockey cheated. Don't pay him; protest the race."

"Harlan wasn't riding Belle, it was his jockey. They were running close together. It might have been an accident."

"Dad, Roses would have won if the jockey didn't strike her!"

"Maybe," Glen said quietly. "I am a man of honor and I pay my bets. I do not try to wiggle out of them. Harlan would do the same. He is a good friend."

Harlan approached them, a big smile on his face. "Well, Glen, looks like you lose. It was closer than I thought it would be. They might even have touched."

"Tell you what, Harlan, I've got Sultan running in the stallion race later in the day. I don't think your horse can hold a candle to him. Want to go double or nothing?"

Harlan chuckled softly, then replied, "You're a sly ole dog, aren't you, Glen? Why, we both know there hasn't been anyone in the county with a horse faster than Sultan for the last two years. I don't think he'll lose today, either, but I'll tell you what I will do. I'll bet my two-year-old will beat Star's Pride, and I'll go double or nothing on that one."

Glen swallowed hard. He knew Star's Pride had trained well, but he was untested in an actual race. "I don't know how good my horse is, but I'll take your bet. It's double or nothing."

"It's a maiden race, Glen. None of us know what these two-year-olds will do. That's why we call it gambling." Harlan laughed. "One thing for sure, one of us will wind up happy."

"This is just a side bet between your horse, Prince of Heaven, and my horse, Star's Pride, right?" asked Glen. "All that counts is which horse beats the other. I hope whichever of our horses comes in first will also win the race."

Calvin and Jessie fumed over the results, but knew it wouldn't change anything.

The word passed down the line of spectators. When the news reached Cassandra and her friends, Gilbert started whooping and hollering in delight. "Cassie, you've got an escort for the ball tonight."

"I guess so, Gil, but even if I'd won, I still would have had to spend the evening with you to collect."

"Yes, I know. That was the whole idea."

"Tonight it is, then."

Katlin said thoughtfully, "Maybe I need to go down and make a bet with Jessie."

"The way he's been eyeing you, I don't think you will need a bet to get his attention. It's more a question of how you could keep him away if you wanted to. Just give him time to finish assisting Father with the horses, and he'll be around."

Katlin smiled coyly. "I hope you're right. He's so handsome.

Leon guided Red Roses back to the meadow where the horses were prepared for the races. He swung off Red Roses while Jethro grabbed the reins to the mare. "Jethro, take care of that cut on Rose's neck. I'm gonna have a little talk with that dumb-ass nigger, Buster. He ain't gonna hit my hoss like that and get away with it!"

Leon marched across the meadow toward Buster, who was locked into conversation with another jockey. Leon grabbed Buster's shoulder and roughly jerked him around.

"Buster, I ought to ram my fist down your throat! You pull another trick like that and I'll be all over you like fleas on a dog."

Buster twisted himself free from Leon's grasp. "I ain't goin' nowhere, Leon," Buster growled. "You think you can handle it, farm hand, you just bring it on."

Leon didn't hesitate. As the last word tumbled out of Buster's mouth, Leon levered a swift upper-cut, catching Buster under the chin. Buster's feet lifted clear off the ground, landing him flat on his back. Buster lay in the dirt, staring up groggily.

Leon towered over Buster, his hands doubled into fists. "Don't call me 'farm hand,' nigger! I got more if'n you wanna come and get it." Buster rubbed his jaw, but stayed on the ground.

"You try somethin' like that again an' I'll stomp a hole in you so big you'll be able to see daylight through it. You hear me, boy?" When Leon realized Buster wouldn't get up he turned and walked back to Jethro.

The races continued throughout the morning. As expected, Sultan ran away from the field, finishing fifteen lengths ahead of the nearest horse. The Kimbroughs didn't enter horses in every race, but there were many races left and no shortage of horses or owners. Bets and wagers were quickly swapped among the spectators and participants of the festivities. By two o'clock it was time for Star's Pride to run his race.

Elizabeth made her way from the porch of the great house where she had been playing to stand by Cassandra. "Mama says for you to be sure and keep on your sun bonnet. She says she doesn't want you red as a ripe tomato at the ball tonight."

"Why don't you run on and play with your dolls, Liz." Cassandra said sarcastically. "I know enough to keep my bonnet on."

"You say!" Elizabeth replied as she stuck out her tongue and ran toward the house.

Cassandra looked up from her squabble with Elizabeth, and caught sight of the strutting Major Benton Bartok. He had spotted her. She shuddered. He was the one person she had hoped to avoid. She turned her attention to the track. Gilbert and Katlin were discussing the upcoming race.

Bartok walked up and touched Cassandra lightly on the shoulder. "Excuse me, it's a pleasure to see you again, Miss Kimbrough."

Cassandra swallowed hard, then reluctantly turned to face Bartok. "Good afternoon, Major, I didn't know you were here."

"It's my duty to keep track of events in my district, and with this big of a gala, it is my pleasure to attend."

Gilbert and Katlin finished their conversation and turned to greet the intruder.

Cassandra motioned to her friends. "Allow me to introduce Gilbert and Katlin Thomas from Riverview Plantation."

"We're familiar with the major. We see him often in Dover," Gilbert said.

"Yes, I've been trying to get Gilbert to join the militia, just as I've tried to encourage your brothers to enlist. I hope you might use your influence to encourage him, Miss Kimbrough."

"I believe it is entirely up to Gil to decide with whom he serves, and when," replied Cassandra coolly.

Bartok tried to ignore her remark. "I hope you will allow me the honor of a dance tonight, Miss Kimbrough."

"I am afraid that will be up to Gilbert, sir. You see, he is my escort to the ball."

"Oh, I'm sure Gilbert would spare one dance for a guest." Bartok shifted his gaze to Gilbert. "Won't you, Gilbert?"

Gilbert glanced at Cassandra nervously. "I suppose one dance would be all right," Gilbert said hesitantly.

"Till later, then. I bid you good day." Benton bowed deeply, sweeping his hat off before him, then excused himself.

"Lordy!" Cassandra complained. "I believe I'd as soon dance with a rattlesnake. I don't think it could be any more slimy or dangerous."

"Quiet, Cassie, he might hear you," snapped Katlin. "I was

afraid he might ask me to dance." She rolled her eyes. "I'm glad he picked you."

"Don't start feeling too secure. That man is like a coyote loose in a hen house. Mark my words, he'll try to dance with you, too, before this evening is over." The trio turned their attentions to the next race—the long-awaited race between Star's Pride and Prince of Heaven.

At the starting line, jockeys were up and the horses were milling around behind the rope. The riders jostled around desperately, trying to get a good break at the start on the other horses. Leon stayed on the opposite end of the rope from Buster, who was riding Prince of Heaven.

Star's Pride snorted and pranced nervously, as he strained against the reins. "Steady, boy," Leon whispered in the big bay's ear. "It'll start soon, sure enough."

The report rang from the starter's pistol and down dropped the rope. Nine horses broke quickly from the start. Star started well and broke into the lead early, closely followed by Battle Axe and Mistletoe. Two lengths back trailed Prince of Heaven, Sporting Edge, and Leverage in a closely grouped pack. The rest of the field trailed behind the leaders. As they neared Cassandra, Katlin, and Gil's position, Buster kicked Prince of Heaven into full stride. The big black stallion ate up the distance with his powerful legs. He pulled away from Sporting Edge and Leverage and moved between Mistletoe and Battle Axe. Star's Pride stretched his lead slightly as the second and third horses faded toward the pack. Prince of Heaven gained momentum and fell in behind Star's Pride.

Gilbert lost his composure in the excitement and shouted, "Get your big black butt in gear, Prince! You can catch him!"

Cassandra quickly elbowed him in the ribs. "Gilbert! You watch your language. You're with a lady." She smiled mischievously. "Go Leon! Go Star! Show 'em your tail." Gilbert exchanged glances with Cassandra and Katlin and they laughed.

The horses barreled into the turn. The sound of the pounding hooves resounded off the walls of the great house, rolling like an invisible tidal wave. Before Leon even realized Prince of Heaven was there, Buster slid the big horse by on the outside to take the lead. Leon slapped his riding crop down on Star's flank, encouraging him to greater effort. Before the end of the turn, Star's Pride regained the lead in the see-saw battle. As the horses entered the straightaway, a barking dog chased by a small boy passed near the ropes and spooked Star's Pride. He shied away from the commotion, snorting in fear. Instantly, Prince, followed by Leverage and Battle Axe, blazed by the startled Star. Leon quickly regained control and dug at Star with his heels.

"Easy, boy, ain't nothin' but a dog and a little boy. Go on now, you can do it, Star," whispered Leon into the horse's ear. Partly because of Leon's urging, and partly because of his fear, Star regained his speed.

He quickly ate up the distance in ground-pounding strides. Star's Pride moved between Leverage on the inside and Battle Axe on the outside. Both horses moved toward the center of the lane, pulled themselves away from the noisy crowd, and closed in on Star's Pride, running strong up the middle. Star was pinned between the two closing chargers. Leon felt the crushing weight of the two stallions as his legs were smashed between the other horses and Star. The horses bounced and rebounded against each other until, slowly, Star emerged from the pack.

Leon and Star's Pride still narrowed the gap slightly on Prince of Heaven despite the crushing impact of the collision with the other horses. Leon felt pain in his legs as he rode on. The finish line was less than an eighth of a mile away and closing fast. Prince of Heaven, still in the lead, looked like a tired horse. Prince of Heaven was game, but he was used up and running out of steam. Star's Pride drove by, followed closely by Leverage.

They were neck and neck. "Come on, Star! You ain't gonna let this hay burner get by, are you?" Leon urged.

Star made a gallant last effort just before the wire and pulled out to win by half a length at the line.

Leon stood up in the saddle and eased back on the reins.

"You did it, Star! You done showed who be the cock of the walk 'round these parts." Leon patted the bay on his withers and turned him back toward the finish line.

Glen, Calvin, and Jessie jumped around, pounding each other on the back to celebrate the victory. Glen hobbled toward Leon and Star as fast as he could with the aid of his cane. Calvin and Jessie passed their father and ran to greet Leon near the finish line. Congratulations were passed all around.

Harlan Thomas approached the group. "Well, Glen, I guess I should know by now not to bet against your horses. Your breeding program is very strong. You've always had an eye for good horse flesh." He pulled a wad of bills from his pocket and handed them to Glen Kimbrough. "Here's your money on our little bet, and when we finish the races, we'll pay the winner's purses."

"Thank you, Harlan. It's been a good day. We brought three horses down to race today and had two wins and a second." The two old friends shook hands warmly.

"Some guest you are," kidded Harlan. "Coming to my jubilee and winning so much. To top it all off, you're walkin' away with my money."

By three o'clock in the afternoon the racing was completed and the crowd dispersed from the lane. The ladies, outfitted with sun bonnets and umbrellas to protect themselves from the searing heat, headed for the great house to rest for the evening's festivities. Cassandra and Katlin went upstairs to their bedroom to rest and prepare for the ball. There they joined Ellen and Elizabeth, who had stayed to watch the day's racing from the house. Fanny helped the ladies ease out of their day dresses and corsets.

Meanwhile, the gentlemen gathered in the garden behind the house to talk beneath the shade of stately maples and oaks. They gathered into informal groups with drinks in hand to discuss the day's racing and politics. When they were sure the Yankee officers weren't listening, the discussion turned to the war and the tricky situation in Missouri.

Calvin, Jessie, and Gilbert found themselves in one such

group. Calvin, with drink in hand, turned toward Gilbert. "I know you were in the Missouri Home Guards until your unit disbanded. I was wondering about your opinion of Governor Gamble's new proclamation. I understand all men between the age of eighteen and forty have to enlist in the state militia."

"First off, let me say Gamble isn't our true governor to my way of thinking, and I bet you'll agree." The group chuckled at this comment, and Calvin noticed those in the group were listening intently. "Gamble is only the governor because the Feds put him in office. Governor Jackson is the man we elected, but he's hiding in exile with his cabinet in Arkansas. Jackson cast our lot with the Confederacy and, in truth, that is where my heart is."

"I think we all agree Gamble is not our rightful governor, but the point is he is in control. He has an army to enforce his policies." Calvin shifted his weight and looked around at the members of the group before continuing, "We're going to be forced to take some kind of action, and soon."

"I know what I'm going to do. I'm going to join up with Shelby's company and fight with my brother." Jessie's outburst riveted the attention of the group. "Rumor has it Shelby is on his way back to Missouri. When they leave here, I'm going with them. What about you, Gilbert?"

"I've been giving it some thought. You know I fought against the Yankees with the State Home Guards last year. I was there when we beat them last summer at the battle of Lexington, right here in Lafayette County. I followed General Price and his boys down to southwest Missouri, and I fought again at the battle of Oak Hills."

"The Yanks called it Wilson's Creek," interrupted Jessie.

"I don't care what they call it, boys, but I saw hell up close. I got my fill of war right quick." He looked around the circle and eyed those watching him, hanging on his every word. "It isn't full of glory. It's just killing and good ole boys dying." There was an uneasy hush in the group, for they saw the truth in his eyes.

"When I joined the Home Guards we enlisted to fight only

in Missouri. When Price decided to take our boys south into Arkansas to link up with the Rebels, it gave us an honorable excuse to leave. Some joined regular Confederate units, but the rest of us decided to disband and come home. I'd seen all the fighting I wanted. Army life and living under the stars, well, it just wasn't for me." Gilbert Thomas smiled. "Hell, boys, I'd trade a nice feather bed in Riverview any day for the army." A nervous laugh passed through the group. "I was just really glad to be alive and happy to come home." He cast his eyes to the ground, unable to look his friends in the eyes.

He took another pull on his glass of bourbon. "Well, you know what happened. Those who signed on fought at Elkhorn Tavern, then they shipped them east of the grand old Mississippi. I'm glad I wasn't with them." He looked at his friends again, conviction burning in his eyes. "If I have to fight, I want to fight on Missouri soil! I don't give a damn about the war in the East. It's my home, my state; I'd shed my blood to protect it. I'll fight again if I must. I only hope they don't force me to make that choice."

Calvin said, "I think we all feel the same. I never had any grand illusions about war. I knew it would be dirty, bloody work. I have to admit, I've let others do my fighting for me—like you, Gil, and my brother Ross. I've felt guilty about not volunteering. I just hoped the war would be over quickly and I could avoid having to kill anyone. I've tried to straddle the fence. You know, not get involved, but I know I can't. Missouri is worth fighting for, and I can't fight against the South." His words trailed off as he stared into his drink.

"You sound like a coward," Jessie said tentatively.

"You know I'm not afraid of any man, Jess. I just couldn't agree with leaving the Union. I know the government has been unfair with us, but I won't be forced into taking up arms against my friends and fellow Missourians. If Shelby comes back, I'll join him rather than the Yankee militia."

Jessie couldn't believe his ears. His brother and the others sounded like they didn't want to fight. He had spent countless nights dreaming about a chance to be a hero in battle. Personally, he couldn't wait to strike a few blows at the Union soldiers.

Calvin nudged Gil in the ribs, "Yankees coming."

The conversation shifted to the evening's pleasures as the Union officers passed near the group. When they left the talk turned to a new topic: Major Benton Bartok and his Third Kansas Cavalry.

"It really burns me that we have to put up with these Kansas Jayhawkers. Why, Bartok and his men are nothing but legalized outlaws. Most of these Jayhawkers have been raiding and stealing from Missourians for years," Jessie said in disgust. His anger flushed his cheeks. "The bastards are nothing more than Red Legs sent here to steal and lay waste to whatever they can't haul away!"

Calvin said angrily, "It appears Governor Gamble's proclamation is going to give Bartok the excuse he has been looking for. By the end of the summer he can start his legalized plunder and intimidation on anyone he feels is disloyal. You can bet if you don't do some serious brown nosing to the good Major, he'll make you pay for it."

Calvin's statement drew positive responses from the group as they nodded in agreement. They all knew the truth of the situation.

Dance Toward the Shadows

"Fanny, would you please help me with my dress? I can't reach the buttons," shouted Elizabeth demandingly.

"You're gonna have ta wait a minute, Miss Lizzie, I'm busy helpin' your sister," exclaimed Fanny, struggling with the buttons on Cassandra's dress.

Elizabeth shrugged her shoulders and glared at Cassandra in disgust. "Just because you're the oldest, I always have to wait for you."

"That's right. I am the oldest and that gives me some privileges. Besides, you're not old enough to court yet and it's important for me to get downstairs early to meet the gentlemen."

"So you can see G-i-l-l-b-e-r-r-t-t, you mean!" Elizabeth drew the words out with exaggerated emphasis, teasing her sister. "I think you are in love."

"Stop it, Elizabeth!" demanded Cassandra. "Sometimes you act so immature!" Cassandra felt her anger building at her young sister's taunts. "I like Gilbert. He is nice, but I certainly don't love him. I haven't met the man that can claim my heart, but I have met several I enjoy seeing." Cassandra gave an ornery smile. "How about you, Liz, do you have a boy friend?"

Elizabeth threw a hairbrush at Cassandra, but Cassie quickly ducked the flying object. Fanny wasn't as lucky. The brush struck her on the shoulder.

Anger spread across Fanny's face. Her eyes widened, emphasizing the blackness of her skin and her sudden anger. She shook a finger for emphasis. "Chile, you watch what you're doin'! You know no lady gonna act like that." Fanny turned toward a laughing Cassandra. "An' you, Miss Cassie, you know you be settin' a poor example for your sister! I 'spect better of y'all."

Fanny's speech took its desired effect and the girls got busy with preparations. With renewed effort, it wasn't long until the girls were ready. Elizabeth wore a white muslin dress with tiny pink nosegays of roses worked into the design. Cassandra wore a gown that belled out with large flowing hoops. The color blue matched her eyes. It was an off-the-shoulder creation with a plunge that emphasized her breasts and showed just a hint of cleavage, as was fashionable these days. The dress was accented with white lace and a large matching blue bow.

"My, oh, my!" said Fanny proudly. "Some of them boys gonna be mighty pleased."

"Thank you, Fanny. You have done such a wonderful job sewing these dresses."

"Now, Miss Cassie, you don't need to be carryin' on so about it. I just do it to make you happy."

Cassie and Elizabeth ran over to the large housekeeper. She hugged both girls, one arm encircling each girl.

"Your mama gonna be mighty proud of both of you. Now, git on down there. You gonna be late for the party!" Fanny watched proudly as the girls left the room.

The sisters met other friends in the hall. Each was busy checking each other's hair and studying the placement of bits of lace and a ribbon here and there. There were the usual cries of "You look lovely," and "You, too," and, "What a beautiful dress." Cassandra and Elizabeth made their way past them and down the stairs.

They joined other guests gathering near a long supper table set up outside, brimming with food. The girls got in line and began filling their plates with food. The table offered fried chicken, ham, and bowls of mashed potatoes, rich egg noodles, green beans, and biscuits. For dessert there was a variety of cherry, apple, peach, and gooseberry pies.

Good food and pleasant company made the supper pass quickly, and soon it was time for the dance. The guests gradually left the dining area and the shade of the stately maples and oaks.

The furniture had been removed from the large sitting room, and the wide doors opened to the veranda that adjoined the dining room and created a large dance floor. A small orchestra brought in by steamboat from Lexington began to play.

Harlan and his lovely wife, Caroline, began the dance. The first number was a waltz, and soon they were motioning to Ellen and Glen Kimbrough to join them.

Glen, feeling depressed and leaning on his cane, waved off Caroline's attempt. Ellen would not accept Glen's reluctance or allow him to feel sorry for himself. She pulled her crippled husband slowly onto the dance floor. They couldn't move normally because of Glen's injury, but Ellen proudly helped her husband. Soon Glen was smiling despite himself.

Ellen never allowed Glen the time to wallow in self-pity. She believed it was far better to do the best you could, accept your limitations, and go on enjoying life. Watching her parents made Cassandra proud.

Cassandra glanced over at Jessie and Katlin. They were oblivious to those around them. It was easy to see their infatuation. Each lost in the other and sharing their conversation. Cassandra had known for over a year Kat was crazy about her brother. He had resisted for a while, preferring to play the field with the many pretty girls in Lafayette County. This weekend, it looked like his resolve was caving in. He'd finally noticed how much the seventeen-year-old beauty had blossomed. Cassandra wondered why it had taken her brother so long; she always regarded Katlin as one of the fairest beauties in the county.

Cassandra envied the contrast of those big blue eyes against the flowing tresses of dark brown hair. Katlin was striking. Cassandra wondered why she always envied the others, rather than being happy with what God had given her.

Gilbert took Cassandra's arm and led her to the dance floor. There they joined the milieu of couples swirling around the room.

"You look lovely tonight, Cassie." Gilbert looked deeply into her eyes as he swung her around the room. "This has to be one of the happiest moments of my life."

"And why is this moment so important to you?" Cassandra teased.

"A beautiful day and the company of one of the loveliest girls in the whole world. It's enough to make this or any other day special," Gilbert said with conviction, and Cassandra felt sure he meant every word.

"You flatter me, Gil, thank you."

The song ended, and they reluctantly left the dance floor. Benton Bartok forced his way through the crowd to join them.

"Excuse me, Gilbert, may I have this dance with Miss Kimbrough?"

Cassandra watched Gilbert flare up like a fighting cock. She moved quickly to smooth the sudden tension caused by Bartok's request.

Cassandra smiled sweetly at Gilbert, "I'm sure Gilbert would spare one dance for a guest, wouldn't you, Gil?" She paused. "Would you mind getting me some punch? I am quite thirsty."

There wasn't much Gilbert could do. He couldn't turn down a direct request from Cassandra, but he would do so with the greatest reluctance. Gil hurried toward the punch bowl.

Bartok took her hand and led her to the dance floor. His

eyes burned into hers, then dropped to peer at her cleavage. As he again looked into her eyes, he said huskily, "Miss Kimbrough, I believe you have everything a man might desire in a woman." He slid his hand tighter around her waist, drawing her closer as they danced. "You're quite lovely."

Cassandra felt her stomach turn. It was bad enough to have to dance with this jackal, but having to contend with his leering, lecherous actions were nearly unbearable. She pulled away from him, trying to get the proper distance between their dancing bodies. She didn't like the feel of his hot breath on her, emanating from his large, hawk-billed nose. He pulled her even tighter, relishing his momentary control over her. The moments seemed to slow to an unbearable crawl for Cassandra as the dance lingered on. For Cassandra, it seemed like time was as slow as honey poured on a cold winter day. "When will this dance end?" she thought. By the end of the dance, Bartok maneuvered her to the edge of the dance floor and near the doors leading to the open veranda. She lost sight of Gilbert, and Cassandra wondered if he was still lost in the crowd attending to the punch bowl.

"I'd like you to walk with me in the garden, Cassandra. I have some important matters to discuss concerning your family. I am afraid it requires your immediate attention."

Benton Bartok didn't allow time for her to object. He grabbed her, circling his arm around her back and grasping her tightly by the back of her elbow. He used a painful, pinching pressure to control and guide her through the open door and out into the moonlight.

Cassandra felt uneasy about his intentions. She implored, "I can't leave Gilbert. He'll be waiting for me. I told him it would be just one dance."

"Nonsense, I'm sure he's cornered by some guests and won't miss us for a while. I really must talk to you alone."

He continued to guide her away from the house. Cassandra tried to resist, but he was too powerful. He propelled her quickly along the garden path.

"You mentioned you had something to say concerning my family. What is it?" she asked nervously.

"I must tell you their personal welfare is at stake here. They don't know it, but great personal tragedy could strike them in these difficult times. Unless, of course, your family had a powerful friend with influence to protect them."

"Protect us from what?" Cassandra asked, already guessing at the answer.

"There is a war going on and there are plenty of Union sympathizers in these parts, eager to punish those who side with the secessionist rabble. I suppose the worst hazard lies in the uncontrolled, roving bands of Red Legs and Jayhawkers making raids from Kansas. They love to target fine plantations like Briarwood. You might find it helpful to have me as a special friend to look out for your personal interest and to protect Briarwood and your family from these unruly elements. As commander of this district I wield considerable power and influence. A word from me could do much to save you and your family from suffering any unfortunate harm."

He leered at her as he spun her around in the moonlight to face him. She could feel his eyes undressing her, his hot breath on her chest as he drew her close. His breathing was becoming rapid and more irregular. She stiffened, put her hands on his chest and tried to push him away.

"All you have to do to save your precious family and that plantation of yours is just be very nice and do as I ask without question." He tried to kiss her, but Cassandra darted her face away from him. Benton didn't hesitate. He buried his lips at the base of her neck and began kissing and licking his way down into the darkness between her breasts, while he pinned her arms behind her. She struggled, but he was too strong for her. He slid his hands to her upper arms and tried to force her dress off her shoulders. She resisted more urgently until Benton, in frustration, reached his hand to the front of her gown and tried to pull it down.

Suddenly, Bartok found himself spinning around to face a man who grabbed him by the shoulder. Bartok's right hand still clutched Cassandra's dress. Before he could respond, Bartok felt the impact of a heavy blow to his nose. He let go of Cassandra in shocked pain as his eyes filled with tears from the blow and his blood began to flow. The next punch caught him full on the chin and sent him sprawling on the grass. He tried to clear his vision by rapidly blinking his eyes. His hands grasped at his broken nose. The blood streaming through his fingers coated them.

Towering above Bartok stood Cassandra's fiery brother, Jessie. "You sorry son of a bitch! You try to touch my sister again and it'll be the last mistake you ever make."

"How dare you hit me! I'm the district commander. I'll have you arrested."

"You'll have to catch me first, Bartok, and if you don't I might find you sleeping some night and cut your sorry throat."

Bartok suddenly realized he was all alone and extremely vulnerable to continued attack by Cassandra's brother. Fear gripped his belly as he searched for some way out of this predicament.

Cassandra came to his rescue, afraid of what the major and the Union troops might do to her brother. She tugged at her brother. "Come on, Jessie, I'm fine. Let's return to the party."

Jessie stood, legs spread, with his hands doubled into fists. Slowly he relaxed when he realized the major would not fight. He turned to follow her.

Cassandra knew Jessie had saved her. She wasn't sure she could have fought Major Bartok off much longer. She was certain he would have forced himself upon her had not Jessie intervened. Thinking about it sickened her.

"I saw him guiding you outside and thought it might be wise to follow. Katlin was busy powdering her nose, anyway."

"I'm grateful you did, but I'm afraid we haven't heard the last of the major. He can make life extremely difficult for us all."

"I don't care! He can't treat my sister that way. Besides, he doesn't know how lucky he was. If Gil had been there he might have killed him."

Cassandra didn't doubt her brother's words, but she worried about the consequences. She feared the major would want quick revenge for his embarrassment and for not having his way with her.

Upon reaching the great house, Gilbert came to her, drinks in hand. "Where have you been? I couldn't find you after the dance ended."

She told him what had happened between her and Bartok and how Jessie had come to her rescue. It was difficult, but she talked Gil out of hunting for Bartok. She was glad the major didn't try to rejoin the party, and the remainder of the evening went smoothly.

She knew Bartok was not the type of man to give up easily—he would seek revenge. She knew she would have to face him again. She shuddered at the thought and tried to keep her mind on the remainder of the evening's pleasures.

9

A Ride Through a Scorched Land

Nothing in Ross Kimbrough's life had prepared him for the blackened landscape. It was as if the very fires of hell had belched forth its destruction on the land. For miles they rode past charred chimneys surrounded by piles of smoking rubble. Not long ago these were homes for hard-working Missouri farmers. Now, from beds of smoldering ash, only silent sentinels stretched their lonely shafts to the open sky. Someone viewing the scene might think a great prairie fire had swept the land, consuming all in its path. Fields were gone, livestock dead or absent, and homes destroyed.

The people, grim-faced with hollow eyes reflecting sorrow and loss, shuffled slowly south toward Arkansas. These were the homeless and dispossessed, the refugees from a brother's war, or a neighbor's war, gone berserk. Vengeance followed vengeance, wrath topped wrath, until Bates County, Missouri, was reduced to ruin.

Ross Kimbrough, Jonas Starke, and Rube Anderson led the way through this desolation. For miles the scouts rode through sweltering heat. The sun beat down on the riders and pasted their ash-covered uniforms to their bodies as the pungent odor of death filled their nostrils. Ross thought even a bird flying over this land would need to pack its own food to survive.

Ross felt a rising swell of disgust and hate, and fought back the bitter taste of bile. Bates County was an easy target for the raiding Jayhawkers from Kansas. The raiders, often Union troops under the command of Lane, Jennison, and Anthony, would strike fast and run their plunder across the border into Kansas, just a few miles west. Lying on the western border with Kansas had sealed the doom for Bates County, Missouri.

Shelby's cavalry traveled fast, anxious to keep moving north toward their homes in Lafayette County. They hoped their homes had not suffered the same fate. Each man felt himself buoyed along by his desire to know and by his fear of what he might find ahead.

Ross pulled down the brim of his slough hat and wiped the sweat from his brow as he thought about their journey. It had taken them five days to cross the Boston Mountains. Those rugged roads and passes took a heavy toll on the poor quality horses and pack animals they had received in Arkansas. Along the way, Shelby's men replaced the dying mounts with better horses, purchased with Confederate bank notes from farmers.

After crossing into Missouri they had fought a small skirmish with Major Hubbard's men of the Union First Missouri, killing three of the Yankees. The remainder holed up behind heavy fortifications and refused to come out and fight. The company had rested and, after a short while, left the enemy to their barricades and continued to move north.

Now they were three-quarters of the way home. Ross felt weary, but the thoughts of home and family kept him going. As the three scouts approached a rise in the road they split their formation. Ross went up the road; Jonas flanked to the left of the hill, and Rube to the right. Ross slowed his horse, giving his flankers time to circle the hill. It wouldn't do to ride into an ambush. When he was certain he had allowed them time to get into position, he followed the road over the hill.

Not more than a quarter of a mile ahead stood the recently burned out remains of a homestead. The chimney jutted out of the ash like some forbidding tombstone, marking the earthly remains of a once-proud home. Smoke still curled in tiny, lazy columns from smoldering wood and danced lightly on the breeze.

Next to the cabin a woman in a dirty, shabby dress lay upon the mound of a freshly dug grave, face buried in her arms. Ross Kimbrough's first impulse was to investigate, but he waited, letting his men get into position.

As Ross approached the burned-out cabin, he guided his mount away from the road and rode directly to the woman. Ross skirted a stand of trees and rode by a thicket of brush as he neared her. She should have heard his horse approaching, but she didn't bother to look up. He watched her shoulders heaving as she sobbed loudly. "Excuse me, madam, are you all right?" She ignored him; wailing and crying as she lay in the dirt.

Out of the corner of one eye, Ross saw a blur of motion. He twisted toward the movement, but it was too late. Ross felt a heavy blow to his ribs and he found himself tumbling from the saddle toward the ground. He struck the earth hard. Through his blurred eyes, he caught a quick glimpse of his assailant, a blond-headed boy approximately fourteen years old.

He felt the boy raining down quick jabs to his chest and face and was thankful the boy wasn't carrying a knife. The shock of the sudden attack made it difficult for Ross to protect himself. They rolled and struggled on the ground with Ross desperately trying to regain his wind. Thankfully, Rube pulled the young wildcat off. Rube struggled valiantly to calm down the boy. Just as Ross rose, with effort, to his feet, Jonas rode up.

"What in hell is wrong with you, boy!" Ross wheezed, still straining to suck more air into his lungs.

"You dirty bastards, I'll kill you! I'll kill every one of ya. Ya killed my pa. Ya killed my pa!" the boy yelled.

"Wait a minute, boy, we ain't killed nobody in these parts. We just rode in here," Rube said, as he spat a stream of tobacco to the side for emphasis. "Suppose you calm down and tell us what happened." Rube turned to the woman, but still held the boy tightly. "Ma'am, maybe you could explain it a mite." The woman refused to respond, carrying on with her heart-wrenching sobs.

"Leave her alone!" shouted the boy. "She's been like this for two days."

"Okay, calm down, boy. Nobody here wants to hurt you. Just tell us what happened," Ross pleaded.

The boy relaxed a little and cast his eyes at the ground.

After a moment, he glanced up and stared at Ross directly in the eyes. "I wanna know if you're Yanks or Rebs."

"We're Rebs; Lafayette County Cavalry," Ross replied after a short hesitation.

The boy eyed them, then relaxed even more, the intensity of his anger decreasing. "My name is Billy Cahill. That's my Ma. Jayhawkers rode in here two days ago near sunset. They dragged Pa and me from the barn and took us over to that patch of trees over yonder. They got a rope out and put it around Pa's neck. Then they pulled him off the ground so his feet dangled in the air. He tried to take the weight off his neck by using his hands on the rope, but he was gagging something awful. They would let him down once in a while and ask him questions. They made me and Ma watch." His jaws began to twitch and tears welled up in his eyes and spilled silently down his cheeks. "Someone here abouts told them Pa had fought with Price's Missouri State Guards and that he favored the South.

"He came back last winter with his discharge and told us he was through with the war. Someone musta told them Pa had some money hid somewheres and they wanted it. Pa tried his best to hold out, but they beat him. They kept him up there until he'd start turning blue and his eyes would start to bulge."

The boy broke down in heavy sobs. After a minute his face flushed red and angry as he screwed up his face and shouted, "Damn them! Damn ever last one of 'em!" he yelled. "Please, God, let me kill them. I wanna see them all dead." He slumped on the ground, sobbing heavily.

They waited a few minutes until he could continue. "Pa finally told them where the money was hid in the house, after they promised they wouldn't hurt Ma and me. Weren't much. Pa told them we only had a little more than twenty dollars. We growed most all we needed," he explained. "Well, that made 'em even more angry and they set fire to our cabin. They wouldn't let us save nothin'. They stole our horses and our milk cows. They killed our hogs and chickens and stole 'em. Then they burned the barn and the outhouse. They made us watch all the slaughter and stealin' and poor Pa still with a noose around his neck.

"He was standin' there pulled mostly up on his toes. When everything was burnin' real good, Jennison's boys pulled Pa up into the air and yelled, 'Look close at your Pa, boy! The next fires he'll see will be the fires of hell!' And they left him hangin' there till he was dead.

"They wouldn't let us help him. We begged 'em to let him go, but they just laughed at us. Pa struggled a long time, maybe twenty minutes 'fore his strength gave out. The heat of the cabin fire was bad and we could see the firelight dancin' off him.

"He choked and gagged until his tongue came out and his eyes bulged, then he just went stiff and quit kickin'. They left him there, hangin' in the tree. His feet danglin' just inches from the ground." The boy grabbed his stomach as if someone was twisting a knife in his gut. "They wouldn't let me help him. They killed my pa! The bastards killed my pa!"

The boy wiped his sleeve across his face; and, after a pause, began talking again, slowly and in a much deeper, calmer tone. "Took me two days to dig the grave. I found a shovel in what was left of the barn, but most of the handle was burned off. I found an old knife in the ashes of the cabin. I untied Pa and got him down from the tree. The rope cut deep into his neck and I had to use the knife to cut the rope from him. Pa's eyes were just starin' at me, like he was beggin' me to help him. Askin' me why I hadn't stopped them. So I closed his eyelids with my fingers. Ma, she wasn't any help. I guess her mind musta snapped or somethin'. I made the cross from dead tree branches and some twine I found."

The men shuffled their feet uneasily. Rube kept doubling his fists and clenching his jaw tighter. Tears flowed silently down the big man's cheeks until they disappeared into his beard.

Ross asked softly, "Where's the rest of your family?"

"I got an older brother, Jimmy. He's in the Reb army with General Marmaduke's cavalry. We ain't heard from him for a while. Last we heard he was in Arkansas." He hesitated. "Don't know how I'm gonna tell him about Pa."

"Isn't there anyone else, boy?" asked Rube.

"That's all I've got livin'. I lost a brother and two sisters to whooping cough 'bout three years ago. They're buried a couple of hundred yards behind our cabin."

"Rube, Jonas, better ride on ahead. We've got to keep someone in front of the column. I'll wait for Captain Shelby and check in with him."

" 'Spect you're right, Sarge, we best move out. If Cap'n Shelby finds us lollygaggin' around here leavin' the column unprotected, God help us!" Jonas remounted his horse.

Rube slapped the boy's back in sympathy. "Wish there was somethin' I could say, somethin' I could do, Billy, to make it better, but there ain't nothin'." His voice trailed off, then after an awkward silent moment, he turned and swung into the saddle.

Just before Jonas touched his heels to his horse he said, "Sorry about what happened, boy. If I ever find any of Jennison's Jayhawkers, I'll kill a bunch of them for you and take pleasure in it." Then Jonas and Rube spurred forward and rode out.

After a short wait, the column appeared and Captain Shelby was briefed. Shelby ordered horses, food, and water to be left for the boy and his mother. Shelby walked over to the lad and put his hand on his shoulder. "If I were you, Billy, I'd take advantage of the food and horses and get out of here. I'd take your mother to Arkansas. The war hasn't touched the country as hard down there."

"I appreciate your thoughts, Cap'n, but as soon as I can find shelter for my mother I'm going to fight the Yankees. This was my home an' they took it away. I'm gonna make 'em pay."

"I understand how you feel, son, but unless you want to be a drummer boy you're too young to fight in the army. Besides, war is a terrible business for a youngster your age. Take care of your mother and try to forget about it until you're older."

Billy's face twisted red and angry as he pulled away from Shelby's hand. "You don't know how I feel and you never will unless it happens to you! I'm not gonna wait till I'm older, I'll fight now! The Jayhawkers brought war here and they killed my Pa. We didn't ask for it and we didn't do anything wrong. I'll be damned if I let 'em get away with it. If the army doesn't want me, then I'll fight on my own."

"I admire your gumption, Billy, but I beg you to take a couple of days to cool down and reconsider. Things might look different then."

"I know what you're thinkin'. You think I'm just a kid someone would have to look after. It ain't so. I know how to shoot. I've been huntin' squirrels and rabbits since I was ten and I'm strong for my age. Nobody is gonna have to watch over me."

Shelby, aware his words were useless, nodded his head sadly and walked away. After the brief stop the column moved on, leaving behind the boy and his mother. It was a terrible tragedy, but common up and down the border. Shelby and his troopers tried their best to put it behind them.

The column rode on until they left Bates County and made their way almost through Johnson County, before word reached them that John T. Coffee, a Confederate recruiting officer in southern Missouri, needed help south near the

Osage River. The command quickly counter-marched back through Johnson County and across the burned district of Bates County to reach Colonel Coffee's command. They found him safe despite the reports. He had been in Missouri several months, and after defeating several small Union units he was well equipped and had plenty of captured horses.

When Shelby's command continued their march, they were equipped with the best the Federal army had to offer— captured Union booty now served the Southern soldiers. There was even some left over for Vard Cockrell's command, although they were not as short on equipment as Shelby's men.

The combined force of Jo Shelby's, Vard Cockrell's, and John Coffee's commands continued toward Lafayette County. Again they crossed the burned district. As they reached the banks of the Grand River, Coffee and his men left the column and moved in the direction of Independence and Lone Jack to recruit and provide a distraction for Cockrell and Shelby.

Ross Kimbrough and his band of scouts rode on ahead and returned with the information the column needed. The Third Kansas, led by Bartok, were camped near Dover. Nothing blocked their path as far as the Redd farm. Shelby's men marched at an accelerated pace.

10

The Lafayette County Cavalry
Comes Home

Ross Kimbrough, Terrill Fletcher, Jonas Starke, Bill Corbin, and Rube Anderson rode again in the advance. They passed by miles of beautiful corn fields and turned in at the familiar home of Mrs. Rebecca Redd. Mrs. Redd was Jo Shelby's aunt and well known throughout Lafayette County. As Ross and his men approached the farm, he saw men stirring near the house. Rebecca stood on her porch, anxious to greet her guests.

As the scouts neared, her eyes brightened in recognition and a smile broke across her face. "Ross Kimbrough, I'm so happy to see you again!" Her eyes twinkled with delight as she smiled mischievously. "I think we have someone staying here you'd like to see." She turned and whispered to her housemaid, who quickly entered the house.

Ross watched the departure of the maid with interest. "I never liked surprises, Mrs. Redd. Why don't you just tell me who it is?" He swung his leg stiffly out of the saddle and tied the reins to a nearby rail.

"You'll see!" she answered, smiling at him.

The front door slammed open and out strolled his younger brother, Jessie. "Ross, is it really you?"

Ross couldn't believe his eyes. "Jess, what in thunder are you doin' here?" Ross blurted out, hugging his younger brother tightly and nearly toppling them both to the ground.

"Mrs. Redd has been hiding me here. I got in a little scrape with the local Union commander on the Fourth of July, and I've had to keep moving ever since to keep from being arrested."

"What did you do, Jess?" Ross looked his brother in the eyes as he pulled himself free from his grasp.

"Oh, not much, I just knocked him down and broke his nose," said Jessie, grinning.

"I suppose he did something to deserve it other than just being a Yankee."

Jessie's expression turned serious. "Yeah, he was busy trying to rape Cassandra."

The smile faded from Ross's face. "She's all right, isn't she?"

"You know Cassie, she's pretty tough. She probably could have handled him herself, but I've been looking for some excuse to flatten that pompous bastard, and I knew I'd get few better excuses than this one!"

"So, what happened after you punched him?"

"He didn't try anything that night, but the next day he sent troops to arrest me. He's been looking for me ever since. But so far, I've managed to stay ahead of them. Rumors have been floating around here for weeks that Shelby was coming. I knew if I could hold on, I could join your company." Jess eyed Ross's arm sleeve. "What's this, are you a sergeant now?"

Ross beamed proudly. "I'm in charge of Shelby's scouts, little brother." Ross studied Jessie from head to toe. "I guess you're not so little anymore. How's the rest of the family?" His face betrayed his anxiety.

"They're fine. They've been worried about me and the Feds have searched the place twice, but I understand they are okay. Father is getting around pretty good now. He still has to use a cane, but he is much better than the last time you saw him."

"How is Mother?"

"She's worried about you and the war, but she's in good health."

Ross introduced Jessie to his scouts, then sent word back to Shelby's column to continue the advance. He posted the rest of his men on all approaches to the farm to protect them from surprise attack. Jess spent the next hour filling Ross in on Governor Gamble's decree and Bartok's actions in the county. Shelby's company camped at the Redd farm for the night. Mrs. Redd got her people busy and fed the entire company. The next day, a Southern sympathizer brought word that Bartok and his men had marched out of Dover, moving north. Apparently, Bartok had decided it was a very good time to patrol neighboring Saline County and to look for guerrillas. Ross speculated the major was afraid to face the wrath of Shelby and his men.

After Captain Shelby was filled in on the latest information, he assigned pickets and details to guard the roads and set up his headquarters at Waverly. The town was within easy distance of his home on Mount Rucker. He gave the majority of his men leave to visit their families, including Ross Kimbrough and his brother.

Since Evan Stryker was not originally from Lafayette County, Ross invited him to stay with them at Briarwood. Evan gladly accepted, anxious to enjoy a hot bath and a few days' rest in a real bed. The party of three rode in high spirits to Briarwood.

Ross wanted to surprise his family, but word had spread quickly. It seemed the whole county had heard Shelby and his boys were coming home. As they rode down the lane leading to Briarwood, Ross felt tears welling in his eyes. His heart soared at the sight of the large white columns and the wide stairs leading to the portico. How he had missed home!

Ross had often wondered if he would ever see Briarwood again. Now the happiness of being home was almost unbearable. It was the dreams of family and home that had sustained him through all the misery and desolation of a soldier's life. It was the one guiding light that kept him fighting. All the suffering he'd endured was worthwhile if it served to protect his home and family.

He watched a young girl on the porch bounce up and down with excitement, and he saw her yell toward the house. She scurried down the porch and grabbed at the hem of her skirt. She pulled the dress above her knees and ran toward the three riders as fast as she could go. He marveled at how quickly she moved.

Ross halted his horse and slid out of the saddle. He waited, a wide smile on his face, as Elizabeth ran to him.

"Ross! Ross! You're home. You're home!" She leapt into his arms and hugged him tightly around the neck.

Ross slowly spun her around in a circle. "My Lord, Sis, I really have missed you. I can't believe how much you've grown."

They clung to each other for a moment, before she broke free to hug Jess.

"I see the Yankees haven't caught you yet. Major Bartok keeps sending his patrols here looking for you. I bet they have searched our house at least once a week since we got back from Riverview." She smiled. "He's disappointed every time he doesn't find our wayward Jessie."

Jessie laughed as they walked toward the house. "It would take a better man than Benton Bartok to catch me. That hawk-billed Jayhawker couldn't find his butt with both hands, so how's he gonna find me? Every time a patrol has come even close to me, our friends have helped me escape."

By now the rest of the family, and Fanny and Jethro, were rushing to greet the boys. Hugs were passed around generously. Evan Stryker, feeling a bit out of place and fearing he was intruding on the homecoming celebration, stood back a little.

Ross noticed and turned to introduce him to his family. "Pardon my manners, Evan. I guess in all the excitement we've ignored you. I'd like to introduce you to my family. This is my father, Glen Kimbrough; my mother, Ellen; my sister, Elizabeth; and my brother, Calvin." Ross paused. "I'm proud to introduce Lieutenant Evan Stryker, formerly with the Sixth Texas Cavalry, now attached to the Lafayette County Cavalry. He's from San Marcos, Texas."

"It is a pleasure to welcome you to Briarwood, sir," responded Glen, shaking Evan's hand warmly. The rest of the family followed.

Ross continued, "I would also like you to meet Fanny and Jethro." Evan stepped forward and shook hands with both of them.

"Fanny practically raised us since we were in diapers. She's been the head housekeeper and cook for many years. Jethro works with the horses and sees to the other slaves. They make this plantation run smoothly."

Fanny turned to Ross. "Ross Kimbrough, you get yo'self over here, an' give this ole black mama a hug now fo' I box your ears!" Fanny stood, arms outstretched, a big, happy grin on her face.

Ross let her give him a mighty hug. While he was still in her grasp, he reached over and shook Jethro's hand. "How have you been, Jethro?"

"Fine, suh, an' I'm mighty glad to have ya home."

Cassandra stood at the top of the stairs watching her brother's introductions. She wore one of her favorite red day dresses, and when she saw the handsome guest from Texas, she was very glad she had taken the extra time to make herself look special. When he glanced up at her, his brown eyes danced and twinkled. His face broke into an easy smile, revealing dimples and nearly perfect white teeth. Ross took her attention away from the gentleman by giving her a hard squeeze. She embraced him just as firmly.

"Welcome home, Ross, I can't tell you how much I have missed you."

"Cassie, I would like to introduce you to a good friend of mine, Lieutenant Evan Stryker from Texas. Evan, this is my other sister, Cassandra Marie Kimbrough."

Evan took her hand and bowed low. "It is indeed a pleasure to meet you, Cassandra. I have heard Ross talk of you often."

"I hope Ross hasn't told you too many tall tales about me."

"He's told me a few funny stories about things you did growing up together."

"Well, I hope we'll have time to even things out a little while you are here. I've got several stories I can tell you about Ross I'm sure you will enjoy." She looked at Ross impishly.

The next two days at Briarwood were like heaven for Ross. He hadn't realized how much he had truly missed home until he had returned. Cassandra found herself more attracted to Evan Stryker than she had been to any other man. Relaxed and comfortable in his presence, she felt as if she could listen to him talk forever.

Meanwhile, men poured in from every direction to enlist in Shelby's command, keeping the recruiting officers for Shelby busy signing up the new enlistees. Union Governor Gamble had given the all-important push to those trying to avoid the war. Tired of the injustices and forced to choose sides, many were ready to fight for the Confederacy. These grim, determined young recruits enlisting for war would make ideal troopers. The cream of the Missouri River Valley poured into the command. These men were mad as hell and ready to fight the Union army, these invaders of their native soil, and they were anxious to right the wrongs.

Shelby enlisted one thousand men in just four days at Waverly. Among them were Ross Kimbrough's brothers, Jessie and Calvin, and their friend, Gilbert Thomas.

11

Sudden Proposal

Gilbert rode with Jessie and Calvin to visit Briarwood after enlisting in Shelby's command. Gilbert knew his duty was clear. He must fight again for the Confederacy. The prospect of returning to war both excited and filled him with dread. He also didn't want to leave Cassandra behind.

Cassandra meant everything to him. If he didn't go, he feared she would think him a coward. He still didn't know how he stood with her, but Gilbert fervently hoped she loved him. He was hoping he could proceed slowly to build upon their relationship, to slowly increase her love for him, but the war was not going to let him. He sensed he must make his move now. He decided he would ask for her hand in marriage. By heaven, he would do it! But in his heart, he felt an ever-tightening knot of doubt.

They reached Briarwood and, after securing their mounts in the barn, they entered the great house.

Gilbert was shocked to find Cassandra in the sitting room engaged in happy conversation with a stranger, her hand in his. Her eyes were filled with affection and tenderness—the very look Gilbert had hoped she would some day share with him. Gilbert fought for control of his emotions, realizing he needed his wits about him. "Cassandra! How have you been?" Gilbert asked, a little too loudly, as he strode quickly to the couple.

Gilbert's sudden and unexpected appearance startled Cassandra. She had been so totally involved with Evan that she hadn't noticed Gilbert's entrance. She quickly withdrew her hand from Evan's and rose. "Gilbert, I am surprised to see you. I didn't know you were planning to stop by."

Gilbert tried to maintain a measure of control, but he found himself glaring at the intruding stranger. "I've just returned from enlisting in Shelby's command. I met Jessie and Calvin there, and they suggested I spend the night at Briarwood before returning to Riverview. You know I welcome any chance to see you again." Gilbert, towering over the shorter, more compact Texan, tried to use his height to intimidate this stranger.

After an awkward, extended pause, Cassandra regained her composure. "Gil, I would like to introduce you to Evan Stryker of San Marcos, Texas. He is a member of Captain Shelby's staff. Evan, this is Gilbert Thomas of Dover, Missouri."

Evan extended his hand. "Pleased to meet you, Gilbert. Ross has mentioned you."

Gilbert was slow to respond, but clasped the offered hand in a firm handshake. The two men tightened their grip, each trying to intimidate the other.

"Pleased to meet you, Mister Stryker. May I ask what a Texan is doing serving with a Missouri unit?"

Evan already disliked this brash Missourian. "I was wounded at the battle of Elkhorn Tavern. I was nearly healed and preparing to rejoin my old unit when I had the pleasure of meeting Ross and Captain Shelby. I was informed that they were planning to fight on this side of the Mississippi and, even more to my liking, they were cavalry. Just what I have been looking for, so I asked for a transfer and was lucky enough to get it."

Plainly unhappy with the situation, Gilbert wanted to be rid of the interloper. Forcing a smile, he asked, "Would you please excuse us, Mister Stryker? I'd like to discuss some personal matters with Cassandra for a few moments. If you don't mind?"

"Please, call me Evan, Gilbert." Evan was enjoying the obvious discomfort of the taller man.

"Yes, of course, Evan." Gilbert turned toward Cassandra. "Cassandra, would you please walk with me to the veranda?"

Smiling apologetically to Evan, she wrapped her arm around Gilbert's. "Please excuse us, Evan." They strolled toward the door.

"Just what are you doing with him?" Gilbert demanded.

"We were just talking. As if it is any concern of yours!" Cassandra shot back at him. She was angry with his rude display. He was acting as if he owned her.

Gilbert sensed her anger and tried to calm the raging jealousy burning within him. "I'm sorry, it's just that I care for you and I get jealous when I see you with someone else."

"Yes, I could see it upset you, Gil, but you shouldn't let it overpower you."

Gilbert pulled her toward him. "I don't know really how to say this. . . . I have so little time."

"Please don't Gil, I——"

"Please, I must tell you how I feel. Cassandra, I . . . I love you."

Cassandra turned away and looked toward the wide Missouri River. "I know you do, Gilbert, but I'm afraid now is not the time."

Gilbert gently turned her to face him. "Damn it, Cassandra! When is there going to be time? I've enlisted in the army, and very soon I'll have to leave. I have to know . . . if you will wait for me." He hesitated, gathering his courage, then plunged ahead. "Cassandra, will you marry me?"

She could not return his gaze and lowered her eyes. "I cannot marry you, Gilbert," she said slowly and softly. "I do care for you. You mean a great deal to me, but I don't love you enough to become your wife. I love you more as a brother and as a very dear friend."

She could see the hurt on his face. Gilbert didn't know how to respond. At first he was stunned. Then the fear of losing her gripped at his throat—it was as if someone was choking the life from him. He turned away. He didn't want her to see his disappointment or pain.

Quickly, the rejection Gilbert felt channeled into anger. Gilbert needed someone, something, to blame for his misfortune. He spun to face her. "Is it Evan, that damned Texan, who has changed you?" he shouted.

"No, Gil. No one changed anything. My feelings for you have never changed."

"It's because I failed to protect you from that Yankee, Bartok, isn't it?"

"No, it wasn't your fault. You had no way of knowing his intentions. I don't think any of us truly did."

"It *is* Stryker, isn't it? He came in here with his damn Texan accent and his fancy uniform and he just swept you off your feet." If she didn't love Gilbert, it must be someone else's fault.

"I will not lie to you. I find him attractive and I do enjoy his company, but, honestly, he has nothing to do with the way I feel about you. Gil, please. Don't be angry. Try to understand . . ."

There was a long pause. Gilbert's mind raced. "Make my excuses for me. I'm feeling very tired and tomorrow I must ride home to Riverview to say my good-byes." He spun on his heels and quickly walked away, not looking back.

Cassandra was alone. She was standing, gazing at the river, trying to sort out her thoughts when her mother came to her.

"Are you all right?" Ellen asked. "Gilbert stormed past me and went upstairs to his room. Did you quarrel?"

"Gilbert asked me to marry him, Mother." She hesitated, fidgeting with her skirt. "I like Gilbert, but I don't love him."

"Perhaps, in time; things have a way of changing." She touched Cassie gently. "Your father wants all the children to gather for a meeting in the sitting room. He asked Evan to allow us to have this time alone, and Evan has gone up to his room. Fanny is visiting Jethro this evening at his cabin."

"Yes, Mother." They turned and walked back to the house, arm in arm.

12

Family Meeting

Glen stood as Cassandra and Ellen entered the room, then eased himself into his armchair once they were seated. Jessie stood by the windows, Ross by the fireplace. Calvin sat in the chair beside his father; Elizabeth sat on the floor.

Glen began, "As you all know, our situation has become dangerous. We are caught in the middle and forced to choose sides despite our wishes. I have considered our options and, if we must fight, our choice is obvious. However, we must remember we live in an area often occupied by our enemies. This presents dangers that must be addressed. I have made some conclusions and decisions that concern us all and I'd appreciate it if you would hear me out without interruption until I've said my piece."

Glen paused to study the faces of his wife and children. He pulled a cigar out of a box beside his chair. He leaned forward and began again. "First, you know I am opposed to the war and have done all I can to stay out of it. Ross, you know I wasn't happy about you joining the army, but I felt you were old enough to make your own decision. I have to tell you, although we worried about you, we were proud of you for following your convictions.

"It has become clear in the last several months that no one is going to be allowed to stay out of this conflict. Our hope for survival must lie with the Confederacy. I'm proud of each of my sons. Each one has joined Shelby, and I'm proud you made your own decisions."

He paused, stuck the cigar in his mouth and lit it. Once the tip glowed cherry red, he continued. "When Shelby's command rides out, the Feds will ride back in. When Bartok hears you've enlisted in the Confederate army instead of his Yankee militia, he's going to be furious. I expect him to hurry out here and seize most of our horses for his army. That's why I've offered to sell all the horses I can to Shelby. I'll even give our extras away to those too poor to purchase a good mount. I want you boys to take our best horses with you into the army. I'm sending Sultan with Ross, Star's Pride with Jessie, and Red Roses with Calvin."

Ross couldn't remain quiet. "Father, you don't want to send your best stock to war. Horses die quickly in battle and they don't receive the food and care they should while on duty."

"Son, I asked you to let me finish. Now please, let me continue." Ross walked to a chair and sat down.

"I am well aware of the dangers to horses in battle, but would I refuse to risk my best horses, yet send my sons? There isn't a thing I own that is more precious to me than my family. I'll feel better knowing that you are mounted on the very best horses available. They might save your lives in combat." He shifted the cigar to his mouth and took another draw. Exhaling, he said, "I insist. I'll send Bright Star and three or four more of our better mares to the Thomas plantation. I don't think Bartok is as angry with the Thomas family as he is with us, and I don't think he'll realize the horses still belong to us."

Jessie quickly blurted out, "I'll help Gilbert take them over in the morning, Father, if it's all right."

Glen smiled as he blew out another rolling cloud of cigar smoke. "I thought you might want to go. You might want to say good-bye to Katlin while you're there." Glen winked at Jessie, who smiled shyly and looked down at the floor.

"Elizabeth, I think it is time for you to go upstairs to bed," her father said.

"Why can't I stay up with the rest of you?"

"Do as your father asked, Liz," Ellen said sternly. Elizabeth, still pouting, went reluctantly upstairs.

"I think what I'm about to tell you is too important to trust to a young girl. I want to keep this secret until she is older." He paused. "We've been blessed with several good years here at Briarwood. The last two years have been particularly good for business. We have amassed quite a fortune in gold and Federal greenbacks. With things as they are in this country, I long ago lost faith in keeping our money in banks." Glen sat forward in his chair. "You must tell no one outside this room what I am about to tell you."

He paused, looking into each face. "I have buried most of our money in the northeast corner of the barn. I buried it in an iron chest I bought a few years ago from a freight company in Kansas City."

Glen motioned toward his son Calvin. "Calvin helped me dig the hole and bury it just a few days ago. We placed a layer of boards just above the chest and covered it with dirt. The chest is buried about three feet deep.

"We will bury another box tomorrow night with the money from the sale of horses to Shelby's command. I want to include our important papers, jewelry, and best silverware. We'll wrap the money and papers in oilcloth and place it in a box inside the chest. I hope it will protect our valuables until the war is over. The second box will be buried in the southwest corner of the barn. The bedding straw and the horses will pack the ground, so our hiding place will be well concealed."

He stood. A soft groan escaped him as he moved behind his chair and rested his hand on it for balance. "I'll feel better knowing that despite what might happen in this war, those of us who survive will have the means to continue. If the Yankees can't find it, they can't steal it."

"Glen, may I speak now?"

"Yes, of course, Ellen dear."

"I just want to say how proud of you I am, my sons. Cassandra, Elizabeth, Fanny, and myself have kept ourselves busy sewing. We will have new uniforms completed before you go. In the inside lining of your jacket, near the button row, you will find two twenty-dollar gold pieces sewed in. These are for emergency use. We have also sewn in the same amount into the linings of our slips for Cassandra, Elizabeth, and myself. This way we will all have money available to us if things should become desperate or we are away from home. We have extra socks, an extra shirt, and pair of pants for each of you. Your father wants you to take your pistols." She stopped and smiled sadly. "I want you to be careful and come home to us safe and well," her voice quivered as she spoke, and her eyes became moist as she fought to maintain control. "We love you ..."

Glen spoke. "I want you to know that no matter what the outcome of this war, I feel slavery is doomed. Our slaves have served us well. If anything should happen to Briarwood and the slaves are no longer needed, I want them freed." He shifted his cigar in his mouth and took another drag, blowing out slowly. "To tell you the truth, I can't see how we can keep them here much longer, anyway. We have lost far fewer slaves than our neighbors simply because we treat our people well. Now that we have Union troops living in this area most of the time, this could change at any moment.

"We fight, because we must, to defend our homes. We fight for the privilege of choosing our own government, for our rights." Glen shifted in his chair. "I wanted to work things out within the Union, but I see it's no longer possible. You boys have made your choices, now I expect you to do your duty. I'm proud of you all. You have given me great joy.

"Well, enough of speech making. If you'll excuse me, I'm feeling very tired." He looked with tenderness at each of his children in turn. "I'll talk with Elizabeth in the morning and fill her in, leaving out the hidden chests. Good night to you all." Glen left the room and headed upstairs, followed silently by Ellen.

The others looked at one another solemnly, then quietly went to their rooms. They didn't question and they didn't argue. Glen was still the head of this family. His decisions were final and they would abide by them.

13

Return to Riverview

It had been one hell of a difficult trip to Riverview. The roads were full of new recruits flocking to Shelby's command. It didn't help matters that Gilbert had been melancholy, keeping mostly to himself. He was handling his disappointment with Cassandra poorly. If he could channel some of his anger toward the enemy, God help them! The horses brought along to store at Riverview hadn't been cooperative either, but Bright Star and the others were now safely hidden in the stables.

For Jessie, the only thing that had made the ride bearable was the anticipation of seeing Katlin again. He was going to miss her terribly, but she was worth the wait. Besides, he couldn't miss this once-in-a-lifetime chance to take part in a grand adventure. He knew war would be thrilling and glorious and he'd never forgive himself if he missed it for a woman—not even the beautiful Katlin Thomas. Sleep was difficult as he anticipated marching away with the army. He pictured himself returning after the war—an officer, a victor, receiving a hero's welcome. There would be many brave tales he could tell his grandchildren as they gathered around a cozy fireplace on a cold winter's night. Chances for glory come only once. He was going to seize the moment and savor every opportunity.

His excitement for joining the war was not shared as enthusiastically by Katlin, which caught him off guard. They were alone, strolling under the moonlight in the garden.

The first stars were out, still faint against the skyline, and the breeze off the river sighed through the stately oaks and maples. They walked in the garden through rows of scented flowers. Jessie felt Katlin's hand reach for his. They walked hand in hand without a word until they reached the gazebo. He knew Katlin was crying.

"It's going to be all right, Kat, don't cry," Jessie pleaded.

"Oh, Jessie," she sobbed, flinging he arms around his neck and holding him close.

He entwined his fingers in her hair and held her warm body next to his. He laid his cheek against her head. "Don't cry, Kat, I'll be okay," he whispered softly.

"Jess, you could be killed or hurt. I . . . I might never see you again."

He felt her warm breasts pressed against his chest move with her every sob. His hand moved down to grasp her waist and pull her even more tightly to him. "Damn!" he thought, his senses filled with the sweet smell of her perfume. "This is going to be harder than I thought."

"Jess, I . . . I have to tell you," she hesitated for a moment, then let the words pour out, "I love you."

Until that moment he had not realized how deep his feelings for her ran. He felt his heart pounding in his chest when he heard those tender words. "I love you, too," he said firmly, giving her another squeeze. He was almost as surprised as she was.

She leaned back, studying his eyes. Her face showed her anxiety as she searched his eyes looking for the truth. "What did you say?" she questioned.

"I said, 'I love you, too!' " he replied, smiling broadly.

"Oh Jessie, you don't know how I have longed to hear

those words." She clung to him for several minutes and then lifted her face up toward his.

He bent down and kissed her on her lips. Her warm, moist mouth sought his. He could feel his passion rise.

They entered the gazebo and sat together. Katlin cuddled to him. "Do you have to go?"

"Yes, I must go."

"You don't have to leave; you could stay here with me."

"You know I can't stay. Bartok has been hunting for me ever since the Fourth of July. When Shelby rides out, Bartok and his men will ride in. I can't keep hiding like a coward."

"But, I'm so afraid you'll be hurt before we can even share a life together."

He lifted her chin and looked into her eyes. "I have stayed out of this war too long. I can't let others fight my battles for me. Don't you see, this is a chance to do something really meaningful, to be a part of history in the making. I have to go. There will be a time for us, believe me."

She knew there was no stopping him, no stopping this horrid war. Yet she so desperately wanted to be with him. "We could get married right away before you have to leave, Jessie—we could." Her words were full of hope.

"It wouldn't be right. I still have to go, who knows for how long. It wouldn't be fair to you."

"But I want to be with you, if only for just a little while," she pleaded.

He wanted her, wanted her desperately. He could feel the hunger for her as a painful dull ache in his loins. Yet he knew this wasn't the time. He loved her too much to dishonor her before they were married.

"Shelby's men are forming to leave tomorrow and I have enlisted. I will leave tomorrow with the command. There is no time to ask permission from your family, to get a preacher, and to gather the family. We simply have to wait."

"I don't want to wait. I want you now, tonight!" she cried.

"The Lord knows how much I want you, how much I would like to take you right here and now. But I want it to be right between us when we start our life together. We'll get married when I come back, I promise. If I know Jo Shelby we'll be back here before too long. We'll whip the blue bellies and drive them clean out of the state. But if it's getting to be too long, maybe you can travel to our winter camp and we can be married there."

"I'll wait for you, Jess. I'll wait as long as it takes!" She began to cry again. "Jessie, please. I want you to love me, tonight."

He kissed her again, and his hand gently cupped her breast through her dress. She twisted toward him and he fell over on the bench on his back with Katlin on top of him. He could feel her passion, her lust rising, and he wanted her just as desperately, more than he could ever remember wanting anything else. Even though he fought it, he felt his animal desires taking control. His hand caressed her hips through her dress. He squeezed gently.

"We've been gone for a while. They might come looking for us," Jessie whispered.

"I don't care," she replied.

"I do," he said sadly. "I like your family, and I don't want to dishonor them. I want their respect. As difficult as it is, I will wait for you until we're married."

Katlin sat up. "Are you sure, Jess?"

"Yes, I think so." He secretly questioned his sanity. He knew getting this worked up and not carrying out this act to completion was going to make him very uncomfortable tonight and for many nights to come, but Kat was worth the wait. "I think we'd better go back to the house. I need to talk to your father."

She hugged him tightly. "I love you, Jessie Kimbrough."

14

Birth of a Brigade

The Kimbrough family gathered on the lawn in front of Judge Plattenburg's residence to say their farewells. Captain Shelby was finishing final arrangements to move his newly recruited army south. Orders were issued for the soldiers to gather, and veterans mixed freely with those new to the ranks.

Ross couldn't believe the maelstrom swirling about him as the throngs of families said good-bye to their loved ones. Everywhere around the judge's house groups of people gathered to say farewell. It was a strange milieu of soldiers, some dressed in worn uniforms and others wearing shiny new ones. Some older veterans wore Union blue captured from the enemy, though most of these wore only the Union pants. The majority didn't wear uniforms at all, but instead wore their homespun garments. A few wore their Sunday best, some complete with top hats.

Ross was amazed at the variety in the new recruits. Weapons were just as varied and ranged from the latest carbines and military muskets to shotguns and squirrel guns. Many carried pistols. Every kind of knife was represented. Most had brought their horses, but men like Glen Kimbrough had provided horses for many of those on foot.

Jessie completed his good-byes to his family and found his way to the Thomas family, who were saying their good-byes to Gilbert. When Jessie thought it appropriate, he stepped in.

Just the evening before Jessie had asked for Katlin's hand in marriage, and Harlan had given his permission. Jessie spent the night at Riverview and rode in with the Thomas family in the morning. Katlin took his hand and led him away.

She pulled him behind a huge oak tree and threw her arms around him. Her lips eagerly sought his in a passionate embrace. She cried softly as she held him tightly to her. "Oh, Jessie, please be careful and come back to me," she pleaded.

"I can take care of myself, Kat. Don't worry, I'll be back; and as soon as we can, we'll be married."

"If you can't come here, I will come to you, Jess. Just tell me where, and I'll come."

"I'll write as often as I can, I promise. Will you write to me?" His eyes studied hers.

"I'll try to write every day, Jess, I promise." She unfastened the gold chain around her neck and gave the necklace, on which hung a small golden locket, to Jessie. "I want you to wear this. It will keep me close to your heart."

He held it in his hands. "Go ahead and open it." She smiled sadly, tears glistening in her eyes.

He popped the catch and the oval locket opened to reveal a small tintype photograph of Katlin. "It's beautiful. Where did you get it?"

"I had it taken for my father's birthday as a surprise gift for him. He has me to look at every day, but you'll be far away. Besides, he doesn't know about the locket and I want you to have it. I'll get him another gift and he'll never know." She embraced Jessie again.

"I'll wear it always and look at it every day."

"I hope it brings you good luck and guides you safely back to me."

"Everyone must be worried about me today. Mother gave me a pocket Bible with a metal cover and asked me to carry it inside the breast pocket of my uniform jacket. She says God will protect me in battle if I have His holy word with me." He laughed and patted the pocket where the small bible lay. "I'll take all the help I can get."

"I will pray for you each and every day. Oh, Jessie, I can't wait for this war to be over so that we can start our life together." He held her close and caressed her cheek and hair until the bugle blew for the cavalry to mount up.

It was difficult for Ross to leave Briarwood. Thoughts of family and home had sustained him in many a skirmish and battle, and his homecoming had been sweet. It had felt so good to put the war away, if only for a brief time. He took one last lingering look at the great house with its white towering columns before riding Sultan from the lane to the road leading to Dover.

His thoughts drifted to his time at home. He was glad he had taken the time to tell his parents about Vanissa Covington, the lovely belle from the White River Valley. She was on his mind whenever he had time to think about matters outside of the war.

Ross didn't know exactly where he stood with her. He only knew she was constantly on his mind, and he longed to see her again. He hadn't received a letter from her since Shelby's company left Arkansas. When the army moved, it was hard for the mail to keep up with them. He hoped there would be mail for him when he reached Arkansas. He might even find time to see her again.

Each time he left home, it occurred to him he might not live to see his family again. This fear, even now tucked as deeply as he could bury it, made the leaving bittersweet. Now he found himself torn between leaving home and looking forward to seeing a girl he had known only briefly. No matter what his feelings were, orders were orders, and now he must return to duty.

Ross stood, the battle-hardened veteran with tears streaking silently down his cheeks as he embraced his father, mother, and sisters good-bye. The hug from Fanny nearly pulled the air from his lungs, but her promises to watch over his family made him feel better.

A dark-haired soldier with a deep, Southern drawl said, "Sergeant Kimbrough, Captain Shelby told me to bring you to him immediately."

"Yes, of course, I'll be right with you," answered Ross. He faced his family. "I'll try to get back before we leave, Father."

"Go, Ross, we'll be here. If you find time to return we'll be happy and if you can't, we'll understand. Do your duty, son."

Ross followed the soldier through the crowd. He didn't recognize him, but figured he was probably a new recruit with prior military experience with the Missouri State home guards. These veterans would be useful to the new command. They entered the home and Ross hurried into the living room.

"Ross, thank God we have found you! A courier arrived less than an hour ago with a message from Colonels Coffee, Hays, and Cockrell. They have captured Independence, Missouri, and won a battle against Union forces at Lone Jack, Missouri, in Jackson County. They killed and wounded two-thirds of the Federal force of one thousand two hundred and captured two cannons.

"They drove the Yankees away, but the Feds have troops on the march from Lexington and St. Joseph, Missouri, and from Fort Leavenworth and Kansas City. Cockrell's actions kept the Yankees tied up in Lexington and off our necks. He feels he has insufficient arms and ammunition to fight another battle and is retreating rapidly for Arkansas with his captured supplies and new recruits. He sent word the Yankees are sending troops from Fort Scott, Kansas, to intercept our march to Arkansas.

"Troops are also marching west from St. Louis and Jefferson City. They mean to surround and destroy us. It is imperative we get south as fast as possible, so we can train and equip this army into a fine fighting force. I propose that we follow a parallel line of retreat to Cockrell's." He stabbed his finger at the map on the table for emphasis. "We must move at utmost speed, day and night, until we are safely away from this circling mass of armies."

"If we were ready, and the men organized and trained, we could give them a good fight." Shelby paused, then breathed a heavy sigh, "Now is not the time. This time we are going to run, by heaven, but we will be back!"

He straightened up from poring over the map. "Ross, I need you and your scouts to lead us out of this mess. Find me a way out of here and I'll see you get an officer's commission. Take Lieutenant Stryker with you. Use him as a courier to carry information to us on the best route and on any intelligence you can gather."

"You can count on us, Captain. I'll send my men south and check the routes. How long before you march?"

"I hope to get the men mounted and in column in three hours. We've got to move fast before the Yankees can spring their trap on us. Tell Lieutenant Stryker you're in charge. If he has a problem, send him to me. Good luck, Ross."

Ross left the house and returned to his family. He managed to share a few final words with them. He located Evan Stryker standing near the front gate with Cassandra.

"Lieutenant, hustle up. Captain Shelby wants you to ride south with my scouts and act as courier. We have to find the best route south and report our findings to Captain Shelby. We've got two minutes before we ride." Ross pulled Cassandra to him and gave her a tender hug. "Sorry, sis, but we gotta go. Take care of Mother and Father for me."

Cassandra wished to herself that he didn't have to go, that none of them had to leave. "You take care, Ross, and try not to worry; we'll be okay." She turned to Evan. "I have enjoyed meeting you, Evan, and I've enjoyed your company. If you like, I'll write to you."

Evan smiled broadly as she offered her hand for him to kiss. He pulled her to him. He held her close and whispered in her ear, "I certainly hope you will. I'm coming back for you when this war is over." Evan pulled back slightly and made what he knew to be a bold move to kiss her. Normally in front of friends and family she would have resisted, but this time she let him. She didn't know how long it would be before she would see this handsome Texan again, and she wanted to leave a lasting impression. The kiss was tender and she could see in Evan's eyes he would spend many restless nights thinking of her. She felt a sadness at his parting, and she watched him as he followed Ross, mounted his horse, and rode away.

Gilbert had fought his way through the crowd, trying to locate Cassandra. He found her in time to see her kiss Evan Stryker. He seethed with anger and clenched his fists. His anger turned into pain, as if someone had buried a dagger deep in his heart, and he felt the rise of panic as he realized she didn't love him and there was absolutely nothing he could do about it.

"You'll pay for this, Stryker! I'll get you for this, you son of a bitch! Somewhere, sometime you'll pay for taking from me the only one I have ever loved." He couldn't talk to her now, not after he had seen her betray his love for her. He felt an urgent desire for strong drink.

Turning away, certain she hadn't seen him, he began to shove and dodge his way through the crowd. "I still have time if I hurry to get a few drinks and maybe buy a bottle before we ride out. I need it."

Calvin spent his last few minutes, before departing, with his parents. He didn't want to go, but could find no honorable way out. Living in the outdoors, from the back of a horse, was going to be a far cry from the life of luxury in which he was raised. Still, a small part of him looked forward to the adventure ahead—an uncertain future, waiting to be discovered. Would he be brave in battle or break like a coward? Inside he was still uncertain.

Ellen Kimbrough was taking it hard. It was difficult to let her three sons ride off to war. Their lot was now cast solidly with the Confederacy, and there would be no turning back. She was proud of her boys and the decision they had made, but she feared the consequences. War, she knew, was a terrible and tragic business, fraught with danger. She was well aware of the peril and acknowledged her inability to provide any protection for her loved ones. All she could do was put her faith in God and pray for their deliverance. She brought them into this world, gave them love, and did her best to teach them what she knew. It was for now and forever out of her hands, and she accepted the fact reluctantly. "God's will shall be done," she thought.

All she could do was give each of them a hug and tell them she loved them, then let them go. That remained the hardest part: letting go. Would she ever see them again? When, and in what condition? She stood beside her husband and waved good-bye to the column riding away, watching through tear-blurred eyes, choking back her sobs. The soldiers headed south, taking her sons with them. She turned away, knowing the loss only a mother can feel.

15

Fatigue Stalks the Trail

Ross, Stryker, and Shelby's scouts pounded down the road at a gallop, headed south. It was hard to leave, but each mile brought Ross closer to Valissa. This time, he felt, would be different for Shelby's command. This time the core of veterans was boosted by the finest men available in Missouri. He felt good knowing his brothers now rode with him, but it also gave him more responsibility. To protect them he must find the best way through enemy lines for Shelby's column. His brothers and the rest of the command were depending on him. He would not fail them for any lack of effort.

Events went smoothly; Evan Stryker and Terrill Fletcher kept shuttling between the lead scouts and the column, keeping Shelby informed about the best route.

Jessie stood in his stirrups, lifting his body out of the saddle as Star's Pride galloped along. His butt felt numb and asleep and his legs ached from being shaped around the sides of his horse. He took his free hand and slapped his hips, trying to bring circulation into the area. It was now late in the afternoon of the first day. The heat waves shimmered and danced over the dusty road, heated by the late summer sun. They had made good time for a new unit unaccustomed to marching in column. The dust coated his new uniform and the heavy wool pants hung wet with his perspiration, especially where the pants touched the saddle and his horse. He had folded his new jacket up in his bedroll at the last rest stop. It was just too hot to wear. He could feel sticky wetness on his back and under his arms.

When they had first started out on their mission there was loud talking and banter among the new recruits. Later, they sang some patriotic songs. He really enjoyed singing "Dixie" and "Bonnie Blue Flag," but it didn't take long for the heat and the pace to sap the energy from these riders. The men soon fell silent.

The predominant sound he heard was the constant pounding of thousands of hooves striking the ground and the creaking of saddle leather. Every now and then a horse would snort or whinny. The sound of bits and equipment rattling and the slap of sabers and swords against the men and horses added to the general din. As Jessie glanced behind him he could see the long, serpentine line of riders winding down the road. They rode in columns three deep, but the lines were ragged and loose. These men were raw recruits, mixed with the company of veterans. One glance at the jumbled, mixed-up column was enough to frustrate Shelby. Once he reached Arkansas he would whip them into a suitable fighting force.

The column stretched as far as he could see, until they were lost in the cloud of dust. The hard, packed road had already been pounded into a layer of powder. It lay in thick clouds, coating all with its deep, dusty brown color. Occasionally, veteran troopers riding alongside the ranks would pass by. It was their job to keep everyone moving and from falling out of the column.

Jessie tugged at the edge of his wide-brimmed hat. It didn't match his uniform, but a man couldn't be in the sun without some kind of protection. He looked ahead, straining to see through the clouds of choking dust. He glanced over at his brother, Calvin, riding on Red Roses next to him. Calvin had his left leg thrown over the neck of his horse, passing just in front of the saddle pommel, so both legs were on the same side. He sat almost facing Jessie, and Jessie could see Calvin's head droop, as if he were about to fall asleep.

"Got any water, Cal?" Jessie asked him.

"Got a little. You out?"

"Yeah. When I got my chance at the last stop to get water the well was already dry. This many men and horses take a lot of water, and I guess I was too far down the line. Next stream we hit I'm stopping for water."

"Sure, if the water isn't too muddy."

Cal passed over his cloth-covered, wooden canteen. Jessie sat back in his saddle and pulled the stopper from the canteen with his teeth, then spat it out. He took a long pull of the warm water. It felt good to ease the dirt and dryness from his throat. He pounded the stopper back in and passed the canteen back. Jessie would have liked more, but he didn't want to use up his brother's supply. They would surely hit another stream soon.

The column rode on, rest stops few and far between. About every two hours the call would come down the line for the column to dismount. The men would slide wearily from their saddles, and march on foot while leading their horses. The horses needed the rest and the men needed to work out the kinks. Usually, they walked for thirty minutes to an hour before the order for remount came. Jessie looked forward to the walking because he was already saddle sore, although it was a seemingly endless cycle.

Nightfall came and still the column continued. They traveled that whole night, only stopping to water the horses and men. The men were allowed only brief breaks to eat and relieve themselves. The riders kept praying for a halt to be called, for a chance to sleep. They were sadly disappointed.

For the first three days Shelby drove them hard, but no harder than he drove himself. He was determined to save this new army. They never stopped more than two hours, day or night, and those two-hour stops were spaced far apart. Ross and the older veterans had spent long periods with little sleep and less food before; but for many of the new recruits, fresh from a comparative life of ease and the comforts of home, it was a devastating ordeal.

The cohesive power of danger is stronger than most, and pride would not let them fail. By the third day, strange sensations caused by lack of sleep began to affect the men. Calvin noticed that every sound became distinct and painfully acute. At times he began to hallucinate, and the air seemed filled with exquisite music. At other times he thought he saw great cities and towns spring from an earth crowned with sparkling lights. Many men, including brother Jessie, became paranoid. Some thought the woods were full of armed men ready to pounce on them. It became so real that Jessie thought he could hear the bugles and orders to charge.

By the fourth day, total exhaustion set in and horses and men were asleep on their feet. Jessie never realized how much he could sleep in the saddle. A couple of times he fell off, but he would awaken as he slammed into the dirt. It took some quick moving to keep from being trampled by riders and horses following, equally asleep. Once he was stepped on by a horse. The animal stumbled. Three horses and riders fell in the pile before it was over. Jessie escaped with only a deep bruise and wounded pride. Those behind him were so tired they only halfheartedly muttered a curse in his direction.

It became increasingly difficult to keep lead riders awake long enough to guide the column. Jessie began to notice his almost total insensitivity to pain. His feet were blistered and sore from walking, and he was saddle sore from four days of constant riding with only brief respite. His belly was empty; all the prepared food they had brought with them had long since disappeared.

Misery was not his alone: every man in the column was experiencing like effects. By the fifth day, men fell from their saddles without waking up. They could be prodded with sabers, until their blood spouted, without stirring. Those in such a condition were thrown over their saddles, as if they were dead, and led on. Rest breaks, out of necessity, became more frequent. Still, Shelby kept them moving for three more days until the army could no longer function and collapsed into camp on Coon Creek in Jasper County, Missouri.

The men struggled to take care of their jaded and weary horses. Coon Creek had the water and feed they so desperately needed. For eight days and nights they had endured forced marching with little food and often a shortage of water. Rest had been in very short supply, never more than two hours in a twenty-four hour period. They had taken the rest of their sleep from the back of a horse. Men didn't do anything more than absolutely necessary, and most fell asleep wherever they happened to be. Because the men had been pushed beyond their limit, the command was caught off-guard. It was now early in the afternoon of August 24, 1862.

16

Encounter at Coon Creek

Jessie lay caught in the black depths of total fatigue. Deep within his mind he heard the first stirring of consciousness. He resisted at first, wanting to ignore the world and regain his needed rest. Unidentified sounds like popcorn popping made him think of home. He was abruptly awakened by searing pain in his back and arm as someone stumbled and fell in a pile on top of him. He awoke with a curse, angry with the fool for not watching where he was going. The Confederate soldier staggered to his feet and moved away. Despite his wishes, his mind was forced to accept the world around him. Wood splintered from the tree beside him, and Jessie recognized Calvin, sitting with his back to the tree, gun at the ready.

"Jess! Keep your head down—we're under attack!"

Jessie rolled over quickly and pulled the thirty-six caliber pistol from under his saddle. He tried to make himself smaller, hiding as best as he could behind his saddle and accoutrements. Blue uniformed soldiers on foot appeared across the clearing, charging at them.

The surprised Confederates fired a ragged volley into the Yankees as the blue-bellies swarmed among them. Calvin was unprepared for this sudden introduction to war. He leaned away from the tree and snapped a couple of shots off with his pistol. One Yank dropped his carbine and grabbed his stomach as he fell in a heap. Another pitched onto his back, still quivering.

A burly Yank charged Jessie from his blind side, arm extended and sword ready to strike. Calvin spun and, without hesitation, jammed his pistol into the face of the onrushing bluecoat. Calvin felt the recoil as the pistol fired point blank into the startled face of the Yankee. The man's head snapped back violently as he was slammed backward from the impact. His sword fell tip first into the dirt. The hilt landed harmlessly on Jessie's back.

Calvin knelt beside the Union soldier, now lying flat on his back. Eyes stared back blankly at Calvin, open but seeing only eternity. In the center of the man's forehead was a dime-size hole with blood welling from it. Black powder burns covered much of the man's ruddy face. Blood began to pool from the gaping hole in the back of the man's head, where the bullet had made its exit.

Calvin's confused mind fought to grasp reality. He began to shake and tremble and turned away while his gut revolted and heaved up the contents of his stomach. The bitter acid burned his throat.

"Cal, you okay?" It was Jessie.

"Yeah, I'm okay, I think. I've just never killed a man before."

"Well, if you hadn't, he would have killed me and maybe you, too. Hell! It's war, you didn't have a choice."

They looked around them. The skirmish had swirled around them for at least five minutes, but the Union troops had withdrawn. The surprised Confederates swarmed forward, forming their ranks along a heavy fence. On their left, firing erupted as Confederates waded Coon Creek and attacked the flanks of the Union force. Soon after, the Yankees withdrew.

The sudden attack had accomplished one thing; it had awakened the exhausted Southerners. Driven by the unrelenting force of surprise and fear, their veins pumped a full supply of adrenaline.

The camp organized itself. A search through the Union wounded and dead yielded a talkative Yank. They were attacked by a detachment of two companies of the Sixth Kansas Cavalry, led by Colonel Cloud. The Rebels were lucky, their only casualties were three seriously wounded men. Miraculously, not one Rebel soldier was killed. The most important casualty was orderly Sergeant Oliver Redd of Shelby's original company of volunteers. Also wounded were Private John Oliver and Private Hunt. The Rebels lost several horses, and most of the wounded horses had to be destroyed.

The Yankees, even blessed with the surprise of the attack, left eleven dead and five wounded. Calvin and Jessie searched the body of the Yankee soldier killed by Calvin. Calvin took the man's Sharps Carbine, sling, and cartridge box while Jessie took the Yankee's saber and scabbard. Veterans of Shelby's original company took the man's boots, leather belt, coat, haversack, and canteen. One old Johnnie threw the gold watch he found in the dead man's vest pocket to Cal.

"Here ya go, Cal! I reckon you earned it, and this here fella sure ain't got a use for it."

Calvin looked at the watch. It wasn't as nice as the one he already owned, so he threw it back to the bearded soldier. "You keep it, friend. I've got a better watch than this one." Cal thought, "Every time I looked at the watch, it would remind me of the first man I killed." He knew he couldn't handle the guilt, but wondered why he didn't feel the same about the soldier's weapons. Perhaps because they were less personal.

The old Johnnie smiled broadly. "Thanks, Cal. That's mighty kind of ya." He pocketed the watch and walked away.

Burial details for the Yankees put the men quickly to work. The wounded Yank prisoners were left water and made comfortable. There was no reason to keep them. It would slow down the column, and the Union troops would take care of them after the Rebels were gone.

They ate supper uninterrupted. When darkness came, the men mounted and rode out in columns of fours. Regulars were deployed to the left and right of the column for protection, and the command forged ahead. It was Shelby's plan to cut through any opposition to reach the relative safety of Arkansas. The men felt inspired by surviving the unexpected attack and proud they had driven the enemy away.

Evan Stryker, again attached to Shelby's staff, knew how lucky they were. They were caught napping by a couple of companies of the enemy probing for their position. By sheer will and a little luck, they had turned potential disaster into a victorious minor engagement. Had the Union attack included a large force, such as a brigade or more, it could have ended in disaster.

From Coon Creek the command moved south into Arkansas, traveling all night and through the next day. An order arrived from General Rains commanding Shelby to report to Elm Springs, so from there the column went to McKissick Springs. Then the order came to march for Pineville. They rode fifteen miles north to a place on Elkhorn Creek, where they joined the camp of Colonel Hays and Colonel Coffee, who had taken over for the wounded Cockrell.

On September 9, 1862, General Hindman assigned the three regiments to be one cavalry brigade under the command of the newly promoted Colonel Joseph Orville Shelby. The company of Colonel Upton Hays, known as the Jackson County Regiment, was officially designated the Twelfth Missouri Cavalry. The Lafayette County Cavalry became the Fifth Missouri Cavalry under Colonel Jo Shelby. The Southwest Cavalry, under command of Colonel John T. Coffee, was designated as the Sixth Missouri Cavalry. A section of artillery utilizing the captured cannons from Lone Jack, Missouri, was assigned to the new brigade from Bledsoe's Light Artillery under the command of Captain Hiram Bledsoe and Lieutenant Richard A. Collins. Because Colonel Shelby would now command the fledgling brigade, Lieutenant Colonel B. F. Gordon would lead the Fifth Missouri Cavalry.

True to his word, Jo Shelby made Ross Kimbrough a lieutenant in charge of the scouts. Evan Stryker was appointed a captain and attached to Shelby's personal staff. Jessie Kimbrough became a private in company E, Fifth Missouri Cavalry, led by newly appointed Captain Gilbert Thomas. Calvin Kimbrough, intrigued by the big guns, volunteered for Captain Bledsoe's mounted artillery battery and was assigned to the gun section under the command of Lieutenant Richard (Dick) A. Collins.

General Hindman ordered the new command to ride across the border into Missouri and set up camp within six miles of Newtonia. In a skirt of timber bordering the open rolling prairies, the new command began to drill and train. Shelby had his brigade at last and the Yankees would soon know and fear him. To mark his promotion, Jo added a black plume to his black felt slouch hat. The brim was anchored on one side by a gold buckle and the black, curling plume flowed in the wind behind him. It gave him the air of distinction he deserved and became one of his trademarks.

The march had toughened the soldiers, now Shelby trained them. Led by the tireless example of Shelby's original veterans and the addition of the old veterans of the Missouri State home guards, their skills improved quickly. The horses, with rest, began to fatten and regain strength. Lost mounts were replaced and the brigade equipped the remainder of the men with what they could find.

Captain Bledsoe began training his new volunteers in the art of firing the big guns. The artillery pieces were easy enough to learn, but it was the drill that made them effective. Officers needed practice to learn to use the Pendulum Hausse sights to aim the guns. Lieutenant Collins, a long-time friend of Jo's, and one of his original company, soon found he had a special knack for the cannons. It was not his first time with the artillery; he had served for a short time in the Missouri State home guards as part of Hiram Bledsoe's battery, clear back at the battle of Carthage in the early days of the war. He had left Bledsoe, even though he loved the big guns, to stay with Jo Shelby.

Calvin began to understand the lure of artillery. He, like Dick Collins, was fascinated by the power wielded at the end of a lanyard. With one quick pull, devastating power could be unleashed on an enemy over a mile away. One good blast of canister turned the cannons into giant shotguns that could cut broad swaths through cavalry or infantry. They felt the power in their hands. They felt the ground tremble as the cannons spoke, and they realized they could make the difference in a close contest. Artillery could open an avenue of escape where there hadn't been one or dismantle an enemy charge. It was power; raw power. It took teamwork to succeed, and the men learned the lesson well.

Being a part of a team working toward a common goal was part of the attraction for Calvin. Soon, Lieutenant Dick Collins and Calvin Kimbrough were grinning ear to ear as they worked with the powerful weapons. Calvin may have had reservations about going to war, but he had overcome them. He enjoyed the roar of the big guns and the power they wielded. Calvin knew he was in love. His new mistress was a six-pound field artillery piece.

17

A Coward or a Fool

The young, baby-faced orderly snapped the door open and held it for Major Benton Bartok. Bartok noticed the orderly's contemptuous smirk as he stepped into the temporary headquarters of General Daniel Kessington. He felt a dryness in his throat and his stomach tightened into knots when he approached the General's desk. The orderly closed the door. Benton dashed off a lazy half-salute as he called out, "Major Benton Bartok reporting as requested, sir." He stood impatiently, waiting for a response.

The general didn't look up at first, his eyes still locked on his paperwork. "Major Bartok, so good of you to come." He glanced up at the major. Bartok sensed the hostility in the general's eyes. General Kessington stood up and leaned over his desk. "I just wanted to check with you to see if you enjoyed your little ride up in Saline County?"

"Field operations are seldom fun, General, and I'm afraid those bushwackers gave us the slip, sir. We just couldn't corner them."

"Major, I don't believe you gave me a proper salute when

you entered my office," the General said softly. "Do it now!" he snapped out crisply. "I don't want to see you move until I'm finished. Is that understood, Major?"

Bartok drew himself to attention, snapping off his best salute. "Yes, sir!"

The General began pacing. "Major, I have read the report on your raid into Saline County to investigate reports of bushwackers, and I must say your timing on this little jaunt was, at best, ill-advised. You rode out of Lafayette County at the very time Jo Shelby and his bunch of Rebel cutthroats were riding in. While you were out chasing shadows, based on some vague reports of bushwackers in Saline County, you let Shelby waltz in here and recruit a full brigade of men under our very noses!" He stopped his pacing, turned to his desk, and leaned forward as he looked into Bartok's eyes. "You knew Shelby was coming, didn't you, Major?"

"No, sir! I had no idea he would be bold enough," Bartok protested.

"Do I look stupid to you, Major? Do you really expect me to believe you didn't know Shelby was heading this way?" The general's face flushed crimson with anger. "Surely you have Union sympathizers in this area who keep you informed of rumors and enemy movements. If that wasn't enough you might have read the telegraph dispatches we sent you. While the rest of the Union commands were organizing to march here, you were busy moving in the other direction!" General Kessington slapped his hand hard on the desk in frustration, sending a shower of paperwork scattering across the floor.

Benton swallowed hard, sweating under the glare of his commanding general. "We received reports he was moving north, but thought he would stay with Coffee's command in Johnson County. I thought we might keep the guerrillas in Saline County from supporting the Rebels."

"You, sir, are either a fool or a coward," Kessington growled in a menacing tone. "To tell you the truth, I think you are both." Fire burned in Kessington's eyes as he glared at Bartok. He slammed his knuckles into the desk; his jaw muscles strained as he spoke. "By God, Major, if it was up to me I would have you court marshaled and shot for cowardice!" General Kessington took two deep breaths and slowly exhaled before he said more calmly, "I can't prove you were aware of Shelby's movements because your junior officers are covering for you. It disappointed me to find them supporting you." General Kessington resumed his pacing. "Since it seems unlikely I could get a conviction against you for cowardice, with so little evidence, I wonder what I should do with you. Do you have any ideas, Major?"

"Sir, I must protest your charges against my conduct. I was only following what I thought was the proper course of action at the time. If you'd only allow me——"

"Shut up, Bartok!" The General whirled to face him. "I'd love to replace you with a good officer. Unfortunately, it seems all the best officers are shipped back east and I get stuck with every dandy that had his daddy get him appointed as an officer. I'd love to send you into a real battle instead of letting you hide back here. You'd run or break—I can smell the fear in you. But it just wouldn't be fair to your men."

Bartok smoldered with anger, but he was uncertain how he should respond. He opted for silence.

"I don't have anyone to take your place at this point, Bartok, but you get this straight," General Kessington pointed his finger at Bartok, threateningly. "One more incident and God himself won't save your ass from me! Is that clear enough for you, Major?"

"Yes, sir!"

General Kessington clasped his hands behind his back. "You'd better be sure, Bartok, because I'm going to be watching you." Kessington turned his back to Bartok and stared out the window as he spoke. "I want you to set down hard on these people. I want them to know we won't tolerate support for the Rebels. I don't want any more recruiting done by the Southerners in this area. I think letting them outfit an entire brigade in this county is enough—don't you, Major?"

"Yes, sir!" Bartok responded; his cheeks flushed with shame and anger.

Kessington spun around and faced the red-faced Major.

"You get a handle on this county, or you'll find yourself shot for cowardice or fighting in the real war. Now get out of my sight. Your stinking incompetence makes me ill." The General stopped, turned his back on Benton, and gazed out the window. "You're dismissed, Bartok."

"Yes, sir!" Major Bartok saluted again and held it, not moving.

After a long, silent pause, the general turned, "Are you deaf, Major? I said you are dismissed. Get out of my sight!" General Kessington's veins were popping out from his temples, and his jaw began to twitch as he watched Bartok.

"Yes, sir! I had to wait for you to return my salute, sir!" Bartok shouted, smiling with a sarcastic curl to his lips.

The general returned a sloppy salute. In a low, menacing voice he replied, "Don't push me, Bartok. It would be a serious mistake."

Bartok spun smartly on his heels and marched out, mounted his horse, and rode back to his command. He thought he was being treated unfairly. Why, he should be a full colonel instead of a major. When Colonel Hurlbut had gotten ill and had to resign his post, Benton had taken over. He should have been promoted to a colonel when he took over the command of the Third Kansas Cavalry. If he didn't deserve that promotion, then he should have been increased in rank to Lieutenant Colonel when Lieutenant Colonel Boyce was killed. That happened even before Hurlbut got sick with the pneumonia. No, they had always conspired against him to keep him from obtaining his proper rank, and now this gross insult by General Kessington.

One week later, Benton Bartok rode ram-rod stiff in the saddle with revenge on his mind. "I'll show them all," he thought. "They made me look like a fool! They helped those Rebels and now they will pay. I've got a score to settle with the Kimbroughs. I know they supplied cavalry mounts, housed a Reb officer, and their sons left with them." It irked Bartok most that Jessie had slipped through his fingers. He had hoped to make an example of him, but knew the chance was gone. "I didn't get to settle my score with him, but they will pay!" he thought. "That bitch, Cassandra, thinks she's so high and mighty. She thinks she is too good for the likes of Jayhawkers like me. Well, we'll see who has the last laugh. Before I'm finished she'll be begging me for help. She'll do anything I want." He smiled wickedly, anticipating the joy he would have by paying back those who had betrayed him and made him look foolish.

"Captain Anders, please join me," Bartok shouted over his shoulder. Bartok's gaze returned to the road ahead as he shifted a cigar and clenched it tightly in the corner of his mouth.

Captain Bob Anders of A company of the Third Kansas Cavalry rode alongside Major Bartok. "Yes, sir." He saluted.

"Captain, I want you to take A and B companies straight through to the barn and corral areas of the Briarwood Plantation when we arrive. I want you to clean out every horse, mule, and cow they have. Have the men round up any chickens and pigs they find as well. If we can't take it with us, I want it destroyed. Have Captain Rodgers of D company bring up the empty wagons from the rear of the column and load out all the grain and hay we can carry. Burn the rest. I want all the work wagons seized from the plantation and filled. Do you understand, Captain?"

"Yes, sir!"

"Anders, send word to Captain Shay of C company—I want to talk to him."

"Yes, sir." Captain Anders saluted briskly, wheeled his horse and rode to the rear.

Shortly, Captain Shay made his way to the head of the column. "Good afternoon, Major, I heard you wished to talk to me."

"Yes, Captain, we are about to set an example for the rest of the Rebel sympathizers in this county." The cruel smirk returned to Bartok's face. "I want your men at the head of the column as we approach the Kimbrough Plantation. Have one of your lieutenants take a squad to make sure no one escapes the house. I want the rest of your company to line up on the lawn in front of the main house. Your company will be in charge of the house. Is that clear, Captain?"

"Yes, sir," replied Captain Elias Shay, as he snapped off a salute.

"Then return to your men, Captain."

Shay wheeled his horse, and returned later with his company to the head of the column.

18

The Devil's Due

Cassandra sat at the writing desk in the family room. She was writing a letter to her brother Calvin. She had just finished a letter to Evan Stryker.

Fanny came bursting into the room, her eyes wide with excitement. "Lordy, Cassie, you best come! There's Yankee cavalry comin' up the road and they're in one powerful hurry. Your Papa is on his way to the portico."

Cassandra quickly put her letters and writing supplies away. She spoke to Fanny as she worked. "Thank you, Fanny, run and tell the others. Hurry!"

Cassandra rushed out to the portico. She felt the involuntary tightening of her stomach muscles, and a shiver of fear ran through her as she felt the unmistakable presence of danger.

Before her rode Federal troopers, surrounded by swirling columns of dust raised by the steel-shod hooves of the Union cavalry. The sound of the hooves striking the ground, the metallic clank of metal from guns, swords, canteens, and creaking leather made such a racket that it flooded her senses.

Near the head of the column rode Bartok. She began to tremble.

Bartok smirked. His men were deploying as he had ordered. Like a grand parade, Shay's company lined up in front of the great house, wheeled right on command, and stood at attention. Bartok snapped a crisp command to his orderly, Sergeant O'Leary: "Dismount."

O'Leary rose up in the stirrups and turned to look back at the line of C company in double ranks. He yelled in his best Sergeant Major's voice, "Dis-mount!" As if they were one machine, the dusty men in blue swung from their saddles. Bartok waited as Captain Shay joined him.

When Major Bartok looked up he could see Glen Kimbrough on the portico leaning against the rail, his hand resting on his cane. Ellen stood beside him with Cassandra.

"To what do we owe the honor of your visit, Major Bartok?" Glen drawled out slowly, with just a hint of sarcasm.

Benton Bartok pulled himself upright in his saddle and in a loud, clear voice said, "As the military commander in charge of this county, it is my duty to confiscate needed supplies for my command. It is common knowledge that you and your family are Rebel traitors and have been aiding the enemy. We know your sons have joined the Confederate army and you have helped by furnishing horses and supplies to Shelby's command. By Federal authority it is my duty to confiscate your property for the Federal forces without compensation, because you have aided and abetted the enemy."

"Oh, in other words, Major, you and your blue-belly Jayhawkers are here to steal everything you can get your thieving hands on!"

"Shut up, you Rebel bastard! Or I'll have you hung on the spot!" Bartok snapped back angrily. "I'm in charge here. I'll take great joy in making an example out of you to the rest of this county."

"Do you think you brought enough men to subdue an old cripple, a few slaves, and some women?"

Red faced and boiling with anger, Benton screamed his reply, "That will be enough of your insolence! Sergeant O'Leary, take a squad of men and arrest him immediately. Bring him to me, now!"

"Yes, sir!" Sergeant O'Leary turned, motioned for a few men to follow him, and headed for the stairs.

When Bartok flew into his rage and started shouting orders, Glen turned and limped into the entryway of the house. Cassandra, now joined by Fanny, Jethro, and Elizabeth, moved near the top of the stairs to stand by the railing.

"Take what you want, Major, but leave us alone," yelled Cassandra. "Surely you can do better than let a crippled man's anger make you look like a tyrant."

Bartok remained stolidly silent, while the sergeant, followed by his group of seven soldiers, reached the stairs and began to run to the top. The women moved to obstruct their path.

"Out of our way!" the sergeant yelled. He shoved his way through the women. When he reached Fanny, he tried to move around her, but whichever way he went, she moved also.

"Excuse me, suh, I jus' don't know which way to go," Fanny said.

After several seconds of maneuvering, the sergeant, frustrated and in a hurry, roughly shoved Fanny backward, spilling her onto her back. Her dress and apron flew upward as she fell heavily on the veranda.

Glen Kimbrough limped through the door, a double-barreled shotgun held at waist level and aimed directly at the non-commissioned officer. "Sergeant, I don't take kindly to Yankees riding in here and mistreating my housekeeper. You and your men better leave before I blow you into the next county."

From down below, Bartok watched the action on the veranda above him. He barked out his orders. "Sergeant, I want him captured, now! Troopers prepare to fire; horse holders to the ready." The soldiers lifted and aimed their carbines. Every fourth man, as the standard cavalry regulations specified, became a horse holder, took the reins of the horses belonging to the other troopers and led them to the rear. The other troopers stood, weapons at the ready, eyes on the veranda. Sergeant O'Leary kept his hands free, but hovering near his pistol holster. His squad of soldiers spread out, hands tightly gripping their carbines. The view was partially blocked for those down below by the women and the soldiers on the stairs and the veranda.

"Well, now," began Sergeant O'Leary, "it seems we have a bit of a problem. I have me orders to arrest you and you don't appear to be a willin'," he said in a thick Irish brogue. "Be careful now with that scatter gun, me boy. Ye might hurt the womenfolk."

Ellen moved toward her husband. "Please, Glen, let them take what they want. It isn't worth dying for." He took his eyes away from the sergeant and glanced at his wife, distracted by her sudden plea. Their eyes locked. She could see the determination in his eyes.

The sergeant lunged forward, taking advantage of the distraction. O'Leary's hands grabbed the shotgun as he tried to yank it away from Glen Kimbrough. In the brief struggle, the barrels pointed directly at the belly of the Yankee sergeant. The sudden pull on the barrels was enough—the gun jumped from the recoil as the shotgun triggered from the sudden pressure against Glen's trigger finger. Flame and buckshot blasted through O'Leary's stomach, lifting him from his feet and flinging him against the railing. He slid down into a bloody, convulsing heap.

Shrieks pierced the air as the women screamed, frozen in place by fear. The soldiers on the veranda raised their weapons. Glen spun the barrels toward the nearest trooper and jammed the shotgun inches from his face. The color drained from the white-faced soldier. He stared in wide disbelief into the black chasm of the deadly gun barrels from which smoke still curled in a slow, lazy pattern. Glen's trigger finger firmly caressed the second trigger.

"Appears to me we have a stand-off. The rest of you clear out, or I'm going to blow this soldier's head off!"

The soldiers looked at each other nervously, uncertain of their next move.

"For God's sake, fellas, do as he says!" the frightened soldier yelled. The other soldiers started to ease away, but kept their carbines aimed at Glen.

"What in hell is going on up there!" Bartok shouted. "Why are you backing up? Shoot him, you cowards! There's only one of him."

Still easing away from Glen, a soldier backed into Jethro. Startled, the trooper squeezed the trigger of his carbine. Kaboom! The shot went astray, striking a column on the house. Nerves on edge, the keyed-up Union soldiers opened fire on Glen in a ragged volley.

Several bullets found their mark. In response to the sudden pain, Glen's finger jerked the trigger on the last barrel. It all happened in a split second: As the bullets tore into him, Glen was slammed onto his back; at the same instant, the blast from Glen's shotgun ripped the top of the head off the Federal soldier. The shotgun pellets hitting his head made a ripping, hollow, squashing sound as if his head were an exploding, ripe watermelon. The soldier pitched backward jerkily and rolled head-over-heels down the stairs, taking another soldier down with him. Those standing on the stairs and the veranda were splattered with gory speckles of blood, brains, and hair from the dead trooper. The soldier's hat, propelled by the blast, sailed up and floated gently down, landing near the body at the bottom of the stairs.

Screams split the air as Cassandra yelled, "Nooooo ... Father!" She ran to him, breaking free of the others. Ellen stood screaming, blood and residue clinging to her face and dress. Her anguish echoed off the portico as she pressed her hands against her head.

Fanny stepped in, using her body to shield the young girl from the awful carnage. Elizabeth sobbed, "I want my Papa! I want my Papa!"

"No child, you can't help him now." Fanny held the struggling girl in her arms until she no longer fought to get away.

Elizabeth buried her face in Fanny's large shoulder and sobbed in despair as she clung to the housekeeper.

Another soldier stepped forward. Grabbing the smoking shotgun, he heaved it over the railing. Several troopers stood in stunned silence; others reloaded their weapons. One Yankee kept his carbine trained on Glen Kimbrough's crumpled body.

Cassandra knelt at her Father's side and Ellen, recovering from her shock, joined her. Tears spilled down their cheeks. "I love you, Father," she whispered, hugging his heaving chest.

He looked in her eyes and ran his fingers tenderly along her cheek. "I know you do, Cassie, and I love you." His hoarse voice wheezed over the sickening sound of a sucking chest wound. He fought to stay conscious and talk. "Don't let them beat you, Cassandra. They can take away everything, but they can't take away your pride or your honor." His breathing became more ragged as his voice fell to a whisper. Cassandra leaned her ear close to his lips. "Cassie, take care of Elizabeth and your mother; they'll need your strength." Ellen moved to the other side of Glen, and he pulled his arms up to embrace both women simultaneously. He began to cough and choke on his blood, his chest heaving. He whispered, with one final effort, "I love you, Ellen." His words faded as his body relaxed, his arms sagged, and his eyes rolled up in death. Cassandra and Ellen clung to Glen's body weeping, his blood mixing freely with the blood of the soldier already splattered on their stained dresses.

The soldiers, enraged by the deaths of their two comrades, used their carbines to crowd and shove Fanny, Jethro, and Elizabeth toward the edge of the veranda. They dragged Ellen and Cassandra away from Glen's body and forced them to join the others.

Ellen kept trying to break free from the soldiers as she cried, "My husband, my husband, oh, please God, let me go to him!"

Captain Shay and Major Bartok were now at the crowded, bloody scene at the top of the stairs. Benton took a long look at the carnage and the dead body of his friend, Sergeant O'Leary. He was livid before, now he felt pure rage and hate burning through his soul.

He barked out his orders briskly: "Remove the bodies from the veranda and place them on the front lawn. Captain Shay, tell the men to help themselves to anything they want in the house, then burn it! I want everything we can use removed and everything else destroyed."

Captain Shay looked at the major as if he didn't believe his ears. "Yes, sir, you want us to burn the house?"

"I gave you your orders. Now get on with it, Captain! I repeat, clean this place out of anything valuable, then burn down this house and all the rest of this damn plantation."

"Excuse me, sir, couldn't we spare the slaves' houses so the negras have somewhere to live?"

His jaw muscles tightened, as Bartok mulled it over. "I suppose so, Captain, if it will ease your conscience."

Cassandra struggled, finally breaking free of the soldiers. She screamed as she ran toward Benton Bartok, "You bastard! She succeeded in reaching him and drumming her fists against his chest. He reacted swiftly, slapping her hard across the face, splitting her lip. Soldiers restrained her arms, pinned them behind her and dragged her away. She spit at him, but missed her mark.

Major Bartok looked at her with contempt and broke into a cruel smile. "I'm going to enjoy burning down this traitor's den, and I'm going to make sure you have a good view of it, bitch! We'll soon see if you're so much better than me when everything you own is gone or in ashes. When you and your precious family get hungry enough you'll come begging for my help." Bartok looked around as he sniffed the air. His smirk widened. "Winter is coming."

"I'd rather die than take any help from the likes of you! My brothers will hunt you down and kill you for this!"

Bartok pitched his head back and laughed viciously. "I doubt they'll even survive the war." His laughter faded as disgust twisted his face. "Get this white trash out of my sight and under guard below," he shouted to the soldiers on the ve-

randa. "I'm going to take a last look around this house myself. Maybe I can find a souvenir or two." He smiled a little
at Captain Shay. "When I come out, turn the soldiers loose."
He turned and entered the house.

Benton strolled into the parlor and approached the bar. He
removed a bottle of fine bourbon and a glass. He found a box
of cigars in the desk.

He saw the photograph of Cassandra on the mantle and
knocked it to the floor. He ground his heel into the glass and
felt the satisfying crunch as the glass shattered underneath his
boot.

He took writing paper and envelopes from the desk, and
shoved them into the breast pocket of his uniform. He
paused, striking a phosphorous match on the Kimbroughs'
fine woodwork, and he lit a stolen cigar. A couple of good
puffs brought the tip to a fine, cherry red. Bartok walked out
of the house puffing on the cigar and carrying the cigar box,
a glass, and a bottle of bourbon.

He smiled broadly as he blew out a cloud of smoke. He
thought, "Kimbrough might not have been good for much,
but he did know good cigars and bourbon." His eyes studied
the scene below from the vantage point of the veranda.

The dead bodies were laid out on the lawn and the
Kimbroughs and their house slaves were crowded into a small
circle, surrounded by guards. Beyond, he could see his soldiers restraining a group of slaves near the slave cabins, while
others scurried about killing livestock, gathering horses and
food. A herd of fine thoroughbreds were driven past, while
wagons rushed in the opposite direction to load grain and
hay. More empty wagons were brought near the great house
steps. Bartok smiled in satisfaction as he started down the
stairs.

He stopped his orderly. "Soldier, I fancy that clock on the
mantle in the family room. Bring it down for me and see that
it arrives safely at my headquarters. Tell Captain Shay I want
him to gather anything he finds of real value—such as
money, jewelry, silverware. We will confiscate the items for
the government." Bartok tried to keep a straight face, for he

knew the government would never see a penny of it. Anything stolen would go to Bartok and his junior officers.

He strolled to the front lawn, and sat well away from the confusion swirling about the plantation. The bodies of Sergeant O'Leary and the dead private were being loaded into an empty wagon drawn by a team of mules.

"Funny," Bartok thought, "I don't even know the trooper's name. I guess it wouldn't change anything if I did."

Captain Shay gave the orders. Except those involved with other duties, the rest of C company charged the house in a ragged group, their cheers piercing the air.

Captain Shay sauntered over and joined Major Bartok for a drink of bourbon. They watched the obvious joy of their soldiers, swarming over the house like a colony of ants discovering an open cupboard.

Soon soldiers were staggering out of the house with all kinds of items such as cookware, bits of clothing, liquor bottles, and food. Large items such as clocks, vases, and lamps were carted out on the shoulders of the men. A chair shattered the glass of the dining room window and sailed out onto the veranda.

The loud, raucous laughter of the bearded soldier who threw it drifted to the ears of those witnessing the scene. Another trooper could be seen through the gaping hole of the shattered window, dancing on the dining room table while swilling down pilfered liquor.

By now, the slaves from the slaves' quarters and from the fields had gathered to witness the downfall of their masters. Union troopers, their carbines at the ready, kept them huddled in a cluster, straining to watch the excitement. The slaves stood in quiet groups, uncertain how they should feel. A few showed joy and triumph, but most seemed disturbed and fearful. Wagons moved past them, filled with confiscated oats, hay, and corn.

The Yankees drove the last of the Kimbrough horses from the barn. Harsh flames leapt from the open barn doors just as the last horse trotted out. Smoke curled upward in dark, ugly swirls. Clouds of acrid smoke drifted toward the captive Kimbroughs and stung their eyes.

Never before had Cassandra experienced the maelstrom of emotions engulfing her now. She seethed with anger and hate, more intense than she ever thought possible. She felt grief twisting away at her insides over the death of her father. She felt utterly powerless and helpless to stop the destruction racing around her. The world was a sick and cruel place. She disdained fear of death, because it was preferable to this living hell. She tried to remain strong as she bit back the tears and remembered her father's last words.

19

Burn, Missouri, Burn

Elizabeth was in shock, hugging her knees to her chest and rocking back and forth as she sat on the ground. Ellen was overcome with grief. Fanny attempted to comfort her, but she continued to wail loudly causing great, heaving, convulsive shudders of her shoulders. They could do nothing, surrounded by armed Yankee troopers who would not let them pass.

Additional empty wagons came down the road and were sent to the front and back of the great house, where they were loaded with plunder and supplies. Soldiers ran everywhere, chasing chickens and pigs. The squawking of the chickens and the death squeals of the pigs added to the ghastly spectacle. Many Union soldiers staggered under their heavy loads of plunder, and around many a cavalryman's saddle lay a brace of dead chickens hung by strings looped around their feet.

Cassandra glared at Bartok, who was locked in heated debate with a circle of his junior officers. From time to time they glanced in her direction. Their conversation was animated and often seemed angry. Major Bartok broke away from the group and accompanied by one of his captains approached the prisoners. On his orders, two troopers grabbed her and brought her before him.

"My men have gone through your house with care, yet we located only a small amount of money. We found mostly cheap costume jewelry and no real silverware. We know you must have it hidden somewhere. Where is it?" Bartok demanded.

"Go to hell!" she screamed. "If I knew, I wouldn't tell you." He leaned forward, hoping to intimidate her, and she spat in his face.

The smirk left Bartok's face and, in one swift move, he back-handed her across her cheek, snapping her head around. The stinging slap resounded in her ears, making them ring. If she hadn't been held by the two soldiers, she would have fallen.

"You damn bitch!" Bartok raged, wiping the spit off his face with his sleeve.

Cassandra felt the blood flowing from a laceration inside her cheek. She tasted the salty iron tang of her blood from the cut, yet she glared at him with proud defiance.

Captain Shay tried to restrain Benton by grabbing his arm. "Major, I don't think this is necessary. She's a woman, for God's sake!"

"Elias, get your hands off me or, so help me, I'll have you court-martialed."

"I know you're in command, sir," they struggled briefly, "but I don't think General Kessington would approve of one of his commanding officers beating a white woman, even if she is a Rebel."

"Don't try to threaten me, Captain, I can break you."

"No, sir! I wasn't trying to threaten you. I was trying to point out a possible consequence of your action."

The reasoning behind Elias Shay's protests penetrated the anger and greed of the hawk-nosed Major. Benton turned away from Cassandra, walked a few paces, then spun on his heels to face her. "So, you won't tell me where you've stashed your valuables. So be it. They won't do you any good anyway because we are going to burn everything but the slave houses on this plantation." A mad, taunting gleam came into his eyes. "That's right! We are going to burn it all down and somewhere in all this your little fortune will go up with it!" He lifted his head back and let loose a crazed laugh. As it trailed off, his grin turned into a wicked, vicious snarl. "You get to watch," he said slowly, in a deep menacing tone. "Right down front so you won't miss a thing." Bartok slowly turned and walked away.

Captain Elias Shay watched Bartok's display, then watched him walk away as the distance between them grew. He turned his attention to Cassandra and the guards restraining her. She stood proud and defiant and glaring after the major.

He couldn't help noticing her beauty, despite the swollen and blood-encrusted slit on her lower lip. Her cheek was bruised and beginning to swell. Even in her simple day dress, smudged with dirt and dried blood, he could see the ample curves of a woman with a classic figure.

He also had witnessed the power of her will and the strength of her hate. He felt a twinge of desire, mixed with a feeling of guilt. He would take little pride in his part in this action and felt remorse for what was happening. "Still," he thought, "this is war and punishment must be dealt to the guilty." It was a rotten, stinking job, but he had his orders. "I just wish old man Kimbrough had gunned down Bartok instead of Sergeant O'Leary."

"Return her to the others, but keep them under guard," Captain Shay said to the soldiers still restraining her arms. He turned and followed the path taken by Major Bartok.

As the shadows began to lengthen and evening approached, the ravaging of Briarwood was near completion. All that could be taken away had been loaded, and much of it was on its way to Union headquarters. Flames were already lighting up the sky from the burning barn and carriage house, and the outhouses, grain sheds, hay stacks, and tool sheds of the great plantation.

The house was a shambles after the soldiers finished looting and returned to their mounts. The men gathered to watch the last act that would destroy the heart of the plantation—the burning of the great house itself.

"Please!" Fanny begged to Captain Shay. "We been slaves of these folk fo' far too long! Before you burn that house, would ya let me and Jethro get our things. I got everything I own in the maid's room of that place. Please, suh!"

Bartok overheard her plea. He liked the idea of the slaves recovering their belongings while the Kimbroughs watched theirs go up in smoke. It was another way to punish them. "Give them ten minutes; then burn it down, Captain."

"Yes, sir!"

Just before the two slaves were released, Fanny turned her back to the soldiers and gave Cassandra a knowing wink. Fanny and Jethro moved quickly, disappearing into the front door of the house. Cassandra was amazed how fast the large black woman could move.

They came out once with bundles of things wrapped in blankets and deposited them on the grass. They went in again, even as soldiers with torches entered the house. Jethro and Fanny worked feverishly to gather whatever they could salvage. The Yankees seemed uninterested, having already taken anything they found of value. Cassandra watched as Jethro stood in the doorway, motioning for Fanny to join him outside.

Flames were already visible in the windows of the upstairs bedrooms. Smoke billowed up from the roof to mingle with the already acrid gray smoke from the other burning structures. Smoke also appeared from the back of the house, the kitchen area. The last soldier left the house and returned to his horse.

A window exploded from the heat, sending shards of glass tinkling down form the upper story to the ground. Bright orange and yellow flames licked around the shattered window and danced along the ceiling. Sparks from the burning interior floated in lazy circles and drifted away from the house. Working together, Jethro and Fanny dragged what they had rescued away from the burning home. Flames burst from the doorways and windows of the lower floors. Additional flames began to lick the sides of the white house, turning it first a dingy gray, then a sickening black. The roof was now completely in flames. The great columns of the portico began to succumb to the ravages of heat and fire, adding to the conflagration.

Cassandra witnessed it all from her vantage point. Tears streamed silently down her cheeks as all that she had called home burned. There was nothing she could do but watch and grieve. The light from the fire cast lengthening, eerie shadows. The sweltering heat, even at this distance from the house, was almost unbearable. The fall weather was still mild, but the heat of the fire made it as hot as any day in hell.

Great spirals of hot sparks lifted from the roof and floated away like angry fireflies. Thick, rolling smoke continued to build and boil upward.

Over the roar and crackle of the fire, and captured in the harsh yellow light of the flames, Cassandra watched and heard Bartok's drunken laughter as he swigged on what remained of his stolen bourbon. She could hear his voice clearly as he laughed and shouted at the top of his voice, "Burn, Missouri, burn, damn you! Burn out all these damned Rebels!" He pitched the empty bottle at the house.

Cassandra, warmed by the fire that she would never forget, vowed someday, somehow, she would even the score with Major Benton Bartok. "If there is a God in heaven," she prayed, "then let me have my day of justice."

By midnight the walls and roof had tumbled in, and only a great glowing ash pile occupied the space once held by the great house of Briarwood Plantation. The last of the soldiers were now gone, leaving the Kimbroughs alone with their misery and despair. Gone was their home, gone was their plantation, and gone was the spiritual head of their family. They lay down in exhaustion to sleep on the cold ground, emotionally drained and full of pain.

20

A Briefing from the Colonel

Come in, Lieutenant Kimbrough, the Colonel is ready to see you." The master sergeant held the tent flap open. Ross stepped through the opening and entered the large wall tent being used as the temporary headquarters of Shelby's brigade. His gaze fell on the familiar face of Jo Shelby. Ross halted, saluted, then stood at attention. "Lieutenant Ross Kimbrough, reporting as ordered, sir."

The colonel looked up from studying the maps spread out on the table before him. A smile creased his face as he recognized Ross. "At ease, Ross," he said, returning the salute.

Ross relaxed and dropped his arm. "Good afternoon, Colonel Shelby. I must say, sir, those three stars on your collar look mighty good. They are long overdue."

"Thank you, Ross, I'm proud to command at any level, but I've got to admit there would have been hell to pay if they had tried to give command of this brigade to someone else." A twinkle of mirth sparkled in his eyes as he chuckled softly.

"Yes, sir. I suspect the men would have hung General

Hindman from a tree if he'd tried to appoint someone else to command the brigade."

"I don't think the government in Richmond would take kindly to Confederate soldiers hanging their generals. Do you, Ross?" Colonel Shelby's amusement was obvious.

"No, sir, I don't think ole Jeff Davis would be pleased."

Both men laughed loudly as they joked about the general. "Well, Ross, you've given me the first good laugh I've had in a couple of days."

He shifted himself in his chair and leaned back. "I want to bring you up-to-date on what has been happening, and I need you to gather some more intelligence for me. As you know, enemy activity has increased. While you were out scouting, I sent Captain Ben Elliot with I Company over to near Carthage. Terrill Fletcher said there was a large party of Pin Indians and runaway slaves engaged in robbing, raping, and pillaging the people there. Fletch led Elliot's men right on top of them, and I think they killed most before they could escape.

"We lost Colonel Hayes while you were gone. He was killed in a clash with Yankee cavalry while on patrol."

"I already heard, Colonel. The men were pretty upset by it."

"I hated to lose Upton Hayes. He was a good officer, but I have promoted David Shanks to take his place."

"I have heard he's a good man and popular with the men. I'm sure he'll do a god job, Colonel."

"He already is. He just returned from his first raid. We received word from a local that the Yankees were mining lead and smelting it at Granby. I sent Colonel Shanks with the Twelfth Missouri Cavalry to see if he could stop them. He not only ran the Yankees off, but he captured all the lead they had processed. He's hauled it into camp and we are busy turning it into bullets, pistol balls, canister balls, cannonballs, and cannon shells from our molds. It should be enough to supply our needs for quite a while."

"Sure is nice of those blue-bellies to do all the work and provide us with the lead we need to shoot at 'em."

Colonel Shelby smiled mischievously. "I consider it only a loan. I intend to give as much of the lead back as possible to the Yankees . . . fired from the barrels of our guns."

Ross smiled. "Seems fair to me."

"Problem is, they aren't very happy about us wiping out their mining and garrison troops. Word is, they intend to send an army after us. That's why I've sent for you. I want you to take your scouts north to capture some prisoners for interrogation. We need to find out what they're planning. Do you think you can bring in prisoners by tomorrow?"

"No problem, sir. I'll round up some men and hit them at daylight." Ross hesitated, then said, "Colonel, have you had time to look over my last scouting report?"

"Yes, I'm glad to see things are quiet to the east. It frees us to deal with other areas. I'll look for your prisoners tomorrow. Good luck, Ross, and good hunting!"

"Thank you, sir." Ross turned and left the tent. "Well," he thought, "I've got the rest of the day to relax. I can round up my men tonight and hit their pickets in the morning. With any luck, we ought to be back by noon." Ross decided he would check with his brother, Calvin. He hadn't seen him for several days, and he hoped he might talk him into going along for the ride. It would be good to spend time together again. Ross returned to Sultan and rode for Bledsoe's battery.

A few minutes later he found Lieutenant Collins drilling the battery in a vacant field nearby. "Okay, men, let's go through artillery drill again. I know if you try, you lamebrains can get this right! Assume your positions; prepare to fire! Crewman position one, what is your responsibility and actions?"

"I'm in charge of ramming and sponging, sir! On the command 'load' I run a wet sponge swab down the length of the interior of the barrel. Then I prepare to ram home the powder charge and projectile."

"Very good, Private. Position number two, what is your job?"

"On the command 'load,' I take the ammunition from Bill here and shove it in the barrel."

"No, Private, that isn't what you do. How many times do I have to tell you, number two, we use crew position numbers, not names. Suppose in battle Bill gets killed. If you don't know to look for your man by position you might not know what to do. Now try it again, and do it right this time."

"Yes, sir. I take the ammunition from crewman number five; I lay the ammunition flat in the palm of my hand and insert the charge into the muzzle of the cannon."

"That's better, number two. Now what is your job, number three?"

"Sir! I hold my thumb over the vent at the rear of the barrel, and close it to help extinguish any sparks, while number one swabs the barrel and rams home the ammunition."

"That's correct. I want to remind you, gentlemen, of the importance of number three holding the vent closed with his thumbstall. If air gets to any hot sparks while number one is ramming home the load, we are going to lose number one and possibly number two when the cannon blows them to pieces! I get very upset when someone blows up my crewmen. Do I make myself clear?"

A loud mumbled reply came from number one. "I reckon I'd be a mite more sorry about it than Lieutenant Collins!" The entire crew broke into laughter, including the lieutenant.

"Okay, men, let's settle down," Dick Collins said, smiling broadly. "What is your job, gunner?"

"After the gun is loaded I step forward to the breech and sight the cannon. I shout aiming directions to position number three who, after covering the vent during loading, has moved to the trail handspike at the rear of the gun carriage. He then can shift the cannon to my shouted aim point."

"Very good, Corporal Kimbrough," shouted Lieutenant Collins. "What are you doing during this time, number five?"

"Sir! After giving the ammunition to number two I return to the limber and get a new round and powder charge from six and seven."

"Excellent, number five. What is six and seven doing?"

"Sir! Position six removes ammunition from limber and hands it to seven. Position seven takes the ammunition and, if it is an exploding shell, I cut the fuse to the directions shouted to me by the gunner, sir! Then when number five approaches I put it into his leather haversack to carry forward to number two."

"Very good. Now what is supposed to happen, gunner?"

"After the gun is sighted I move behind the gun to observe the effects of the shot. I then give the order, 'Ready!' "

"When the gunner yells 'Ready!' what happens, number three?"

"Numbers one and two stand clear of the muzzle. I step forward from the trail spike and, using the vent pick, ram it down through the vent in the breech and through the powder bag, sir!"

"Number four, what is your function?"

"I attach a friction primer to the lanyard and insert it into the vent. I then step back and hang on to the lanyard leaving it slack. Number three stays at the breech and holds the primer in place."

"Corporal Kimbrough, what happens next?"

"I give the order 'Fire!' and number three steps away from the wheel. Number four pulls the lanyard firing the piece, sir."

"That's close, gunner, but you left out one little detail. Do you know what you left out, Corporal?"

"No, sir!"

"You have to wait to yell 'Fire!' until I give the order. Unless you have received an order to 'Fire at will.' "

"Yes, sir! Sorry, sir!"

"That's fine, gunner. Now suppose you tell me what happens next."

"Yes, sir! As the gun fires and then recoils, number five gives the next round to number two. The crew pushes the cannon back into position and the sequence starts again."

"Excellent, gunner. If you work as a team you should be able to fire this piece in battle, twice every minute, and do a reasonable job of hitting your target. Men, this requires concentration and teamwork.

"The safety of those in your crew, the men of your artillery battery, and the men in your army depend on you. It is your responsibility to do your job quickly and accurately. You must practice and drill so that when you are in battle and men are wounded or killed in your battery, you can still do your job. I expect every man to know every position so you can keep this weapon firing until a replacement can reach any vacant position on the crew.

"It is not your responsibility to take care of any wounded men. That will just leave more spots open in your crew and further erode the efficiency of your team. You can do the most good for the members of your crew and our battery by continuing to inflict heavy damage on the enemy. Is that clear, gentlemen?"

A chorus of "Yes, sir!" met his question.

"We'll practice our drill for ten minutes without live ammunition, followed by five minutes with live ammunition. Gun number one, prepare to fire!"

Ross sat on the rail fence and continued to watch his brother, Calvin, and gun number one practice their drill. He saw the crew for gun number two standing and observing the practice. Like him, they were interested observers

The number one crew worked their way through the drill until ten minutes had passed, then began their live fire practice. Ross could see they were taking aim on a section of rock fence running along a ridge road nearly half a mile away.

The first shot went high. The second went high again. The third shot was low, but it threw dirt on the wall. The fourth shot hit home, scattering stones into the air. A cheer went up from the number one crew. Shots five and six scored hits, and then the seventh shot went a little high again. Shots eight, nine, and ten either hit the fence or landed near the base of it.

Ross watched the crew as the lieutenant gave a review of practice, then dismissed them. Crew two took their turn at their cannon.

Ross yelled at Calvin as he walked away from the cannon, "Hey, gunner, got time to talk to another lieutenant?"

"Yes, sir!" Calvin snapped to attention near Ross and gave him a quick salute.

Ross grinned back at his brother and said, "At ease soldier. Hey, little brother, I see they made you a corporal and a gunner already. How did you rate?"

"Just luckier at aiming than most when we were training, that's all."

"Yeah, I figure it had to be luck." Ross tried to keep a straight face, but he just couldn't do it. He began to laugh and slapped Calvin on the back, then gave him a brotherly hug.

"So, Ross, what brings you over here?"

"Colonel Shelby wants me to go out in the morning and bring in some Yankee pickets for questioning. I thought you might come along to see what it's like to be a scout."

"I'm not on duty tomorrow, so let me check with Lieutenant Collins. If he says yes, I'll ride back to your camp with you."

There was no opposition to the request, and soon the two brothers were on their way to camp to join the scouts. As they rode, Calvin, feeling curious, asked, "Have you heard from that girl from Arkansas you told us about?"

"Valissa? Yes! Two days after we made camp at Elm Springs, I had two letters delivered to me; another caught up with me at Elkhorn Creek; and another came yesterday with mail call."

"So, don't keep me in suspense. What did she have to say?"

"Ah, you know, the usual stuff. She talked about her family and what's been happening to them."

"Is that all?"

"Well, no, she also wrote about how much she enjoyed our time together and how she hopes I'll come see her again."

"Sounds like the girl took a fancy to you. It's about time you found someone that can gentle you down a mite. The gals back home from the Missouri River valley have been trying to catch you for years, but it took a belle from Arkansas to get the job done."

"Now hold on a minute, little brother—I'm not married yet."

"I've seen that faraway look in your eyes. I've seen you lost in thought so badly that you didn't even notice others around you. You might fool others, Ross, but you can't fool me. You're in love with her. It's as plain as day to me."

"I admit she's on my mind more than I'd like. It's downright dangerous. If I get to daydreaming too much, there'll be a hole in the ground with my name on it."

"Ah, the dangers of love."

"She's one of the most beautiful women I have ever seen, Calvin. She has eyes the color of new bluegrass in the spring. I can get lost in those eyes. I only met her once, and we spent only a short time together, but I can't keep her off my mind. Sometimes I dream about her, and when I ride I find myself thinking about her. I've even thought about sneaking away for a few days just to see her again."

"It must be wonderful to be so much in love," Calvin said. "Maybe when the war is over, I'll find someone. Ross, I know it's hard, but right now, you must put duty first."

Their thoughts were of romance and love, and each brother struggled with his thoughts and memories of the past as the conversation faded away. They rode on in silence until they reached camp and joined Shelby's scouts.

21

No Game for Gentlemen

The scouts rode out just past midnight, galloping cautiously up the road, shrouded in the black veil of night. The deepest shadows carried an unfathomable black inkiness to them. Ross's eyes did their best to adjust to the dark, but to see anything at all there had to be some movement within the shadowy areas. The eerie sensation was heightened by the necessity to move as quickly and quietly as possible. They knew Jonas Starke was ahead and would warn them when they reached his location. When they found Jonas they would be near enemy lines.

After a tense ride that seemed to last far longer than the three hours it took, they spotted the signal lamp. In the depth of the shadows, the appropriate passwords were exchanged and the small band of scouts followed Jonas off the road and into a small clearing. Once there, Jonas reported.

"Ross, I've checked things out and I've located a picket camp just up the road about three quarters of a mile. They have one man standing guard along the road and another one along the creek. I figure I could lead another man in, and if we move quietly between the road and the creek, we might surprise them. Once we take the night guards out, we can capture the others while they are asleep." Jonas's thin, scraggly features appeared almost grotesque in the yellow glare of the hooded lamp.

"Since you know the lay of the land and the situation better than we do, I'm gonna let you take out the guards. You pick a man to help you," said Ross.

"Hell, I figure me an' Rube can do 'er."

"I'll bring the men up the middle behind you. Signal when the area is cleared and we'll move on the sleeping men."

Jonas and Rube nodded in agreement. Both scouts lightened their loads, leaving all extra equipment behind. They carefully tied down anything else that might make a sound as they moved through the woods. The two men moved out when they were ready. Ross used the light from the oil lamp to read his pocket watch. No wonder he felt tired. It was already near four o'clock in the morning. A late-rising sliver of moon cast a faint glow through the foliage.

They waited quietly while Jonas and Rube moved into position, then followed. Ross led the others until they caught Jonas. Jonas gave a slashing motion across his throat, indicating that the picket guards had been permanently silenced.

Ross held up his hands in tight fists, then opened them and spread his fingers. At this silent order the scouts quickly spread out and advanced on the sleeping camp. Ross pulled Double Twelve from the holster behind his neck. He could sense Calvin following behind him as they moved silently. He could smell the smoke drifting through the trees from the dying embers of the campfire.

Before them lay several cavalry troopers, still snug in their bedrolls. The horses stood picketed among the trees to the north of the camp, and he heard their faint nickering and snorting, disturbed by the approach of the Confederate scouts through the woods.

Most of the Yankees seemed fast asleep, but as one of the scouts snapped a twig, Ross saw a trooper roll over and sit up. He still looked half-asleep. He might have heard the snapping twig, or, perhaps, the man was just heeding the call of nature, but it could spell disaster if he had time to alert his friends.

Ross shouted the order at the top of his lungs, "Charge!"

At his command, seven Confederate soldiers entered the sleeping Union camp. The Yankees spilled from their blankets and groggily tried to mount some kind of defense. For most it was near impossible to even rise. Others groped about, trying to find their weapons.

Ross and the scouts yelled, "Drop your weapons, hands in the air!"

The embarrassed enemy pickets surrendered, their hands reaching for the sky as they dropped their weapons. Ross, amused, eyed the rumpled Yankees standing in various states of dress.

Calvin bent down to pick up an enemy carbine, twisting his back to the prisoners as he reached for the weapon. Ross's shotgun roared and Calvin involuntarily flinched. He glanced up to see the body of a Union trooper fly through the air and hit the ground with a heavy thud. The soldier's right arm was pinned beneath his body. Minute splatters and droplets of blood lingered in the air with a small cloud of dust, stirred by the fall.

Calvin stood in amazed silence as Ross ordered Jonas and Fletch to keep an eye on the rest of the prisoners. He saw Ross and Rube stand over the dead body, laughing and smiling.

"Would ya look at that! Double Twelve must have thrown him back three feet and left a hole in him big enough to see daylight through!"

"Damn, Ross! You could almost put your arm through that hole!" Rube pushed back his slough hat with the barrel of his navy Colt, then spat a stream of brown tobacco juice into the dust. "Damn fool thang he tried."

Calvin felt anger and disgust well up within him. He pushed alongside the two scouts and looked down at the dead Yankee trooper.

The trooper's eyes were open, staring at the dark void of

death. Blood pooled under the body, soaking into the dry dust. One foot still quivered.

Calvin turned and grabbed his brother by the arm, "Why, Ross? Why did you shoot an unarmed man?" He stared into Ross's hardened eyes. "Damn you! You kill an unarmed man and you act like it's some kind of joke."

The smile faded from Ross's face as he jerked his arm loose from Calvin's grip. His jaw muscles bunched and tightened as his eyes burned with anger. "You think I shot down an unarmed man just for sport? Why don't you look before you go shooting off your mouth, boy?" The words rolled out hard and edged with contempt. Ross shoved Calvin closer to the body. "Roll him over, Cal," Ross ordered.

Calvin hesitated, then reached down and grabbed the body by the left arm and tugged until the soldier rolled over on his stomach, exposing the right arm. His hand loosely gripped a cocked Remington thirty-six caliber pistol.

"He had a gun stuck in the back of his belt. When you turned your back on him, he went for it and I spun and shot." Ross jammed Double Twelve back into its holster. In one stride Ross reached Calvin, grabbed him by the lapels, and jammed his face inches from his brother's nose.

"Listen to me good, boy! This ain't a game for gentlemen. This is war! There aren't any rules, and if you try to play it like there is, you're going to end up as dead as he is."

"You've grown hard, Ross. Doesn't killing a man even bother you anymore?"

Ross let go of the lapels and, for a second, Cal could see the turmoil behind his brother's eyes. Ross said, "This is all new to you, Cal, and sooner than you think, if you live long enough, you'll be like the rest of us. I've fought at the battles of Oak Hills, Lexington, Elkhorn Tavern, and Corinth. I've watched good friends die, some of them in my arms. I've killed many men and wished I'd killed more.

"I've come along after the Yankee Jayhawkers burned entire villages, like Oceola. They took everything—food, clothing—and burned the homes and buildings. I've seen innocent women and children left with nothing to eat and no place to live. I've found fathers and young boys left hanging at the end of ropes.

"I've found the bodies of black women raped and murdered by Union men. These same men who say they want to grant them freedom. Hell, I've even killed freebooters in the act of raping white women! While I've been out here fighting and killing, you were warm and safe at home in Briarwood. You went to the university and learned all the rules of being a gentleman." Ross continued sarcastically, "Hell, Cal. You have no idea what war is. Where do you think you earned the right to be passing judgments on me? You'll learn, boy." Ross slowed as his anger spent itself. "You'll see, it's different after you've been here a while. We came here to take these prisoners back to headquarters for interrogation, and that's what I aim to do. Then I'm going to return you to the artillery where you belong." He turned to Jonas, barked out his orders, and the men moved out. Ross turned away and ordered the horses to be brought forward.

Rube Anderson walked over to Calvin. "You're wrong about Ross. If it hadn't been for him, that Yank would have tried to put a bullet in yer gizzard. Ross ain't really hard; every time we lose a man under his command, he cries. I've seen the tears running down his cheeks. But war toughens ya up. You get used to seeing men slaughtered like animals. After a while it don't mean nothin', you'll see." Rube turned and started gathering captured weapons.

Calvin stood, stunned. He felt sorry for the things he had said, and wished he could take them back, but now it was too late.

The scouts mounted up and led the procession of Yankee prisoners toward the Confederate camp. Upon returning to the Confederate lines with their prisoners, the scouts received an unexpected surprise. Scattered around them on both sides of the road new camps were springing up filled with fresh reinforcements.

These men represented a strange conglomerate. They were but a fraction of over three thousand Confederate Indian troops of the civilized nations led by General Douglas

Cooper. The Indian command was composed of Choctaws, Cherokees, and half-breeds from the Indian territory.

It was not the first time the veterans of Shelby's scouts had served with Indian troops. They had fought alongside of Albert Pike's Indian Brigade at the battle of Elkhorn Tavern.

The white troopers had mixed opinions on the worth of the Indian soldiers. Many recalled how they stalled, then stampeded in retreat when faced with artillery fire. During the battle of Elkhorn Tavern, once they faced the 'thunder wagons,' the Indians fled to the security of the woods and could not be induced to venture forth again for an attack. Ross recalled they had been largely ineffective as troops, because they lacked the discipline to follow orders. No one could deny they were fierce in battle until faced with the cannons.

Serving with the Indians was a blessing for Ross, for he learned how to track and read signs. He owed much of his ability as a scout to this association with the Indians. "Any reinforcements are welcome," he thought.

For Calvin, seeing the Indian troops was a new experience and he wasn't prepared. They were dressed in a mixture of uniforms and buckskin and beads. Some wore Confederate gray uniforms with war feathers in their hair. Long ponytails or braids frequently extended well below their hats. Some wore a mix of Union blue and Confederate gray. Uniforms were always at a premium in the Confederate army. Try as they might, the commanders of the Indian brigades seldom had the material to uniform their troops properly. Though the Confederacy had a shortage of man power, the Indian troops were always the last to get what they needed. This accounted for the hodgepodge of dress among the troops. The mix of different weapon types was even more diverse.

Most of these troops were of the civilized tribes and lived as the white man in cabins and homes. They adopted some European-style clothing. Still, when Calvin viewed these allies, he felt fear gripping his heart. All his life he had heard of the atrocities and savagery committed by Indians on the frontier. The stories drifting back from the plains and Texas reached the settlements in Missouri where the tales were retold. Just recently, pin Indians were killed by Shelby's Confederate troopers as punishment for their grisly murders and rapes. The pin Indians had wreaked havoc among the scattered population of southwest Missouri. Calvin knew he would sleep uncomfortably having Indians camped so close.

The scouts rode into headquarters and turned over their prisoners for questioning, then returned to camp where they collapsed in exhaustion. Calvin rode on to find Bledsoe's battery. His parting with Ross was brief, and he could still feel tension between them.

22

A Baptism of Fire

The next morning, Ross sat by the campfire sipping some rare coffee when Evan Stryker of Shelby's staff approached. "Good morning, Captain Stryker. Care for a cup of coffee this morning?"

The aroma of the fresh-brewed coffee filled his nostrils as Evan inhaled. "Don't mind if I do, Ross, smells great. I don't know how you always manage to find good coffee."

"It isn't much of a problem when you're a scout. This coffee is compliments of the Sixth Kansas Cavalry. We just helped ourselves when we captured those prisoners yesterday morning. We figured we needed it more than they did." Ross grinned broadly. "What did the boys find out from those Yank troopers, anyway?"

"That's why I'm here. Colonel Shelby told me to tell you General Salomon is headed our way with the Sixth Kansas Cavalry and five thousand Dutch troops. He's got a few Indian troops with him acting as scouts. We know some of his German troops came from Wisconsin."

"Those damn foreigners really get to me. They can't speak

English and they're down here putting their noses in our business. They're the same as hired mercenaries the way I see it. I can't wait to ride over some of them kraut eatin' Dutch!"

"The Dutch are fine fighters, Ross."

"Yeah, I suppose they are, but we made Siegel and his Dutch run at Oak Hills."

"That we did. Probably the best thing that's happened for the South in these parts was the death of General Nathanial Lyons at Oak Hills. He was a tough Yankee. Ole Dutch Siegel couldn't fill his shoes and ran like a scalded dog. Yankees called it the battle of Wilson's Creek. Funny how most times we can't even agree on the names of the battles."

Ross took another sip of his coffee. "Heard you and Gilbert Thomas had a fight. Is it true?"

"I'm afraid so. I gather Gilbert is in love with your sister, Cassandra, and I don't blame him. She's a spirited and beautiful woman. Your sister doesn't love him and he figures I'm somehow to blame. Gilbert thinks if I hadn't come to Briarwood, it might have been different between them."

"Evan, I know you didn't do anything to change how Cassandra felt about Gil. Their relationship has been a one-sided affair from the start. Gil has chased after her since they were children. She's always liked Gil as a friend, but I know she never felt anything more for him. Gil just hasn't accepted it. He knows Cassie is interested in you—I guess that makes you a target for his disappointment."

"We've already had one argument. Right after the brigade was formed, he got drunk and came looking for a fight. He had too much to drink, and I tried to talk my way out of it, but there was no way I could get him settled down. I punched him several times, but he just kept coming until I knocked him out."

"I'm afraid you've just made a worse enemy out of him. Be careful, Evan. I don't know what he might do to settle the score."

"I hope, with time, he'll come to realize that even if I hadn't come along she would never have loved him."

Ross nodded in agreement. "He's blinded by his emotions

right now. He is a good officer when he's not drinking, and a hell of a good man to have with you in a battle. I hope he'll come to his senses soon."

"Me too, Ross, the Confederacy needs every man she can get right now. He's a captain and in charge of the same regiment your brother Jessie belongs to. I know his men wouldn't have voted for him if they lacked confidence in his leadership. If he reaches a point where his drinking is endangering his regiment, I'll be forced to report him to Colonel Shelby."

"Evan, I hope it doesn't come to that."

"I hope not. Well, I didn't come here to discuss my problems. I've been sent here by Colonel Shelby to give you your orders."

Ross sighed heavily. He was enjoying the campfire and the coffee, and hitting the trail again wasn't very appealing. "Well, let's hear it."

"Colonel Cooper has taken over command by virtue of his seniority. Colonel Tresevant Hawpe has also joined us with his Thirty-First Texas Cavalry regiment of nearly four hundred men. From information brought in by Southern sympathizers and the prisoners you captured, we know General Salomon's Yankees will reach us by tomorrow.

"Colonel Cooper wants to put the Texans in Newtonia to hold the town. He has ordered a two-gun section of artillery under Bledsoe posted on the plains in front of the town. They figure the flour mill is what the Yankees are after, but we need it to feed our troops. Colonel Cooper has ordered Jo to hold our brigade behind the town in support. The Indians are to be positioned on both flanks of our brigade. The Colonel wants you to scout to the west. We know Salomon is to the north of us, and the east is clear."

"Tell him we'll ride out tonight. Tomorrow is the thirtieth of September, isn't it?"

"Yeah, I think so. Another month gone and winter is fast approaching." Evan stood, stretching his legs before he left. "Have a safe ride."

"You too, Captain—watch your hide."

Captain Evan Stryker gave the empty tin cup back to Ross and hurriedly left the campfire as he continued his rounds delivering orders to the scattered commands.

The rumble of galloping hooves echoed off the buildings of Newtonia as Bledsoe's battery thundered down the street. They were moving under orders to take up position in front of the town to stem the advance of Salomon's army.

Calvin hung tightly to his reins as he bounced along on Red Roses. He strained his eyes trying to see through the dust raised by the passing of the limber pulling the number one gun. He must stay close behind, because the number two gun and crew were following on their heels.

He tried to make sense of it all: the blur of the passing buildings, glimpses of women and children taking cover, and the choking dust clogging his eyes and throat. His palms were sticky with sweat; his stomach was in knots, and he could feel every beat of his heart surge blood through his temples.

On they rode through Newtonia, onto the road leading to the prairie bordering the small town. They galloped for half a mile before Captain Bledsoe gave his orders to deploy.

Calvin quickly swung out of the saddle. He handed the reins of Red Roses to a horse holder so that she could be led back with the reserves and away from the danger of the battery. Eager hands rapidly gripped the cannon, and the barrel was swung in the direction of the enemy. Horses were unhitched from the limber and led away. The ammo chests in the limber were opened, and all the equipment was prepared for battle under the watchful eyes of Captain Bledsoe and Lieutenant Collins.

"Load!" came the order. They went through the now-familiar drill. They could see the advancing enemy. Infantry was marching in line formation to the distant roll of the drum. The bright sunlight glinted off the gun barrels as the soldiers marched. The artillery crew watched as sharp pinpoints of light danced from the reflections on the iron bayonets. Calvin heard the piercing sound of bugles and shouted orders muffled by the distance. Two six-gun batteries of

Union blue faced off against the single two-gun section of Bledsoe and Collins. The deep boom of the battery on the right signaled the attack was on.

"Sight on the battery on the left," ordered Captain Bledsoe. Calvin stepped forward to sight the gun. His hands shook so badly he could barely rest the pendulum hausse sight into its bracket. He peered through the sight and across the barrel. Solid shot was loaded in the big gun since their target was an enemy battery. The steel balls could destroy the tubes or crush spokes or carriages with a solid hit.

Aiming down the barrel was enough to send shivers of terror through his body. He winced as he saw the enemy battery fire, almost as one gun. He saw the smoke and flame jump from the big guns and heard the deep boom of the explosions. He ducked as the shells screamed overhead on their way toward Newtonia. He gave the elevation screw a couple of turns until the barrel lined up level with his target.

"Swing it right . . . More!" Calvin shouted to Henry Hawthorne at the trail spike. The target lined up, Calvin turned and walked to his position—clear of the gun and slightly behind it.

"Ready!"

At the command Brady Dobler strode to the vent and jammed the vent pick through into the powder bag. Delmar Pickett stepped forward and inserted the friction primer into the now open vent. He stepped back, lanyard at the ready. Positions one, two, and three leaned away from the cannon, hands covering their ears. All was ready.

"Gentlemen, ready; commence firing!" shouted Lieutenant Collins.

Calvin swallowed hard then shouted out the command, "Fire!"

The cannon roared in defiance. Smoke and flame belched forth from the muzzle as the wheels lifted from the ground. The ball blasted from the barrel; the gun rocked back but was instantly rolled into position by the crew. The sound of the ball ripping through the air rang in Calvin's ears as he watched the path of the projectile. It sailed harmlessly above the enemy battery, disappearing into the woods. Calvin made a mental note and again went to the task of correcting his aim. Gun number two's shot hit in front of the enemy battery, showering the Yank gunners with dirt.

Calvin was glad they had spent so much time on drill. The discipline helped him do his job despite his fear. He was really too busy to think about the dangers they faced. Fortunately, the enemy infantry was reluctant to confront the battery head on and stayed out of effective musket range. On the third shot Calvin's crew hit a limber of the target battery. The resulting explosion caused havoc among the Union battery. The Yankees began to direct less fire at the town and more at the Rebel cannons.

Bledsoe and Collins urged the men of the battery on, and they continued to blast the enemy. Twice a minute the big guns belched out their deadly cargo. For an hour the duel continued as shells screamed overhead. Shells impacted in front and to both sides of their position, hurling geysers of dirt into the air.

Miraculously, the shelling did little damage. Solid shot skipped through their position twice, like someone skipping a flat stone over water. Their luck held. The constant roar from the cannon made Calvin's ears ring, and smoke burned his eyes. The cannon tube became so heated from constant use that to touch it for more than a moment was unbearable. Soon, the inevitable happened—the ammunition was exhausted, and both guns fell silent.

"Hold your positions, men!" came the shouted order from Bledsoe. "I know we're out of ammunition, but the Yankees don't."

Calvin began to feel fear washing over him in overwhelming waves. When they were busy, he hadn't had time to be afraid. Now, with the guns silent, he had time to observe the danger around him. He began to shake.

Charlie Jasper yelled out to Lieutenant Collins, "All we have left in the chest is canister rounds."

"Charlie, run back to the reserves and send someone to

bring up some more ammunition," Collins shouted above the roar of enemy shelling. Charlie started jogging to the rear.

The enemy, reluctant to charge the cannons, began to try to maneuver around them. The troops of the Ninth Wisconsin began a flanking movement on the town of Newtonia, still held by Hawpe's Texans. The action had shifted to the right and behind the Rebel battery. Calvin nearly panicked as he realized the enemy was now on three sides of them, and they were in danger of being cut off from the rest of the Confederate forces. The Union army began to deploy skirmishers.

On the southern outskirts of Newtonia, Colonel Jo Shelby and Colonel Douglas H. Cooper studied the battlefield and planned their troop deployments. Both realized the danger to Bledsoe's battery. Holding the center of the line was imperative if they were to hold Newtonia. The battery must be saved.

"Colonel Shelby, I want you to take a regiment of your cavalry and drive off those skirmishers before we lose that battery."

"Yes, sir! I'll see to it immediately. Might I suggest we immediately resupply our artillery?"

"Yes, of course, send one of your staff to give the necessary orders."

Colonel Shelby turned. "Stryker, ride to Lieutenant Colonel Gordon. Tell him to bring up the Fifth Missouri Cavalry. Tell him I want my boys to ride over the damn Dutch. Drive 'em into the ground, or off this field, but by heaven, I want the Dutch to see what hell looks like! These Yanks ain't seen nothing till they come up against my boys."

Evan looked into the fiery eyes of his commander and saw a determination and zest that was unstoppable. He could not help but smile proudly as he snapped his hand up in salute. "Yes, sir." Evan wheeled his horse and rode at a gallop to find Colonel Gordon and his regiment. It was a short and swift ride. Immediately upon receiving his orders, Gordon had his troops on the march.

Jessie Kimbrough sat on his horse nervously. His heart was pounding; he was so excited it was nearly impossible for him to sit still in line. Star's Pride was just as nervous, hoofing and snorting, occasionally bumping another horse on either side of them. The constant booming of cannon and the whine of minie balls sounding like terrified bees filled the air.

Sweat poured from under the band of his hat and streaked a course down his face. The salty taste of sweat dripped onto his lips. Before him on the grassy plain lay the battlefield. He could see the hated enemy soldiers advancing on the town, like miniature soldiers with tiny toy muskets.

The Rebel cavalry waited in line. Soldiers held their weapons at the ready. Some of the Fifth Missouri held pistols gripped firmly in their hands; others held swords. For now, most of the carbines and muskets remained sheathed, for it was too hard to shoot them from the back of a running horse.

Colonel Gordon rode down the line in front of his regiment. He showed an air of confidence and looked strikingly military on his charger. He stopped near Captain Gilbert Thomas, who was positioned directly in front of E Company. Lieutenant Colonel Gordon pulled his sword from its scabbard and pointed it over his head in a slow, circling motion. Then he pointed it toward the enemy while shouting his order. "Boys! Give them hell! Forward at a walk." The line of cavalry advanced in line. After a few yards came the order they had been waiting for: "Charge!"

In an instant the soldiers cut loose with the Rebel yell. The line became ragged as the galloping men and horses raced forward. The sound of the thundering hooves and the clang of bit and metal filled Jessie's senses. He felt as if he was part of an overwhelming wave as he rode with his friends into his first real battle. Excited and pumped with adrenaline, he was heedless of the danger awaiting them.

Before the onrushing tide, the Union troops hesitated, then held their line. Officers frantically tried to straighten their formation. The Ninth Wisconsin knelt as one man and poured a fierce volley of fire into the ranks of the hard-charging Fifth Missouri Cavalry. Jessie watched the line of blue coats stop and make their adjustments. He watched with detached wonder as he heard the sound of their muskets explode like a string of firecrackers and saw the clouds of expended smoke roll from their barrels.

He heard the whining sound of musket balls furiously wing their way past him. He felt the tug at his sleeve as a musket ball tore at his jacket. Besides him, a horse stumbled and flipped with a hoarse, throaty groan. The rider was tossed head over heels from his dying horse. Other saddles around him suddenly emptied. Star's Pride moved on, closing the gap between him and the enemy at every stride.

A burly German in his blue uniform loomed in front. Star's Pride tried to halt, but could not check the momentum of her charge and rode over the wide-eyed soldier. He wheeled Star's Pride to the right. A Union soldier ran and Jessie stroked his sword across his back. The German screamed in pain, dropping his musket as he fell on his face.

Another Yankee thrust his bayoneted rifle at Jessie, who parried the thrust with his sword. He felt the bayonet slam against the curved hilt of his sword, jarring his arm. Jessie kicked the man in the chest as Captain Gilbert Thomas drove his sword deep into the Yankee's back. Jessie saw the shocked, unbelieving look on the face of the Union soldier as he dropped his musket and both hands grabbed the blood-stained blade protruding from his chest. Blood started to run from his mouth as his eyes glazed in death and he fell forward into the grass, ripping the sword out of the hands of the captain.

Like a tidal wave crashing on a shore, the Yankee line disintegrated. First one, then many fled in retreat. Some were captured; others died on the spot. Many ran in terror, relentlessly pursued by Shelby's cavalrymen.

The Confederate troops circled and tried to reorganize after the short pursuit. The captured Union soldiers were rounded up and marched to the rear while care for the wounded was initiated. Although the skirmish line was repulsed, the enemy had not abandoned the field. On a nearby hill, one of the six-gun batteries began concentrating its fire on the Fifth Missouri Cavalry, now dressing its ranks for another charge. A direct assault on the battery was impossible because of intervening fences in the fields. Despite the obstacles in their path, the Rebels charged the exposed Union battery.

The Yankee cannoneers, terrified by the sight of the charging Rebels and scattered by the retreating Ninth Wisconsin infantry running through their battery in wild retreat, began to limber up and withdraw from their position. They galloped quickly to the rear. The Fifth Missouri Cavalry was kept from capturing the artillery only because the fences slowed their advance.

Seeing the German troops of the Ninth Wisconsin in route and the danger to their battery, the men of the Sixth Kansas Cavalry came up boldly and tried to attack the Rebel cavalry from the left and rear flank.

Lieutenant Colonel Gordon quickly gave the command to his men to wheel half-way around to face this new challenge. The Confederates again loosened the bloodcurdling Rebel yell as they charged among the Yankee cavalry. In the circling mass of men and horse flesh, Jessie waded in to do battle.

His sword flashed again and again as he bobbed and weaved his way through the lines. He felt his sword jarred loose from his grip as he blocked a blow from a Union trooper. Flame danced before his face as a pistol aimed at him missed its mark. He hugged Pride's neck as he broke clear and wheeled her again to face the enemy. His fingers pulled his pistol from its holster. Jessie raised the weapon, cocked the hammer, and felt the reassuring kick as the pistol recoiled against his hand. The Sixth Kansas Cavalry broke as the infantry had before them and retreated for their line of reserves. At least the Union cavalry withdrew in an orderly fashion.

General Salomon formed his reserves into a solid phalanx at the edge of the timber line. From this point he rallied his retreating infantry and cavalry. On both flanks he supported his line with his two artillery batteries.

Colonel Cooper and Colonel Shelby saw what was happening and ordered the withdrawal of Gordon's victorious cavalry troopers. The Rebels prepared for an all-out assault.

In the diversion created by the charge of the Fifth Missouri Cavalry, Bledsoe's battery was resupplied. Calvin felt some of his fear drain away as he watched the menacing enemy infantry driven from the field. Collins's battery began to hurl well-directed shells into the enemy line.

In less than two hours, all was ready. The entire Confederate army hurled against the Union line. Salomon's men, demoralized and weakened by their losses to the Ninth Wisconsin and Sixth Kansas Cavalry, could not withstand the murderous weight of the attack. The entire line gave way under the powerful momentum of the Rebel assault. There was no question of reforming the line this time. The scared Union soldiers were terrorized by the yells and chants of the Indians and by the equally murderous Missourians and Texans.

They scattered in wild disarray to the rear, pursued by the screaming Confederates. They chased the running Yankees to the north from Newtonia for a distance of over twelve miles. Many were captured. The Union units not captured were disorganized and scattered. Only stubborn resistance by the Union cavalry kept Salomon's whole Union army from annihilation.

It was long after midnight before the Rebels completed gathering the plunder left by the retreating Yankees. Blankets, coats, guns, and provisions left in the abandoned Union supply wagons were welcomed. Fall was closing fast and cooler weather would not be long in coming.

Jessie and the Fifth Missouri participated in the pursuit. When finally a halt was called, Jessie barely had enough energy to take care of Star's Pride before he fell asleep on the ground. The adrenaline had worn off, and in its place was mind-numbing fatigue.

Calvin camped with Bledsoe's battery on the prairie, now littered with the still forms of the dead and the cries of the wounded. The carnage was horrible to witness. Salomon had lost over one thousand men—either killed, wounded, or taken prisoner. The Rebel losses had been much lighter, but they had plenty to mourn. The Union wounded and dead were left in cabins, and abandoned along the road for miles along the retreat route.

October 4, 1862, dawned bright and clear. Shelby and Cooper still firmly held Newtonia. On the highest building in town proudly floated the Confederate flag given to Shelby by Mrs. Lightfoot.

The quiet didn't last long. Shelby's scouts and Southern sympathizers soon brought dire warnings of the approach of the army of the Union General Schofield. The Union general, angered by the defeat, advanced his larger army down to drive the Rebels from the Missouri border and back into Arkansas. Colonel Shelby and Colonel Cooper prepared their troops and awaited the approach of the next Union threat.

23

Farewell to Briarwood

"Miss Cassie, Miss Cassie, it's time to wake up!"

Cassandra rolled over. "What is it, Jethro?"

"Miss Cassie, Me an' Leon done some lookin' down by our cabins an' we found a couple of shovels the soldiers missed. If it's all right with you, I think we should bury Massa Kimbrough this mornin'."

Cassandra looked through sleep-blurred eyes. She felt cold and stiff from sleeping on the ground with nothing but blankets for a bed. The reality of the tragedy of the day before was inescapable; the pungent scent of burned buildings still drifted on the winds. "Yes, I suppose he must be buried soon. What does Mother want to do?"

"She's still pretty upset, Miss Cassie. Fanny took her over to Leon's cabin to get her cleaned up. She ain't makin' much sense yet. I think you gotta be the one to make the decisions, Miss Cassie, cause Miss Ellie is all mixed up."

"Where is Elizabeth? Is she all right?"

"Yes, Miss Cassie, she's still sleepin'."

"Let her sleep. It probably will do her the most good."

"Miss Cassie, where do ya think we should bury Massa Kimbrough?" Jethro asked softly.

"I suppose in the family plot near Grandma and Grandpa. Father always said it was so peaceful there. From that hill you can see the sunrise in the morning and the sunset in the evening. He always enjoyed watching the Missouri River and the riverboats passing by."

"I'll take Leon and a couple of the other men, an' we ought to have it dug before noon."

Cassandra rose slowly from her sitting position. "Thank you, Jethro. We always could count on you. I'll check with Mother and Fanny and decide what else has to be done. We must make some decisions about our future soon."

Jethro bowed, then turned and walked toward the slave quarters. Later, Jethro led Leon and two others toward the family burial plot on the hill near the river.

Cassandra looked around her; a dark, dreary sadness weighed her thoughts. "What should we do? We can't stay here. We must move on. Until this war is over the plantation can't be rebuilt, and it would be useless to try." She looked over to where her father's body lay on the grass, covered with a blanket Fanny had rescued. "I must get everyone ready for the burial, take stock of what we have, and arrange to leave here," Cassandra thought. "Thank God Father told us to sew some money and jewelry into our petticoats. God knows we will have need of it. I must make some tough decisions quickly and get us away from here. But first I'd better check on Mother."

She made her way slowly to the slave cabins. Only these buildings of the once-great Briarwood Plantation remained. Cassandra tapped on the door of Leon's cabin. She heard "Come in," opened the door, and entered.

The cabin consisted of two rooms, a third of it used as a kitchen and dining area. The table was made from rough wood and the chairs were plain and ordinary. The other room held the sleeping quarters and family room, dominated by a small, stone fireplace. It was not fancy, but it was clean and functional. Cassandra saw Fanny brushing Ellen's hair, trying to comfort her. Ellen sobbed softly. Fanny stopped brushing and turned to greet Cassandra. "Miss Cassie, you're up! Are you feelin' all right?"

"Yes, Fanny. Leon, Jethro, and the boys are going to dig a grave for Father." Cassandra looked out the window. "Looks like some cabins are empty." Then she turned her eyes toward Fanny.

Fanny's expression showed an unusual mix of anger and sadness. "Yeah, some of them done gone an' run off. Heard some of them shoutin' it be the year of Jubilee a comin', and they be free! I'd say a third of them packed up an' followed them Yankees wherever they was a goin'."

"Yes, I know the soldiers have been encouraging them to run off, so I'm not surprised."

"You wait an' see, Miss Cassie, first sign a bad weather and the food runs out, an' they'll be comin' back here beggin' for you to take care of 'em again. If I was you, I'd just tell 'em to hightail it on down the road, cause we don't need no no-account, ungrateful niggers hangin' around here!"

"I don't know what we would do without you, Fanny. The truth of the matter is, now with Briarwood destroyed, I can no longer take care of them. Father said he thought the days of the plantations were numbered and eventually the slaves would be freed. He hoped some might work as sharecroppers on the land. He made us promise that if anything should happen to the plantation, we would free the slaves."

"Miss Cassie, I know they all like you givin' them their freedom, but how they goin' to take care of themselves?"

"They will learn, for that is part of the price for freedom."

"What they gonna do, an' where they gonna go?"

"With their freedom papers they can go wherever they like and wherever they can find a place to work."

"Miss Cassie, I don't want to stay here, an' I don't have no place to go. Your family an' this plantation been my whole life! Please, Miss Cassie, can Jethro and me go with ya?"

"Sure, Fanny, we would be pleased to have you stay with us, but you'll have your freedom, too."

"Thank you, Miss Cassie, I'm sure Jethro will want to go

too. We gonna be a big help to you, same as always." A big smile spread across her face, as Fanny's tension eased. They might not have a fine plantation any longer, but she could stay with those she loved and those who loved her. "I'm worried about your mama, she don't talk at all, an' when she ain't cryin' she just sits an' stares out yonder."

Throughout the conversation Ellen Kimbrough, head in her hands, sat glaring at the table. Her eyes were red and puffy and her cheeks were still wet with tears. It was as if Cassandra wasn't even there.

Cassandra approached her gently. "Mamma, are you all right? Mamma, please, look at me."

Ellen lifted her eyes to Cassandra, "What am I going to do without him? Where are we going to live?"

Cassandra could see the same deep hurt in her mother's face she herself felt. Somehow, they had switched roles—now the daughter was the strong one. Cassandra knew she would have to make the family decisions.

For years Ellen had left the tough, day-to-day decisions of running the plantation and indeed, the direction of their lives, in the hands of her husband. Now Glen was gone and she couldn't deal with the depth of her loss and grief sufficiently to handle the decisions that must be made. Glen's words came back to Cassandra clearly now. "Take care of Elizabeth and your Mother. They're going to need you. Don't let the Yankees beat you and don't let them take away your honor or your pride."

"I don't know, Mamma, but we have to go on. Jethro is digging a grave for Father near Grandma and Grandpa Kimbrough. As soon as we can we must leave here."

"Where will we go? We can't go too far without horses or a carriage."

"I've been thinking about it. I think we should go to the Thomas Plantation, then maybe, after we are better equipped, we could head south. In the Confederacy there might be a place we could live until the war is over. We might even be close enough to see the boys more often." Cassandra leaned over her mother and whispered in her ear. "I think it would be best to leave everything buried under the ashes of the barn until the war is over. If we try to dig it up now, someone will notice and take it away from us. I think we should leave it behind."

With a heavy sign of resignation Ellen said, "Whatever you think best, Cassandra." With that simple statement, Ellen let control of their destinies slip into her daughter's hands.

The rest of the morning was spent with Fanny and Cassandra organizing what little was rescued by Fanny and Jethro from the plantation fire. All they had left were a couple of changes of clothing for each of them. The outfits were not the ones she would have chosen, but Fanny had had little time and the house had been badly pillaged. Many of the finer dresses had been destroyed or stolen. The simpler day dresses were going to be of more value and use now in their current situation, and she was grateful that anything was spared.

Only Fanny's quick thinking had rescued these meager possessions. They studied the rest of the items rescued from the house. In the pile were a couple of well-worn quilts and a few blankets. All the better ones had been stolen by the Yankee soldiers.

Most important to Cassandra were the photographs saved by Fanny and Jethro. She looked lovingly at the family tintypes and daguerreotypes. Included were the pictures of both sets of Cassandra's grandparents and the last family picture taken at Lexington. It meant so much to her now because it would be the last picture taken with the family complete. A few letters had been rescued, along with the family Bible.

She smiled as she caressed the cover of the old Bible. It held the records of the births, deaths, and marriages of the various family members for two generations. She smiled sadly as she realized she would need to add the date of death to her father's name in the book.

A small amount of writing paper and a fine pen and inkwell was saved, and for those she had a use. She needed paper and pen to write out the letters giving each slave his or her freedom. Whatever remained would be used to write to those in the army.

How was she ever going to tell her brothers this terrible news? How was she going to tell them of the death of their father and the destruction of Briarwood? It was a matter she would have to deal with, but it would have to wait. There were more pressing matters.

A knock echoed, startling those inside. Fanny answered the door. "Honey chile, you don't have to knock, just come on in."

Elizabeth walked through the open doorway. "I wasn't sure if you were here. I woke up when I heard a wagon coming up the drive. Andrew Burke and his son James are outside. They want to talk to Mother."

"I'll handle it, I don't think Mother is up to it yet," said Cassandra. The others followed her outside. She eyed the men in the wagon. Andrew Burke, an old friend of her father's, owned the farm next to Briarwood. His son, James, sat next to him. Seeing a familiar, compassionate face comforted Cassandra.

"Good afternoon, Cassandra. We heard the Yankees when they rode past our place yesterday. We saw the fires last night and decided it wasn't safe to show up with the soldiers still here. I'm sorry."

"We understand, Andrew. There really wasn't anything you could have done."

"Just the same, I feel terrible I didn't come."

"Please don't feel that way. If you had come they might have burned you out, too. Believe me, one man could not have stopped what happened here."

"Well, we're here now. How can we help?" His son smiled shyly. The boy was almost fourteen and starting to stretch out. If he kept growing at the rate he had been, he was going to be taller than his father who stood over six feet tall.

"We lost most everything when they burned us out and killed Father." She tried to say it without emotion, but her chin quivered involuntarily.

"God! I didn't think they would go that far. I'm sorry, Cassandra."

"Well, at first they were going to arrest Father and he

wouldn't surrender. There was no way he could win against so many, but he wouldn't let them take all he had without a fight. He killed two of their men before they got him." She hesitated, giving him a chance to comment; but when he didn't, she continued. "Well, in any case, they took everything they wanted and burned us out."

"Times are hard and I haven't got a lot. You know our farm isn't any plantation, but I'd like to help if I can."

"If you could spare us some food and sell us a wagon and a couple of horses, it would help. We also don't have any tools or wood left to make a coffin for Father."

"I've got some boards you can have, and I'll bring some nails, a couple of saws, and hammers for your slaves to use. They can build a casket, but it won't be fancy."

"Anything would be better than nothing. Right now, the best we can do for him is a blanket."

"Sure. I'll send James back with the things you need. I'll see what food we can spare. I have an old freight wagon over at my place. It ain't in too bad a shape. It has a spring seat and it's rigged for two horses or mules to pull her. She still has some bows so you can rig up a canvas over what you're haulin'." He scratched his chin thoughtfully. "I don't have any animals I can spare to pull it."

"I don't think we are in a position to be choosy, Mister Burke." She thought for a moment, then said, "I think I can get horses from the Thomas family, if we can get that far. Could you lend us a pair of horses or mules just till we reach Riverview?"

"I'll lend you a pair of my mules and I'll send James with you. He can return my mules from Riverview."

"You don't know how much we appreciate your help. I don't know what we would do without it. How much do you want for the food and the wagon?"

"I don't want nothin' for 'em, and if I could spare the mules, you could keep them too, but I can't work my ground without 'em."

"I don't expect you to give us the wagon. It's far too expensive for you to replace. Won't you let us pay you something?"

"Cassandra, your father helped me out of some tough spots over the years. When I was hurt and couldn't harvest my crops two years ago, he sent over some of his slaves to help me and wouldn't accept a nickel in payment. He helped me many times. No, sir! You all been good neighbors over the years, an' I'm just glad I've got the chance to even things out a mite."

Cassandra's eyes glistened at Andrew's kind words. A sad smile crossed her lips. "Thank you, Mister Burke, we are very grateful."

"Don't you worry none, James and the wagon will be here shortly. Good-bye, Cassandra. Tell your mother our thoughts and prayers are with her, and we wish you good luck."

She smiled gratefully. "Thank you, I will."

With a quick snap of his whip, Andrew Burke turned his wagon and team and headed down the lane.

Several hours later, the people remaining at Briarwood Plantation gathered in the family cemetery, overlooking the Missouri River. It was, by necessity, a modest funeral. Glen's body now rested in the simple wooden box constructed by Jethro and Leon.

They had removed his personal items—a pocket knife, a gold watch, and two rings. These items were now safely hidden in the skirts of the Kimbrough women. They couldn't embalm him; there simply wasn't time or anyone with the equipment and knowledge available, and they couldn't wait for a preacher or for friends to gather. Glen's body was already showing signs of decomposition. The burial had to be done quickly.

They used ropes to lower the rough-hewn casket into the grave. Cassandra and Elizabeth read passages from the Bible. Then Ellen led the gathering in singing "Rock of Ages" and "Amazing Grace." Fanny and a few of the slaves sang "Swing Low, Sweet Chariot." Her sweet voice mixed with the beautiful harmonies and echoed across the river valley.

Before the slaves left the burial, Cassandra made her announcement. "I want to thank each of you for your loyalty these past years. I know you could have left with the Yankee soldiers, but you chose to stay. I know Father would have been proud of you. We are granting your freedom in appreciation for all your hard work here at Briarwood. You have earned your freedom through your labor and your devotion.

"I wish our family could continue to take care of you, but it is impossible with Briarwood destroyed. Those of you wishing to stay on and live in your cabins are welcome to them. You have our permission to farm the land for your own use until the end of the war. If we still own the land after this is all over, we will try to work out a sharecropping deal with those who have remained. Once I give you your freedom papers you may stay or go. The choice is up to you. There is nothing else I can offer you."

She looked around the circle of the familiar faces of hardworking people she had known for most of her life. "Please come by Leon's cabin in the morning to pick up your freedom papers. Godspeed and good luck." A loud chatter arose among the group, then they quieted and lined up, one at a time, to give condolences to the Kimbrough women.

During the evening, by the weak light of a lamp and the glow of the fire in the hearth of the slave cabin, Cassandra wrote a letter for each former slave, granting them their freedom. That night, the Kimbroughs slept in the quarters of their former slaves. It was a far cry from the comforts of Briarwood, but it was far better than sleeping another night on the cold, hard ground.

Morning came and amid jubilant and tearful joy, the former slaves of Briarwood enjoyed their first moments of freedom. Most were nervous about the future, yet anxious to test their newly found liberty. A few planned to strike out boldly into the new world, while others decided to stay and work the land.

Jethro, as Fanny predicted, asked to stay with the Kimbrough women. He was glad to be free, but he knew Fanny would not abandon the Kimbroughs. Where Fanny went, his heart would follow. He asked Cassandra if he could work for them and Cassandra was pleased to say yes. Fanny absolutely beamed with excitement when she heard the news.

"I'd be pleased to have your help, Jethro, but it might not be right us spendin' so much time together, with us bein' single and all." Fanny's voice trailed off coyly.

"Yeah, gal, I've been givin' it some thought. An' if it's all right with Missus Ellie and Miss Cassie, I thought maybe we could jump over the broom together." His look was hopeful but uncertain of her response.

"You no longer need our approval," said Cassandra tenderly. "But I would be pleased to attend if Fanny says yes."

All eyes turned to Fanny. She glanced shyly at her feet as her hands smoothed out the front of her dress. She lifted her chin slightly and looked at Jethro. "I reckon I need time to think about it, Jethro."

Jethro's face was a picture of desolation. Disappointment crowded every facet as his eyes dropped to the floor. "Okay, Fanny."

With a mischievous smile, Fanny said softly, "Yes."

Jethro perked up, uncertain of what he had heard. "What you say, gal?"

"I said 'Yes,' Jethro."

"But I thought you said you'd have to give it some thinkin'."

"Well I did, an' now I say 'yes'!" She smiled brightly.

Jethro understood she had accepted his proposal. He grabbed Fanny in his arms and swung her around, nearly knocking Cassandra off her feet. "Oh, Lordy! Fanny, you done made me a happy man!"

Cassandra beamed. Even in the midst of terrible family tragedy there were moments of triumph and joy. "I hope when we arrive at Riverview, we can arrange to have a minister perform a proper ceremony. You two deserve more than simply jumping over the broomstick."

"Did ya hear that, Fanny? Thank you, Miss Cassie." Jethro held Fanny tightly.

Fanny's grin lit up her whole face. She said, "I know you

goin' to make a fine husband, but we got work to do. The sooner we get it done, the sooner we gonna tie that knot."

"I already loaded most everything we got left into the wagon Massa Burke brought over. Massa James been watchin' the mules."

"I guess we'll move faster with a light load. It's the only good I can see in all of this. Will you help me make a bed in the back for Mother?" Cassandra asked.

"Sure, Miss Cassie, I'll fix it right up, an' I'll help her get comfortable, too." Jethro headed for the door.

"Elizabeth, would you take a walk with me, while Jethro finishes?"

The fourteen-year-old, with strawberry blond hair and a dusting of freckles spilling across her nose, looked surprised and vulnerable. "Yes."

The two young women left the cabin and strolled at a leisurely pace across the grounds of Briarwood. Cassandra felt the warm breezes caress her hair and fit the day dress softly against her body as they walked. "I know what I have to tell you might not help much, Elizabeth, but you must try to understand. Mother is not handling this very well. She's always taken care of us, and now I'm afraid she needs our help."

"I know, but I'm scared, Cassie!"

"I understand, I'm scared too. I promised Father I'd take care of Mother and you, and I don't want to let him down."

They reached the burned-out remains of Briarwood's great house and stopped, staring at the ruins. The blackened brick chimneys jutted into the air like giant, bony, skeletal fingers. Smoke still drifted from the ash piles in lazy circles until it drifted away on the gentle breezes from the river. Cassandra leaned against a smoked portico column. Her father had died near this very spot.

"Elizabeth, some day when this war is over, perhaps one of us will live to see Briarwood rise again from the ashes."

"No, Briarwood is dead and gone—just like Daddy!" Elizabeth broke into racking sobs, as tears streamed down her face. Cassandra stroked her sister's head as she held her close. "Don't worry Elizabeth, when this war is over, God willing, we'll find a way to build Briarwood again. You just wait and see."

They lingered among the smoky ruins, saying good-bye to Briarwood, just as they had said their good-byes to their father. After a while, they walked away from the ash pile of their childhood home and rejoined the others at the wagon.

Leon Pepper, the former jockey and exercise rider, walked over to them from a cabin. "Pardon me, Miss Cassie. Before you all leave, I want to say my good-byes."

"Thank you, Leon. Will you be staying here in the cabins?"

"No, Ma'am, I reckon not. I figure me an' the missus will load up what we got an' head down the road."

"Where will you go?"

"I don't rightly know. But this be the first time in my whole life where I'm free to go wherever I want without askin' no one." He took his hat off and held it in his hands. "I got to know more about this freedom. I'm thinkin' it would be a good time to see what it's like."

"I think I understand, Leon, and I wish you and your family the best of luck." She offered her hand. He studied it for a moment, then glanced at her, smiling his big toothy grin. He took her hand and shook it warmly. "Best wishes, Leon. Thank you for all you have done for us."

"Thank you, Missy." He smiled, bowed slightly, and headed toward his cabin.

24

Fragile Sanctuary

The wagon rolled along noisily as the iron wheels crunched against the occasional stone lodged in the ruts leading from what was Briarwood Plantation. Nearly loaded to capacity, the wagon held Cassandra, Ellen, and Elizabeth Kimbrough, Jethro, Fanny, and James Burke, and their meager belongings. Jethro and James Burke sat on the spring seat in front, the rest sat on boxes or blankets in the back. Cassandra and Elizabeth dangled their legs over the back of the wagon.

Briarwood's former slaves stood in the lane, waved, and watched the wagon roll away. Elizabeth stared at the ground, too depressed even to take a last look. Cassandra could hear Ellen sneezing and coughing behind them.

"Wrap another blanket around you, Mother, it's best if you keep warm." Cassandra knew from the sound of her coughing that Ellen was catching a severe cold. The combination of exposure to the cold ground and the emotional stress they had endured weakened her.

Cassandra knew the ride to Riverview would not be too

difficult, but she was worried about the reception they might receive from the Thomas family. Of course they would be helpful and take them in, at least temporarily, but she worried about the danger they posed to the plantation, should Bartok learn of their stay. Major Bartok burned Briarwood, and she knew he would not hesitate to burn and pillage others should it suit his whim. She tried not to worry, but it seemed impossible as she pondered their position. Cassandra tried to weigh her options, but the more she thought, the more sure she was that Riverview was their only hope. They must pay a visit to Riverview and hope Harlan Thomas would help them. She tried to sit back and relax as the miles slowly rolled past.

"We's almost there, Miss Cassie," Jethro announced. Cassandra moved to the front of the wagon. Leaning over Jethro and James, she watched the stately oaks and maples pass, touched with soft hues of gold, browns, and red as the leaves turned to fall colors. They pulled into the circular drive and stopped beside the wide stairs leading to the veranda. A house servant stepped forward to hold the mules, and another offered his hand to those in the wagon to help them down.

Katlin Thomas cried to them from the top of the stairs. "Oh, Cassandra, it's so good to see you. Please come in and bring the others."

They made their way to the veranda and into the great house.

Two hours later, Cassandra felt more relaxed. They had just completed a delicious meal and sat before a roaring fire. The large, over-stuffed chair wrapped comfortably around her, and a weariness began to seep into her body and mind. She felt as if she were back home at Briarwood, before the war entered this valley. Harlan, Caroline, and Katlin had gone out of their way to make them feel welcome. Arrangements were made and accommodations had been provided for Fanny and Jethro to stay in the slave cabins. Ellen ate lightly at supper and, still feeling under the weather, turned in early. Elizabeth went with her, in case she needed further care, as did Caroline.

James Burke had also turned in. He was to take the mules back to his father's farm in the morning, and he wanted to get an early start. Only three remained to enjoy the comfort of the fire, sip brandy, and visit. Harlan sat to Cassandra's right and Katlin to her left, the chairs forming a half-circle before the fireplace.

"I appreciate your offer to let us stay here, Mister Thomas, but we simply can't put your family in that kind of danger. If Bartok finds out we're here he'll be after your plantation next."

"I suppose there is a measure of truth in what you are saying, Cassandra, but whether you are here or not, the Yankees will get to us eventually. Bartok knows we are friends, and I am sure he remembers his humiliation at your brother's hands here at Riverview. No, it's just a matter of time before he pays us a call."

Harlan swirled the brandy in his snifter and took a sip. "In truth, we've been expecting it ever since we heard they burned out your family. The Yankee cavalry have already helped themselves to some of our livestock and feed supplies to outfit their units. We have managed to save a few horses, but we know they will be back. We have no illusions about the major. He is mean and he is greedy, so he'll get around to us."

"Please, take time to prepare before they strike. Try to hide your valuables and foodstuffs."

"Don't worry, we have hidden some things and we have a wagon loaded with personal items under the protection of one of our most trusted slaves. He hides in the woods when we hear there is danger approaching."

"Aren't you worried your slave will run off with your things or turn it all over to the Yankees?"

"I believe we can trust him, but I do worry the Yankees will discover our hiding place, or bushwackers or Jayhawkers. They are as anxious to rob us as the government is."

"Judging from our experience, I'd suggest you bury some of it away from your buildings in case they try to burn you out, too."

"I'll see to it tomorrow. But enough of our problems, what are your plans?"

"Ever since we were burned out I have been trying to come up with a solution to our problem. I know Bartok will not stop until he can't reach us any longer. That leaves us little choice. I intend to head south to Arkansas."

Harlan was stunned by the announcement. He leaned forward in his chair and twisted himself around to face Cassandra. "I don't know if that's such a good idea. The trip down there is going to take quite a long time. The country you must travel through is crawling with bushwackers, Yankees, and outlaws. You're going to ride through a war zone."

"I know the trip is dangerous, but I think we will be as safe traveling south as we are here in Lafayette County." Cassandra shrugged her shoulders. "I don't think we have any other viable choices. We simply can't stay here."

"All right, suppose you can get through, where are you going to go? You've got to have some place to stay."

"I have been thinking about it and I believe we should head for Little Rock. It's still in Confederate hands. Ross is rather serious about a girl from Arkansas. He said her family was from Batesville. I have her address, and maybe they could help us find a place. All I know is that I want to get as far away from the Yankees as I can."

"Do you think you'll be close to where the boys are?" Katlin asked.

"I hope we'll be close to where the army will spend the winter. That is another reason I want to head south. We'll have much more of a chance to be near Shelby's command in Arkansas."

"I want to go with you," Katlin said excitedly, rising.

Harlan slammed his fist down hard on the arm of his chair. "No! I won't let you go traipsing off across Missouri and down to Arkansas with a war going on. I won't hear of it!"

"If I can be near Jessie and have a chance to marry him, I'm going to take it and you won't stop me!" She stood defiantly.

Harlan rose from his chair to face her. "Katlin, I won't allow you to talk to me in this way."

She stood nose to nose with her father, her hands on her waist. "Father, stop treating me as if I were a child! I'll soon be eighteen years old. I know what I want, and more than anything else I want to be near Jessie. I love him."

Harlan could see the determination on her face. He knew she meant every word. His anger flowed away. He placed his hands on her shoulders gently. "I know you love him, Kat; but kitten, it's just too dangerous out there. Jessie wouldn't want you on the road either."

"Father, you know what has happened to the Kimbroughs. It is happening to others in the county as well. You're just kidding yourself if you believe it is any safer here than it is on the road. It is worth the risk to get away from these awful Yankees." She twisted out of her father's grasp and stepped back.

"Look, Katlin," Cassandra explained, "I really have no other choice. I must go south, because every moment I stay around here I endanger others. I don't want to be responsible for causing problems between you and your father. I just would not feel right exposing you to the dangers of the trip."

"I'll go to Arkansas with or without your help, Cassandra. My place is near Jessie and nothing is going to keep me from being near him!" She whirled abruptly and stormed from the room.

"I must apologize for Katlin's outburst, Cassandra. I'm afraid she is headstrong and loses her composure."

"You have no need to apologize to me, Harlan. Indeed, I am grateful for all the help you have given us." Cassandra paused, then said, "I'm proud she cares so deeply for my brother."

Harlan began to pace. "Yes, I am afraid the timing of her falling in love with him is ill-fated. This damn war! I'm afraid it will not end until it has destroyed us all." He stopped his pacing and turned back toward Cassandra. "If you insist on this bold plan of yours to head south, how do you plan to make the journey?"

"I'll go by wagon. We have very little to take with us, so we should be able to handle the trip in the wagon Mr. Burke gave us. Do you still have Bright Star and the other mares father sent you?"

"I still have three of the mares, including Bright Star. The Yankee's last detail stole one of them while they were here looking for supplies."

"The wagon is rigged to be pulled by a two-horse team. We'll use two of them to pull and the other horse as an extra we can take turns riding. We have transportation; all we need now is to gather a few supplies, some food, and we will be ready. We have some money we can take with us to buy what we need along the way."

"I still have reservations about your trying this trip, but I doubt that I can persuade you to do otherwise. What about your mother? She seems to me to be too ill to travel that great a distance."

"I hate to admit it, but it is my greatest concern." Cassandra sipped at her brandy as she thought. "I know it is risky, but I see no other choice than to try. We have no right to endanger our friends, but Bartok will give us no peace as long as we are within his grasp."

"I understand, and I admire your courage and determination. Please allow me to help you by providing some of your supplies. I can give you a pistol and a shotgun to take with you."

"I appreciate the offer, and we will gladly accept your help; but I couldn't possibly accept your weapons—you may have need of them yourself."

"Nonsense! Don't be ridiculous. I would not have made the offer if I couldn't spare them. I have a few extras." Harlan smiled broadly. "You know, long before the war, I enjoyed collecting fine weapons, and Gilbert and I enjoyed hunting together. I have kept them well hidden so the Yankees couldn't find them." Harlan winked at Cassandra.

"Thank you. I appreciate your generous offer and we will gladly accept. Might I ask for another favor?"

"Of course you can! Your father was my closest friend,

and I think Jessie and Katlin will marry some day. That practically makes us family, so out with it, Cassandra."

"It's our former slaves, Fanny and Jethro. It seems they have fallen in love and want to be married. I was hoping before we left they could be married here at Riverview."

"Yes, of course; they are as fine a pair of darkies and as loyal and hard working as any I've ever seen. I think we can arrange a nice little ceremony for them. Are they planning to travel south with you?"

"Yes, they are. I have to admit I would be afraid to make the trip without them. I know Jethro will do all he can to guard us, and Fanny always takes good care of us."

"Loyalty such as theirs is rare these days and should be rewarded. God knows most of my slaves have run away. I'll make arrangements first thing in the morning."

Cassandra walked over to Harlan. She put her arms around him and gave him a big hug. "Thank you so much, Harlan. I don't know what we would have done without you." She kissed him on the cheek.

Harlan blushed. "Cassandra, you are a charmer. I can see why Gilbert is so crazy about you. Why, if I were a mite younger, I'd be chasing after you myself." Harlan smiled brightly.

"I don't doubt it for a minute. You've always been an ornery one, Harlan. Well, I guess I'd better get some sleep. We have much to do in the next two days. If we are to reach Arkansas before hard winter sets in, we must do it quickly. The hazards of winter travel would make the trip almost impossible."

"Yes, I have to agree. If you are determined to try this, it's best you start as soon as possible. Good night, Cassandra, sleep well." Cassandra turned and moved up the stairs to her room.

25

Unwelcome Intrusion

Cassandra sat proudly in the front row during the small wedding held on the lawn behind Riverview Plantation. Try as she might, she could not hold back the tears of joy as she watched Fanny and Jethro repeat their wedding vows. Cassandra had never seen Fanny more radiant or happy as she stood beside Jethro in her best dress. Jethro couldn't quit smiling as he shyly looked at his bride.

The minister had ridden in from Dover after being sent for by Harlan. He was pleased to have a handsome fee and was doing a fine ceremony to earn it. The wedding was of course small, but it was an important occasion for those attending. Ellen, Elizabeth, Cassandra, and Katlin were there to witness the event.

The Riverview plantation slaves that could be spared from doing essential duties served as guests. Altogether, they numbered twenty-three slaves. While she watched, Cassandra took time to ponder the events of the last two days.

Harlan had sent for the minister and Fanny had made her plans. Cassandra and Harlan had set to the task of gathering equipment and supplies for the trip south. James Burke left the day after they arrived at Riverview. She thanked James for his help and sent word of their gratitude to his father. Time had moved quickly with so much to accomplish. With any luck they would be on their way south in a day or two. First, however, they would enjoy today.

Katlin and her father were still arguing over her wish to travel south with the Kimbrough women. Harlan still opposed the idea. Cassandra told Harlan that she was welcome to come, but the final decision would have to be made between Katlin and himself.

Cassandra's mind returned to the wedding ceremony as the groom kissed his new bride, and the minister pronounced them man and wife.

Cassandra congratulated the newlyweds. More tears of joy followed. The couple had just reached the wedding cake when the celebration was interrupted.

A house servant, dressed in his finest clothing, came at a run toward the gathering. "Yankees! Yankee horse soldiers are a comin'! Miss Katlin, your daddy wants you to come to the house right away."

Katlin turned ghostly white as fear gripped her. "Cassie, what should we do?"

Cassandra swallowed hard. "Don't panic, it might be a patrol, or a party foraging for food. Panic will not make the situation better. I'd best go with you." Cassandra glanced over at her mother, Ellen. Ellen was shaking violently. "Elizabeth," Cassandra ordered, "take care of Mother."

Cassandra turned and followed Katlin to the great house, while Elizabeth tried to comfort Ellen.

Jethro and his new bride were stunned at first. Then Jethro took charge of the wedding party. "Y'all take it easy. Soldiers ain't likely to mess with our weddin'. They got other stuff to do. Be best if we just go on 'bout our business like there ain't nothin' wrong. Let's just let Massa Thomas handle it." The couple continued with their celebration as they prepared to eat cake, although the guests remained subdued and tense.

Jethro winked at Fanny. "Don't you worry, gal, I ain' gonna let no soldiers mess up our weddin'."

Fanny smiled with pride at her new husband. "Whatever you say, darlin'."

Cassandra and Katlin rushed to the house through the back doorway and made their way to the sitting room. On first sight, the scene in the house shook Cassandra to her very soul.

Harlan Thomas was involved in a heated discussion with a dark-haired Union captain with brown, brooding eyes. To her dismay he looked very familiar. Recognition quickly gripped her. Yes, he was among the officers that had destroyed Briarwood.

The soldier noticed Cassandra and Katlin as they entered the room. "Well, if it isn't the Rebel bitch from the Kimbrough place. I thought you'd be begging in the streets by now."

Harlan's jaw tightened and he clenched his fists in anger. "I'll ask you to refrain from using foul language in my home, Captain."

The captain's eyes flashed deep and angry. "I'll talk any way I wish, sir! No damn Southern gentleman is gonna tell a member of the Union army what he can or can't say! I give the orders around here, not you. Do I make myself clear, Mr. Thomas?" He paused, then realizing he held the upper hand, he laughed loudly. When he stopped he said gleefully, "I think Major Bartok will be very interested when he finds out who is staying here." His eyes twinkled with amusement as a sarcastic sneer crossed his face. "He has shown great interest in the whereabouts of this lady."

Harlan fought to regain his composure. He choked back his pride and continued, "Cassandra, Katlin, I'd like to introduce you to Captain Bob Anders of A Company, Third Kansas Cavalry." Harlan looked at the women and then back at the captain and said, "The captain is here to get some food for his men and horses. I have given my people orders to supply his requests."

Captain Anders said sarcastically, "Yes, Mr. Thomas is being most helpful. It is a pleasure to see such cooperation from the locals." Anders stepped closer to Katlin. He stroked his hand through her hair and touched her cheek. "My, but aren't you a pretty thing. I bet we could have some fun together, you and I." He leered at her.

Katlin's face showed clearly her distaste for him as she recoiled from his touch. "I'm not feeling well. Perhaps another time, Captain."

The Union officer smiled. "I hope you have a swift recovery. For one as pretty as you, I'll make sure I stop by again soon. If I were you, I'd think about how nice it might be to have a good friend able to intercede on your behalf with Major Bartok. It might make things easier around here." He moved near her again and ran the palms of his hands down her upper arms. "In turn for my protection, I expect you to be extra nice and friendly to me." Anders winked at her suggestively. "Sure would be a shame to see this place end up like her daddy's." He motioned to Cassandra.

Cassandra felt pure hot anger well up within her, freely mixed with fear. She felt her stomach tighten and grew clammy and queasy. She began to tremble, but held her silence.

The moment was saved by the entrance of a Union lieutenant. He marched in and saluted. "Captain Anders."

Anders turned to face the young officer. "Yes, Lieutenant." He returned the salute.

"Sir, we've completed rounding up the food and supplies."

"Thank you, Lieutenant. Have the men mount up and prepare to march to camp." He turned back to face Harlan and the girls. "Well, as much as I hate to leave the company of women so pretty, I have my duties to attend to. Good day, ladies; good day, Mr. Thomas, I'm sure we'll meet again." He bowed slightly, then marched out the door.

As his footsteps echoed then died in the distance, Katlin ran to her father and threw her arms around him. "Oh Father, what are we going to do?"

"I don't know if there is anything we can do. I get so damned frustrated! They can walk in here and do anything they want to us and there's absolutely nothing we can do about it. One thing is certain, I have changed my opinion on your going south with Cassandra and her family."

"Do you mean you will let me go?"

"Yes. The captain made himself very clear. He intends to use his position to force you into doing as he wishes. I would kill him or die myself before I'd allow that to happen." Harlan began to pace, clasping his hands behind his back. "Not only that, but we are a prime candidate for robbery. We have a son in the Confederate army, we have sheltered the Kimbroughs, and we have property worth stealing. I am afraid Major Bartok will not hesitate to destroy us. He is just biding his time. If he doesn't come here, Anders or other Yankee Jayhawkers will come."

He stopped his pacing as he looked at the women. "I can't protect you here, even though I'd like to think I can. You'll be in less danger moving south. I'm hoping it will be safer for you in the Confederacy."

Katlin ran to her father. He held her in his arms. "Papa, why don't you and Mamma come with us?"

"I'd like to go, but I'm afraid your mother's health would never permit it." He looked around the room, still holding his daughter. "My whole life, everything I own is invested in this plantation. I can't abandon her, if there is hope she can be saved. I was wrong, earlier. I want you to go, Katlin." he let go of her and looked at Cassandra, then back at his daughter. "I need to go upstairs and tell your mother what has happened. I don't like to expose her to these visits, so I sent her upstairs when I knew they were coming. She isn't going to like it, but I must tell her of our decision." He looked at Cassandra. "Cassandra, is it all right if Katlin travels with you?"

"Of course it is, Harlan."

"Tomorrow I'll help you outfit a wagon that can be pulled by four horses, and I'll supply the extra ones. I have a bigger, better wagon I can trade yours for."

"That won't be necessary."

"Nonsense! My daughter will be traveling with you and

you are our closest friends. I want you to have the best I can give you. Time is growing short—tomorrow you must leave." He turned and climbed the stairs two steps at a time.

Cassandra and Katlin embraced each other tightly. Tomorrow, tomorrow! What new challenges would the new day bring?

26

Journey South

The sun felt soothingly warm on Cassandra's neck. She rode Bright Star through the grass alongside the dusty road. The rest of her party rode in the wagon, slightly ahead and to her left. It was much too dusty to follow directly behind the wagon, and this way she could watch the road. The wagon creaked slowly with its heavy burden as the horses pulled against their harnesses in unison. Prince of Heaven, Katlin's black two-year-old stallion, pranced along behind the wagon where his halter rope was tied. Elizabeth dangled her legs over the hanging tailgate, near where the horse was tethered.

Cassandra wore a riding dress and sat in a sidesaddle provided by Harlan Thomas. She would have much preferred to use an English riding saddle and wear the English riding boots and pants she had worn fox hunting before the war. It still wasn't readily accepted for a lady to be riding astride a horse; so to keep from being lectured by her mother and Katlin, she agreed to use the sidesaddle.

It was just too cramped traveling in the wagon day after

day. For her sanity, she had to ride on horseback once in a while. She loved the feel of the sun on her cheeks and the wind in her hair. When she was riding she felt truly free. It had a calming effect on her and brought back happy memories of days astride a horse along the great Missouri River and across Briarwood Plantation. The back of a horse was a place from which to daydream and remember, and her mind wandered over the days since they had left Riverview Plantation.

The plans for leaving were made with haste. Every plantation member joined in to see that all the necessary tasks were performed. Harlan Thomas insisted they be outfitted with the best he had to offer. He supplied them with a large Conestoga-type freight wagon, rigged with canvas and equipped to be pulled by four horses. Harlan traded the Briarwood horses he had been keeping at his plantation for a trained horse team, except for Bright Star. An extra spring seat was installed by the plantation carpenters and blacksmith. With so many people riding in the wagon, it would help. Necessary food and camping supplies were provided.

Harlan gave one double-barrel percussion shotgun and two six-shot navy Colt revolvers to the women. Cassandra also talked him out of a small thirty-two caliber percussion cap derringer she could easily hide on her body. Luckily, Cassandra was trained to shoot by her brothers and father. She knew Jethro was a good shot and had spent many a day with her brothers before the war doing target practice at Briarwood. It was not a common practice to let slaves handle guns, but then her brothers always favored Jethro and seemed to delight in teaching him how to shoot. It never hurt to have an extra trained man to help protect the plantation, what with all the border problems with Kansas and their marauding Jayhawkers.

Unfortunately, Katlin hadn't shown any previous interest in guns. She felt knowledge of weapons was unladylike. The changing circumstances and the uncertain swirl of the war around them changed her mind. Her father and Jethro spent a few moments before she left teaching her how to load and fire the pistols and the shotgun, but she was clearly frightened of them. She wouldn't keep her eyes open when she pulled the trigger, and she still couldn't hit the broad side of a barn. Hopefully, with time and practice she would improve. For now, she could load for the others if the need should arise.

It was uncertain how long the war would last, and Harlan wanted to be certain his daughter would have the money necessary to provide for herself in the Confederacy. He had a false bottom installed in the base of a water barrel that hung on one side of the wagon. A canvas drawstring bag, wrapped in waxed paper, holing a supply of gold coins and Federal greenbacks was placed in the compartment. Gold coins were also sewn into her hooped skirts and underwear. Money in too accessible a spot would likely be stolen on the way south.

Cassandra, although eager to have Katlin come with them, was less excited about having Becca along for the trip. One of Cassandra's greatest concerns was the number of people sharing one wagon. She resisted strongly, but Harlan was just as determined to send Becca with them.

Becca was a sixteen-year-old slave who had practically grown up with Katlin and, for the last year, had been her personal servant. Her given name was Rebecca, but Kat couldn't pronounce it when they were both very young, so she shortened it to Becca—the nickname stuck. Becca was an extremely attractive girl with large dark eyes and fine features. She had flowing, black, straight hair and full, sensuous lips. Her skin was a medium tan tone, the color of liberally creamed coffee. She stood nearly five-feet five-inches tall with a slender but well-developed figure.

Her mother, Callie, a great beauty in her own right, had been a maid at the Riverview Plantation house when Katlin was born. Becca was just ten months younger than Katlin. Harlan always took great interest in Becca and was truly fond of her.

Harlan bought Callie at a slave auction shortly after his marriage to Caroline, and she cost him dearly. A slave woman of her beauty and figure always brought premium prices, but he insisted she was worth the cost because he would have only the best for his new bride.

Callie died of pneumonia in 1860, just a year before the war began. Her death left Becca alone at Riverview. Callie had given birth to other children besides Becca, and all were much lighter complexioned than their mother. However, only Becca survived the bouts of childhood disease the children were prone to—the rest died in infancy or at an early age.

Cassandra remembered the lecture Harlan gave Katlin about taking good care of Becca. Under no circumstances was she to part with or sell the girl, and it was her responsibility to take good care of her property.

Harlan sent a letter with Katlin only to be opened if he died. It was understood it was his will, and he wanted Katlin to have a copy in these uncertain times.

So, despite her misgivings, Ellen and Cassandra had agreed to take along Becca. With the addition of Becca and Katlin, the party had grown to seven.

The parting from Riverview was bittersweet. On the one hand, Cassandra was eager to leave for Arkansas, but on the other, she hated to leave the comfort of her friends and Lafayette County.

Caroline took the departure of Katlin, and even Becca, with great difficulty. The tears came freely, and the scene was so touching to the rest of those watching that soon all were crying. So much uncertainty lay before them and this fact, combined with the grief of separation, made for overwhelming emotions. No one could know with any certainty if they would all survive the war and live to see each other again.

Harlan lingered with the girls. He pulled each one close and looked into their faces for what seemed a long time. When Katlin asked why he was studying them so hard, Harlan responded he was trying to memorize every feature and burn them into his memory. He didn't know how long it might be before he laid eyes on them again. This brought a flood of new tears to everyone and another round of hugs and kisses.

Eventually the party got under way, but they watched

Harlan and Caroline until they disappeared from view. The couple continued to wave, even as they turned from the long, oak-lined lane. Katlin was quiet for a time, but when they cleared Higginsville she began to talk of seeing Jessie again.

The first day of travel went smoothly. They stopped for the night at the home of one of Katlin's Higginsville friends. The following day they began their journey early, and two days later they passed through Warrensburg. The thirty-one miles between Warrensburg and Clinton passed without incident, taking only three days to travel. Because they were passing through higher ground, the river crossings came less often and they moved at a more rapid pace. The party maintained a course running directly south.

Upon reaching Clinton, they spent a night in a local boarding house, and all enjoyed sleeping in real beds. Each one took a hot bath, a luxury no one had enjoyed since leaving Riverview. While standing in the lobby of the hotel, the ladies were surprised to meet some local boys they recognized from Dover and Waverly, Missouri. One was a neighbor from near Briarwood and a good friend of Calvin's. Cassandra was surprised to find Wash Mayes so far from home, but he explained they were traveling south to join Shelby's brigade. Cassandra was ecstatic to hear of their plans and asked Wash to take letters to her brothers. Wash agreed.

In a letter, she told the boys of the death of their father and the destruction of Briarwood. She knew it was going to be a horrible shock to them, but they needed to know. She also wrote about their journey south to Arkansas and her hopes of finding them. Her goal was to reach Fayetteville, Arkansas, by early December. If the boys could meet them there, all the better. If not, then maybe they could direct them to where they should go. She asked them to leave a letter of instruction at the post office in Fayetteville. Katlin sent a letter covering much of the same details to Jessie. She wrote of her love for him and how glad she would be to see him again.

They spent a few days resting in Clinton before beginning their journey again. From this point they would angle southwest toward Nevada, Missouri. They were warned to avoid the border counties near Kansas City, including Jackson, Cass, and Bates counties. That was the local stomping grounds of a band of already famous guerrillas led by Captain William Clarke Quantrill. Any area where Quantrill was to be found would be swarming with Union troopers searching for him. The area had been plagued by raids and pillaged by Kansas Jayhawkers and Union troops.

When Ross came home he related his stories about the terrible scenes of desolation and destruction he had witnessed when traveling north through Bates and Cass Counties.

Cassandra's plan was simple. They would pass around the outskirts of the desolated counties, then swing southwest until they reached the roads going south and parallel to the Missouri border. It was best if they stayed west of the Yankee stronghold at Springfield, Missouri. The best information and latest rumors suggested it was likely the Confederate army, including Shelby's brigade, were operating in northwest Arkansas. This was their destination, for they hoped to spend the winter somewhere near the brigade. Two more days of travel brought them through Appleton City, then through the village of Rockville. They hoped to reach the riverbanks of the Little Osage River before nightfall.

Cassandra urged Bright Star alongside the wagon. She leaned over and shouted above the wagon's creaking to Jethro, "How far do you think it is to the river?"

"I don't know, Miss Cassie. Seems to me we ought to be gettin' pretty close. Shouldn't be too much farther."

Cassandra scanned ahead. Before them rose a gentle upgrade, which lead to a hill crest, about half a mile away. "Maybe from there we can see the river."

Fanny leaned forward on the seat beside Jethro and yelled, "Lordy, I hope so, Miss Cassie. If I ride on this seat much longer my rear end goin' to be paralyzed!" Fanny's eyes widened to emphasize her statement.

Cassandra wanted to laugh, but she held it back and said, "I know how you feel, Fanny. I'm a little saddle sore myself. I hope we can find a place to camp near the river."

The sun moved lower in the sky, and the evening chill increased. Now, in the first week of November, the days were getting shorter and the nights colder. So far they had enjoyed good weather on the trip; only one day had been very cold.

Gradually, the wagon made its way up the incline and mounted the crest of the hill.

"There she is, Miss Cassie," exclaimed Jethro proudly.

They looked into the river valley, now less than a mile away. "Ought to be down there in thirty minutes or so, and I bet we find us a campsite inside of an hour." He turned to Fanny. "Woman, you think you could fix us a pot of pork an' beans with some sorghum in 'em? I'm powerful hungry for your beans."

"I got the fixins. All ya gotta do is get me down by that river, build me a fire, and peal my bottom out of this hard ole seat. Lord a' mercy! I think my behind done died an' gone to heaven."

Katlin laughed from the second seat, and Becca sat grinning beside her. "Fanny, if you'd get out of the wagon an' walk alongside part of the way like Miss Liz and Miss Kat and I do, you wouldn't be so seat sore," said Becca.

"Chile, this here body made for cookin', cleanin', and lovin', but it sure ain't made for walkin'. I'll leave that to you younger gals. I just need time once in a while to shake every thing out a little."

Two hours later, as they sat around a warm fire, Jethro leaned back against a log and held his toes near the fire. "Man, oh man, that sure feels good! Those were good beans, dear. You done yo' self proud."

Fanny smiled proudly, "I knows it. An' we got enough for some more tomorrow, if'n you ready for 'em by then." She spoke to Becca. "I got a pile of dirty plates that needs a cleanin'. This here been the first time in a couple of days we camped near a fresh stream. Fetch some water and get started washin' up this mess."

Becca raised herself from a log near the fire. She set down her empty plate and walked over behind Jethro. The young woman leaned over Jethro's back and embraced him around the neck, pressing her breasts into his upper back. She spoke sweetly, "Jethro, would you mind haulin' me a couple of buckets of water up here so I can do the dishes?" She smiled at him innocently.

Jethro grinned widely. "Sure, I'll be back in a jiffy." Becca let go of him and sat down to scrape the plates. Jethro walked to the wagon, grabbed two water buckets hanging from the side of the wagon, and headed for the river.

Elizabeth sat in the wagon with her mother, Ellen, who still showed no signs of improving. Cassandra, sitting with Katlin near the fire, glanced up and noticed the anger on Fanny's face as she tidied up and put the food away.

When Jethro returned with the water, Fanny cornered him. "I want to talk to you right now."

Jethro was caught off guard, but replied, "Well, go ahead woman, what do you want?"

"Not here, let's take a walk. Miss Cassie, is it okay with you?"

"Sure, Fanny, you don't have to ask my permission. Newlyweds need some time alone." Jethro smiled shyly and tried to take Fanny's hand. She jerked it away quickly and stormed away from the fire in the direction of the river. Jethro looked puzzled but followed. He caught her near the river.

"What in the world got into you, Fanny?"

Fanny crossed her arms across her ample chest. "Don't pretend you don't know! I seen the way she hugged all over you and how you just smiled so big an' said, 'I'll go down an' bring you a couple buckets of water, no problem at all.' "

"So what's the matter? She asked me to help, an' I did. It don't mean nuthin'."

Fanny, faced flushed and angry, rested her fists on her hips. "I've been watchin' her battin' those big eyes an' flirtin' with you, an' you're just eatin' it all up. The way she been swinging herself around and stickin' out that little chest of hers!"

"Fanny, ain't nothin' for you to be gettin' all fired mad about. Why that girl only sixteen, an' she's young enough to be my daughter."

"I know how old she is, and I also know she ain't your daughter! You the only man in this here party for her to chase after. She's so young an' pretty. I won't have none of it, ya hear!"

Jethro tried to console her, but Fanny was still too angry. "Fanny, don't worry. Becca is just at that age when she does a lot of thinkin' about men an' boys. She's just practicin' her flirtin' on an ole man, so she be ready when she gets near some young man she takes a fancy to. She is a sweet young thing, but I need a woman that's got some meat on her bones. I needs somethin' I can hold on to that can keep me warm at night. Besides, there ain't no one can out-cook you. Good cookin' gonna last a lot longer than being skinny. You know I love you."

Fanny felt the anger drain away. "I guess I'm just a jealous ole wife. I love you so much, Jethro, an' I guess I got all worked up over nuthin'. You ain't mad at me, are you?"

"Nah, I ain't mad, it makes me proud you love me enough to care." They embraced near the river and, under his loving kisses, Jethro laid her down gently on the riverbank.

It was much later when Cassandra heard Jethro and Fanny return. The soft sounds of the two trying to be quiet woke her from her bed beneath the wagon, but it was the deep, hacking coughs of her mother in the wagon above that kept her awake. She rolled over in her blankets. Cassandra worried about her mother—her cough just seemed to be getting worse.

27

Captured!

They forded the river the next day. In the afternoon, they passed through Fair Haven. The weather was cool and crisp and the travelers bundled up more tightly in coats and blankets. They made camp again and suffered through a frosty, cold night. When the first rays of sunlight penetrated the cold gloom of night, they were on the move again.

Today, with luck, they would reach Nevada, Missouri. Once there, they would try to spend a night in a boarding house. Everyone looked forward to sleeping once again in a real bed and to enjoying another hot bath if it was available. Maybe they could find a doctor for Ellen. The cold air had further compounded her symptoms, and it was apparent she was growing weaker.

Noon came and went, and on they traveled. The sun began to warm the hills of western Missouri, and the brittle white frost disappeared quietly from the landscape. The trail wound through the hills, and it was around one of these bends that trouble found them.

Suddenly—in one mad, startling explosion—horses ridden by dusty men in blue darted into the road from concealed positions in the brush. Instantly, riders on both sides of the trail had their hands on the harness leads of the wagon team and forced them to a halt. A dirty, burly, bearded man leveled the barrel of a Remington forty-four pistol at the face of a startled Jethro.

"Hold 'em steady right there, nigger, so's I don't have to give ya a third eye 'twixt the other two!" From where she sat on the second spring seat, Cassandra could see the grin on his dirty, bloated face.

A shrill scream of surprise burst from Katlin's lips, in reaction to the sudden attack. The horses lunged and reared in their traces, frightened by the unexpected riders and Kaitlin's scream. Prince of Heaven and Bright Star jerked their heads around on their lead ropes and shied from the intruders. Elizabeth and Becca had been walking behind the wagon. As both girls turned to run, two more riders appeared behind them from the brush to block their escape. The men herded the girls closer to the wagons.

The man with the Remington revolver was obviously the leader. Cassandra saw the yellow sergeant's stripes on the sleeve of the big man's dirty, Union-blue uniform.

The bearded man spat an amber stream of tobacco juice into the dust of the road, then turned to smile at the people in the wagon as he held his gun on them. "Well now, what have we got here? Looks like we caught some Southerners out for a ride with a few of their niggers." He laughed deeply, amused by the fear he saw in their eyes as they stared down the barrel of his pistol.

"Just where do you think you're going, ladies?" He stopped smiling, and his eyes grew cold and intimidating.

Cassandra replied, "Our home has been destroyed and we are refugees heading south to Arkansas."

"Well now, ain't that a pity. A pretty thang like you homeless an' all." The man grinned again, showing his tobacco-stained teeth, and wiped the spittle from his beard and lips with the back of his free hand. "But you can't be haulin' contraband out of Missouri. You're gonna have to leave your slaves here, unless of course you could pay us a little fine. We might let you keep 'em if you got enough."

"No, suh, we ain't slaves. Me and the Missus here, we free! We just work for the ladies."

"Shut your mouth, boy! I ain't talkin' to you. This here is betwixt me and the ladies here." He glanced back at Cassandra.

"He's telling the truth, Sergeant! They have their freedom papers and they work for us. We're not breaking any laws."

"Maybe you ain't figured it out yet, lady, but this here gun and the Federal government is all the authority I need to collect fines here."

"If it's money you're after, I'm afraid you're too late. We've already been robbed twice since we left Lafayette County. We have nothing left of value that hasn't already been taken from us."

"Yeah, well maybe so, lady, but I figure me an' the boys might just make up our own minds."

Becca found herself pressed up beside the wagon and pinned in by the other riders. "Look at this one here, Sarge. She's damn nice lookin' for a nigger gal!"

"Yeah, Taylor, she is mighty fine. How about it missy, you a slave?"

"Yes suh, I belong to Miss Katlin there, an' I like it just fine."

The sergeant's eyes snapped back to Cassandra. "I thought you said they were free! You been lyin' to me, lady?"

"I haven't been lying to you. Jethro and his wife, Fanny, are free and were hired by us. Becca is a slave, but will be freed when we get to Arkansas," Cassandra lied.

The sergeant bent down, grabbed a handful of Becca's flowing hair and twisted her head around so he could look at her closely. "How about it, Missy? I can free you right now an' take you away from all this." He leered at her. Becca's eyes widened in terror as she strained against his hold and tried to move away from him. "No, suh, please, suh, let me stay with Miss Katlin. I belong to her."

The tall, slender soldier named Taylor spoke up. "Hey, Barnes, let's take her with us. We could have us a ball with her tonight. I need somethin' to help keep off the winter chill."

"Yeah, Sarge, maybe she can cook, I can't handle much more of Taylor's cookin'!"

Another of the riders growled. "Shut up, Brant! You eat it fast enough."

"Knock it off, the two of ya! Brant, take a look in the wagon, and see what we can use." He turned and looked challengingly at Cassandra while still holding Becca a captive. "You seem to be the leader of this group, how you goin' to pay your fine?"

"I told you, we don't have any money. We've been robbed by your kind before."

"Yeah, you said that, but I think a woman of your beauty could find ways of payin' us with somethin' better than money." He smiled, showing those grotesquely stained teeth. He leaned over and spat again.

Cassandra could feel the shake and shift in the wagon as the soldier named Brant swung up and over the tailgate. Before she could respond, a loud bang exploded in the wagon behind her, then another!

Brant dove head first out of the back of the wagon and landed in the dusty road. He screamed loudly, "Jeez-us Christ! There's someone in there with a gun!" At the same instant the shots were fired, the horses tied to the back of the wagon skittered wildly around, nearly trampling Brant. He scrambled quickly to his feet and ran to the soldier holding the reins of his horse.

Jethro took advantage of the turmoil caused by the gunfire and slapped the reins down hard on the backs of the horses hitched to the wagon. "Ho, giddy up!" he hollered.

Those in the wagon clutched at their seats as best they could as the wagon leaped forward. Elizabeth, left behind in the road in the confusion, darted into the brush by the side of the road and ran as hard as she could.

Becca was not so lucky. Still held in the grasp of Sergeant

Barnes she could not free herself, but it was all Barnes could do just to hang on to his horse and his captive.

"There goes that little gal into the brush!" yelled a Yankee.

"Forget her, she's too young to do us any good. Let her go. She'll be too much trouble to chase down." Barnes grabbed Becca roughly and pulled her across his saddle in front of him. She lay on her belly, bottom in the air, draped over the front of the saddle. She kicked and tried to fight him, and his horse shied and circled. Sergeant Barnes reacted swiftly. He slammed the butt of his gun down hard on her derriere once, then again. She was stunned by the pain and the feeling of the air being pounded out of her.

"Don't fight me, nigger, or I swear I'll kill ya real slow."

"Come on, Sarge, ain't we goin' after 'em?"

"Gawd damn, Hanks, sometimes I think you got shit fer brains! By the time we catch up with the wagon, they ain't gonna be surprised no more. They'll likely be armed and ready for us. Besides, I think it's likely the woman was tellin' the truth an' they probably have been robbed before. They ain't got nuthin' we need enough to take a chance a gettin' killed for except a good piece a tail, and we got that right here." He patted Becca on her bottom, lingering and squeezing to feel her hips beneath the cloth. The riders circled closer together on their mounts.

"That ain't the half of it, Hanks," yelled Taylor. "In case you ain't noticed, they're headed in the direction of Nevada, which we just came from. That's got to be the worst direction we can go. I ain't hankerin' to run into Colonel Catherwood. He'll have us shot if'n he catches us after we run off."

"Worse yet, we might run into some of Quantrill's boys, an' they don't take prisoners. I know the bushwackers are suppose to be movin' south toward Nevada, Missouri, but you can't tell where them Missouri boys might go. I sure as hell ain't fer anything that takes me closer to Quantrill. That's why we deserted. Ole Colonel Catherwood can try to cheat the devil, but he can do it without us."

Hanks looked at the others sheepishly. "I reckon you're right."

"You're damn right we are! Now let's turn east and get some distance behind us before dark." They took off at an easy gallop.

Becca felt the air gush out her mouth. The motion of the horse pounded her relentlessly against the saddle and drove the air from her lungs. Already the pain of the saddle digging into her stomach and ribs was becoming unbearable. A surge of panic engulfed her, but the pain superseded all other sensations. She clung desperately to the stirrup and leg of her captor.

28

Tempered Steel, Forged by Fire

Jethro had the horses moving at full speed. The wagon bumped and rocked dangerously from side to side down the rutted road. "Miss Cassie, get in the back and see if they're comin'," Jethro shouted.

It was all Cassandra could do to get over the back of her seat. She practically fell on Ellen lying under the canvas-covered portion of the wagon.

"Mother, are you all right?"

A deep hacking cough answered her, then a familiar voice, "I'm fine, did I hit him?"

"I don't know. In all the confusion I'm not sure what happened." Cassandra glanced out the back of the wagon. "Jethro, I don't see them. I don't think they're following us."

Jethro nodded his head.

"Is everyone all right? Where is Elizabeth, Cassie?"

"She's back there, Mamma. We left Becca too!"

"We have to go back. We can't leave them! I can't leave my baby in the hands of those damn Yankees!" Ellen was trembling now, but her grip on Cassandra's arm showed strength far beyond what she expected given her mother's sickened condition.

"Don't worry, Mamma, I'll get them back. Just try and rest and I'll go back and find them." Cassandra took another look behind, then moved toward the front of the wagon. Suddenly, she was slammed into the side of the wagon. If it had not been for the tied down canvas, she would have fallen out. A sudden turn of the wagon had thrown her off balance.

She heard Jethro yelling to the team as he brought the wagon to a stop. She reached Jethro just as he locked the wheel brake with his powerful leg.

"I have to go back and get them, Jethro. You've got to help me get Bright Star saddled up."

"No, Miss Cassie, you ain't goin' nowhere. You're gonna stay here and take care of Miss Katlin and your Mamma. I'll go get Miss Elizabeth and Becca."

"No, Jethro, I'll go. I need you to stay here."

"No ma'am! Miss Cassie, I belonged to your family a long time, an' your family always done right by me. But Miss Cassie, I ain't your slave no more, I got my freedom papers, an' I says I'm goin' to get them girls back, an' you ain't gonna stop me. This time I'm not takin' orders. Lord a' mercy, Miss Cassie, all we need is another woman in the hands of those men out there. They won't take no runaway slave serious, an' maybe I can get the girls away from 'em."

She saw the proud, stubborn pride on Jethro's face, and she was caught off guard by his boldness. She admired his courage. No matter what her personal feelings, maybe it would be better his way. It just might work. She smiled, "All right, Jethro, what do you need?"

A satisfied look crossed his face when he realized she was going to let him go. "I need a horse, the shotgun, an' I'll take along my knife too."

"You can take Prince of Heaven, but you'll have to ride him sidesaddle—unless you want to go bareback."

"I'll go without the saddle, Miss Cassie."

"Good luck, Jethro." Cassandra turned and walked away. Fanny listened to the exchange from inside the wagon where she was attending to Ellen. What she heard from her man frightened her.

"Jethro, don't you be no fool! You think one nigger can whip five Yankees all by his self?"

"I don't aim to whip 'em, I just want to sneak in and get the gals out, that's all."

Fanny saw the look of determination on her husband's face, and she knew there would be no stopping him from trying. "You're goin' off, an' you're gonna git yourself killed is what you're gonna do." She paused, an anxious, worried look on her face. "I need you, Jethro. You're the only thing I got in this world." Tears welled in her eyes.

"You know I love you, an' I ain't goin' to let nobody keep me away from you long. I'll be back, gal." He gave her a passionate kiss and held her tightly in his arms.

A few minutes later, Jethro headed Prince of Heaven down the road in a gallop. He had the shotgun and a canteen slung over his shoulder and his knife stuck in the back of his belt. In his pockets he had extra powder, shot, and caps for the shotgun.

The big black stallion's gait quickly ate up the ground in long strides. After a short distance, Jethro eased him back. It was good to let him burn off some of his excess energy, but it wouldn't do to ride too hard or too fast toward the unknown.

He was uncertain whether or not the enemy was pursuing them cautiously. In fact, it surprised him the soldiers hadn't run them down already. If they weren't in pursuit, were they lying in wait to ambush them when they came to rescue the two girls? He kept at a steady pace, but his eyes were continually alert to any movement. He utilized the brush and trees along the trail as a screen. He finally reached the area where he thought they'd been attacked. He watched and listened quietly for more than fifteen minutes before he advanced.

Jethro realized he had little time to waste. He must take a chance before losing the daylight. After a few minutes, he spotted the tracks of one of the girls going off into the brush. The feet were small, and he figured it had to be Elizabeth.

The other tracks disappeared in the middle of the road. They must have loaded Becca on one of their horses, he surmised. Now he wondered, did he dare to yell out for Elizabeth? He decided he must take the chance.

"Elizabeth! Miss Lizzie, it's Jethro! Are you all right?" He waited, but there was no reply. "Miss Elizabeth Kimbrough, it's Jethro. Where you at, gal?"

He heard a muffled reply, and Elizabeth burst from the bushes, "Jethro! Here I am, Jethro!"

He swung down from Prince of Heaven as she ran to him. She leaped into his arms and he held her as he spun her slowly around. Prince of Heaven pulled away from the pair and stood alert, staring at them.

"Chile, ole Jethro wasn't gonna leave you. You're gonna be just fine." He eyed her carefully; she appeared unharmed. "Did they hurt ya?" he asked, looking into her eyes.

"No, I ran off into the woods when the wagon took off, and I thought they would come after me, but they didn't. I hid as best as I could, and after awhile I came closer to the road, but they were gone. I haven't been here very long."

"Did you see what happened to Becca, child?"

"No, I just ran as fast as I could. I didn't even look back."

"That's okay; don't worry, we'll find 'em. Your mamma and everyone else is just fine. They hid up the road a little more than a mile. Come along with me for now. We got to find Becca."

It didn't take Jethro long to find the tracks of the soldiers' horses. He figured they wouldn't expect pursuit and he started to trail them. He hoped they would want to make camp early tonight and wouldn't try to travel far. He was no tracker—he knew that once it grew dark he would lose the trail until it was light again. If he lost them he might never find Becca again. The trail led almost due east. He followed it as fast as possible. Elizabeth rode behind him, locking her hands around his middle.

He tried to run the details over in his mind. He figured they were attacked between one or two in the afternoon. The wagon escape and finding Elizabeth must have taken at least until three or half past three. He hoped the soldiers wouldn't ride more than a mile or two before camping for the night.

They had a woman as captive and, if he figured these men correctly, they would be anxious to get at her. He counted on their lust because, if they traveled far, he would lose the trail in the dark before he found them.

The trail continued down the top of a ridge line, then abruptly veered off into a little ravine with a creek flowing through. He guessed the creek would eventually empty into the Little Osage River. Jethro made a bold decision. Instead of following the trail down in the ravine, he would follow the ridge. His hope was that from a higher position he might spot their campfire. It was his best chance to locate them. As he rode the ridge, he spotted curling tendrils of smoke drifting up from the ravine.

"There. Do ya see it, Miss Lizzie? Looks like a campfire to me." He pulled the black stallion over the crest of the ridge, hiding out of the camp's line of sight, and eased Elizabeth to the ground. Jethro dismounted "Miss Elizabeth, I got a real big job for you. I want you to stay with ole Prince here, and take care of him. If something goes wrong, or I'm not back by daylight, you follow our tracks back the way we came. When you reach the wagon road just keep on goin' the way we were headin' before the soldiers came, okay?"

"Jethro, I'm scared. Please don't leave me!"

"Child, I know you're scared, and I'm scared too, but those men got Becca an' only the Lord knows what they'll do to her. I got to try and get her back, no matter how scared I am. Just think how scared Becca must be."

Elizabeth thought about what Jethro said. She looked up at him with eyes filled with hope. "I know, but can't I go with you?"

"No! It's bad enough I gotta go, but I need to know you're safe, gal." His face became more stern. "You stay here. You understand?"

She nodded silently.

"All right then. No matter what, you wait for me right

here. If light comes, you ride out of here. Keep bundled up warm in your coat."

He unslung the shotgun, left her the canteen, and started to work his way toward the campfire. The sun was already setting, splashing the sky with vivid reds, yellows, and golds, as he carefully worked his way down the ridge and toward the campfire smoke. He moved quietly and as rapidly as he could. In some places where the cover was sparse he crawled, and in others he moved in a crouched position. His heart pounded, and his inhalations came in shallow, ragged breaths. Though it was cool and growing colder, he could feel the beads of sweat on his forehead. He finally reached a position where he could peer over the brush and peek into the campsite. He prayed silently just before lifting himself up for his first look. "Oh lawd, please let this be the right camp, an' look out for this poor ole nigra who sho 'nuff got his self in a heap a trouble!"

He eased up and studied the camp. Yes, this was the right one. He recognized two of the soldiers sitting around the campfire. The skinny one was sitting on a log and watching the one he had heard called Brant on top of Becca. Brant's pants were down around his ankles. He was holding her down by pinning her wrists with his hands. Jethro heard Brant's laughter drifting up to him. He watched her uselessly struggle against the weight and strength of Brant's body thrusting away at her. Another soldier sat near the fire, trying to cook bacon in a frying pan, while a fourth man fed and cared for the horses.

Something wasn't right, something he wasn't seeing. He sensed it, then heard the bone-chilling click of a pistol hammer being cocked. The sound came from behind him. It wasn't loud, but he felt the hair rise on the back of his neck as his knees began to tremble.

"Hold it right there, nigger! You make one wrong move and I'm gonna scatter your brains all over those bushes."

Jethro froze in place.

"Ease that scatter gun down easy, butt first. Keep your hands where I can see 'em."

Jethro moved slowly, doing exactly what he was told. He was scared and he knew this could be his last mistake. "Yes, suh, I don't mean no harm. I just seen the fire, an' I was cold, that's all." The gun butt touched the ground.

"Now push that barrel away from you and let go."

Jethro didn't hesitate. He was caught, and he hoped they wouldn't recognize him.

"Turn around real slow, an' keep those hands where I can see 'em."

Jethro turned slowly to face the voice behind him. He recognized the man at once. It was the overweight sergeant that had led the ambush on them that afternoon.

"Well, I'll be damned, if it ain't the nigger driver from the wagon." Barnes smiled wickedly at his prisoner. "I bet yer lookin' for the nigger gal we took, ain't ya. I can't blame you much, she sure is a looker, she is. Sweet little thang, I enjoyed gettin' a piece of her and I can hardly wait till it's my turn again." He licked his lips as he savored his thoughts of Decca.

It wasn't easy to keep his composure. He wanted to kill this fat, repulsive Yankee, but Jethro tried to remain cool. He gave the sergeant his most innocent smile. "No, suh, I don't care a lick for that gal. She was always suckin' up to white folk, like it'd do her any good." He tried his best to look disgusted. "I done run off from those people, I did. I know'd you were Union soldiers, an' I knew it was my chance to be free, so I ran away."

"Oh." A stern look of disbelief crossed Sergeant Barnes's face. "If ya want your freedom, you came to the right place. I'm gonna take great pleasure in stringin' up your worthless carcass from a tree for the crows to eat." His expression turned angry. "You think I'm stupid, boy? You said you was free earlier, an' you had your papers. Now you're changin' your story." He nodded his head as if he knew the truth. "You're after the girl all right. But you got caught, an' now ya gonna pay, boy!"

"I don't think so, Yank! Drop your gun real easy." The

woman's voice rang steady and calm from behind the sergeant.

Barnes flinched at the sound of the woman's voice coming from behind him so unexpectedly. He froze in place, hesitated, then let the pistol drop. He turned around slowly. In the dim light of dusk he saw the beautiful but determined Cassandra holding a navy Colt in a two-hand grip, pointed directly at his chest. She stood a scant few short steps away.

"Jeez-us lady, you scared the shit out of me! Come on now, holdin' a gun on a man an' usin' it is two different things. You know you ain't gonna shoot. You ain't got the stomach to kill no one. Put the gun down, an' I promise I won't hurt ya none, an' I'll let you go." He started to let his hands drop as he took a step toward her.

Outwardly, Cassandra was strangely calm, but inside she was boiling with hate and anger. Before her stood a fat, leering man in a Union-blue uniform, but Cassandra saw much more. In her mind she pictured her father shot down by men in blue. She saw Briarwood in flames ... Bartok wore that same navy blue uniform. She still remembered Bartok's despised face and his evil, lustful grin. It all overwhelmed her in a flash of white hot anger. She smiled, a strange, delightful smile, and she pulled the trigger. She felt the gun buck in her hands and saw the bright flash from the muzzle as the gun fired.

Barnes felt the impact, even as he stepped toward Cassandra. He looked down in disbelief, touching his hand to the wound in his chest. Blood, dark ruby red, pulsed through his fingers. He held his hand up and looked at it, as if it were some kind of illusion. He looked back at the beautiful woman with flowing blond hair; and then his eyes fell on the smoking gun in her hands. "You ... you shot me." He looked puzzled.

She fired again, and again. The second shot hit him square in the middle of his forehead—he was dead even before the third shot hit him in the belly. He slowly pitched over onto his back, like a giant oak tree felled by a lumberjack.

When Jethro saw Barnes drop his Remington revolver, he

grabbed the pistol and the shotgun. He stuffed the revolver in his belt just as Barnes fell dead. He pointed the shotgun at the camp in case the others might be coming toward the sound of the shots.

He didn't know how Cassandra had gotten there, but he could question her later. He was more concerned with the other soldiers. He took a quick look at the camp. The shots had shocked them, and they were scrambling to either leave or reach their weapons. The soldier busy with forcing himself on Becca had rolled off and was simultaneously trying to stand and pull up his pants. Taylor stood up from his log and pulled his revolver from its holster. He crouched as he stared in the direction of the gunfire. The soldier by the horses pulled a carbine from a scabbard on a saddle, while the soldier cooking by the fire straightened up as he tried to fathom the meaning of the echoing shots.

Cassandra didn't hesitate. When she spotted the soldiers in the camp she fired. The muzzle blast flared in the growing gloom of evening, but the bullet missed its mark, whining harmlessly over the heads of those in the camp. Cassandra felt exhilarated. Shooting Sergeant Barnes felt satisfying and offered an outlet for her pent-up anger and pain. From this crucible of danger she was forged anew—stronger and more resilient than before, tempered like raw steel in a furnace.

Brant was still struggling to pull up his pants and run. He looked comical as he tripped and fell, his feet tangled in his clothes. At the next shot, Taylor fixed their position, but he couldn't tell what he was up against. He turned and ran toward the horses.

"Let's get the hell out of here!" Taylor shouted.

"What about Barnes? He went into the woods to look around."

"To hell with Barnes, I ain't in the army anymore. Besides, those shots we heard was probably Barnes gettin' it. It's every man for his self!"

The man with the carbine aimed hastily in the direction of the muzzle flash and fired. Then he sheathed the carbine, untied the reins of his horse from the picket line, and swung into the saddle. Taylor reached the horses and picked up his saddle and tried to get it on the nearest horse. The horse, startled by the men running at him and by the gunfire, pranced wildly, straining against his lead rope.

Another soldier joined them. "Where the hell is my saddle?"

"Where you left it, over by the fire!"

"Well, I ain't goin' back fer it." He jumped bareback on the nearest horse.

Brant, struggling to escape, was still fighting to get control of his pants. Becca caught him as he neared the burning campfire. She gave him a rough, quick shove, toppling him into the fire. He landed on his side.

He screamed as his pants caught fire and the searing heat of the red hot coals bit into his flesh. He rolled over on the frying pan in an attempt to roll free of the flames. His momentum pitched over a coffee pot sitting at the edge of the fire. His flesh sizzled as it touched the red-hot metal of the pot. The smell of his burned flesh mixed freely with the aromatic smell of cooked bacon. He pulled himself to his feet, the flames burning and spreading from his pants and his shirt.

He ran toward the men screaming. "God help me, I'm on fire!" He screamed his agony as the fire blackened his flesh. The flames worked their hellish way up his back, and his sleeves caught fire from pounding at the burning clothes. His hair began to smolder, then caught flame. His cries were now of terror and pure agony as he neared the men.

By now, Taylor had the saddle on his horse. He pulled a revolver out of his belt. At nearly point-blank range, Taylor fired two quick shots into the chest of the approaching, flaming wreck of a man. "Gawd damn it, keep away from me!" he yelled. In the excitement, Taylor's freshly saddled horse broke free from his grip and galloped away. He paused for only a moment, then turned and ran into the woods after his startled mount.

Becca, cold and exhausted, dropped down near the remains of the campfire.

The rider on the saddled horse fired a few wild shots in the direction of Jethro and Cassandra in the hopes of discouraging pursuit. He wheeled his horse and fled in the same direction as Taylor. The last man, riding bareback, followed closely on his heels.

Cassandra and Jethro turned to each other in amazement. Jethro would never have guessed that it would be so easy to stampede these men. The two rose in unison from the bushes and cautiously approached the camp.

The burning man was no longer moving, but the flames were still licking at his charred body. Becca sat with her knees hugging her chest, staring into the glowing embers of the fire. Cassandra ran to her.

"Becca, are you all right?"

She didn't answer at first. Then she looked at Cassandra, and the tears began to roll down her cheeks. She trembled as she replied softly, "No."

Cassandra pulled her to her feet and held her in her arms. The ravaged girl let loose with big racking sobs. "They made me! They . . . they, raped me!"

Jethro heard it all, but he stood at the ready, expecting at any minute to see the Yankees reappear. He yelled back over his shoulder to the women. "Quick, search the camp for what we can use, then let's get out of here."

Cassandra pulled herself free from Becca's arms. Becca's clothing was ripped and hung in tattered shreds. Cassandra knew the girl would freeze to death if she tried to travel in those rags. Cassandra searched hastily through the abandoned bedrolls and gear. She found a shirt that, although too big to fit well, would give Becca some kind of protection. She found a baggy pair of dirty cavalry pants she could slip on. Jethro fashioned a tether rope into a belt and rolled up the pants, which made them serviceable.

Jethro found some ammunition and the weapons belonging to Brant. Cassandra gathered the blankets and a couple of cavalry overcoats. A horse remained tied to a tree abandoned by the fleeing men. It was either the mount that belonged to Barnes or the man called Brant. Neither would have further need of a horse. Jethro saddled it, put the bridle on, and led it to Becca. The extra equipment was tied on the saddle. Jethro hefted the extra saddle left by the campfire. "I can use this on Prince," he said. "Miss Cassie, I was sho' enough glad to see you, but I don't know how you found us."

She smiled at him. "I couldn't stay behind and do nothing. I knew Katlin and Fanny could take care of Mother and the wagon. I was afraid you might need help searching for the girls. So I left shortly after you did. I just followed your tracks and those of the other riders."

"I guess if ya hadn't I'd be dead now, and Becca would still be held prisoner by them Yanks."

"I found Elizabeth with Prince, just after you left her. I left Bright Star with her and followed your footprints."

"I don't like stayin' here," said Jethro, wrinkling his nose. The sweet, pungent odor of Brant's roasting flesh turned his stomach. "They might get brave an' come back for their stuff. I reckon we ought to leave."

"I agree, there might be more of the Yankees nearby, and Elizabeth must be scared back there all alone with the horses."

Becca spoke softly, "I don't think there are any more soldiers to help 'em. They're Yankee deserters. I heard 'em say they was afraid to fight Quantrill, so they ran away."

"That's why they ran—they're yellow!" shouted Jethro.

"They might have stayed and fought but they didn't know who or what they were facing. We could've been Yankees coming after them for desertion or some of Quantrill's men for all they knew."

"They sho 'nuff lit out like scalded dogs," Jethro said.

"Becca, did you say they were part of an army looking for Quantrill?"

"Yes, ma'am, I heard them say their colonel thought Quantrill and his men was movin' south toward Nevada."

"If we could locate Quantrill and his men we could travel south safely. We've got to hurry and tell the others."

The three soon reached Elizabeth, who was relieved to see them all safe. Darkness had descended on them and the cold seeped through their clothes, but there was a partial moon lighting the way. They agreed it would be better if they moved on a little farther before they camped. Jethro saddled Prince of Heaven with the extra cavalry saddle taken from the camp. At least the ride back would be more comfortable. In the morning they would return to the wagon and head for Nevada, Missouri.

29

Bartok's Scheme

The orderly sergeant stuck his head into the room. He took one quick glance at Major Benton Bartok. "Captain Anders is here to see you, Major."

"Very good, Sergeant, send him in." Captain Bob Anders sauntered to the desk and gave a half-hearted salute.

"At ease, Captain, make yourself comfortable."

Anders grabbed the closest chair and slid it up near the desk. He seated himself, kicked the chair back on the rear two legs and rested his boots on the corner of another chair.

Bartok finished shuffling through paperwork and moved a large stack to the side of his desk. He looked up at Captain Anders and waited expectantly for him to report.

Anders waited until he saw Benton look up from his papers. "I think we ought to burn out Riverview," Anders said flatly.

"Why? Didn't ole man Thomas come up with the money?"

"Yeah, he came up with it, but I don't like his attitude."

"Come on, Bob, we both know why you want to burn him

out. It still rankles you his daughter got away before you could get a piece of her."

An amused smile creased Anders face when he realized Benton Bartok knew exactly what was bothering him. He shook his head and then laughed. "Yeah, well I guess that has a lot to do with it. Still, I think it would be good to set an example for the others. It wouldn't look good if they think they can do whatever they want."

Benton pulled a cigar out of his desk, bit off the end and spit the stub into the waste basket. He clamped the cigar in the corner of his mouth. "Bob, you and I have got a good thing going for us here. If we want to keep things going smoothly, we need to use our heads." He paused, fished a match out of his coat pocket and struck it on his fingernail. The match flared brightly and he held it to the end of the cigar. "I don't think it will look good to the locals if we burn a man out even though he came up with the money we requested. If they figure we're going to burn them out anyway, they won't come up with our money."

"Yeah, I suppose ya have a point, but I don't like the idea they got away with it."

Benton stood up, walked to the front of his desk, and sat on the corner. He rolled his cigar in his fingers and stared at the burning tip. "They haven't gotten away with anything, not yet. We have time to get even. This war looks like it will drag on for a while, and, if it does, we can make ourselves rich. We just have to remember to keep General Kessington happy and off our backs. The best way to do that is by not causing a general uprising."

He looked up at Bob, who was now staring at the mud on his boots. Bartok continued, "We've already burned out four plantations and picked them clean. Those examples have kept the others in line. Most of the landowners have made their protection payments on time, and at this rate we could become rich beyond our wildest dreams. They know what will happen if they don't."

Anders eyed Benton. "Yeah, the money has been good."

"Not only the money, but you haven't had so many women

in your entire life as you've had since you were assigned to this county, have you?"

A broad smile lit up Captain Anders's face. "No, sir, I can't complain there. I don't mind a bit if a man doesn't have the money to pay to keep his place if he has a good-lookin' daughter or wife instead."

"Yes." Bartok laughed. "I remember the Banberry woman. You arrested her husband for suspected aid to the guerrillas and threatened to have him shot. I'll bet she came in here three times that week."

"Hell no, you're wrong! I had her in here every day for a week, and she was very accommodating. She did everything I asked and more just to keep her husband alive. It was the best lovin' I ever had. I had her six ways to Sunday, I did!" He eased the chair down on all four legs and slapped his hand down on his leg. "Hell! She was so good I had to let him go. Damn it though if he didn't run off! If my men ever find him again I've got standing orders to have him arrested. Next time I'm going to hold him longer." Both men laughed.

Benton wiped tears from the corners of his eyes. "I've done all right for myself and had some good times, too. That's why we must take it easy and play the game. We don't want to kill the cow as long as it gives us sweet milk."

"I can't argue with your logic, so I guess I'll square things with Harlan Thomas later." He reached into his pocket and pulled out a leather wallet. He opened it and extracted a stack of Union greenbacks. "Here is the payment from Thomas. It's all here."

Bartok reached for it, looked it over casually, and stuffed the wad of money into his pants' pocket. "I'll deposit the money into our account at the bank." He glanced up at Anders. "By the way, I sent a detachment to Lawrence today with our goods."

"How much did we ship this time?"

"Four wagons full of goods and around fifty head of cattle."

Anders smiled at the news. Then he asked, "Who's in charge?"

"Captain Rodgers is leading a detachment of D Company."

"You sure we can trust him?"

"I made sure we don't have to. I wired my brother a list of what we shipped to Lawrence. Jacob will let us know if anything is short in the shipment."

"You think of everything, Major. If your brother keeps selling our goods at top dollar prices in Kansas and adding it to our bank account, we have it made."

"We can depend on Jacob. He has a knack for finding a buyer for almost anything." Bartok took another drag on his cigar and exhaled slowly. "He is my brother, but he's not doing this out of the kindness in his heart. He's in it for the money, just like us. He'll keep working if we keep paying him a good commission, and he'll stay honest with us as long as it serves his best interest."

"I'm glad we have most of the money stored in Lawrence. Around here you never know when the guerrillas or the Rebels might come through and clean out the bank."

"Don't worry, Bob, when the account builds up enough in the bank from our cash deposits, I have the local banker telegraph a transfer of funds to Lawrence. It's much safer that way."

Anders smiled, satisfied with the way Bartok was handling things. If things stayed as they were he would be wealthy when the war ended. "Well," he said as he stood up and stretched. "I guess I'd better get back to my quarters and get cleaned up. It's been a long day and I could use a hot bath up at the hotel." Anders headed for the door. He turned to look back at Bartok. "If you don't have anything urgent for me, Major, I'd like to take a day or two to relax."

"No problem, Captain. If anything comes up and I need you, I'll send someone after you."

As the door closed, Bartok walked back to the window and stared out at the activity in the street. His mind was on other things. He understood Anders's disappointment with the Thomas woman. He himself was disappointed with his failure to bed Cassandra Kimbrough. She was a beautiful woman and he wanted to force her to bend to his will, giving herself to him to protect her family and home like so many others had. It hadn't work out the way he planned. She was spirited and proud and wasn't intimidated by his threats. He lost control of his anger, and it cost him his advantage and leverage. Her damned father had pushed things totally out of control when he dared to fight back. Even Glen Kimbrough's son Jessie had interfered.

He felt the bitterness and disappointment rise within him. By God, he had made her pay for her insolence! Her home was nothing but a pile of ashes and her father lay dead in his grave. It helped soothe his anger, but it didn't ease his discontentment. "Damn! If I could have taken her just once before she got away." He stared into space, thinking thoughts of lost opportunities and possible new conquests.

30

Dark Journey
Nevada, Missouri;
November 1, 1862

"Miss Kimbrough, the doctor will see you now. Would you please follow me?" Cassandra followed the matronly woman down the hall to an open door. The woman motioned for her to enter. "Please have a seat, the doctor will be with you soon."

Cassandra stepped past her into the room and took a seat in the closest of the two wooden chairs. The woman closed the door behind her. When Cassandra was alone, her mind drifted back over the last few days.

She first recalled their encounter with the Union deserters and how it had transformed them all. Becca was no longer the carefree girl of before, eager to flirt with Jethro. She was quiet and withdrawn. She kept to her chores as she tried to come to terms with her ordeal.

Elizabeth had lost her childhood innocence and grown up considerably. In a few short weeks she had witnessed the murder of her father, the destruction of her home, an attack on her party, and the rape of Becca. She realized how easily it could have happened to her had she not gotten away. Because it did happen to Becca, she somehow felt a measure of guilt. She had stayed behind in the forest while Jethro and Cassandra rescued Becca, and she had survived unscathed.

Jethro had shown great bravery in going after the girls. He felt a new pride and self-confidence that showed in the way he carried himself.

But what of the changes in herself? Cassandra realized she was forever changed. She had shot a man at point-blank range and had killed with no remorse. The lack of guilt, in a way, bothered her. True, he was a man who deserved death, and only God knows what would have happened if she hadn't shot him. Yet even in her wildest dreams she would never have imagined she could so easily kill someone. What worried her more was realizing that she enjoyed it. It was as if the repulsive man in Union blue represented all the hate and despair the war had forced upon her. The experience had forged a new strength in her, fueled by the fires of hate and injustice. She felt renewed confidence in her ability to face danger and to do what must be done.

The joy of knowing everyone was safe was tempered by the discovery that her mother had taken a turn for the worse in their absence. The illness had settled in her lungs, and now she suffered from sustained coughing fits. There was little they could do. They decided to push on as fast as possible for Nevada, where they would try to find a doctor.

The party made very good time with no further delays until Ellen experienced a severe coughing fit. The color drained from her face and her eyes widened in terror as she gripped her throat with both hands. She tried to breathe in, but she could only wheeze. It was like watching someone drowning and being unable to help.

Ellen turned blue and passed out, collapsing on the floor of the wagon. Elizabeth screamed in terror and Cassandra felt a rising tide of panic. Finally, Ellen began to breathe again and regained consciousness. Cassandra and the others were paralyzed by the incident and didn't know how to respond.

Ellen herself was scared. She described the terrible panic of not being able to breathe, as if someone was smothering her and she was utterly helpless to prevent it. They were all puzzled why, after one of these severe coughing fits, her throat or lungs just seemed to close, only to open again after she passed out.

That was the first attack. There were two more before they could reach the doctor. Each time they wondered if she would survive, and each time they were relieved when she recovered.

They placed her in the hotel in a sunny room on the second floor and summoned the doctor. He came to the room to examine her and asked for a little time to make his diagnosis. It was this very morning that he had requested Cassandra to come to his office, and now she sat there, waiting.

There came a light tap at the door and a gray-haired gentleman entered. She recognized him at once as Doctor Johnson, the same kind man who had examined her mother.

"Good afternoon, Miss Kimbrough, so good of you to come."

"Good afternoon, Doctor, have you figured out what is wrong with my mother?"

"Yes. I wanted to check my medical books and to send a telegram to a doctor I know in Saint Louis. Between the two of us, I think we know what her problem is."

Cassandra sat anxiously on the edge of her chair. "What is it?"

"I believe your mother has bronchial pneumonia."

Cassandra swallowed hard. "Is there any cure?"

"No, I'm afraid there is little we can do for her. As you know, pneumonia is usually fatal. I wish there were something I could give her, but unfortunately we lack any effective medicine or known treatment for her affliction."

"Well what do we do?"

"I can give you some laudanum to help her rest. A little whiskey and honey can cut the phlegm in her throat and ease her pain."

"Does she have any hope of getting better?"

"I'm afraid there's not much hope. It's in God's hands now. I expect her lungs will begin to fill with fluids and eventually she'll die. I can't really tell you how long she has. Something like this can happen quickly, and sometimes it can drag on for weeks. I just wish there was something we could do, but there really isn't."

Cassandra sat in stunned silence. Her mind raced, but there were no answers. Lord, she was going to lose her mother and there was nothing she could do about it. She stood up and shook the hand the doctor held out to her. "Thank you, Doctor Johnson."

"I'll check in on your mother each day. For now, keep her head elevated with pillows, give her the laudanum, and keep her in bed. You can get the medicine at the front counter." He turned and walked out the door.

Cassandra walked to the front of the office and picked up the medicine. She made her way toward the hotel. How was she going to tell the others? They all knew Ellen was seriously ill, but they had hoped the doctor might help her. Worse yet, how was she going to tell her mother?

As she turned the corner, she glanced up at the hotel and her mother's room. She eyed the balcony and the stairs leading from the ground to the balcony, hugging the side of the hotel.

She was startled to see her mother suddenly throw open the door to her room and rush out to the balcony. Ellen stood near the top of the stairs. Cassandra watched her long white nightgown billow behind her in the breeze. Cassandra was close enough to see the panic etched on her mother's face, her fingers grasped at her throat. Ellen was suffering through another coughing fit.

Elizabeth followed her mother out onto the balcony and had nearly reached her when Ellen's legs began to buckle. Cassandra screamed and ran toward the hotel.

Ellen sagged to her knees, then tumbled down the stairs like a limp rag doll. Elizabeth tried to catch her, but grasped nothing but air. Ellen's progress down the stairs was brutal—her head and body slammed against wooden railings and stairs. She finally spilled out onto the street and lay still.

To Cassandra it was as if everything had slowed down. She

felt like she was trying to run through a tub of molasses. Elizabeth was the first to reach her mother and yelled at startled passersby to fetch a doctor.

Fanny ran out onto the balcony. "Oh Lawdy, Lawdy!" she cried in shocked disbelief as she raced down the stairs.

Cassandra found her mother lying on her side in the street. Elizabeth was trying to roll Ellen over onto her back. "Don't move her, Liz! She might have broken bones!" But it was too late—Elizabeth cradled her mother's head in her arms. Ellen's face was bleeding from the nose and from a cut on her forehead. She had scrapes and bruises on her cheeks.

Cassandra knelt beside her in the dusty street. "Is she breathing, Liz?"

Elizabeth was in shock. Cassandra saw the scared look on her face and the tears streaming down her cheeks. "I don't think so. Oh God, what are we going to do!"

Cassandra felt for her mother's wrist. Her hand was limp. She felt for a pulse as a swell of panic began to rise in her throat. Fear and hopelessness gnawed at her guts as her heart raced.

Fanny reached the bottom of the stairs, but was unable to get past Elizabeth or Cassandra. "Miss Cassie, is she all right?" While the women were crowded around Ellen, a man standing near the front of the hotel sprinted for the doctor's office.

Cassandra felt her mother's chest. "Please," she prayed to herself, "breathe!" She felt nothing. She looked into her mother's face, and it was pale. Ellen's eyes were rolled up and stared vacantly at nothing. She knew the truth then, but she refused to accept it.

Doctor Johnson came running with his black doctor's bag in hand and knelt beside Ellen to examine her. After a brief analysis he looked into Cassandra's eyes. He shook his head. "She's gone," he said softly.

"Dead," screamed Elizabeth. "No, she can't be!" Elizabeth laid her head on her mother's chest.

Cassandra's eyes clouded with tears. "Oh, dear Lord! Did she just stop breathing?" she asked.

"No, it wasn't her lungs or the pneumonia that killed her. Her neck is broken."

The words hung in the air. None knew how to respond. The Kimbrough women felt the enormity of their loss.

The doctor stood. "If it's any comfort to you, she was dying. It was just a matter of time." He paused and looked thoughtful, then began again. "This shortened her suffering. It has to be better to die swiftly than to feel yourself slowly suffocating from pneumonia. It's hard to see it now, but it's probably best for her."

Cassandra heard the doctor speak, but little registered in her mind. Grief was flooding her senses. She rose and fell into the comforting arms of Fanny.

"Now, now, child, it's gonna be all right. Miss Ellie, we gonna miss her, but she ain't hurtin' no more. She's gone to be with the Lord an' your daddy now."

Katlin, Becca, and Jethro reached the scene. All the commotion on the street had brought Jethro out of the stable. He swept his hat off and held it firmly gripped in his hands. "Is there anything I can do, Miss Cassie?"

Cassandra could not speak. She just looked at Jethro and shook her head.

The doctor turned to the gathering crowd of people. "We could use the help of a few men to carry this woman down to the funeral parlor. Who will help?" Jethro stepped forward and three others joined him.

Cassandra pulled herself from the arms of Fanny and turned toward her sister, who sobbed heavily and clung to her dead mother's body. "Elizabeth, you have to let go so these men can get her out of the street. Come here," Cassandra said softly.

Elizabeth looked up at Cassandra, her eyes wet and red. "Cassie, Cassie!" She could say no more, the words refused to come. Cassandra half lifted her younger sister up and locked her in a long, tearful embrace. "Cassie, there is so much I wanted to say to her. I loved her!"

Cassandra held her sister close while rubbing her back. "I know you did, and Mamma knew it, too."

The men gathered around and gently lifted Ellen's body. "Wait, please, just one minute," Cassandra requested.

The men held Ellen as Cassandra bent down and gently kissed her mother's cheek. "Good-bye, Mother, I ... I love you." She felt weak but was also relieved to know that she still had Fanny.

"Why don't we go upstairs for a bit an' think things through. Jethro gonna see they take good care of your Mamma." The women ascended the stairs as the crowd began to disperse.

31

Fire Storm

The wagon bumped and rocked along the southern trail. Cassandra sat in the front seat beside Jethro. Elizabeth and Becca napped in the back, and Katlin and Fanny sat in the second spring seat, lost in their thoughts.

Cassandra was still in grief. She felt irritable and depressed. Was there no end to her troubles? She recalled her mother's small funeral. They bought the best casket available in Nevada, Missouri. It was made out of a lovely rich cherry wood and lined with satin. They hired a local minister to officiate over the proceedings. The most difficult aspect of the funeral for Elizabeth and Cassandra was burying their mother in a strange place, far from home. They wished she could have been buried beside their father at Briarwood. Unfortunately, with a war going on, it just wasn't possible. So they laid her to rest in the Nevada cemetery. Elizabeth and Cassandra vowed they would have their mother buried at Briarwood when the war was over. This war had already extracted a heavy toll on her, and Cassandra felt the anger twisting her emotions.

Jethro jarred her from her dark thoughts. "Miss Cassie, I do believe I see Lamar."

The wagon crested the rise, and they saw before them a town. Cassandra was alarmed to see smoke billowing and rolling from several structures. For most of that day they had observed black clouds smudging the skyline. They were unsure of the source of the smoke until now. Jethro stiffened, anticipating trouble. He shifted himself in the seat, his shoulders hunched forward to face whatever was to come.

Cassandra reached for her purse and felt the hard reassurance of the gun's cold steel. She turned and spoke to the others. "Elizabeth, Becca, wake up! There might be trouble."

Katlin asked, "Maybe we should find another route around this town?"

"No," Cassandra said firmly. "We'll lose too much time. We've got to continue. We can handle whatever is up ahead. We turn around now and we will lose at least two more days."

"The time might be better spent backtracking, rather than running headlong into trouble," replied Katlin.

"We'll lose too much time, Kat. Shelby's command might leave northwest Arkansas before we can find them. Do you want to risk it?"

Katlin hesitated before she answered resignedly, "No." Katlin didn't want to look for trouble, but she would risk almost anything if it would speed up her chance to be in Jessie's arms again. The wagon continued down the rough, rutted road. It entered a gentle curve in the trail and, as they exited the turn, they approached a cemetery. Union cavalry troopers impeded their path as they manned a temporary road block. On their right, they noticed other soldiers busy unloading a wagon of dead bodies at the cemetery. A few of the bodies were dressed in civilian clothing of a distinct style. Cassandra counted six bodies in shirts adorned with unusually fancy needlework and embroidery. The shirts were cut low in front, the slit narrowing just above the belt into a rosette. All the shirts were covered with large pockets in various colors ranging from vivid reds to shades of brown.

Separated from these bodies were a few dressed in Union blue. The Union soldiers were carefully placed in individual graves, but the others were simply thrown together into a common trench.

"Hold up there. Whoa!" yelled a soldier. He stepped out from the makeshift barricade. "State your business."

Cassandra laid her hand on Jethro's arm and said softly, "Let me handle this, Jethro." She turned to the soldier. "We are traveling and bound for Arkansas."

"Turn that rig around, and go back the way you've come. I'm sorry, but this road is closed!"

Cassandra's eyes narrowed in anger. "Why can't we pass?"

"Listen, lady, I don't have to explain anything to you. I told you to turn this rig around and get the hell out of here."

She arched her back and sat up defiantly. "No. We've spent two days on the road since we left Nevada and I'm not going back. We are going through!"

"I ain't tellin' you again, lady. I got orders to keep people out of this town till we get things cleaned up, and I will carry out my orders."

An officer watched the exchange from the shade of the trees along the road. He stepped forward. "Private McCoy, I'll handle this." The officer was handsome, with strong angular features. He wore a flowing brown handlebar mustache with tips that turned up at the ends. The rest of his face was clean shaven. His eyes were pale blue and seemed to sparkle. He walked toward the wagon and smiled politely. "May I help you, ma'am?"

"Yes, you may. You can tell this soldier to let us pass."

"We have experienced some difficulties ahead, and there might be some sights unfit for a lady to witness." The officer flashed a sincere smile. "I'd advise you to postpone your trip or to go around this area."

"We have seen plenty of misery already in this war, and I very much doubt we could see anything ahead that would be worse than what we have already lived through."

"I would have no way to verify that, ma'am, but I would find it difficult to question the word of such a beautiful woman." He pulled the doe skin leather gauntlet from his right hand, reached up, and offered her his hand. "Allow me to introduce myself. My name is Captain Kenton Doyle of the First Batallion, Second Wisconsin Cavalry." His hand remained awkwardly in the air as Cassandra ignored his gesture.

She glared at him angrily. "I have suffered quite enough at the hands of the Union army already, sir, and I don't want to shake hands with you." He let his hand drop to his side.

Cassandra's words shocked Katlin. "Cassandra, shame on you! I don't think you should be so rude to the good captain." Katlin stood up. "Please allow me to introduce myself," Katlin said sweetly, eyeing Captain Doyle. "I'm Katlin Thomas." She motioned toward the others. "This is Cassandra Kimbrough, her sister Elizabeth, and Becca is in the back. Jethro is driving, and his wife Fanny is with Becca. You must forgive Cassandra, she has endured a great deal. I'm sad to say her home was burned by Northern troops and her father was murdered."

Cassandra was livid with anger. "I don't need you to apologize for me, Kat!"

Jethro reached for Cassandra's wrist and squeezed it firmly. He said in low tones only she could hear, "Please, Miss Cassie, let Miss Katlin talk." Cassandra fumed in silent, contained rage.

Katlin continued, "Please, sir, forgive her anger. On top of her other troubles, her mother died just five days ago, and it has been quite a shock."

Captain Doyle looked embarrassed, yet he showed no anger. He responded calmly. "I'm sorry to hear of your mother's death, and I can understand how you must feel about our army. I'm sure if the situation was reversed, I'd feel the same way. No words I can say will right any wrongs that might have occurred to your family."

Cassandra glared at him and said icily, "I don't want your sympathy, I just want to pass through your lines and continue our trip south."

"Cassandra!"

"No, Miss Thomas, it's all right. She has a right to feel the way she does. If it's safe passage through our lines that you desire, then you shall have it. I will assign a patrol to escort you through, and I will take personal charge of it."

"Thank you for letting us pass, but we don't need an escort."

"I'm afraid you do, ma'am. You see, Quantrill's guerrillas attacked our garrison last night. They were unsuccessful in trying to drive our troops out of the town, so they set fire to over a third of it. There were losses on both sides, and a house-to-house search is in progress to round up any bushwackers left behind."

"I'm not surprised you attribute the fires to Captain Quantrill's men, rather than to your own."

"Despite what you would like to believe, ma'am, it wasn't Federal forces that started these fires."

"I find it hard to believe, sir. Captain Quantrill has made a habit of attacking towns in Kansas, but I have never heard of him attacking Southern people or towns. If he did attack Lamar I'm sure it was to liberate it from Yankee control."

"I see nothing I can say will change the way you feel or what you believe and I understand why. However, time is of the essence for both of us, so let's be on our way. If you will excuse me while I talk to my men." The captain bowed slightly and touched his fingers to his hat. "Ma'am."

When the officer walked away, Katlin touched Cassandra on the shoulder. "What in God's name do you think you're doing?" Katlin whispered. "Are you trying to get us shot? I can't believe he is willing to help us at all after the rude way you treated him. Please, Cassie, let's just get through here without any more confrontations!"

The captain returned with a squad of seven mounted troopers. "Will you please follow me?" They pulled their wagon in line behind the Federal cavalry and rode toward town. When they reached Lamar the clean-up was well under way. Soldiers and civilians were working together to extinguish the fires, or they were fighting to contain the fire to one structure to keep it from spreading to adjacent buildings. On one block, where the fires were still out of control, groups of women and soldiers were hauling as many personal belongings out of homes as possible. They were racing to save items from the path of the uncontrolled fire storm.

The wagon took a zigzag path through the town in order to dodge and bypass the worst fires. Still, the heat was intense and the acrid black and white shrouds of smoke wrapped their tendrils over them. Their eyes watered and their throats burned. Sparks borne by the wind glowed and danced through the air. Here and there they could see smoking ruins of homes standing next to homes untouched by the torch. There seemed to be no rhyme or reason why some were burned and others unscathed. They finally reached the town square.

Captain Doyle motioned for them to stop in front of the county courthouse. The structure was an imposing brick building that looked as if it had been turned into a fortress. Bullet scars in the bricks and in the woodwork were evident.

Captain Doyle rode up beside the wagon. "Please wait here a minute. I need to confer with Captain Breeden." He dismounted and handed the reins to a nearby private standing guard.

Cassandra studied the area surrounding them. Near the wagon an old man with a long gray beard sat near the door of a café, his chair tilted back against the wall. He eyed the ladies intently. He looked harmless enough and Cassandra was curious. "Pardon me, sir, do you live here?"

"Yes, ma'am, I reckon I do. Been livin' here in these parts for nigh on twenty years."

"Looks like things got pretty hot here."

"Yes, ma'am, it did. An' I was in the thick of it, I was. I was tryin' to sleep in my room above the inn when all hell broke lose!"

Cassandra interested, leaned forward. "Would you tell me about it?"

The old man tipped his chair down on all four legs, tapped the fire out of his pipe and then leaned forward and said, "Last night, about ten o'clock, Quantrill's men rode in an' attacked the Yanks. The Union soldiers expected an attack, so they holed up there in the courthouse. Ole Quantrill's boys tried powerful hard to run 'em out, but them blue bellies were dug in like ticks on a fat dog. They knowed if Quantrill's boys got a hold of 'em, they'd likely be dead anyhow."

The old man began to warm to his story as his face lit up with excitement. "The Yankees had the advantage of the courthouse, an' they killed at least six of Quantrill's boys an' wounded a pile more of 'em. I guess I shouldn't have watched, but I kept lookin' out that window up there. I had a ringside seat, I did. The Missus, she kept tellin' me to keep my fool head down, but I ain't seen such excitement around these parts before, and I'd be danged if I was gonna miss it!"

"It sounds like you were lucky you weren't shot."

"Yes, ma'am, my wife hid under the bed except when she was a yellin' at me. I stayed right there near the window, an' I saw most of it." He pointed the stem of his pipe at the window above the café. "I even heard ole Captain Quantrill himself, screamin' mad. The Yanks killed some of his favorite boys, an' he was fit to be tied. I heard Warner Lewis an' his Rebel boys were to join in on the attack, but they didn't show like they planned."

The gray-haired storyteller poked new tobacco into the bowl of his pipe, tamping it down with his finger. "I heard Quantrill cussin' him somethin' awful for bein' a no good coward an' leavin' 'em hangin' out to dry. Said it was Lewis's own damn plan an' then he goes an' don't show up! Excuse me, ma'am, for the strong language."

"That's all right," she said, then paused. "Mister . . . ?"

"Meeks, ma'am, name is Gabriel Meeks."

"Mister Meeks, the Yankees tried to tell us Quantrill's boys burned the town. It isn't true, is it?"

"I'm afraid it is, ma'am. Never thought Captain Billy would ever hurt a Southern town, but he was in a rage. He was screamin' so loud I could hear him over the gunfire. He even spent time in our café for a while. I heard them break the door lock, an' they were shootin' from our front windows there. Time they were done, didn't have any glass left in 'em." He turned and gestured to empty windows near him, devoid of glass.

He fished a match out of his pocket, and he held it in his hand as if he might strike it on his fingernail at any second. "I heard Cap'n Quantrill tell his men if he couldn't free the town, he'd burn it down around their ears! He tried to burn 'em out, but it didn't work." He lit the match and touched the flame to the bowl of the pipe: two quick puffs and smoke rolled out of his lips.

"Are you telling me that Quantrill's men did set the fires?"

"Yes, ma'am! If'n I'm lyin', I'm dyin'! Them young boys of his were so angry they got carried away. I guess they plumb forgot they weren't in Kansas this time. I don't know why, but he spared our place." The gray-haired gent took a deep pull on his pipe and exhaled through his nose.

Cassandra was shocked by the news. Until now, most of the destruction she had witnessed she could attribute to the Federal forces—but this was clearly different. This time wanton destruction was done by men supposedly on the side of the South. It didn't sit well, but she realized Captain Doyle had been honest with her. She looked back at Gabriel Meeks, who stood slowly, stretching his muscles, tired from sitting too long. "Thank you for telling us your story, Mister Meeks."

"Shucks, ma'am, it was my pleasure. I been dyin' all day long to tell somebody, but I ain't had the chance till you come along. Seems everybody that's fit an' able is out fightin' fires or helpin' others, but I'm too old fer that." He gestured with his pipe toward the café door as he smiled. "My wife is inside cookin', but there ain't been many in to eat it."

Their conversation ended with the reappearance of Captain Doyle, followed by another officer. "Ladies, I'd like to introduce you to Captain Martin Breeden of the Eighth Missouri Cavalry, Federal forces."

The man was obviously tired. The strain from the night was etched into his face. "Well, you're right Captain Doyle. They are indeed beautiful. Ladies, I'm pleased to meet you."

Katlin smiled pleasantly. "How very nice to meet you, sir. I'm so glad you have allowed us to pass through Lamar."

"That's why I'm here, ma'am. You see, Quantrill's men were here last night. We don't know where they are now, but we do know they were headed south. I felt it my duty to warn you of possible danger if you and your party continue south. We don't expect Quantrill will attack us again, now that Captain Doyle has arrived with his troops. Colonel Catherwood and his Sixth Missouri Cavalry are now in hot pursuit of the guerrillas."

"We appreciate your concern for our safety, Captain Breeden, but we wish to continue. As you know, there are few safe places since the war began. We'll take our chances, if you will allow us," said Katlin sweetly.

"As much as the captain here and I would like to detain you, we won't. I can assure you we would welcome the company of women of your rare beauty in our midst, but sympathize with your feelings."

Captain Doyle, staring at Cassandra, added, "I have secured permission from Captain Breeden to accompany you a safe distance from the town and to see you to the correct road to Carthage. Most of my men will stay here to continue helping with the clean-up. We will head out at dawn in pursuit of the guerrillas."

Cassandra felt his appraising glance. She looked at him, much of the anger gone from her. "Thank you, Captain Doyle and Captain Breeden, for your assistance and kind words. We are most grateful."

"Please, ma'am I'd feel more comfortable if you would call me Kenton."

"All right, I'll call you Kenton if you wish." For the first time she smiled at him—a small, shy smile. She continued. "I . . . want to apologize for my behavior back on the road. It's just we've been through so much and I have gotten to where I expect the worst when I see Union soldiers."

"No need to apologize, Miss Kimbrough. I know the war has hurt so very many people already." He touched his fingers to his hat. "Would you ladies be so kind as to accept our hospitality and allow us to buy you dinner here at the inn?

Then, after we eat, we can escort you safely south of the town."

"I think it is a good idea, Cassandra. It is well after noon, and we should eat something," Katlin said quickly.

"Yes, I think it would be good for us to eat and to stretch a little. We've been in the wagon all morning." Cassandra made her mind up and smiled at the captain. "We accept, Kenton, but please, call me Cassandra." She offered him her hand, and he helped her by lifting her then the other ladies down to the sidewalk. They entered the windowless inn.

Three hours later, after sharing a pleasant meal and a mile's ride in the wagon, they parted company with Captain Kenton Doyle and his patrol. She hated to admit it, and would not to anyone other than herself, but she had enjoyed the meal and the conversation.

Kenton Doyle was well educated and charming. He had displayed his ability to command men, and yet he was understanding and sensitive in the face of her anger. She could not help but like him, once she let down her guard. He was as fine a gentleman as she had ever met, and he had a sense of humor that was disarming. Throughout the meal she could feel him staring at her and felt his approving interest, but he treated her like a lady. She could still see his angular, handsome face when she closed her eyes. "If only he hadn't been a Yankee," she thought. "If there wasn't a war, things could have been different."

She hadn't felt this strongly attracted to anyone except Evan Stryker. In many ways they looked similar, she mused. Both had thick, flowing mustaches, but Evan's eyes were brown, while Kenton's were pale blue. Evan's face was not so angular, and his cheekbones and jaw line were not as pronounced as Kenton's. Kenton lacked delightful dimples in the chin and both cheeks that delighted Cassandra. Nor did he have the deep southern drawl of the Texan. Despite his drawbacks, though, she knew she was attracted to this soldier of the North. The acknowledgment of it, even if only to herself, was disturbing.

During dinner they confirmed a Southern army was gathering in northwest Arkansas. After the pursuit of Quantrill was completed, the Second Wisconsin would be joining the Union forces deployed to oppose the Southern army. If they could find their way through the lines of both armies, perhaps she would be reunited with her brothers. One thing was for certain, having a few friends in the Northern army might help them pass through the lines.

She turned from her thoughts and let her mind rest. She prayed silently for a safe trip and for those fighting for the South. She added to the end of the prayer: "Mother, I hope you told Father we love and miss him. If you can see us down here, I hope you'll do what you can to guide us safely south." She drifted off into a deep sleep of exhaustion.

32

Whiskey Rage

Gilbert Thomas tipped the flask of sour mash bourbon back and felt the burn as it slid down to his stomach. He set the flask down and let the coolness of the earth caress his hand. It felt good to sip sour mash and relax a little. He felt the hard, rough pressure of the bark of the tree at his back. Time ... time to think.

This damn war! So busy in stretches, you don't have time to eat or even relieve yourself. Other times, like now, nothing but the endless monotony of camp life. It was these times he had the most trouble handling. Too much time to think and too much time to ease the pain with whiskey.

Always there were thoughts of Cassandra drifting in his mind and filling his dreams. He could still picture the blue-eyed blonde in his mind. It was as if she were forever burned into his memory. The love he felt for her was always tainted by the hurt of her refusal of his marriage offer. The thought of the rejection and the anger he felt, the shame of it, still glowed like fire in his gut. If it weren't for that damn Texan stealing her affection, she would still be his! Stryker with his damn Texas accent ... because he was someone new he swept her off her feet. Well, the captain would pay for it. Nothing meant more to him than Cassandra. By God, he would pay.

He tilted the flask up and chugged down a few long drinks. The glow of the bourbon warmed him and his self-assurance grew. Gil Thomas no longer feared the war. He had faced the elephant and survived. He enjoyed the battles because there he didn't have time to feel sorry for himself or to think about Cassandra.

In battle, and yes ... even in killing, he could pour out his anger and frustration. He could inflict pain as terrible as the pain he himself felt ripping at his guts. He didn't need the solace of a bottle of bourbon when he was in the midst of combat. Action was drug enough.

"All I want from life is the undying love of a beautiful woman like Cassandra," he thought. She was his ideal of everything a woman should be. In his dreams she ran into his arms and welcomed him home after the war. She would hug and kiss him as he lifted her and swung her around. She'd whisper words of love in his ears, the very words he longed to hear. That was all he wanted—her love. He wanted to know she was waiting for him, looking out for his return with open arms filled with love and tenderness. He had read of such love in books and dreamed of such wonders for himself. Still, the burning desire for the beauty of Cassandra beckoned him and drove his desperation and anguish. Was it so much to ask for? The world could deal out whatever it would. All Gil asked for was the love of a woman, one woman—Cassandra.

He felt the pulsing surge of anger rising, fueled by the fire of bourbon in his belly. As the last of the drink slid down his throat, Gil tried to rise. He fought for his balance and stumbled on unsteady feet. It was time to find Stryker and settle it.

It took him a while before he found Evan currying his horse. He approached the smaller Texan without hesitation.

"Stryker, I want to have a word with you!"

Evan turned around slowly. One look told him that Gilbert was drinking again and looking for trouble. "You again, Thomas. I'd have thought the last beating you took would have been enough, even for a man like you."

"You got lucky last time, Stryker. You never would have beaten me if I hadn't been drinking."

"Yes, so what's the difference this time? You've been tipping the bottle plenty. You reek of it."

Gilbert Thomas, moving closer, eased his leather gauntlets from his belt.

"Go back to your camp, Gilbert, and sleep it off. I have no quarrel with you, and I hate to take advantage of a drunk."

Gilbert stepped in close and with a fluid swing struck Evan a hard, stinging blow on his cheek with his gloves. "I challenge you to a duel, you coward," Gilbert taunted, his voice filled with whiskey-soaked anger.

Evan was startled by the sudden move and the sting of the blow. His face flushed and anger colored his cheeks. He felt his hands tighten into fists as the curry brush slid from his hand to the ground. Evan rubbed his cheek with his left hand and turned away, as if to ignore the blow. He twisted, cocking his right arm, and in a blur of motion turned to face the taller Gil Thomas. Evan's right fist caught the surprised Gilbert flush on the chin. The wound-up, right-handed roundhouse punch lifted the taller man off his feet. Gilbert landed on his backside in the dust.

Evan, still clenching his fists, towered over the shocked and dazed Thomas. "I accept, Gil! Sorry I didn't have the gentleman's glove handy to return the favor. Since you challenged me, I believe I then have the honor of selecting the weapons. I pick cavalry sabers at dawn tomorrow. I'll meet you on the other side of the creek, behind your company's camp. No one calls me a coward, Thomas. Tomorrow, you'll eat those words or die!"

Gilbert stared up at Stryker, his vision clouded by the blow. "I didn't expect a gentleman's reply and you didn't disappoint me. I won't be drinking tomorrow, Stryker, and I'll take great pleasure in finishing you then."

"You have what you came for. Now drag your sorry hide out of here, I have work to do." Evan turned his back, picked up the curry brush, and returned to his work.

Gil picked himself up, dusted himself off, and left for his camp.

Evan finished grooming the horse, but all the while his mind whirled with things he could have said, or should have said. He fed and watered his horse. When he finished he went to see Ross Kimbrough.

"What the hell do you two think you're doing? Are you telling me you're going to fight a damn duel in the middle of a war? No!" Ross shook his head. "I don't want anything to do with it. Count me out of this. I'll tell you something and you'd better listen. If Cassandra knew what you two idiots are planning to do, she wouldn't have anything to do with either one of you."

"Come on, Ross. I know it's crazy, but Gil won't let me alone. I'm tired and I want it to end. There is only one way he's going to stop, and I want it to be a fair fight. Come on. You know us both, and we trust you. I know Gilbert won't object if you second the match." Evan looked at Ross with frustration clearly etched on his face. "I'm going to do it with or without you. What do you say?"

"I don't like it at all. I've known Gil for most of my life, and his father is one of my father's best friends. To top it off, I think my sister might be in love with you. Hell! I even like you despite your being a Texan." Ross grinned and shrugged his shoulders. "I just don't want to see this happen. Either way you'll both lose. Cassandra could never abide the idea that one of you killed the other over her. She will never forgive the winner, no matter who it is. Don't you see, either way you'll lose?"

"I suppose you're right. I know you are . . . but I couldn't live with myself knowing I ran from this fight. I have to keep my self-respect, right or wrong."

"You two are just plain, mule-headed fools! I know there is no stopping this, so I guess I'll be there to pick up the pieces. Promise me one thing though, Evan—if you can end this without killing him, I'd appreciate it."

"I'll try, but if it comes down to him or me, he's dead."

"Fair enough. I'll be there in the morning."

"Thank you, Ross, I appreciate it. I'll see you tomorrow." Evan Stryker turned and left. Ross, still shaking his head in disbelief, watched the Texan fade into the gloom of the night.

33

Crossed Swords

Gentlemen, cross swords!" Ross ordered.
    The two men stood toe-to-toe with the blades of their swords crossed at the tips. Both stood right foot to right foot.

"At my command . . . begin!"

The scraping sound of blade on blade followed. Then the clang of metal as Gilbert swung a vicious cut at Evan. Evan blocked the blow and Gil's blade slid to the hilt of Stryker's sword. They stood inches apart, until Evan shoved Gil away. Evan followed Gil with thrusting advances, swinging his sword skillfully, but each blow was parried by Gil as he masterfully retreated. Gil was startled when he abruptly backed into a tree. Evan seized the advantage and leveled a sweeping blow for Gil's head. Gil ducked the blow, and the blade of Stryker's sword bit deep into the bark of the tree. Gil ducked the blow, moved to the right of Stryker, and spun to face him.

Evan tried to pull his sword free, but it was wedged solidly in the bark. Gil kicked his cavalry boot into Evan's chest, shoving him away from his sword, still stuck in the bark.

Evan felt the sword ripped from his fingers as he staggered back, fighting to regain his balance. He stood unarmed and facing a smiling, advancing Gil Thomas. Gil made quick, slashing cuts at Stryker, but each time Evan danced free of the swinging blade.

Gil advanced, aiming the tip of his sword at Evan's chest. Evan tried to avoid the blade as he lunged rapidly to the right. Evan felt the burn as the sword scratched his ribs and then punched through his cavalry jacket.

The movement of the lunge carried Gil forward as Evan spun right. The quickness of the move further entangled the tip of Gil's sword into the material of Evan's cavalry jacket. The quick twist was enough to yank Gil's sword loose from his grip. As Evan continued his spin, the sword, propelled by the momentum of Stryker's move, pulled free of the material and went skittering across the ground.

Both men stood disarmed. Gil eyed Evan's sword still stuck in the tree bark. It was the closest weapon and he ran for it. Evan charged him and made a diving tackle. Evan's shoulder drove into Gil's back, throwing him off balance and throwing him to the ground. Evan grabbed a generous amount of Gil's hair and tried to turn the larger man onto his back.

The echoing sound of a revolver split the morning air. Both men froze in place, startled by the sudden gunfire. In shocked disbelief they stared into the angry, bearded face of Colonel Jo Shelby.

"Atten . . . hut!" Ross shouted. He had been watching the combatants and was as startled as they by the appearance of their commanding officer. He pulled himself erect. Gilbert and Evan rose quickly to their feet, and the three stood side by side at rigid attention.

"Gentlemen, what is going on here?"

Gilbert spoke first. "Just a little disagreement, sir."

"Just a little disagreement, is it." Shelby faced the two and glared at them. "The rumor going around camp is that you are fighting a duel. I'd say that's a little more than just a little disagreement, wouldn't you?"

"Pardon me, sir, but I think Captain Thomas meant this is

an affair of honor concerning just the two of us. We wished to handle it privately."

Anger flashed in Jo Shelby's eyes as he listened to Evan Stryker's reply. His face became strained as he fought to control his temper. "Captain Stryker, you are a member of my personal staff. Anything you do reflects personally on your commanding officer. Do I make myself clear?"

"Yes, sir!"

"Captain Thomas, you are a company commander for a regiment in my command. Is that correct?"

"Yes, sir!"

"Then, gentlemen, what you are doing and anything else you might do is my business. Is that understood?"

Both men responded quickly and in unison. "Yes, sir!"

"You listen to me and you damn well better listen good. You two self-centered fools are busy fighting a duel between two gentlemen in the middle of a God damn war! If you're looking for a fight, then I've got good news for you. Just a little north of here there are at least two Yankee armies with somewhere in the neighborhood of ten thousand men. Beyond that, Missouri is swarming with Union troops. Do you really think we have the time, or the men to spare, for you to have your little affair of honor?"

By now Colonel Shelby was shouting loudly in the men's faces. His veins were bulging in his temples, and his face was growing purple as his anger mounted. "You men, get this straight. The day you signed on with me and received your commissions, gentlemen, is the day your ass belonged to me! I need every capable officer and soldier I can get in my ranks. The South needs every man in her service we can get and we can't afford to squander even one. I'll not have two candy-ass gentlemen fightin' any God damn duel in my outfit! Is that understood?"

"Yes, sir."

"What was that? I didn't hear you."

"Yes, sir!"

"That's more like it. I want to make this clear to you both

so there isn't any way you might not understand my meaning. Are you both listening carefully?" Shelby said more calmly.

"If I hear of any more incidents involving you two, I will personally court-martial you both. Any argument you might have can wait until after the war. If the Yankees don't kill you first, you can fight it out then, and I won't give a damn. Don't even think about crossing me on this, gentlemen, or I swear there won't be a place big enough, or far enough away, to hide your sorry asses from my wrath! Now I want you two to turn and shake hands and promise you'll settle this after the war has ended."

The men hesitated. They looked at Colonel Shelby, then at each other. Neither wanted to make the first move.

"By Gawd, I gave a direct order—I'll not ask again!"

The two captains turned and faced each other. Gilbert spoke first. "Since I first offered the challenge, then I ask for a postponement until after the war has ended. If that is acceptable, Captain Stryker?"

"I don't think we have any other choice. I accept the postponement."

The two reached out their hands and shook hands firmly. The group began to disperse.

"Lieutenant Kimbrough, might I have a word privately with you as we walk back to camp?"

"Yes, sir."

When they were alone, Ross said, "I want to thank you, Colonel Shelby, for the way you handled this."

"I'm just glad you brought this to my attention last night, Ross. You did the right thing."

"Thank you, sir, but I must admit I was beginning to wonder if you would show up before they killed each other."

Colonel Shelby smiled as he gave a sideways glance at Ross. "I know I could have broke it up a little sooner, and by delaying my entrance one of them might have been killed, but they needed to work off a little of their anger." The two men stopped walking and turned to face each other, as Jo Shelby leaned against a tree. "I seriously doubt they would have followed my orders if I hadn't allowed them to fight first. A man needs his honor and a chance to prove his mettle. I gave them an honorable way out of this mess and I'm glad they took it."

"I am too, sir."

"I think secretly they are, as well. I doubt deep down they really want to kill each other. Besides, the South truly is in need of her sons." The two friends started walking toward headquarters.

"I'm not so sure, sir, Gilbert's anger runs deep. He will keep his word, because he is a man of honor, but when the war ends he'll have his duel."

"You know, Ross, chances are they both won't live to see the end of the war, anyway. If they do, then maybe they'll find another way to resolve their problems."

"I hope so, Colonel, thanks again." Ross left Jo Shelby in front of his headquarters tent and returned to his scouts.

34

Camp at Cross Hollows

As Ross arrived at his scouts' camp, he noticed men gathering in clusters, watching the road, and murmuring in low voices. Curiosity getting the best of him, Ross ran to join Jonas Starke and Rube Anderson. "What's everyone gawking at?"

"Company of horse soldiers comin' in, and they're a mite peculiar in dress. Better see for yourself," Jonas answered.

Ross elbowed his way through the crowd and looked down the road at the approaching riders.

At the head of the column rode a man of average height in a dusty regulation captain's uniform. It was easy to tell he was an experienced horseman; yet his posture was slouched, as if he had a great weight upon his shoulders.

Beside him rode another man, wearing an unusual rust-colored shirt cut low in front, the slit narrowing to a point just above his belt and ending in a rosette. The shirt had four large pockets on it, two of them located over his breasts. Protruding from each of these pockets were revolvers. Both men rode excellent mounts that were well muscled and in fit condition.

Following the first two riders rode two more men dressed similarly to the one in the fancy shirt riding in the lead, but in shirts of different colors. The rider directly behind the officer carried a large, black flag, fully displayed and snapping briskly in the wind. The man beside him was obviously a bugler. Behind them in columns of four riders abreast followed the remainder of the company.

Ross stood in amazement, watching the parade pass before him. Nearly all the men were dressed in fancy shirts, with colors ranging from red to butternut brown. Many had very elaborate needlework displayed on the shirts. Guns protruded from all over the boys, draped over and on their saddles. Bowie knives were crammed into belts and sticking out of boot tops on most of the riders. It struck Ross that this was the heaviest armed band he had ever seen, but there were very few rifles or carbines among them. Revolvers, and lots of them, were the standard fare upon these hard-eyed riders. Most wore wide-brimmed, nonregulation hats in various colors of black, brown, and gray.

"Who the hell is it?" Rube asked.

"I'll bet my eyeteeth, boys, that you're lookin' at William Clarke Quantrill's company," Ross whispered with some reverence. Rube and Jonas both turned to look at Ross, then swept their eyes across the column of riders.

"I 'spect you're right, Ross, but what in blue blazes are they doin' here? I thought they was an irregular outfit that stayed in Missouri? Ain't they a mite far from home?"

"I don't know what brings them this far south, Jonas, but I bet we'll know the reason soon enough."

Rube spit an amber stream of tobacco into the road. "I'm guessin' they just needed a breather from the Yanks an' they figured if they'd join us a while, they'd get a rest."

As the column continued to pass in front of them, Ross scanned the faces of the passing soldiers. Already these men had a legendary reputation for daring, vicious attacks against the enemy. To most Confederate Missourians who'd felt the

stinging injustice of life under Union rule, his band of guerrillas striking back in daring raids upon the enemy were seen
as heroic. While most of the Missouri Confederates had been
driven from the state, Quantrill and a few other bands stayed
behind.

As he stared at them, Ross was struck with the realization
of how young most of them were. They were a tough-looking
unit—most were young boys without beards—yet there was
no denying they had the look of men used to danger and killing.

One rider looked familiar to Ross, but he just couldn't
place the face. The boy was young, no more than fourteen or
fifteen years old, but he wore a hard-eyed look of experience
many years beyond his age.

"Hey, ain't that the boy we met when we were headin'
north to Lafayette County?" asked Jonas.

Now Ross remembered. "Yeah, that's the boy who jumped
me back in Bates County. He knocked me clean out of the
saddle."

"I remember," Rube said, "His ma had gone half crazy,
and the Jayhawkers had burned them out and kilt his pa."

"An' now he's ridin' with Quantrill," Jonas said in amazement.

"Boys, you stay here. I'll see if I can get that young wildcat to come back here and visit with us a spell." Ross turned
and jogged down the road, trailing the column of riders toward the headquarters of the brigade.

The column stopped and the men remained in their saddles.
Ross ran down the line until he reached the boy they had recognized. Ross approached him and touched him on the knee,
"Excuse me, you look familiar, and I was wondering if you
were the Cahill boy from Bates County?"

The youthful boy eyed him. Then a spark of recognition lit
his eyes and he smiled and replied, "It's you, ain't it. You and
your company come along right after I buried Pa."

"You almost stove in my ribs when you knocked me out of
the saddle. I thought I'd been attacked by a wildcat!"

The boy smiled, then began to laugh. When he quieted

down, his look became more serious. "Yeah, I reckon that was the only funny thing I can look back on durin' those times."

"What happened to your ma?"

"She's fine." The boy's eyes clouded a little as he thought about his mother. "She didn't want to leave Missouri, an' she went to stay with my aunt. She snapped out of her grievin' and gets along fine. My aunt knew one of Quantrill's boys an' took me to him. I've been payin' back them Jayhawkers a lick, an' I hope to kill more of 'em before I'm through. Captain Quantrill don't cut them any slack, an' that's just fine with me."

"What are you doing this far south? I thought you boys fought close to home?"

"Shucks, I don't make the orders, I just follow them. I heard Captain Billy is plannin' to go to Richmond for a spell, an' until he gets back we've got orders to ride with your brigade."

Ross smiled at the news. These men and boys were known for their reckless daring in combat. He knew they would be a welcome addition, and he was very glad they were on the same side. "When you get your camp set up, just follow the road down to our camp. My boys would be proud to hear about Quantrill's raiders and your adventures."

"You can count on me if you've got somethin' to eat. I'm real tired of my cookin'."

"You're welcome to eat, such as we have." Ross shook his hand and turned away.

Evan Stryker stood next to Colonel Shelby as the head of the column approached headquarters. The officer in command wore a Confederate officer's uniform, but he rode in stark contrast to the rest of his men who seemed to have their own uniforms. The rider pulled his horse to a halt and signaled to the column to stop. The slouching officer slid wearily to the ground and handed the reins of his horse to the man behind him.

"Lieutenant Gregg, have the men remain mounted." Without waiting for a response he turned and strode toward Colonel Shelby and his staff. He stopped in front of the colonel and snapped off a loose salute. "Are you Colonel Jo Shelby?"

"I'm Colonel Shelby, now who the devil are you?"

Although the officer smiled, his thin lips still curled down. "I've been called a devil and much worse I suspect. I am Captain William Clarke Quantrill and these are my men." He glanced back over his shoulder at his troops then turned to face the colonel. He reached in his pocket, withdrew an envelope, and handed it to Colonel Shelby. "I have orders from General Marmaduke assigning my men to your command. My orders are included."

Jo Shelby took the papers and studied them. The rest of the men waited patiently for him to conclude reading the communication. After a pause of a minute or two, Colonel Shelby folded the letter and replaced it in the envelope. "This letter from the general is very interesting, Captain. It says you are on your way to Richmond and, until you return, your men are to be assigned to my command. Might I ask what business you have in Richmond?"

"I don't mind telling you, Colonel Shelby. I'm going to Richmond to ask for a promotion. I believe if I were made a colonel or even a general and given command of a brigade, I could drive the Yankee scum clear out of Missouri."

"Pardon me, Captain Quantrill, but I think you'll find it one thing to have success with a small band of renegades playing hit and run before fading off into the night, and quite another to operate in the field as part of an army."

Evan watched Captain Quantrill pull himself up to his five foot eleven inches. His eyes, a strange gray-blue color that seemed full of threat and danger, burned with a quick and sudden fury. Quantrill's curled lips and Roman nose were not the sort of features one would expect to find on a man considered rather handsome, but there they were. He was a young man—in his mid-twenties, Evan guessed. Quantrill was slender of build, weighing maybe one hundred seventy pounds soaking wet. He had blond hair and bronzed features from days spent in the saddle. His side whiskers and mustache had a reddish cast to them.

Quantrill responded to Shelby's remarks. "On the contrary, Colonel. I see a brigade in my command operating as I do now and using the same tactics, only on a larger scale. Hit the enemy, then run, then strike him repeatedly. I already strike terror in the hearts of my enemies. Think of the panic I could cause with a thousand men!"

"I don't doubt the courage of you or your men and I don't care a damn about politics, or politicians. So I'm glad it is you who are preparing to face those political scalawags in Virginia and not I. Meanwhile, I welcome your men to my command while you make your trip to Richmond." Shelby turned toward Captain Edwards. "Captain Edwards, assign Quantrill's men to a regiment, and find them a place to set up camp."

"Yes, sir!" Captain John Edwards stepped forward to join the captain and colonel. "I'd like to assign them to Major Shank's regiment. His regimental numbers are the lowest."

"That will work just fine, Edwards; see to it. Good day to you, Captain Quantrill. I have other duties to attend to, and I'm sure you'll need to see to your men and prepare for your trip." Colonel Shelby reentered his tent. Quantrill returned to his horse and swung into his saddle.

"If you'll follow me, Captain, I'll show you where to set up your camp."

"Just lead the way, Captain Edwards."

One hundred and fifty of Missouri's toughest guerrillas followed Quantrill into their new camp.

Ross listened to the fat pop and sizzle in the pan as the aroma of fried bacon mixed with the fragrant scent of burning pine logs. The smell made his stomach ache with hunger. Jonas hunkered over the pan, prodding the bacon with his Bowie knife.

Ross said, "You're going to worry that bacon to death, Jonas. It won't cook any faster by fiddling with it."

"Who's doin' the cookin' here, you or me?"

"You are."

"Then I guess I'll do'er my way, if'n it's all right with you, Lieutenant."

"Now don't get huffy, Jonas, I'm just making conversation."

"Instead of criticizing my cookin', why don't you make yourself useful and check on them biscuits there in the Dutch oven. They oughter be about ready, Lieutenant."

Ross moved to the Dutch oven resting on the fire and looked in on the biscuits. "They look ready to me." He slid one of his leather cavalry gauntlets on, pulled the tin out, and placed it on a rock to cool.

Jonas moved over and gave his final approval. "Yep, they look good an' brown. Too bad we don't have honey or jam to put on 'em. I'll just slice them in half, an' we can lay bacon in there." Ross, occupied with the biscuits, didn't notice the three soldiers approaching their camp.

"Smells mighty fine, Lieutenant. I hope you can spare some biscuits." Ross turned to see Billy Cahill standing with two companions. "I brought along some friends. I hope ya don't mind. We brought along extra food we can cook up on your fire."

"No problem at all, Billy. Good food and good company are always welcome. Give me a hand and we'll drag another log up close to the fire for y'all to sit on."

The work was quickly done, and Billy pulled a ham and a jug out of a gunny sack. "Slice some of this up, Lieutenant, and put it on the fire. Ought to be mighty tasty with that bacon an' biscuits. I got us a jug of apple jack we can wash it down with later." He handed the ham to Jonas.

"Lieutenant, I'd like ya to meet Frank James an' Riley Crawford." The boys both stepped forward. Ross eyed them while shaking their hands firmly and watched as they eased themselves down on the log. What he saw surprised him. Frank was the taller of the two and looked rail thin and about nineteen years old. Riley looked even younger than Billy. He was only a boy, short in stature with a baby face. Both boys wore the guerrilla shirts, every pocket stuffed with a revolver.

Ross couldn't resist commenting on Riley's youthfulness. "I'm mighty surprised to see Quantrill lets young boys ride with him in a man's war."

Ross watched Riley's hands ball up into fists, while his eyes narrowed, angry and hard as flint. Frank laid his hand on Riley's shoulder, holding him back. Ross shifted his gaze to the flat gray eyes of Frank James.

"Looks can be deceiving. Riley is the same age as Billy, an' they got more in common than ya think. Riley has killed as many men as anyone in our company, an' he's only fourteen."

"Settle down, boys. I didn't mean to rile you. I didn't mean anything by it. I've heard so much about Quantrill's bushwackers, and you're just not what I expected. Somehow, I pictured you all to be ten feet tall and meaner looking than a mountain man." Frank and Riley looked at one another and broke into smiles. "Let me introduce you to a few of my scouts. This is Jonas Starke, Rube Anderson, and Terrill Fletcher—we usually call him, Fletch." The men nodded and exchanged handshakes. "Shouldn't take Jonas long to finish cooking."

"I'll put some more biscuit batter in the oven, if you'll slice the ham for fryin', Rube," Jonas said. "That ham is gonna taste great fried in bacon grease."

Ross said, "Riley, I want to apologize if I offended you, but I have to admit I'm curious how you started riding with Quantrill."

Ross watched the last of Riley's anger ease out of the boy. "It's all right, Lieutenant, you're not the first to say somethin' and I reckon ya won't be the last." Riley picked up a stick and started scratching designs in the dirt by his feet as he talked. "Jayhawkers came to our home and killed my pa, Jeptha Riley, same as they done to Billy's daddy. Ma took me to Captain Billy an' begged him to let me ride with 'em. Quantrill did cause he figured I had a right to pay back them Yankee murderin' scum. I ain't let him down. I've killed every Yankee I've come across, an' I give them the same chance my pa got—none." He stared at Ross with the cold, cruel eyes of a deadly killer.

Frank said, "Riley is a crack shot with a pistol and an excellent horseman. The Yanks let him ride in close to them sometimes. They don't expect any trouble from a boy, an' that's usually their last mistake. Riley doesn't take prisoners."

Ross thought about the cruelty of war and how it could take mere boys and turn them into blood-thirsty killers. These boys might be young in years, but they were clearly more dangerous than rattlesnakes. He was glad he didn't have to face them in a gunfight. "How many men does Quantrill have with him?" Ross asked.

Frank James answered, "We brought nearly one hundred and fifty men, but some of our boys refused to leave Missouri. One of my best friends, Cole Younger, stayed there. A few others stayed with him. Let me tell ya about Cole—we call him Bud, mostly. His father, Henry, was murdered and robbed by Cap'n Walley of the Union Fifth Missouri Militia. Bud hopes if he stays in Missouri, he might get a chance to kill Cap'n Walley. The Youngers have had it rougher than most. In sixty-one, Jayhawkers robbed them. This year Union troops burned their home. Later the Yanks killed their pa, Henry.

"I had a devil of a time makin' up my mind whether to stay with Bud, too, but Ma wanted me to leave. She was afraid I'd get my younger brother, Jesse, mixed up in this— she says he's too young. Jesse's best friend is Jim Younger, Cole Younger's little brother."

"Sounds like most of your riders have had family killed by the Yanks and the Jayhawkers."

"Not all, but most of us have been wronged one way or another."

Rube Anderson bit a good-sized chunk off a plug of tobacco he fished from his pocket. He worked the chaw hard before he cut loose an amber stream and let it sizzle in the fire's red hot coals. "You boys have a powerful reputation. I know the Yankees fear you ole boys worse than death itself." Rube glanced at Frank James. "Tell us about some of your better riders, Frank."

"Well, other than Captain Billy, we generally follow Bill Gregg or George Todd. I think Jim Little is probably Captain Billy's best friend, but he stayed with Bud in Missouri. I think Andy Blount is goin' with Quantrill to Richmond in the mornin'. Jim Little's brother John and Ed Koger got killed back in August. They were both good men. There's John McCorkle, Bill Anderson, Archie Clement, Dick Yeager, David Poole, Fletch Taylor, John Thrailkill, and Larkin Sqaggs," Frank said, straining to remember names.

"Don't forget Perry Hays; Babe, Rufus, and Bob Hudspeth; Ollie and George Shepherd; Ab Haller; Tom, Tuck, and Woot Hill; Bill Greenwood; and Doc Campbell, just to name a few," added Riley.

"These two here are as good as any of 'em, an' better'n most," said Billy Cahill. Frank smiled, his eyes catching the dancing flames of the campfire.

Jonas grumbled, "This bacon is gettin' cold. You boys get to eatin' it, while I fry this ham up." He passed around a plate of bacon and biscuits.

Ross savored the smokehouse fresh bacon and the taste of the biscuit as he bit into it. The boys settled into eating, and soon the ham was passed around in generous slabs. They ate the ham in thick slices, too hungry to wait for the second batch of biscuits to finish. They talked as they ate.

Ross had noticed a few things about Quantrill's men, and he couldn't let it pass without asking about them. "I watched you boys ride in here today, and I noticed all Quantrill's men ride prime horseflesh."

Between mouthfuls, Frank James replied, "Yes, sir. Captain Billy says if you want to survive ya got to have the best horses. We ride the best we can buy, steal, beg, or borrow. We take 'em from the Yankees whenever we can."

"I didn't see many muskets or rifles among your men, and yet I've never seen so many pistols."

Riley chuckled and winked at Frank, then said, "Bill Gregg, George Todd, and Captain Billy are responsible for that. See, they figured tryin' to load a musket or rifle from a runnin' horse was plumb crazy. If you're usin' a musket, you only get one shot. With pistols you get five to six shots before reloading, and if you carry several revolvers, you can lay down a lot more lead quicker than the enemy. The more revolvers you got the longer it is before ya gotta stop and reload.

"A revolver is easier to handle and aim from the back of a horse, anyway, and for close work they are deadly. Much better than a sword."

"We use revolvers ourselves, but they aren't much good at long distance."

"You're right, Lieutenant, but most of our fightin' is in close. We charge right over 'em or catch 'em in ambush. We leave the long distance fightin' to the regular troops. Hit 'em hard and move out quick, that's the way Quantrill's men fight."

"Quantrill's men have a reputation for being ruthless in battle, and I've heard you don't take prisoners," said Terrill Fletcher.

Billy glared at Fletcher as the firelight danced in his eyes, giving him a devilish look. "The Yankees made the choice, not us. General Halleck, that son-of-a-bitch blue-belly, issued his order number two in March of this year. It says any irregular troops or guerrillas will be considered outlaws. If they catch us they hang us, or shoot us down on the spot without a trial. They don't give us any quarter, so we figured to do the same. That's why Quantrill flies the black flag and why we don't take prisoners. When you know it's death if you're captured, you never surrender."

"Yeah, I can see where that would make yer backbone a little stiffer come a fight," Jonas said. "Say, how about passing that jug around. I believe I got a piece of biscuit caught in my gullet."

Riley Crawford grabbed the jug, uncorked it, tipped it up, and took a couple of swallows. He passed it to Jonas. Jonas wiped off the neck of the jug and tilted it back. "Whoo whee! That is smooth applejack! Ya gotta take a shot of this, Ross."

Leave it to his men to call him by name, instead of rank. Well, what did it matter, Ross thought, as he grasped the jug and took a long drink. He felt the sweet taste of apple, smooth and mellow, and felt the glow of the alcohol as it warmed him. "It's mighty fine, Riley. Where did you find this?"

"We picked it up at a little town called Lamar in Missouri. We tried to capture a garrison stationed in Lamar, but they hid in a brick courthouse. They had it heavily barricaded, an' we couldn't get 'em outa there. Hell, we even tried smokin' 'em out, but it didn't work. The boys got a mite carried away with the fire startin' and the winds fanned the flames and it got away from us. Anyway, while we were there I found this jug. I've been savin' it for something special, an' I guess this is good as any."

Ross took another chug on the jug and passed it to Billy. "How long have you been with Quantrill, Billy?"

"I joined in October. We captured a Yankee wagon train and then we hit Shawneetown, Kansas. That was my first fight. We burned Shawneetown to the ground. Gave them damn Red Legs some of their own medicine. We shot down ten of 'em right where they stood. We caught another wagon train in Missouri on our way down here and killed the soldiers escorting it. Then we hit Lamar. We crossed over to Kansas and took the Fort Scott road south till we turned east and reached here."

Riley smiled, then said, "I've been with Captain Billy longer. Cahill missed out on the other two Kansas raids when we hit Olathe and Aubrey. We showed 'em how it feels to be under the torch."

Ross grew silent, and he looked away from Billy and his friends. He heard the laughter from his scouts as conversation swirled on without him. The talk about war against Kansas towns just didn't set right with Ross. Fighting soldiers was one thing, but war on civilians just wasn't right. Wanton destruction and theft in the name of any cause was not justified in Ross's eyes. A man had a right to take what he needed to keep on fighting; but to take for gain or vengeance, just for the sake of hurting others, was something he found personally repugnant.

Maybe, if he'd suffered under the Jayhawkers like Billy or Riley, he might see it differently. Yet, somehow, it seemed all wrong. Maybe he was just getting soft as he got older. During the border wars with bleeding Kansas in his youth, he hadn't hesitated to take the war to the Free-Staters. As he gained in years and faced mounting dangers, life became more precious to him. In his youth he felt invincible, almost bullet-proof, but now he understood no man could dodge bullets forever.

Besides, gentlemen fought war like men, not like wild animals injured and biting, slashing out at anything they could reach. No, war should be fought by the rules. Yet this was a war more like a no-holds-barred, bare-fisted fight to the death. Only one side would walk out a winner—the other would be devastated.

This was nothing at all like the idealistic, chivalrous war among gentlemen that he had envisioned back in 1861 when he first went to war. Somewhere, that war got sidetracked. Now it was all black and deadly and rolling out of control, sweeping all reason before it. This was the hell on earth only the devil and his dark lords could relish.

Ross, warmed by the applejack in his belly, laughed to himself. A couple of good belts of applejack and he was turning into a philosopher. He tried to focus on the conversation through the liquor-induced fog creeping over his brain.

"Ross," he felt someone shaking his shoulder, stirring him from his thoughts. "Ross, can we talk to you alone for a minute?" The familiar voice came from behind him, but the tone of the voice told him something was wrong. He turned around and rose to his feet. In the gathering gloom of the evening, warmed by the light of the fire, Ross saw his two brothers, Calvin and Jessie.

One look at their faces made his stomach tighten. He felt fear grip at his throat as he tried to remain calm. It was serious business when he saw his brothers look that grim. Both had red-rimmed eyes, and neither had a trace of their usual confidence and good-natured humor.

It was Calvin who had spoken, so Ross asked him, already fearing his reply, "What's the matter, Calvin? What's wrong?"

"I'd rather we talked in private, Ross. It's important."

Ross turned back toward the fire. "Gentlemen, enjoy the jug. I'll be back in a few minutes. I have some business to discuss." He turned back to his brothers. "All right, boys, let's take a little walk and get this straightened out."

After walking clear of the campfire to where they wouldn't be overheard, Ross asked, "What in hell is wrong with you and Jessie? I know it's big to have you both this stirred up."

The brothers stopped walking. Jessie stared off into the woods, unwilling to face this moment of truth. The stars were starting to come out. Laughter from men around the campfires and the sounds of horses softly nickering drifted to them along the road. Ross looked away from Jessie, who was avoiding his eyes, and studied Calvin. Calvin tried to speak. He opened his mouth, but the words wouldn't come. He coughed as he cleared his throat, and tears welled up in his eyes. He looked down at his feet.

"Damn it, Cal, tell me what is going on!"

"I don't know any easy way to break this to ya, Ross. Father is dead."

Ross couldn't believe his ears. He stood in disbelief and shock. It was as if someone had hit him with a club. "What did you say?"

"I said, 'Father is dead.' The Yankees burned Briarwood to the ground."

Disbelief and anger filled Ross like a balloon reaching its bursting point. "Where did you get this nonsense!"

Tears streaked down Jessie's face as he shouted, "Shut up and listen, Ross. Cal's tellin' the truth. I've seen the letter."

"What letter? What are you guys talking about?"

"A friend of mine, Wash Mayes, rode into camp this afternoon with a letter from Cassandra. It brought the bad news, and I figured you wouldn't believe me until you read it yourself. I brought it with me." Calvin reached into his pocket, pulled out the wrinkled letter, and gave it to Ross.

Ross took the letter and held it in his hands. Dread filled his heart, for he recognized Cassandra's handwriting. He really didn't want to read it, yet he felt torn by the need to know. "I've got to find some light."

Ross didn't want to go back to his campfire. Too many people there would ask too many questions he wasn't prepared to face. He decided to walk down the road a short distance and look for a campfire with fewer soldiers. He found what he wanted when he spotted a small fire with only two soldiers hovering near the cheering warmth. He moved into the circle of light.

"Pardon me, boys, mind if I use the light of your fire to read a letter?"

He didn't know either trooper, but their faces looked familiar. "Help yourself, you're welcome to the light."

"Thanks, it won't take too long."

Ross opened the letter and began to read in the dim light. Cassandra's words cut him as if someone had stabbed him in the chest with a Bowie knife. Sure enough, his father was dead and Briarwood burned to the ground. The Union officer responsible for this attack was a Jayhawker named Major Benton Bartok.

The letter informed him that Cassandra, Elizabeth, and his mother were heading toward Arkansas at this very moment. Traveling as companions were three slaves—or former slaves—Becca, Fanny, and Jethro. He was surprised to read Katlin Thomas was with them. He knew how Jessie felt about Katlin and realized she must be coming with marriage on her mind. The letter was genuine. There was no doubt it was from Cassandra, and he knew in his heart it was all true. He tried to choke back the pain and tears that clouded his vision as he attempted to finish the letter.

He read about his mother's illness. It sounded like it was serious. He realized the women would be traveling south through hostile territory, and the thought of them facing those added dangers heightened his fears. It was clear they intended to reach Fayetteville, Arkansas, by early December. If the boys could not meet them, they were to leave a letter with instructions at the Fayettville post office telling them where they should go.

Ross folded the letter neatly and stuffed it back into the soiled envelope. He could barely see it for the tears blurring his eyes. His jaw was tightly clenched, fighting back the need to scream. His hands shook and made his efforts more difficult. He handed the letter to Calvin and stumbled away from the fire.

The soldiers watched Ross as he read, and they knew better than to disturb a man trying to deal with bad news. They didn't speak as he walked away.

"Thanks, boys, for the use of your fire," Calvin said.

"You're welcome to it any time." The bearded old veteran motioned toward Ross and said, "From the way he looked I'd say it was a dose of bad news. I hope next time his news is better." Calvin, nodding in acknowledgement, turned to follow Jessie and Ross.

Ross stumbled blindly down the road. Where it lead to didn't matter and he didn't care. He heard his two brothers following him, but neither tried to stop him. He felt the pain of loss welling up within him, threatening to drown him in sorrow. Ross stopped in the middle of the road, tears streaming down his face. He shook his fists into the night and screamed in pain and anger. "Gawd damn this stinking war, Gawd damn it all to hell! So help me, God, I'll make the Yankees pay for this! I'll kill every one of those sorry bastards I can get my hands on!"

Calvin and Jessie were beside him now, but he took little notice of them. Remorse like he never felt before clutched at his guts. "Ah, Father, I should have been there with you," he choked out.

"We both felt the same Ross, but you know Father wanted us to do our duty. Chances are nothing would have been different if we had been there. There wouldn't have been enough of us, and Father was a stubborn man," Calvin said softly, as he gripped Ross's shoulder.

"Cal, I . . . never told him how much I loved him."

"He was always proud of you, Ross. I know you both had words when you went off to Kansas and again when you decided to go off to war. He didn't want you to go, but he was still damn proud of you. He told everyone who would listen about you being in the army. Every time we got a letter, he'd dang near wear it out reading it. He loved you, Ross, and at least you two had time to heal some old hurts when you came home. I know how you feel, but I know Father knew you loved him and I know he loved you. He had room in his heart for all of us."

"Why did he have to go and get himself killed."

"You know the answer, Ross. Father always fought for those things worth fighting for. For him there were only three things that he put above all else—God, his family, and Briarwood. He'd fight the very devil himself before he would give up any of them. I guess that's why we're so stubborn, because of him. It's in our blood."

Ross was becoming calmer now; the sobs had lessened. "Yeah, I reckon you're right, Cal. I loved that old man, and I'll even the score with that Bartok the first chance I get." Suddenly, Ross felt confused. Earlier he'd struggled with the notion of war against civilians, even if they were from Kansas. Now he too had felt a terrible blow struck by the Jayhawkers. He was beginning to understand how Riley and Billy Cahill felt.

"Don't worry, Ross, we all want a piece of Bartok. The time will come and justice will play itself out."

The next few days were hard on all the brothers. They grieved for their father and for their lost childhood home. Each was plagued by self-doubt and guilt about what had happened and wondered if it would have been different if only they had been there. They worried about their mother and sisters on the road and envisioned all sorts of horrible scenarios. Jessie's anguish was increased by worrying about Katlin. Time was their enemy, for time let them fret and chafe about the women.

Ross was relieved when he got the word: Shelby wanted them to move north. North toward Cane Hill; north toward the enemy. North held yet another lure. It would bring them ever closer to the girls and a family reunion.

Ambush

Ross Kimbrough strained his eyes against the impenetrable darkness of the night. He shifted his weight against the tree as he fought to ease some of the stiffness. He might not see them, but Ross knew he could hear Yankees should they come this way.

Ross had been waiting for several hours. He had scouted the area and decided that if the Yankee attack came it would come down this road. At least he'd believed it when he started the vigil. Now, he was beginning to have doubts. Ross checked to see, for what must have been the third or fourth time, if all the buttons were fastened. He pulled his jacket tighter, but the cool, late November air seemed to seep through his clothes no matter what he did. At least the big oak tree he was leaning against blocked the wind. It would soon be dawn. Already to the east he saw the false dawn beginning to lighten the sky, and he could see better with each passing minute.

Sultan stood nearby, trying to find substance out of the dried-out brush around him. Sultan was thinner than Ross would have liked him to be, for the horse had been on short rations since the first frost had killed the grass. Hay and feed were in short supply in the Confederate army, and it was no better for the soldiers.

Ross had recently notched a new hole in his belt to keep up his pants. Even now his stomach growled, reminding him of the added discomfort of hunger. When he first decided to keep watch on this section of road, anticipation of the enemy galloping into view at any moment was enough to keep him vigilant. Now, after several hours had passed, anticipation was replaced by boredom. His mind began to wander more easily.

Try as he might, his thoughts still wandered to the death of his father. It was just two weeks ago that he had learned of the destruction of Briarwood. In his mind he had trouble grasping the reality of it, like a bad dream he wished would just go away. He supposed he would never come to terms with his emotions and the finality of it all until he saw the ashes of Briarwood for himself and stood at his father's grave. A part of him fought to resist believing what had happened. Yet another part of him knew it was true, and he grieved hard over his loss. Anger and pain changed him. The war was now very personal. It was his war now to the bitter end, and he would not stop until it was won. His father's death had to mean something, stand for something. It put a blood-lust for the fight in his heart. The Confederacy must win or his suffering, his loss, would be for nothing. He was determined it wouldn't happen.

Even thoughts of Valissa Covington had been displaced as he dealt with his grief. He needed to write and tell her, but he lacked the courage to face the truth and put pen to paper, as if doing so would make his nightmare a reality. He must write her, even though he had put it off, for he knew he must ask her to find a place for his family to stay.

He looked around his tree to see if Fletch was still alert. Earlier he had dozed off, so Ross thought it wise to keep an eye on him. He knew Fletch was tired—they all were. For the two weeks since they left camp at Cross Hollows they were constantly in the saddle patrolling and looking for the enemy. Even now, Shelby's command stood ready near Cane Hill, just a little south of the Missouri line in northwest Arkansas.

The Yanks would come; of this he was certain. They had fought clashes with Yankee patrols, while rumors and reports of Union movements filtered into the camps daily. Ross and his scouts kept busy constantly making sure they weren't surprised when the expected Union attack materialized. Well, if they were coming down this road today, they would soon know it.

Jonas should have returned by now—how long did it take to check down the road two or three miles? Then he heard the sound of a galloping horse, even before he could see it, coming over the hill. Both men pulled their horses closer to them, and Ross put his hand over Sultan's nose so he wouldn't whinny and give them away. Jonas Starke rode into sight and Ross stepped into the road, leading Sultan behind him. He waited until Jonas pulled up his horse in front of him.

"You guessed it right, Lieutenant. There's a large force of Yankees movin' this way not more'n a couple miles back."

"Fletch, you better ride ahead and tell Colonel Shelby. Jonas, stay with me and give your horse a rest. Looks like you've been riding her hard."

Jonas quickly relayed what he had seen to Terrill Fletcher. Fletch swung into his saddle and rode off at a quick trot.

"How long do you think it'll take them to get here, Jonas?"

"They're movin' in column, Ross, but they got infantry with 'em. The foot soldiers will slow them down a mite. I figure Colonel Jo will have time to set up a right nasty surprise for 'em."

"I'll feel better if we watch the road until they come into sight, then we'll ride back to the command."

Jonas dismounted and walked his horse over to take his place where Fletch had been moments before. Ross returned to his hiding place. They waited nearly thirty minutes in nervous anticipation when, again, the sound of a single galloping horse reached their ears. As before, the men pulled their horses in close to them and waited. Over the hill came a girl riding a blood bay horse at a hard gallop.

Ross leaned out where Jonas could see him and signaled him. Both men swung into their saddles and waited as the girl closed ground swiftly. At Ross's signal both men moved into the road, blocking the girl's path. She pulled up hard on her reins as her horse slid to a halt and shied from the riders, surprised by the sudden encounter. The girl was an accomplished rider and maintained control of her frightened horse. When the dust settled, his eyes looked approvingly at a beautiful blonde. She had ridden in great haste; her hair was in disarray and she was dressed in a long white nightgown. Over the gown she wore a heavy winter coat. Gloves covered her hands, but her shoes were a mis-match with her night clothes. The horse was well lathered from a hard ride and breathed heavily.

"Where you goin' gal in such an all-fired hurry?" Jonas asked.

The girl's eyes, pale blue in the light of early dawn, looked scared. "Are . . . are you Yankees?" she asked nervously. Ross eyed Jonas as they laughed.

Ross said, "No, ma'am, but I can see why you might not believe us." Ross unbuttoned the Union blue overcoat he was wearing to reveal his ragged Confederate uniform hidden inside. "When it gets cold outside, a fella uses what he can get. We took these coats from the Yankees." Ross looked over at the grinning Jonas, who also pulled his coat up at the bottom to uncover his gray pants underneath. They watched relief flood the face of the girl as she relaxed.

"Thank heaven I have found you! I have urgent news for your commander. Will you take me to him?"

"It will be our pleasure to guide you. It must be mighty important for a young lady to go riding so early in the morning dressed as you are, Miss . . . ?"

"Oh, yes. I guess I should introduce myself. My name is Susan McClellan. I live just four miles west of here."

"Pleased to make your acquaintance, Miss McClellan. My name is Lieutenant Ross Kimbrough and this is Private Jonas

Starke. We're scouts for Colonel Jo Shelby's brigade of the Confederate army."

"I'm pleased to meet you, but we'd better ride—we haven't much time."

The three riders rode for Shelby's headquarters. Headquarters was but a short distance away and, since her horse was nearly worn out, they moved out at an easy trot. They found Jo Shelby in a meadow bordering a corn field with his staff gathered around him.

As they rode into the meadow, Ross pivoted on his horse to study the area around him. He saw a long, snaky fence stacked five rails high lying between the corn field and the meadow. Behind the fence stood a line of Shelby's dismounted troopers, weapons at the ready. Behind them about a quarter of a mile stood the horse holders and General Shelby's staff. To their right, partially concealed, were the big guns of a section from Bledsoe's battery commanded by Lieutenant Richard Collins. The big gaping bores pointed in the direction of the corn field, waiting to unleash their fury. Mounted cavalry stood in reserve to the left and were partially hidden.

They halted their horses near the ground of bustling staff officers, each seemingly involved in some important task, like bees in a beehive. Captain Evan Stryker, a smile on his lips, strode toward Ross. He smiled with mischievous delight. "I hate to bring it to your attention so early in the mornin', Ross, but don't you think you could've found a more appropriate time to court so pretty a lady?"

"Miss McClellan, I'd like to introduce you to a wayward Texan, Captain Evan Stryker of Shelby's staff. I'm not sure how we got stuck with him, but despite his wisecracks, he's a good man to have on your side in a fight. Evan, Miss McClellan has some information for Colonel Shelby."

"The Colonel is busy, Lieutenant, but if I know him, I think he'll spare a few minutes for one so fair as this, who has obviously ridden hard to get here. Miss McClellan, if you'll follow me, I'll take you to see the Colonel. And don't believe everything you hear from this ole Missouri river rat who brought you in here. He's a fair to middling scout, but often forgets rank."

Jonas dismounted and hurried to help the young lady down. He stayed with the horses as Ross and Susan followed the captain.

"Wait here a second, Miss McClellan, Ross." Stryker walked over to the group of men and brought Colonel Shelby over with him to meet Miss McClellan.

Jo Shelby said, "Good morning, madam. I understand you wish to talk to me."

"Yes, Colonel. My name is Susan McClellan. I live about five miles west of here. My father woke me early this morning and told me to ride quickly and warn you."

"It was gallant of you to make such an effort, and your father must have felt it was very important to send his daughter out alone in such a hurry."

Susan's cheeks flushed in embarrassment. "Yes, sir. My father wanted me to tell you over six hundred cavalry accompanied by infantry and artillery are advancing in this direction from Fort Smith to surprise you. They were passing our house before daylight."

Jo Shelby laughed heartily, then smiled brightly before he replied. "Tell your father I certainly appreciate his concern and his efforts on our behalf. Tell him also that not only does he have one of the loveliest daughters I have seen in some time, but also the bravest and most noble I have met."

Susan was astonished by the response, and more than a little uncomfortable. "Thank you, sir, but aren't you gonna do something?"

"No, madam. We've already done it. We're going to wait for those Yankees to ride right into our trap. You see, our scouts rode in here and reported the troop movement less than an hour ago. My men are already deployed to ambush them. I hope you'll soon have the pleasure of watching my brigade force them back to Fort Smith. Once we take care of them, I'll send you home escorted by ten of my men. If my men had not discovered their movement, your ride might very well have saved my army. We can't overlook such bravery."

Further words were interrupted as a fast galloping courier reined his horse to a sliding stop before the group. "Colonel Shelby! Major Shanks would like to report that the enemy is advancing through the corn field."

"Tell Major Shanks to have the men hold their fire until they are within a hundred yards, then fire by volley." He turned toward Stryker. "Evan, ride over to Bledsoe's battery and tell them to hold their fire until our dismounted cavalry fire. I want him to open up with the cannons double loaded with canister and grapeshot. At that range he ought to tear holes you could drive a steam engine through."

Both soldiers saluted crisply and rode to deliver the orders. A strange hush fell over the group as all turned toward the coming battle. Ross felt a surge of excitement and his heart began to race. He tried to position himself and Sultan between the enemy and the girl. It just wouldn't be right to let anything harm this beautiful woman.

Jessie Kimbrough stood at the fence studying the old corn field. Harvest had long passed and now only the yellow-brown, broken-down stalks remained in the rows. The soldiers in blue stepped off proudly in line of battle as they advanced through the remaining crop residue. Sunlight reflected off the gun barrels and danced along the razor-sharp edges of the steel bayonets as the Union line advanced.

Jessie instinctively touched the gold locket given to him by Katlin. Whenever he was lonely or scared he rubbed the outside of the case. It was his good luck amulet to ward off danger. His mouth was dry and his hand trembled as he waited. He clutched the navy Colt revolver tightly in his sweaty hand as he stood nervously behind the snaky, wooden fence.

He glanced down the line and saw nearly fifteen hundred muskets, pistols, and carbines held at the ready, waiting to fire on command. He wondered if the enemy knew they were there, waiting to spring the trap. He watched the Union army, their ranks dressed up as if on parade, with their regimental flags unfurled and to the front.

He knew the Rebel flags were concealed so they wouldn't give away the ambush. Behind him, lying on the ground, was a second rank of Rebel soldiers. Those in the second row would rise to admonish the second volley after those in the first row fired their weapons. He had watched earlier as Collins's battery masked their cannons behind cut brush and bushes and he doubted the enemy even knew they were there. He was mighty glad he stood on this side of the fence.

If there was a hell on earth, he felt sure it had to be the area that lay before those deadly cannons when they discharged their fire and fury. No sane man could walk or ride willingly into those harbingers of death and dismemberment.

On the soldiers in blue came, so close now he could hear the corn stalks crunching under their feet. He could make out the individual facial features of the men. He picked out a man in the ranks he figured to be a sergeant. He aimed his gun dead center on the soldier's chest and waited. Seconds seemed to tick by like hours. He could feel the pounding of his heart as the blood rushed through his veins. Even as he faced death itself, he had never felt more alive. Life seemed more precious to him than ever before when he stood so close to losing it. He silently prayed for his safety and hoped he would see Katlin again.

His mouth felt dry as he tried to swallow. He squeezed his legs together tightly, fighting a sudden urge to pee. He hoped he wouldn't wet himself in front of his friends. He knew there was no time left to go and relieve himself. It was all he could do to stand still and not run. In his mind he always thought he'd be fearless in battle, and now he was wondering if he could control his bladder.

When it seemed as if they would wait until the Yankees marched right over them, the command came to fire. He felt and heard a tumultuous wall of sound, like a string of Fourth of July firecrackers going off until the small sounds built into one loud roar that swallowed up the individual sounds of weapons fired. The blue-black cloud of powder smoke hung before them like a foggy shroud, obscuring their vision. Jessie felt his pistol buck in his hand. He felt almost detached, like some outsider observing a dream. He watched the first rank of Yanks crumble and pitch forward, as though some unseen giant was hammering them with a club. Here and there a man still stood, as others fell dying around him.

The Union line shuddered to a halt; the sudden ferociousness of the barrage weakened their will to continue. In a daze, he heard the next order as the last of the Rebel guns in the first rank discharged. "First rank to the rear, second rank to the front. . . . Fire!"

The Yankee front line stood dazed as their second rank mixed with the survivors of the first. They unleashed a sputtering volley upon the Rebels. The man that had taken Jessie's place in the front row pitched onto his back, sending the warm stickiness of blood splattering across Jessie's face. Jessie looked down into the wide, staring eyes of the dead Rebel comrade lying at his feet. A neat round hole he could stuff his index finger into was punched into the man's forehead. At the crown of his head it was not nearly as neat; the distorted musket ball had blown a large hole as it exited the soldier's skull.

Jessie turned and fell to his hands and knees, retching forth the contents of his stomach while his body trembled. He nearly gagged again on the bitter bile as it burned his throat. Jessie nearly jumped out of his skin when the cannons ripped loose their canister charges into the stunned wall of Union troops. It sounded like a thousand bees from hell buzzing through the air. He could hear the rattle as the canister shot hit its target or fell spent to the ground. The effect was as if a huge scythe had swung several quick passes through the Union line. There were large gaping holes in the line where men had been standing before. Now they lay in mangled, bloody heaps upon the earth. The Union line wavered, then broke. Soldiers, once marching bravely, now turned and ran from the deadly hail that greeted them.

The first rank of Rebels were ordered back to the front. Jessie somehow found his way there, firing again at the fleeing Yankees. Seeing the frightened, running Union soldiers gave him confidence. He felt a Rebel yell spring from his lips as all tension and anxiety unwound from him. The sound of hundreds of other Rebels yelling mixed and blended with his voice as it roared down the line—a yell of victory and relief released without any need for a command to do so. He stood trembling as he looked about; some of those around him were wounded. Others lay draped over the top rail of the fence, still in death, the life drained from them.

He glanced at his revolver. He noticed all six cylinders had been fired, but he could only recall firing twice. He knew he must have fired the others during the excitement. He began to reload. To his left he heard the charge of Carroll's mounted cavalry as they galloped by in pursuit of the retreating foe. He found out later Colonel Carroll's troops had failed them again. Although they followed the routed Union troops, they moved so cautiously that they failed to pick up even a single straggler.

Soon after the battle ended, a detail left to escort Miss McClellan home. With them would ride Jonas Starke. After they reached Miss McClellan's home, he would continue to scout the area around Fayetteville, Arkansas, and gather intelligence for Shelby's army. Jonas also would deliver a letter to the postmaster at Fayetteville, Arkansas, to be held for Cassandra Kimbrough.

36

Cane Hill

The next few days flew by quickly as Shelby's command continued to hold the area around Cane Hill. The brigade made a fast march to Ray's Mill to confront Federal troops who held the mill, but the Union troops retreated without a fight. Shelby returned to Cane Hill.

Jonas and other scouts brought in information about General Blunt and a large force of troops near Fort Smith, Arkansas. Again Shelby's men marched on an all-night, forced march. It had been rumored the enemy was bivouacked at Evansville, but when they arrived the enemy had once again retreated. The troops returned to Cane Hill discouraged, tired, and hungry from enduring ceaseless rains, cold nights, and battles that never materialized. They rested for four days at Cane Hill.

While the rest of the command recuperated, Ross and his scouts lived in the saddle, moving between their own and the enemy's lines. Sometimes they dressed in Union blue and rode among the enemy to learn more of their movements and plans.

On December 3, 1862, Union General Blunt was finally reinforced to give him about eight thousand men. He moved slowly and cautiously, so Shelby's command had plenty of warning of the advance. General Marmaduke, in charge of Southern cavalry in the district, ordered every supply wagon sent across the Boston Mountains to safety. On December 4, Shelby's troopers lay all day in line of battle waiting for the enemy to come.

Blunt's army was only fourteen miles away, but still they didn't arrive. By sunrise, December 5, Union patrols drove in the Rebel videttes guarding the road. At last the battle was pending. General Marmaduke, warned by couriers from Colonel Shelby of the advance, come to the front to witness the action with his staff.

Shelby's brigade was formed on the crest of a hill just beyond his camp. Lieutenant Collins's battery, still a section of Bledsoe's battery, was positioned in a large graveyard along the left side of the line. His dark cannons and rugged artillery men moved in and out through the somber gravestones like phantoms in the twilight of dawn. Among them was Calvin Kimbrough.

Calvin bent over the cannon as he sighted on the advancing enemy line. He could see the long lines advance as they had just days before, battle flags streaming in the strong northwest wind. At this distance they didn't look real to him; they looked more like little toy soldiers painted and lined up for display.

He knew they were much more than toys for, after the last fight, he had walked among the dead, the wounded, and the dying. He would never forget the awful carnage he had witnessed—the stench of blood and bowels ripped asunder; men mangled beyond recognition often lying by those that looked merely asleep; bodies and pieces of human flesh scattered across the battlefield as if by a careless child.

What haunted his mind were the pitiful cries and shrieks of those wounded and dying. There was little he could do for them. He offered an encouraging word here and there, and gave some of them a drink from a canteen. He was forced to move cautiously through the enemy, for there might be a wounded man or two eager to take a Rebel with them before they died. He could not stay aloof from their plight though danger surrounded him. He felt too much compassion for his fellow man to allow it. It sickened him that he had been the cause of much of the death and misery on the field before him. His only consolation was that it was better the enemy was lying here rather than his comrades in mangled heaps.

Yankees might have killed his father and burned his home, but he doubted that it was any of the ones that had fought here. Calvin was not the kind of man who could easily shift hate to anyone wearing the blue. In fact, he found it difficult to hate at all. Devotion to duty was the most sacred trust as far as Calvin was concerned. It was his duty to aim the cannon. His crew and his army depended on him to do it to the best of his ability. Like it or not, despite the cost, Calvin would do the best damn job he could do. It was this conviction and devotion to duty that sustained him and kept him at his post.

"Number three, shift the trail left two inches. Good!" Calvin ordered. Satisfied the cannon was aimed properly, he stepped back behind the gun so he could observe the shot and make mental adjustments for the next one. As Calvin reached his position he gave the command, "Ready," to the crew. In seconds, number three stepped forward from the trail spike and, using his vent pick, punctured the powder bag within the cannon breech. As he moved back to stand at attention, number four stepped forward and inserted the friction primer and lanyard to the vent of the cannon. He stepped away from the cannon holding the lanyard at the ready. "Cannon number one ready to fire, sir!"

Beside them he heard the crews from the other guns yell as they were ready. Then Lieutenant Collins gave the order: "Fire at will!"

Calvin gave his command: "Fire!"

Delmar Pickett, standing at the number four position, yanked the lanyard activating the primer. The gun roared to life as it bucked into the air and rolled back a few feet. Black smoke quickly whirled away from them, borne by the strong wind. Calvin looked with satisfaction as his shot tore a ragged gap in the oncoming ranks of the enemy soldiers. They reloaded as fast as they could, and Calvin again aimed the cannon. They fired their second shot less than forty seconds after the first, their shot adding to those of the others.

The Union line wavered, then broke, scattering like chaff on the wind to the woods beyond the field. Confederate skirmishers, encouraged by the Yankee retreat, pursued them across the field. General Blunt was not ready to concede the battle, and, as the Rebels watched from the hill crest, Union artillery began to position themselves in the valley below to return fire. Battery after battery rolled into position to face the lone battery of Shelby's brigade.

Closest and deadliest were the six rifled James guns belonging to the notorious Rabb battery. The enemy unleashed a horrible barrage from their artillery on the Confederate lines. They began to extract a bloody toll as they walked their fire in on the crest of the hill. The artillery duel raged on for over an hour as the Yankees homed in on their target.

Calvin kept his crew diligently to their work as cannon shells shrieked through the air around them. Shells erupted geysers of dirt on the hill behind the cemetery as the shots went high. Many landed in the field between Cane Hill college and the gentle rising slope behind the cemetery. Occasional round shot bounded and skipped through the headstones moving to fields beyond.

Finally, General Blunt added infantry to the assault, supported by the fire of the Union batteries. Three times they came, and three times the Rebels stubbornly held their ground and hurled them back in confusion. Shelby held his strong position, and Blunt could not drive him with a frontal attack. Blunt was not to be stopped when his force was clearly superior in numbers. Soon the Rebels watched hopelessly as new columns of fresh Union troops broke to the left and to the right of their position.

Marmaduke and Shelby conferred. They knew if they did not retreat they would be surrounded. Colonel Shelby ordered the buglers to sound retreat. They moved in an organized and leisurely fashion, as the Rebels brought off the field not only their wounded, but their dead. Covered by the dismounted troopers, the artillery was removed. Then the cavalry companies began to withdraw.

Blunt, jubilant he had finally driven the Confederates from the field, ordered his cavalry to press the attack. Here, in a brilliant flash of strategy, Colonel Jo Shelby began his legend as an unsurpassed cavalry commander. He took each of the thirty companies of his brigade and set them in position on the road. As the enemy approached each position at near point-blank range, the mounted cavalry fired, then fell back in column. After riding past the other twenty-nine companies, they set up again to repeat the maneuver after the rest had passed. This forced the Union cavalry following in pursuit to face a constant barrage of deadly lead. Just when they thought they had the Confederates in full retreat a fresh company would fire into them.

Near the road rose a high spiraling rock formation on a hill where a two-gun section, commanded by Lieutenant Collins, set up to sweep the steep road. Shelby ordered a regiment to support the artillery to further slow the Yankee advance. The Union infantry had been able to keep up with the Yankee cavalry because the cavalry was slowed by the deadly traps the Rebels had sprung on them. Calvin watched the Union cavalry swirling around the base of the hill in wild eddies.

Again the mighty guns delivered death among the ranks of the Union troops; the rebels held until, once again, Blunt's men began to encircle them. The Yankees rapidly pressed the attack. Ten companies of Union blue pressed against the one in Confederate gray like waves breaking on a distant shore.

Evan Stryker had been busy all day delivering orders given by General Shelby to various company commanders, but now he was with the colonel and Captain Martin. Evan was there when Captain Martin's blood splattered Jo's face. He watched as a pistol ball carried Jo's black plume from his hat and first one horse, then another, was shot from under Shelby. The second horse went down with at least eleven musket ball strikes, but Jo Shelby remained untouched. Never one to shrink from danger and believing a commander should be where he was needed most, Shelby remained with the company closest to the enemy. His uniform was torn by musket balls and drenched in the blood of his men and his horses.

The Rebels were particularly hard pressed when Shelby gave the order: "Stryker, ride back and find Majors Gordon and Thompson. Have them locate a suitable place and join up across the road to cover our withdrawal. Jean's regiment needs relief. Be damn quick about it, Evan, I'm depending on you!"

"Yes, sir. I'll see to it, sir!" Evan wheeled his horse and rode hard to give the necessary orders.

Ross Kimbrough had been in the rear observing the enemy attack and scouting for any possible advantage. He joined Shelby as the position was nearing collapse. For the third time a horse was shot out from under Colonel Shelby in the same day. The horse shrieked in pain and rolled on its side, pinning Jo beneath him. Ross rode to Shelby's rescue. He swung down from Sultan and pulled the colonel's leg free of the horse. "Are you all right, Colonel?"

"I've been a damn sight better, Ross. Help me onto your horse." Jo favored the leg as he limped slowly to Sultan. Ross helped him up before swinging behind him. Sultan, not acclimated to the extra burden of two men, protested a little at first. The artillery was withdrawn. Shelby gave the order as the men made a mad rush to the rear and to the protection of Gordon and Thompson.

Ross and Jo raced for safety. Sultan carried them both with ease. As soon as they reached the new lines, Shelby found and mounted his fourth horse of the day. The last of the Rebel cavalrymen raced through the safety of the line of dismounted cavalry. On one side of the road was a turbulent mountain stream, and on the other, the steep, menacing rock wall of the gorge. Southern soldiers had climbed into the icy waters and stood waist deep behind the bank of the stream, aiming their weapons. Other soldiers climbed to positions on the rugged rock wall. Shelby's men stood in the pines and behind the rocks at every turn.

The sunset colored the western horizon as the last fatal confrontation of the day spiraled toward a climax. Ross Kimbrough stayed beside his commander. Beyond them, mounted Southern cavalry acted as decoys to draw the Yankees into the trap.

On they came, the thundering Union cavalry troopers of the Sixth Kansas Cavalry under the leadership of Colonel Jewell. Hooting, swearing, and yelling, their cavalry sabers drawn and ready, they charged. Ross watched with deadly fascination as they rode into the trap. Gun blasts came from the rocks, the pines, and the riverbank, pouring fire as destructive as heavy hail against a ripened wheat field. Ross watched as the Union colonel fell in the middle of the road, mortally wounded.

The Union soldiers, to their credit, tried to recover the body of their commander. Soon, twenty-nine men and nineteen horses were blended in one vast pile of death and agony, shot down in the attempt to extract their commander's body. Again and again, the Union troopers charged with fresh cavalry troops. Each time they were driven back with heavy losses. Night continued to close in upon the field of battle, but still General Blunt would not give up. He advanced his artillery and began a concentrated fire down the mountain road. The roar of cannon echoed off the rock walls and lit the gathering gloom of night. Although distracted by the fire, the Confederates continued to hold.

Every Rebel knew the Kansas troops seldom took prisoners. None knew it better than the company led by William Gregg, known simply as "Quantrill's men."

During the shelling Colonel Shelby lost another horse, killed by fragments. Again Ross Kimbrough helped Jo recover and mount another sorrel. Jo turned toward Ross. Amazement crossed his face. "You know, this is the fourth horse I've lost today. Every one was a sorrel. I'm beginning to believe I can't be killed when I ride a sorrel into battle."

"I guess that's one way to look at it, Colonel. But I'd have to say you're hard as hell on them. If I were the next sorrel horse and I saw you coming, I'd tuck my tail and run for parts unknown, or ask 'em to spare me the wait and just shoot me on the spot!"

Jo laughed hard. It was a release of tension they all needed. He smiled, then spoke softly. "Yes, I guess it must look far different from their point of view, but so far, not one horse could pass on tales of their misfortune to my new horses." He paused. "Still, I have to believe it isn't just a coincidence. It must be a sign from Providence. I believe sorrels bring me luck, and I'll take all the luck I can find."

Further comment was quickly discouraged as Blunt's blue-coated soldiers made one last desperate attempt to break the Confederate position. They came at full gallop, sabers at the ready and screams upon their lips. The narrow, rough road was filled with horsemen hurling down upon them. Soldiers who stood bravely throughout the day broke to the rear under this new assault. The lot of them thundered down the steep hill, pistols cracking, sabers slashing, screams and cussing filling the air.

The war cries of the troops mixed with the sound of hundreds of horses that ran in one mad, uncontrolled rush and broke through every line Shelby's brigade had established. Carried forward by the momentum of the charge and the sheer steepness of the hill, their progress rolled on relentlessly. No barrier could check the headlong rush. The final company pulled out of the way. The runaway onslaught, moving too fast, sent some horses and men over dangerous precipices and onto rocks below. The luckier ones landed in deep pools of water. Those who stumbled were trampled to death in the wild stampede. Only the fall of darkness and the leadership of Shelby and his officers restored order.

Luck remained with them. The Federal troops were just as disorganized and confused as the Rebels whom they'd rolled through like an angry tidal wave. A flag of truce was offered and accepted. The Yankees wanted to reclaim the body of Colonel Jewell and return it to their army. It was done; even his enemies had to admire his leadership and bravery. The battle had lasted all day and covered over fifteen miles of mountain roads.

Colonel Carroll's brigade, poorly led, never rallied after leaving the field and didn't stop its running until it reached Van Buren, its panic stricken soldiers spreading rumors of disaster and defeat. Only the howitzer battery connected with the runaway brigade stayed and fought bravely all day. The small artillery unit reported directly to Colonel Shelby and was led by Huey and Shoup.

The rest of the night was spent without food in exhaustion. Marmaduke had fought with Shelby's brigade of three thousand men against the ten thousand of the Union army and yet had maintained discipline while exacting a heavy toll on a larger army.

In the morning, Shelby's command withdrew to Dripping Springs to lick its wounds. They would not have much time to wait. Confederate General Hindman was on his way with reinforcements to strike a blow at the Yankees.

Union troops hadn't fared much better. They were badly bloodied by the continuous curtain of lead they had ridden into all day. General Blunt decided to withdraw his army of ten thousand to the battlefield at Cane Hill and camp there. He was content for the moment to savor the victory by holding the field they had paid for so dearly.

General Herron, commanding another Union army of six thousand men, held his position at Yellville and Huntsville to the east and did little to maintain contact with General Blunt. Hindman, in charge of Confederate forces in the area, had moved near Fort Smith when the retreat began. He hurried his troops forward. All day he heard the cannon fire, and he rapidly crossed Parson's Brigade to check the Union advance.

General Hindman, General Marmaduke, and Colonel Shelby met at Dripping Springs. There they decided to attempt to strike Blunt before he could be joined by Herron's army. Marmaduke and Shelby both agreed more intelligence was needed. Ross Kimbrough was ordered to find Herron's army and figure out their intentions. Ross hit the trail again. Maybe this time he could find a weakness in the Union lines for Shelby and Hindman to attack.

37

Taken Prisoner

Ross Kimbrough lay on the ridge watching the valley below. He had been there for several hours, and the cold of the frozen earth was seeping through his body and chilling his blood. He shivered, making it more difficult to hold the spy glass steady. He had watched as regiments of cavalry and infantry marched by. Several artillery batteries pulled by crewed caissons were traveling with the cavalry and accompanied by supply and ammunition wagons. No doubt about it, Herron's army was clearly on the move to link up with General Blunt's. Ross turned away from the valley and crawled over the crest, making his way to his waiting horse.

Sultan pricked up his ears as Ross approached. Ross swung into the saddle and spurred the stallion into a fast gallop. "Come on, boy. We've got to warn Shelby and Hindman. General Herron's boys are coming, and if they join Blunt it'll be hell to pay!" Man and horse, working as one, rode hard and fast. No time to ride safely and slowly. Shelby needed to know what was happening, and he needed to know immediately.

Ross found command headquarters at Morrow's farm at the point of divergence of the Fayetteville and Cane Hill roads. The roads rejoined a short distance further at Prairie Grove.

Sultan was heavily lathered and wheezing hard when they reached headquarters. Ross felt remorse over pushing the big stallion so hard, but he knew it couldn't be helped. The information he carried might save the Confederate army. Ross loved the big stallion and he was a special connection to his past. Sultan was a gift from his father and came from Briarwood Plantation. Months on the campaign trail had made a bond of mutual trust between horse and man. Sultan had carried him through tough spots when a lesser horse would have quit. He just hoped he hadn't destroyed his faithful companion.

When Ross arrived at headquarters, he took time to make sure an orderly gave the stallion a good rub down and a double ration of grain. He would see Sultan properly cared for, even if he had to give the order at gunpoint.

It was now the night of December 6, 1862. General Hindman had gathered his officers together for a final strategy session when Ross arrived with his new information. The officers listened to his report carefully and with great interest. Discussion and debate followed as they tried to decide how to deal with the new threat.

Colonels Shoup and Frost desired to make an all-out frontal attack on Blunt's position near Cane Hill. Until Ross appeared with this latest information on the movement of Herron's army, everyone had been in agreement. Now the situation was decidedly different. With Herron's army just twelve miles east of Cane Hill, something must be done to keep the two Union armies from linking up.

Generals Marmaduke and Hindman were for sending Shelby's brigade to Prairie Grove, located directly between the two armies. This might be a brilliant plan, or a total disaster. If Blunt wasn't kept busy, Shelby's command could be crushed between the two blue armies.

Finally, after much haggling, it was decided that one regiment, under the command of Colonel James S. Monroe, a daring Arkansas officer, was to demonstrate before Blunt at Cane Hill and make him believe a full attack was coming from that direction. Parson's brigade was to follow Shelby's brigade and hit Blunt along the Fayetteville road from the rear. The rest of the army, led by Shelby's command, would strike to destroy General Herron's smaller army before he could join with Blunt. It was a bold plan, but the only one that had any chance of succeeding and keeping the two Union armies from joining forces.

Shelby's men left the warmth of their glowing fires at four o'clock in the morning and moved out under a cold and frosty sky. There had been no chance for sleep for Evan Stryker this night. As a staff officer he had delivered various marching orders to the separate commands. He was still awake when a blood-red sun crested the tree tops, lighting a cold and frost-layered landscape. Evan listened as Major Shanks received personal instructions from Colonel Shelby.

Shelby, anticipating the coming battle, sat on his sorrel horse nervously, twirling the tips of his mustache above his luxuriant, russet-colored beard. "You will, Major Shanks, take half your regiment and half Thompson's regiment and establish my advance, keeping two hundred yards interval between your rear and my column. Attack anything and everything in sight. Charge from the moment you see the enemy, and I will support you with my entire brigade. I'm sending some of my scouts with you. Keep me informed and keep moving forward, Major."

Shanks listened carefully to the commands, his eyes glowing with expectation. He lifted his plumed hat in salute and galloped off to obey. Less than a mile from where he received his instructions, Shanks ran squarely into the troops of Major Hubbard of the Third Missouri Union regiment. Hubbard had several detachments from other units assigned to him to help him escort a supply train of twenty-one wagons. Major Shanks immediately ordered his men forward to capture the supply train.

Evan Stryker rode with Colonel Shelby's staff when they heard the unmistakable din of battle not far ahead of them. Shelby galloped toward the sound. Evan knew if he didn't ride hard he would be left behind.

When they arrived on the scene, Shanks had already routed the Union troops and was pursuing them vigorously. The surprised Yankees were doing their best to reach the protection of Herron's army. As they reached the junction with the main road, Shelby ordered Gordon to dismount his men and post them in the dry bed of the creek to hold the road to Cane Hill.

Shelby had outrun the remainder of his brigade, except for a section of his mounted artillery. He pressed forward with them and his staff. Shelby, realizing he needed immediate help, sent Evan Stryker back to urge on the remainder of the brigade. Unknown to Jo, the Yankees had scattered. Shanks divided his force to chase them into the woods and away from the road. Colonel Shelby was unaware that he was moving past his advance, believing they were still before him, when in truth he was now in the lead. Now, nothing stood between the Colonel, his small band of men, and the Union army.

Calvin hung on to the seat for dear life as the caisson he was sharing bounced along the trail. The crack of the whip sang in the air as the driver did his best to keep up with the colonel.

"Hang on there, Cal, I ain't got the time to come back fer ya!" shouted Brady Dobler, handling the whip and leads with ease.

Calvin was already cussing his decision to leave his horse and ride with Dobler. How he wished he were back in the saddle.

Red Roses was being led by Delmar Pickett, who trailed behind them with the rest of the artillery crew. Calvin glanced up as they rounded a bend in the road. What he saw made him feel as though ice water ran in his veins. Cold, naked fear reached out and squeezed his heart. Over one hundred mounted Union cavalry troopers thundered toward them.

There wasn't time to unlimber their cannons. There wasn't time to run. Delmar led Red Roses up beside the caisson, now sliding to a halt in the center of the road. Calvin threw himself into the saddle. He gripped the reins in one hand and grabbed the Sharps carbine with the other.

He rapidly threw the carbine's safety strap over his shoulder, if he let go of the carbine, it would hang at his side rather than be lost. He steadied his aim as best he could. Cal squeezed the trigger and felt a satisfying jar as the carbine recoiled into his shoulder. The rider he aimed for pitched forward on the neck of his horse and slid under the galloping hooves. There was no time to reload. He let go of the Sharps and reached for his revolver. He fumbled for the holster flap, trying to unbutton it, as pistol balls shrieked past him.

Brady Dobler was desperately trying to turn the caisson, horse team, and cannon around, but it was much too late. The Yanks were nearly upon them. Calvin watched in horror as bullets found their mark and Brady Dobler slid from the driver's seat, his body riddled by a dozen shots. The horses screamed in terror and tried to run, but two were already dead in the traces; the others thrashed around madly trying to pull them along.

Over the gunfire, Lieutenant Collins shouted to his men: "Form a circle men. Quickly!"

There was little time—every second the Yankees closed the gap. Billy Jo Paxton, positioned seven on the crew, screamed in pain as he took a minie ball in the shoulder and pitched off backward from his horse. Calvin pulled his pistol free of the holster and fired off a quick pair of shots, both missing the rapidly moving targets. Red Roses, uneasy in the turbulence of the battlefield, skittered sideways, making his aim even more difficult. Then the blue troopers were among them.

One burly soldier took a sweeping swing with his saber. Had it connected, it would have ripped Calvin's head from his body. Calvin ducked beneath the swing and rammed Red Roses into the Yankee horse. He was too close to get his revolver turned and pointed at the soldier, so Calvin used it like a club and crashed the barrel against the man's temple. The man slid to the ground and disappeared under the trampling hooves of the horses.

Calvin spun his horse firing at one, then another, Yank. He saw the second shot strike the target and watched as the rider fell forward on his mount, spurring away wounded from the melee. Calvin watched in terror as a Union lieutenant approached Ed McCann from behind at a gallop. Ed never saw it coming as he battled another Yankee before him.

"Watch out, Ed!" Calvin screamed, but it was too late. Calvin watched as the cavalry sword, extended at arm's length and propelled by the horse moving at full gallop, rammed through Ed's back and penetrated cleanly through his chest. He heard Ed's blood curdling death scream and saw Ed, eyes wide and frozen with shock, grasp the blade of the bloody sword with both hands as it protruded through his chest. Moments later he spilled forward out of the saddle onto the frozen ground.

Calvin tried to shake the horror from his mind, but when he closed his eyes he could still see Ed's hands gripping the bloody blade. The startled, pained death mask of his friend remained etched in his mind. Rage and anger filled him with a power and hate he had never experienced before. He spurred toward the Yankee who had killed his friend. The soldier was now unarmed, the sword ripped from his hand when the weight of Ed's body tumbled to the ground.

The Yankee looked up in time to see Calvin riding directly at him. Scared and unable to defend himself, the Union trooper raised his hands to show he held no weapon. "Don't shoot, I surrender!"

Calvin reined in hard beside him and thrust his revolver against the man's chest. All reason left him as he pulled the trigger once, then twice more. The first shot blew the man out of the saddle and the next shot hit him in the face. On the third try, the hammer fell on an already fired cylinder. "You didn't give Ed any chance, no chance at all," Calvin screamed out in rage. "Try surrendering to the devil, you son of a bitch!" Chaos ruled as the soldiers mixed in hand-to-hand combat around him, each fighting a private war for survival.

Major Hubbard, leading the Union charge, rode directly toward Colonel Shelby.

"You are surrounded and overpowered. Surrender your men immediately, sir," the Union officer demanded.

Shelby, his pistol empty, sat his horse defiantly and refused to respond.

"Surrender," Hubbard demanded, pointing his revolver at Jo Shelby's head. "Surrender, or I fire!"

"Sorry, Major, I can't do that," replied Shelby calmly. "You see, it is you that must surrender. Call off your men and look behind you."

"When the major glanced over his shoulder, the exhilaration of victory quickly vanished and his spirits sank. Closing fast and less than fifty yards away rode Major Shanks with his Confederates.

Major Shanks had Quantrill's raiders among his men. They had finished their bloody work of chasing down the fleeing soldiers from the wagon train and returned to the aid of their commander. Leading the charge were Frank James, Riley Crawford, and Billy Cahill. At nearly the same moment, from the opposite direction rode the men of Thompson and Elliott of Shelby's command. The Union soldiers began to surrender, and those who tried to escape were run down and killed on the spot.

The Union major looked back at Colonel Shelby and lowered his revolver carefully. He tried to smile, but the disappointment was too much. He turned his revolver around and handed it butt first to Jo Shelby. "Well done. I am nicely caught. I offer you my gun and my sword in surrender. I ask only quarter for my men."

"Keep your sword, Major," Shelby replied. "In every encounter your men have fought with honor. I have learned you treated our people with dignity when you were at Newtonia, and I respect an honorable foe."

When the final tally was gathered, three hundred and seventy-three prisoners were sent to the rear with twenty-one wagons of badly needed supplies and clothing. In addition, many killed and wounded were collected. Billy Joe Paxton was sent in a captured wagon to seek aid at the field hospital. Brady Dobler and Ed McCann, belonging to Calvin's crew, were dead. The other artillery crew suffered even higher losses.

General Marmaduke reached Shelby's position and asked him to concentrate his brigade and moved on to find Herron's army, which he knew must be close. The rest of Marmaduke's cavalry division joined with Shelby's brigade for the advance. Two miles beyond Prairie Grove Church they found Herron's advance.

38

Frozen Hell at Prairie Grove

Herron had his Yankee infantry advancing in line of battle—cavalry withdrawn, skirmishers out front and ready for action. Herron, on seeing the advance of Marmaduke's division, halted. He found his Union army in a wretched position. At the same moment, General Hindman put General Parson's Confederate brigade in motion toward Union General Blunt's army to strike him from behind at Cane Hill.

General Herron began to press the attack on Marmaduke's cavalry division. Shelby's brigade had the lead and was falling back slowly before the Union advance until it reached Prairie Grove. General Shoup's Rebels came up to assist Shelby, but then stayed in place instead of pressing the attack as he had been ordered to do. Marmaduke and Shelby now occupied a large hill about two miles east of Hindman's position. In these lines were concentrated over eight thousand Rebel troops facing Herron's six thousand. Only General Hindman leading Monroe's regiment and Parson's brigade faced the ten-thousand-man army of Blunt's Union forces.

Monroe attacked Blunt ferociously, and for a time, Blunt believed his army was the focus of attack. It was the sound of Herron's artillery that finally convinced him where the point of the real attack was located. His scouts told him the direct route to Herron was cut off by Rebels, but he took a chance and began to withdraw to Rhea's Mill, eight miles to the north. Once he crossed the Illinois River, he marched east four miles to Prairie Grove unmolested.

Herron advanced to attack, but took his time, waiting for Blunt to reach him. Luck was with him, for General Shoup of the Confederate army did not follow Marmaduke's orders and failed to press his attack.

The Confederates were aligned around the crest of a large hill that was shaped like a ridge. Shelby's brigade covered the far right. Fagan and Hawthorne's brigades commanded by General Shoup held the center, with Frost and Parson's brigades holding the left. The Confederate artillery was massed at the center. In front of the hill lay a large meadow, and beyond it lay large swells covered in timber.

Jessie watched from his position on the line as the Union troops emerged from the trees and began forming their battle lines. More cannons than he thought possible lined up in the meadow to pound the Confederate line. The firing was relentless upon the hill, and each soldier did his best to dig in or pile up anything he could find for cover.

Shelby tried to counter the highly accurate Union artillery fire by constantly moving his cannons to make it harder for the Yankees to zero in on them. Collins kept moving his guns as best as he could and pressed cavalry troops into manning the positions left vacant by Hubbard's attack earlier that morning.

The Yankee batteries were extremely accurate, especially Rabb's battery with his rifled James Guns. More than forty Union cannons fired constantly at the Confederate position for over two hours. Large trees were knocked down by the cannonballs; branches were severed, and splinters flew through the air. Stone and wooden fences fell before the fury of the artillery. The losses were terrifying.

Jessie watched with morbid fascination as a cannonball bounced along the ground, severed a small tree, bounced over a rock wall, and plowed through a group of soldiers. A Rebel soldier stepped out and tried to stop the rolling cannonball with his foot, just as you would a rolling ball. But he was gruesomely surprised as the cannonball neatly took off his foot and continued up the hill. The soldier fell to the ground and soon bled to death, screaming in agony. Jessie made a silent vow never to attempt to stop a rolling cannonball.

Finally, the Union troops marched a full brigade of infantry into the open led by Colonel Black of the Twenty-fifth Illinois. They marched directly at Shelby's, Hawthorne's, and Fagan's position on the hill. Before the Confederate line lay what remained of Blocher's four-gun Confederate battery of Fagan's brigade. Around it lay every artillery horse belonging to the battery, killed by the brutal Union artillery fire. Over half the cannon crews were already dead or wounded amid the big guns. Most of the surviving artillerymen fought to save their friends, while a few broke to the rear, seeking protection in the orchard. Without horses the cannons could not be withdrawn.

Evan Stryker rode with a communication to Lieutenant Richard Collins from Colonel Shelby. After Lieutenant Collins read the order he called Calvin and the other gunners to him. "Men, I just received orders from Colonel Shelby. He has ordered us to load our cannons with canister and aim them at Blocher's battery. Our orders are to hold our fire until the battery has fallen. When the Yankees capture the battery we are to open up on them. Colonel Shelby doesn't want that battery captured without making them pay a heavy price."

A worried expression crossed Calvin's face. "Even if we hold our fire until the last minute, there's still Confederate wounded and crew around those cannon. We might kill some of our own men. My God, we're only two hundred yards from those guns!"

"The cannons will be a focal point of their charge. They will mass among those guns and present us with an outstanding target. Even if we kill some of our own men it must be done and there isn't any use arguing about it. Calvin, I will give you the order to fire—I expect you to follow it."

"Yes, sir," Calvin replied. He returned to his crew. They immediately loaded the guns with double canister and aimed on the tortured battery. Calvin eyed the battery sitting in the yard of the white framed house of Archibald Borden. Calvin felt a twisting of his stomach. He could see the logic of the order, but he never before had fired into an area that still held Rebels. The thought that some of those wounded Confederates might die at the hands of his battery was more than he could handle. His hands began to shake and sweat beaded on his brow despite the freezing weather.

In beautiful array the Union soldiers advanced up the hill toward the doomed Blocher's battery. As they closed within thirty paces, the remaining survivors of the battery ran for the rear. Some of the wounded tried to crawl away. Some helped their wounded comrades limp away from the guns. Calvin watched as the Union soldiers stopped to fire a volley into the Confederate dead and wounded around the cannons. Then the Union troops swept in among the big guns. The mostly Irish troops let loose a gigantic hurrah as they captured the battery. He watched in shock as Rebel cannoneers were bayoneted or shot down by the Yankee advance.

Calvin was now eager to fire on the battery, for he had witnessed the heartless destruction of the defenders. He aimed his cannon on the gun in the center where a large man was busy running his bayonet through a young boy with his hand held up in the air, pleading for his life. Calvin clenched his jaws tightly together as tears welled in his eyes. "Forgive me, Father," he prayed to himself, "for what I am about to do." Lieutenant Dick Collins gave the order: "Fire!"

Calvin yelled in immediate response, "Fire!"

Delmar Pickett yanked the lanyard hard as the cannon roared to life. Calvin's cannon joined in unison with the other three guns of the battery leveling lead into the Union troops. Above the roar and drifting smoke Calvin heard the rattle of the canister shot strike the barrels, carriages, and wheels of Blocher's cannons. Splinters from wheels and wooden carriages were flung in every direction. Broken bodies covered with blood littered the blast area.

The Union troops paused under the shock of the cannon fire. Quickly Shelby's, Hawthorne's, and Fagan's men fired their volleys into the ranks of the advancing blue line.

Colonel Black, badly wounded, tried to rally his troops, even under that galling fire, but the unleashed slaughter had been too disheartening for the Union line. Officers, soldiers, horses, and riders thundered back in one huge, struggling mass, while Collins's battery fired two more quick salvos into the retreating troops.

Jessie was among those firing at the Twenty-fifth Illinois. He watched as Captain Gilbert Thomas stood and swung his sword over his head and shouted, "Come on, men, let's chase them back to hell!"

Jessie rose and charged down the hill, screaming at the top of his lungs. He held his sword in one hand and his pistol in the other as he raced forward. Around him swept the men of Shelby's brigade, but Gilbert Thomas and the Fifth Missouri led the charge. Soon Jessie found himself fighting to stay on his feet as gravity and the steepness of the hill propelled him out of control. He tripped and fell over a stump. He rolled ten feet down the hill and crashed into another one. The air gushed out of him as he lay stunned on the ground. The Confederate line swept past him. He pulled himself up, picked up his pistol and sword, and followed the charge. The Rebels let their enthusiasm overcome their reason as they pursued the enemy almost to the Federal batteries. The eruption of shot and shell struck them as the Union batteries opened fire and the retreating Federals cleared their cannons. Jessie watched as the ranks before him were raked with the withering fire. The Rebels began to fall back toward the hill. Jessie waited for them and fired his pistol at the new line of fresh blue-coated soldiers breaking from the woods.

Captain Gilbert Thomas came running toward him, yelling to his men over his shoulder, "Fall back, men, fall back to the hill!"

Jessie felt a crushing blow to his chest, as if someone had

hit him with a hard swung axe handle. He felt himself being lifted off his feet and slammed to the ground on his back. His chest ached as he tried hard to suck in air, but it wouldn't come. He felt a pressure on his chest as if someone was sitting on it. His eyes clouded and his vision dimmed as he fought for air. Around him he felt men passing him by, running for their lives. He felt strong hands grab him. Someone threw him over his shoulder. Each jarring step drove the man's shoulder into Jessie's stomach. He faded into blackness until he awoke to find Gilbert Thomas's concerned face staring into his.

"You all right, Jessie? You scared the devil out of me. I saw you go down hard from a shot and I figured you was a goner for sure. Since the damn Yanks were after us I figured I'd better carry you up here and check your wounds later. Good thing a couple of the fellas gave me a hand or I would've never gotten you up this hill."

Jessie could breathe again, but his chest still ached painfully. He hesitated, then asked the question, "How . . . how bad is it? Am I going to die?"

Gil broke into a wide grin, then said, "Well, Jess, you're going to live, but I'm afraid you're Bible isn't. Take a look at this." Gilbert held up the Bible that Jessie had received from his mother. There was a hole punched through the center, clear through to the back where the hinged metal cover was attached. Gilbert opened it to the last page. There, in a dent formed in the metal cover, was the flattened nose of a fifty-eight caliber minie ball. The bullet had penetrated the entire pocket bible until it reached the metal cover, nearly piercing it.

"You're damn lucky you had it in your breast pocket Jess, or we'd be looking for a place to plant you. You have a nasty bruise on your chest, a little bleeding, and a nice big hole in your overcoat and your uniform jacket to remind you of your good fortune, but you'll live."

Jessie felt relief flood through him, knowing that it wasn't serious. He reached up and found the gold locket given to him by Katlin and caressed it lovingly with his fingers. Had it brought him good luck, or had his help been heaven sent? He was uncertain, but glad to be alive.

There was a lull in the fighting as both sides made adjustments. During the Confederate charge, the cannons from Blocher's battery had been pulled behind Rebel lines. Hindman started shifting troops to his right so that he could attempt to assault the enemy left. Before the attack could begin, a Confederate Arkansas regiment under the command of Captain Adams deserted almost en masse, leaving only their officers and a few of the men to fight with other Confederate regiments. This desertion in the heat of the battle shook the confidence of General Hindman, who promptly gave up his planned attack and concentrated on holding the hill until nightfall.

Herron, now reinforced by the arrival of some of Blunt's army, renewed his heavy artillery fire on the hill. A second attack was prepared by the Union commanders using troops from the first attack, bolstered by reinforcements fresh on the field. In the new attack, the troops included the Twenty-fifth Illinois, Seventh Kansas, Fourth Wisconsin, and Ninth Missouri Federal regiments.

Ross Kimbrough rode hard toward the Confederate lines with the latest information on Union movements. All day he and his scouts had been doing their best to keep tabs on Blunt's movements. Now he was certain they had withdrawn from Cane Hill and were moving beyond the Confederate troops set to block his joining forces with Herron's army. He must get the word to General Hindman and Colonel Shelby. It could be disastrous if the Yankees joined forces before the Confederates were aware of what was happening.

He kept low on Sultan, whispering in his ear and urging him on, "Fly, boy, fly; you can do it!" Ross began peeling off his Union blue overcoat as he rode. He should be approaching Rebel lines and it wouldn't do to be shot down by his own army. He threw the overcoat across the saddle in front of him. The cold wind cut through his worn and tattered Confederate jacket.

Cold, so damn cold! Both armies ought to be in winter

camps instead of fighting this insane battle in freezing weather, he thought.

He crossed an open meadow and galloped hard for the hill, waving his hand so the Rebs would be sure to see him. They waved back furiously as he approached. He leaned forward in the saddle as he neared the Rebel lines only yards away and closing fast. Behind him he heard a barrage of musket fire as Union soldiers tried to cut him down. The shots sped harmlessly past him. He urged the big stallion on as the horse bounded over the Rebel soldiers lying in cover. The jar of the landing almost pitched Ross over head first, but he maintained his position in the saddle.

He headed Sultan for the top of the ridge and over the side of the hill where he knew Shelby's command should be.

He had barely cleared the ridge and headed past Prairie Grove Church when the Union army began to fire its new barrage preceding the second assault. Horse and rider were rocked by an exploding shell impacting near Sultan's right side and sending both of them staggering. Ross felt an immediate and intense pain in his right thigh as the shell exploded. He felt the big horse stumble and groan as he tried to keep his feet. The heart of Sultan was strong, but shell fragments had turned the horse's guts to bloody jelly. Sultan stumbled and went down hard on his right side, partially on Ross. Ross felt the frozen earth pound the wind from him as he slammed to the ground. At first he couldn't see because of dirt in his eyes and the shock wave from the exploding shell. His ears ached. Blood seeped from a ruptured eardrum. His head pounded with a terrible ache, compounded with the ringing in his ears.

Ross felt Sultan uselessly trying to regain his feet, but two of Sultan's legs were shattered and he was bleeding heavily internally. Terror was in the horse's eyes as he struggled.

Although Ross was suffering from shock, he knew his leg was pinned beneath his horse. His first thoughts were not for himself, but for Sultan. Tears streamed from his eyes as he rubbed the neck of the stallion. "Easy boy, it's all right. You did your best, easy now." Inside Ross felt the pain of losing a close friend as he hugged and stroked the big horse in his last moments. In minutes Sultan rattled out his last breath and lay still.

Ross cried in anger and cried still more in pain as he fought against his wounds and his grief. His leg was pinned and twisted under Sultan's body. He knew he must have taken shell fragments in the leg, but at least the pressure of the horse lying on it would help control the bleeding. His head hurt and the ringing in his ears seemed to intensify. He was alone and there was little he could do until someone found him.

He tried yelling for help, but above the constant roar of cannon and musket no one heard. He tried to look about him with his limited field of vision, but he could see no one—only trees, rock, and brush. He was fortunate he could reach his water in the canteen and the bedroll tied behind his saddle. The cold felt sharper now as he noticed the lack of his overcoat. He knew where it was, pinned under Sultan as was his leg.

The frozen ground only added to his discomfort. He hugged Sultan close, drawing comfort from the heat still emanating from his dead body. Well, if he could not use his overcoat, he could still wrap the blankets from his bedroll about him. It was difficult going, and the pain was constant, but after a bit he had the blankets wrapped around him. He put the canteen to his lips and was surprised to find the water turning to slush. It felt good to his parched throat.

All he could do for now was wait to be discovered. He only hoped it would be by his army. This thought made him aware of the need to protect himself. He reached behind his neck, pulled Double Twelve free, and pulled the sawed-off shotgun under the blankets. He had to rest from his efforts. He tried to take his mind off the pain, but it was of little use. He had never in his life felt more trapped and alone. It was all he could do to control the rising surge of panic within him. He had lost the best damn horse he had ever ridden or loved. He could think of a dozen men he knew he would have missed less.

39

Lucifer's Inferno

While Ross lay trapped beneath his horse, a half mile behind the front line, the battle raged on. General Blunt arrived on the field with his army and, as every hour passed, more troops were brought into the battle for the Union side. For four hours the bloody battle raged around the normally peaceful country church at Prairie Grove.

Blunt, determined to turn the Rebels left, massed a brigade and advanced toward Parson's brigade. Parson's men, determined to stand their ground, repulsed them with heavy losses. Blunt's veterans retreated through a large orchard and then beyond to the timber. There, lying in wait, General Blunt massed over thirty cannons in one solid artillery park.

In the orchard before the massed cannons stood five gigantic ricks of straw, harvested during the fall. The straw was well dried and dangerously combustible. The wounded lying on the battlefield were mostly Union soldiers injured in the attack on Parson's brigade. The weather was desperately cold and well below freezing. It was impossible to light fires for warmth, so the wounded that could crawl to the stacks covered themselves with straw to keep warm.

Disaster struck when sparks from the Union artillery set the stacks ablaze. The fire whipped quickly through the powder-dry straw. Many wounded were helpless to escape the flames. The screams and cries of the tortured being burned alive in the horrible conflagration twisted the hearts of the strongest soldiers. The heat was so intense that rescue was nearly impossible and few were saved. It presented the perfect picture of hell brought to the earth's surface. Some soldiers ran from the flames, their clothes and hair on fire, begging to be killed quickly by their comrades. The smell of burnt and roasted human flesh with its sickly sweet smell drifted to the Confederate lines. Over two hundred men and boys died in the flames and most died hideous, painful deaths, roasted alive in the fires.

Attracted by the smell of roasted flesh, a large drove of wild hogs made their way to the scene a few hours later. There they dined on the twisted bodies and vital organs of those caught in the fire. The sight was enough to make a man at once enraged and sick to his stomach. While some rooting hogs pulled arms and legs about, others dragged entrails across the ground. Out of anger, the soldiers began firing at the hogs, but the demands of battle limited this, and in the end the hogs continued their unholy feast of human flesh.

Herron, on the right of the battle, had little success and was repeatedly repulsed with heavy losses. Only the approach of darkness slackened the sickening slaughter.

As the sun began to color the sky through the lingering clouds of drifting gunpowder smoke, Jonas Starke located Jessie Kimbrough on the firing line.

Jonas crouched beside Jessie, using what little cover the tree next to him provided. He looked into Jessie's tired eyes. Black powder stains covered his face and made the whites of his eyes stand out in stark contrast. "Jessie, I need to talk to you."

Jessie looked at the wiry little scout, and he could see the deep concern on his face. Only one thing would bring Jonas looking for him. "It's about Ross, isn't it? What's happened, Jonas?"

"Yeah, I'm here about Ross. I don't rightly know where he is. All I know is he's darn sure missin'."

"Do you know where he was going?"

"Colonel Shelby sent him out to scout Blunt's boys 'round noon, I think it was. Well, when he didn't come back I got to thinkin' he might have bought the farm, so's I went lookin' fer 'im. The boys on our left said a fella that matched the way I described him crossed their line betwixt two and three this afternoon.

"He was travelin' in a hurry by himself, but he never reached Shelby. I figure he's got to be down on this ridge somewhere here abouts. Chances are if Ross didn't show up and if he is within our lines he's done been killed or wounded. Don't see much else that would keep that feller from doin' his job. If'n he is wounded, could be he's already been sent back to a field hospital."

Jessie felt his heart sink. His breath came in ragged little gasps as he thought about Ross. He knew Jonas was probably right. Ross had a strong devotion to duty, and if he didn't show up there had to be a good reason. "Thanks for coming to tell me, Jonas. I really do appreciate your checking on him. The fighting looks like it's slowing down now, maybe I can get permission from Captain Thomas to go looking for him. If he's dead I want to see he gets buried properly, and if he's wounded I want to help him in any way that I can."

"I wish I could help you look for him some more, Jess, but I ain't suppose to be here talkin' to you now. The colonel wants me to check and see if the road is open to the south. I guess the generals need to know if'n they got us bottled up in here or not."

"I understand, Jonas. And I know Ross would too. He'd want you to do your duty first."

"Yeah, I reckon you're right, but it don't set right anyway. I hope you find him healthy, youngster."

"I hope I do too. See you later, Jonas."

Concern was clearly etched on the scout's face as he kept

low and worked his way carefully from the front lines. Jessie made his way to Captain Gilbert Thomas.

"How are you doing, Jessie? You look better than you did when we hauled you up this hill earlier."

"I'm feelin' better, Captain; my chest is still mighty tender, but that's not why I came to talk to you. It's Ross—he's missing, and I'd like to get permission to go looking for him."

Gilbert looked away and paused as he thought silently. He turned and answered, "I'm not suppose to let my soldiers go wandering off looking for missing relatives or friends, Jess, but since you're sort of wounded, I guess you should try to find your way to a hospital to have it examined. It might take a fellow a while to find a hospital, I suppose." Gilbert winked at him. "I hope you find him alive, Jessie. Just try to catch up to us when you can. As far as I'm concerned, you've gone on leave to take care of battle injuries. We'll still be around when you get back."

Jessie smiled at Gilbert in relief. "Thanks, Gil, I really appreciate it. If you get the chance, would you let Calvin know I've gone to look for Ross?"

"Sure, I'll take care of it the first chance I get. Now you'd better go and get that wound of yours looked after."

The two quickly shook hands and Jessie made his way toward the crest of the hill behind him. He knew there was precious little light left, and once it was dark, the chances of finding his brother would be slim at best.

Jessie moved to the picket line where the horses were tethered. It was located in a draw that helped protect the horses. Even so, a few of the animals had been killed or injured. Those seriously injured had to be shot. Jessie was glad to see Star's Pride wasn't one of them.

Jessie thought that if he did find Ross he would either be dead or wounded. If he were dead, he would need some way to carry him. If he left his mount behind he might lose him. Horses were scarce and expensive to replace. He sure didn't want to wind up in the infantry for lack of a horse. He told the men why he was taking his horse, then led him away from the lines.

Jessie's first thought was to head for high ground. From the crest of the hill he would be able to see in both directions. He knew he was taking a chance because he would make a good target silhouetted against the skyline. He also knew it was a chance he would have to take.

The last rays of light lingered in the twilight as he moved over the ridge. An unnatural quiet was descending on the battlefield as darkness closed the day and ended the carnage. Jessie could not get over how cold it was. It would be far worse that night. He could see his every breath on the air when he exhaled. On every inhalation he could feel the sharp sting of cold air as he sucked each breath in through his nostrils. He wished for heavier gloves, because his hands tingled from the frigid weather.

It had grown quiet, so he started yelling, "Ross, Ross Kimbrough, can you hear me?" He repeated it every minute or so as he walked, leading his horse behind him. Each time he hollered, Star's Pride would fidget a little behind him.

Only ten minutes had gone by, when he heard, "I'm here, over here!" The sound was slightly muffled, but he recognized the voice. He had found Ross!

Jessie began to run, trying to pinpoint the direction of the voice. Finally, he came to a clearing. He strained his eyes to make out the terrain in the failing light.

Then he heard the voice, closer now. "Over here!" Ross was wrapped in blankets, lying against his horse.

"Jessie, you're sure a sight for sore eyes."

"Ross, are you hurt?"

"Yes, I guess I am. I don't know how bad it is. I've had my leg trapped under Sultan now for several hours. I'm pretty sure my leg was hit when the cannon shell exploded near us. The leg is asleep, so it helped control the pain. I know it's going to hurt like hell though when it wakes up again."

"Just hold still. I'll tie a rope to your saddle and see if Star's Pride can drag your horse off you."

Jessie scurried around hitching the rope to the saddle, then he mounted his horse. He pulled the rope taut and eased the stallion as he pulled against the dead horse.

Ross felt Sultan begin to lift off his leg as Star's Pride began tightening the rope. He used the leg that was on top of Sultan to push as best as he could. He felt himself jerk free, but the shift in the leg sent a wave of pain pulsing through his body. Ross screamed in pain. "I'm clear, Jess! You can slack the rope now."

Working mostly by feel, Jessie removed the overcoat from where the horse had lain. He removed a brace of pistols from the saddle, a draw sack of personal items belonging to Ross, and a Sharps carbine. These he strapped onto Star's Pride. "We can't take the saddle with us, Ross. No way to haul it, but I got most everything else."

Ross put Double Twelve back into his holster, then slipped the blue overcoat on and wrapped the blankets from his bedroll about him. He carefully explored his thigh. Just above the knee he found a ragged wound. He could tell the flesh had been ripped savagely, and he could feel the red sticky ooze still flowing from it. He couldn't reach lower because it hurt too much.

Jessie made his way to him and felt gently down the pant leg. There was a large bump in the flesh near the calf. "Christ Almighty, Ross! I think your leg is broke below the knee. I'll take you to the field hospital. I know it's going to hurt like hell, but do you think you can stand it if I lift you up on my horse?"

"What choice do I have? If I black out you'll have to tie me to your saddle. Jessie, I just want you to promise me one thing."

"Sure, Ross, what is it?"

"Promise me you won't let 'em take my leg off. Promise?"

"Aw hell, Ross, I can't promise you that! They might tell me you'll die if it doesn't come off. I'd rather see you with one leg than dead."

"Damn it, Jess, it's my life! I'd rather be dead than live like a cripple hobbling around on a stump the rest of my days. Promise me you won't let them take my leg, no matter what they tell you!"

Jess gave in reluctantly. "Yes, I promise, but we've got to

get you somewhere and have that busted leg set and get that wound tended to."

"Yeah, sure, but wait a minute. It tingles and hurts so bad it would kill me if you try to move me now."

After a few minutes Ross was ready to try and, after a painful struggle, he was lifted into the saddle. The damaged leg was left to dangle free of the stirrup. Jessie swung up behind and hung onto Ross, steadying him, holding the reins and guiding Star's Pride. Occasionally, Ross would slump over, nearly pulling them both to the ground when he passed out from the pain.

They made their way over the crest and down the other side. They reached Cove Creek Road and headed south, hopeful they would find a field hospital. When they started passing wagons filled with wounded, they knew they were on the right track. Empty wagons were moving north to pick up more wounded. The soldiers detailed to gather the injured worked by the light of dim lantern lights. Jessie could see them walking along the road, swinging their lanterns. Now and then they would stop and check on a wounded man. Those farther away, as they bobbed along, reminded him of fireflies flitting in the distance. Above them, in the bone-chilling cold, appeared the rising battle moon.

All along their route they could hear the pitiful cries and screams of the dying and the wounded. The battle lines were too close, so fires could not be lit. Both sides allowed the use of lanterns to gather the wounded, but gunfire would be directed at any campfire that could be seen.

The eerie, cold, moonlight glare exposed many ghastly sights along the road. Dead could be seen scattered everywhere, like rag dolls broken and discarded. White hoar-frost hardened on the fevered brows of the wounded. The dead stared vacantly into the star-lit heavens; their eyes and clothes, dimmed by the frost, gave them a ghostly appearance. The clip-clop of the horse's hooves sounded unnaturally loud on the frozen surface of the road.

They finally reached a meadow that served as the temporary field hospital. They were far enough away from the battle lines that they could see the cheering warmth of burning campfires. Jessie helped Ross to the ground and found him a place near a fire to rest. The fire would help ward off the night's clammy chill. Ross dozed off and on through the night, the pain in his right leg keeping him from sleeping soundly.

With the coming of false dawn he could see the meadow around him. A short distance to the south of him stood a tent used by the doctors for surgery. All night long he had heard screams of pain and terror.

He lay there for a couple more hours until two soldiers approached carrying a dirty, blood-encrusted stretcher. They laid it beside him, and the older, bearded soldier bent over him to examine his wound. The man's bloodshot eyes showed clearly his fatigue from taking care of the wounded all night. "He's next," he said matter of factly.

"I'm going with him. He's my brother," said Jessie.

"Operatin' tent ain't no place for those that don't need to be there. Sorry, but you'll have to wait outside."

"I said I'm going in there with him!"

"Look, I'm too tired to argue with ya, an' I ain't got the time. Besides, you'll probably faint dead away when they start on him, and then we'll have to carry you out."

"I've seen worse."

"Suit yourself," the soldier said disgustedly.

The soldiers bent down and quickly transferred Ross to the stretcher. Pain shot through his leg. Ross groaned and gripped the stretcher so tightly his knuckles turned white. As they carried him in, Ross saw a large pile of human limbs piled behind the tent. He was amazed at the size of the large stack of grisly remains. Hands, arms, legs, and feet protruded from the pile in every direction. Many were tinged with the dried color of black, coagulated gore, still others were tinted with the scarlet color of fresh blood. Boots and shoes still covered many feet.

Ross felt fear grip his stomach like a giant claw. He clutched Jessie's arm. "Don't forget your promise, Jessie! I'm counting on you to keep your word."

As they walked, Jessie laid his hand over his brother's. "Don't worry, I haven't forgotten."

They were ushered into the operating tent without ceremony. In the center of the tent stood two sawhorses with wooden planks stretched across. The table was wet and stained with blood along the edges. A soldier threw a bucket of water across the boards and quickly pushed the excess liquid off onto the floor with a blood-tinged cloth.

"Hurry up there, Floyd, I haven't got all day," grumbled a man standing near the center of the room. He stood next to a small stand located near the makeshift operating table. On the smaller table were arranged several bloody tools for cutting, sawing, and probing the afflicted. The doctor stood puffing on the stub of a fat cigar stuck firmly between his teeth. He wiped his blood-covered hands slowly across the dirty, stained smock that covered his uniform. Ross looked into the eyes of the doctor as he examined the wounds superficially.

What Ross saw was a man nearly worn beyond endurance, and nearly past caring. The man wore wire-rimmed, round glasses perched high on his nose. His beard was thick and dark. The doctor shifted the cigar in his mouth and said matter-of-factly, "Prepare him, Floyd, this leg needs to come off."

Ross sat upright, screaming. "No, take me out of here! I'd rather die than lose my leg. Don't let him do it, Jess!"

"Settle down, boy, that thigh has been hard hit and the leg is broke too. Chances are if we leave that leg on you you're gonna die of gangrene. Even if we take the leg off you might not recover, but if we cauterize the stump your chances to survive improve."

"I'll take my chances. Just dig that steel out of my leg and set it."

"Listen, soldier, I've got hundreds of men waiting for me to do what little I can for 'em. I haven't got time to waste digging around on a leg that needs to be taken off anyway. If I leave it on, you'll probably die. Now I'm tired and I haven't got time to debate medical procedure with you. The leg is coming off and that's all there is to it! Floyd, get some men in here to help hold him down."

Ross reached behind his neck and slid Double Twelve from its holster and jammed the twin barrels inches from the doctor's face. "I don't give a good, Gawd damn what you think, Doctor. This leg is staying on me. It isn't going to be cut off by you, or by anyone else. I came into this world with two legs, and I'm leaving it the same way. Now dig that metal out of my leg and set it, or so help me God, I'll blow your face all over the side of this tent." His eyes glared with intensity, leaving no doubt he meant every word.

The doctor looked pale and shocked as the blood drained from his face. He held his hand up to calm down Ross. "Take it easy, soldier. That cannon you got in your hand is liable to go off. I'm not about to work on you while you're holding a shotgun on me. First serious pain and you're likely to blow me to kingdom come!"

Jessie had been watching the scene and listening intently. Now he acted. He drew his revolver from its holster and held it in the direction of the doctor. "Doc, this is my brother, and if he wants to keep the leg, then I'll see that he does. Do what he says, or I'll shoot you myself."

The doctor sighed heavily, then replied, "Okay, I'll do the best I can if it's so damned important to you, but I warn you he probably will die anyway. Don't come back blaming me, because I've warned you." The doctor looked at the two brothers with resignation on his face. "He's got to put the sawed-off shotgun away. I won't touch him while he's aiming it at me."

"Put away the gun, Ross. I'll make sure the doctor doesn't remove your leg."

Ross handed Double Twelve to Jessie. Jessie tucked his pistol into his belt and held the sawed-off shotgun on the doctor. "Now get to it, Doctor. There are lots more waiting."

"You know I could have you both shot for this."

"We'll worry about that later, just get busy."

The doctor reached over to the table and grabbed a bottle of whiskey. He reached for a tin cup, poured a generous amount it and offered it to Ross. "Here, drink this; it's the only thing I can offer you for the pain." Ross tilted the cup back and drained the amber liquid down his throat. He felt the burn all the way down as it slid to his stomach. He finished the rest of it while his eyes watered.

"Would you like another cup?"

"No, let's get on with it."

"Well, if ya don't mind, I'll have a little." The doctor took a long pull directly from the bottle, then set it down. He reached across and grabbed a chunk of wood off the table. "Put this in your teeth to bite on. This is gonna hurt like hell!"

The doctor cut off the trouser leg, exposing the wound beneath. He poured whiskey on the damaged thigh. Ross nearly passed out from the searing pain. The doctor began probing the wound for the shrapnel. Minutes into it, Ross slipped into unconsciousness.

When he awoke he found himself lying under a tree near a campfire, just a short distance from the operating tent.

"I see you've finally awakened."

Ross's leg throbbed with every heartbeat, and his head pounded with pain. "How did it go?"

"You were in there almost two hours, and you've been out here for two hours more. The doc probed your wound and found these." Jessie held up two chunks of steel shrapnel from the exploded shell. He handed them to Ross. Ross looked at them, then pocketed them in his overcoat. "Ought to make a nice souvenir. What about the busted leg?"

"Well, Doc Spencer says it was a clean break and he set it. You have to keep your weight off it. He has it heavily splinted. He seems to think you might recover the full use of your leg, provided you don't come down with gangrene. Time will tell the tale. By the time he was done, Doc Spencer cooled off. While he was working on you we had plenty of time to talk. He says he admires your spunk and thought I was brave to risk courtmartial by holding him at gunpoint because of a promise. He decided he wouldn't report it. He told me he wished you the best of luck."

"I'm glad he saw it my way, because even if he hadn't, I still would have done it the same way."

"It's going to take you a while to get over this and, judging by the traffic on the road, our army is retreating south. I've heard we won the battle because we still hold the field, but I suppose the Yankees will claim otherwise. I hear our army is nearly out of ammunition and the closest supplies are at Little Rock. That means we have to pull out soon and all the wounded that can be moved will be; the rest will be left behind. We have to get you out of here."

"I know I need a place to rest and heal up, and I don't want to be in any army hospital. I've got an idea, if you'll help me."

"Sure, Ross, you know I won't leave you until I know you're safe. Captain Thomas said to take however much time I needed. Do you remember me telling you about how I got shot in the Bible? I told you last night as we rode in here. Well, Gil said I should have it looked after and take medical leave for as long as necessary. Doc Spencer looked at it after he worked on you and says I might have a rib separation or maybe a cracked sternum. Doc said it's deeply bruised and will be really sore for a while, but I ought to be fine. I figure it ought to be healed just about the time I see you safely away from here." Jessie winked slyly at his brother.

"Do you remember me telling you about that girl I met, Valissa Covington?"

"I sure do! Isn't that where you sent Cassandra and Katlin in the letter you left for them at Fayetteville?"

"That's right. Do you think you can get me to her home? I've never been there, but she told me it is near Batesville, Arkansas, in the White River valley."

"I'll get you there, Ross. You can count on it."

40

A Gift of Kindness

Cassandra fidgeted in her seat. Her hips were sore from spending long hours in the wagon. It seemed the journey would never end; after a while, one town was rather like the next. Before this trip she had traveled very little and it was a revelation for her.

Her mind drifted to thoughts of her mother. She still grieved, but the hurt was less as each day passed and she adjusted to her situation. She guessed it couldn't be more than a few miles until they reached Fayetteville, Arkansas. She looked forward to that goal with anticipation and concern. She hoped they would find a letter from her brothers there. If not, she was uncertain what to do next. She hoped her brothers had received the letter she had sent with Wash Mayes weeks ago.

After leaving Lamar, Missouri, they traveled through Carthage and Pineville, then through Bentonville, Arkansas. Now they were just a short distance from Fayetteville. Not knowing whether this was the end of the journey or just a temporary rest stop made them all tense. Toughened by adversity, hardship, and suffering, and forced to share close quarters for so long, they were all thin on patience.

They were amazed that there was at least one Union army detachment stationed at any large town. Some were local home guard companies, but most were units in regular Federal service.

They were passed by Captain Kenton Doyle and the Second Wisconsin Cavalry shortly after leaving Carthage. He took a few minutes to exchange greetings before duty compelled him to ride on with his unit. Doyle thought a battle was shaping up and his men were on their way to join General Blunt's Army of the Frontier.

Occasionally, they were forced to travel off the road or to wait for the passing of cavalry and infantry troops heading south. They were plagued with recurring meetings with wagon trains carrying supplies for the army. Cassandra noticed how Becca began to tremble each time they neared blue-uniformed soldiers. Her eyes would show her fear and, whenever possible, she would hide in the wagon. It was clear the rape she had suffered at the hands of Union soldiers had not been put behind her.

Luck was with them, for they had been largely ignored and allowed to continue. Food was plentiful if one was willing to pay the price. As they moved into the month of December, despite traveling south the weather grew increasingly cold and bitter. "Jethro, when we reach Fayetteville, we need to find the local post office. I just hope there is a letter from the boys."

"Yes, Miss Cassie, I reckon ya done told me three times today."

"Jethro, don't you be talkin' like that to Miss Cassie. You show more respect." Fanny turned to Cassandra. "He don't mean nuthin' by it, Miss Cassie."

"He's right, Fanny, I guess I have been repeating myself. I'm just tired and worried."

Katlin said, "I think we all are tired of riding in this wagon. I, for one, am looking forward to a stop."

It seemed to take forever to reach the post office. When

they did, Cassandra quickly jumped from the wagon. "Wait here and I'll see if they have a letter for us."

Katlin, Elizabeth, and the rest waited nervously, all praying a letter would be there.

Ten minutes passed. The seconds seemed to drag by. "What do you think is taking her so long?" Elizabeth asked.

"She probably has to wait her turn. "She'll be out shortly, I'm sure," responded Katlin. Katlin was just as anxious as Elizabeth.

Cassandra stepped from the post office gripping a letter tightly in her hands. "I've got it! It's a letter from Ross."

The entire party unloaded from the wagon and gathered around Cassandra. "Open it, Cassie!" urged Katlin.

With trembling hands she tore open the letter and began reading. After a few moments she looked up at those around her. "Ross says we should head for Batesville, Arkansas. He wants us to go to Covington Manor Plantation on the White River. He writes that his friend Valissa Covington and her family will help us find a place to stay. Ross says he has never met Valissa's parents, but their names are Andrew and Mary Covington. He has been writing to her and knows they are gracious Southerners and will help us. . . . But Batesville is nearly one hundred and fifty miles east of here, according to Ross."

A collective sigh of disappointment came from the group. Disillusionment was evident on their faces. "I know that hearing we still have two or more weeks of traveling is not welcome news, but we all want to be away from the Union soldiers, and they're thicker than fleas around here. I don't see that we have much choice."

They all looked tired but resigned to the fact. "For weeks all we knew was that we were heading south. Now, at least we have a destination," Elizabeth said with optimism.

More was written in the letter questioning the death of Glen Kimbrough and the destruction of Briarwood; Ross mentioned the good health of Jessie, Calvin, Gilbert, and Evan Stryker. It was obvious from the questions and concerns he expressed that he was clearly worried about his mother.

Cassandra knew it was going to be difficult to give him the painful news when at last they met. Ross also said he expected a big battle soon. From what the group had witnessed as they entered town, and the hustle and bustle of many soldiers scurrying about, something big was in the air.

"We've still got several good hours of daylight, so we might as well make use of it. The sooner we start the sooner we will be away from these soldiers." Cassandra turned and walked back to the wagon. "Well, don't just stand there, let's get moving." The rest joined her in the wagon now headed east.

They tried to find the main road heading in the general direction of Batesville. "When we near the edge of town you had better stop and let me ask directions, Jethro," Cassandra said.

"Yes, ma'am."

As they turned yet another street corner, a large church with wagons parked in front of it came in view. They stayed on their side of the street and passed by slowly, observing the activity around the church. Wagons were parked near the entrance and more were pulling up alongside. From the interiors of the wagons they heard the cries and moans of the wounded. They gawked as stretcher bearers unloaded the wounded and carried them inside the building. They were staring so hard they nearly ran into a Union barricade at the end of the block.

"Halt, halt, damn you!" yelled a Union guard.

"Whoa, there!" Jethro hollered at the horses as he sawed back on the reins.

The Union soldier stepped forward, gripping the leads of the horses. "State your business."

"Ain't got no business, suh! We's just headin' our way to Batesville."

"I ain't talkin' to you, nigger! I'm talkin' to who's in charge here. Now who would that be?"

Cassandra leaned forward. "I guess that would be me."

A thin, tall man dressed in a Union officer's uniform

stepped down from the boardwalk. He yelled at the soldier in the street. "Corporal Watkins, what have you got there?"

"Don't rightly know yet, Captain."

"I'll handle it." The voice sounded self-righteous, as if the officer found himself vastly important. He strutted around to the front of the team like a puffed-up peacock. "Now what do we have here? Where do you think you're heading with that wagon?"

"Excuse us, Captain, but we're heading to Batesville to visit family. You see we are refugees and our home has been destroyed. With winter closing in it is important we find shelter with family soon," spoke Cassandra firmly.

The officer stood before them arrogantly, swelling his breast as much as possible. The dark of his uniform accented his gaunt features. He looked over the wagon carefully. "I don't give a damn about your personal problems, ma'am, but the Union army is in need of a wagon like this. Our army has just completed a battle at Prairie Grove, and we have many wounded that need to be evacuated. I should seize this wagon for the Union army."

Cassandra, her face flushed with sudden anger, stood in the wagon. "You can't do that! This is all we own in the world. Without our wagon we'll be stranded with no home and no way to travel."

"What happens to you doesn't concern me. My immediate concern is to take care of our wounded and to see the doctors at the field hospital get what they need." He let the words sink in and take effect. "However, if you were to, say, volunteer to help with the wounded in the hospital over yonder . . . I might reconsider and allow you to keep the wagon. Provided of course, you serve among the wounded for a suitable time."

Cassandra's anger took control. She shook her fist at the captain. "You damned scoundrel! You try to blackmail a group of homeless women to work like common slaves in your hospital, while holding out the mere possibility that you will allow us to keep what is rightfully ours in the first place."

Katlin, knowing the situation teetered on the edge of disaster, stood and grasped Cassandra by the shoulders, then sat her down hard. She whispered quickly into Cassandra's ear. "Cassie, let me handle this! Your temper is going to lose this wagon, or worse. Now be quiet, please!"

The captain was startled by Cassandra's vehement outburst. He took immediate control of the situation. "Corporal, call out the guard."

"Yes, sir!" He sprinted to the doorway and yelled in the door. "Sergeant Smith, bring out the men." Ten men quickly filed out into the street.

Katlin spoke up quickly, "Please, sir! Forgive her comments. It is obvious to me you offer very fair terms. She just doesn't have a complete understanding of our situation. She hasn't been well of late."

"I'll not take that kind of talk from anyone. Is that clear?"

"Yes, sir, I'm sure she didn't mean it. Why don't you apologize to the captain now?" She pleaded with her eyes as she looked at Cassandra.

There was a pause, as everyone held his or her breath, waiting to see how Cassandra would respond. Cassandra, gritting her teeth, finally spoke softly. "I apologize, Captain. I am sorry if I offended you."

The captain looked smug, enjoying his victory. "I will accept your apology and have Corporal Watkins direct you to a place behind the church where you may park your wagon. Report to Doctor Harrison and he'll assign you to your tasks. If you do as you're told, you may keep your wagon."

"Thank you, Captain."

"You're welcome, Miss . . . ?"

"Katlin, Katlin Thomas."

"Thank you, Miss Katlin, until later then." He turned and strutted into the store serving as his command center.

They followed the corporal and his squad to the back of the church. There they unhooked the horse team and fed them. Jethro was left to guard the wagon and horses. Becca, trembling in fear, was hidden in the wagon. The rest, Cassandra, Katlin, Elizabeth, and Fanny, entered the hospital where they were ushered into the church office. There they met Doctor Harrison.

A tired looking man in his thirties entered the office. "What do we have here, Watkins?"

"Captain Matthews found these ladies, and convinced them to volunteer to help in the hospital."

"Tell Captain Matthews I'm very grateful. This hospital is overflowing with wounded, and more arrive every hour. I'm desperately short on help. We'll put them to work immediately; thank you, ladies." He smiled at them.

"We will do our best to help, Doctor. Despite our situation, we hate to see anyone suffering needlessly."

The rest of the day and most of the next the women toiled in the hospital. They changed bandages, carried water and food to the injured, and wrote letters home for some of the men. They even carried out the slop buckets overflowing with human waste, filled by men too injured to seek the outhouse behind the building. The stench of excrement, the iron-sweet smell of blood mixed with the odors of sweat, gunpowder, and dirt sickened them. Many dying soldiers were crying out in sweat-soaked delirium. Their screams of agony pierced the air and unnerved those around them.

Despite her anger at being forced to work in the hospital, Cassandra was affected by the misery surrounding her. Although these men were the very enemy her brothers were fighting against, on a personal level she found herself responding to their suffering. She felt satisfaction as she helped them and enjoyed their appreciative thanks.

On the second day, a young soldier lay dying of a gunshot to his chest. He was near delirium as he pleaded for his mother. Cassandra finished changing the bandage on a soldier nearby. Finally, overcome with pity for the young man, she went to him and grasped his hand. She leaned forward and put her hand gently on the boy's sweaty brow. "Rest easy, son, you'll be all right," she said softly.

"Ma, Ma, is that you?" He searched in her direction with eyes that could not see.

She paused, then answered, "Yes, it's me, son."

"Ma, I'm so glad you came, Ma. I hurt so bad."

"Rest easy, you'll be just fine."

"They shot me pretty bad, Ma, an' it hurts somethin' awful. I ain't never hurt so bad, Ma." He gripped her hand firmly. "I know I left without tellin' you and Pa I was fixin' to join the army. You ain't mad at me are ya, Ma?"

Tears welled in Cassandra's eyes as she looked at his youthful features. He couldn't be more than fourteen. She spoke soothingly, "No, son. We're not mad at you."

"I just knowed Pa would be mad at me fer runnin' off, Ma. He said I'd just go and get myself killed if'n I went." The boy's breathing became more ragged. "I didn't run, Ma. I stood there and I fought 'em until I got shot. I laid out there all night. Coldest night I ever spent. Tell Pa I'm real sorry an' that I love him, Ma. I don't think I ever took time to tell him."

She began to sob. Tears began streaming down her cheeks, her heart tore. She wished there was some way to save this boy, "Try not to speak, son. You need your rest."

"I can't, Ma. I can't hardly breathe." He coughed deeply; a froth of blood lingered on his lips. "I'm scared to go to sleep. I'm afraid that I won't wake up, Ma."

"Close your eyes and sleep now. God will watch over you while you rest." She held and stroked his hand.

His breathing slackened as he wheezed for air. Then he stopped breathing as his hand relaxed in hers. He stared at the ceiling with vacant eyes. She continued to cry as she reached up and closed his eyelids with her fingers.

She turned to the soldier in the bed next to her. The man had a bloody stump where once his leg had been. "Do you know what his name was? I want to write his family and let them know what has happened to their son."

"No, ma'am, I surely don't. All I know is they called him Tommy when they brought him in this mornin'. I never heard a last name. Maybe when they search his body before they bury him they'll find something with his name on it. If they don't I guess it won't make much difference to him anymore.

A grave is the same whether you've got your name on it or not."

She searched the boy's body for some clue. In his breast pocket she found a blood-tinged letter. In it she found a tintype with the youthful boy standing proudly in his uniform sternly grasping a musket. When she turned it over she saw the name: *Tommy Benson, Twentieth Wisconsin Infantry. Picture taken at Springfield, Missouri.* The letter had his hometown of Madison, Wisconsin, addressed on it. She neatly folded it away, vowing to herself to write and send them the tintype. She found a piece of paper and wrote his name on it with a pencil and pinned it to his shirt. He wouldn't be buried in an unmarked grave. She turned away and walked toward the room's entrance.

A familiar voice spoke as she neared the door. "That was kind of you to stay with that boy while he was dying, Cassandra."

She whirled to face the voice. In the bed, with his back braced against the wall, sat Kenton Doyle. His shirt was loosely buttoned and she saw bandages beneath it. Pain was clearly visible in the pale blue eyes. "Captain Doyle, I'm surprised to find you here."

"You can't be much more surprised than I am. You're one of the last people I would expect to find working in a Union hospital."

"As you might have guessed, it certainly wasn't by choice. We have to work in this hospital or lose our wagon."

"I know we need the help, but I don't approve of forcing civilians to work by threats. I want to know on whose authority you were treated this way."

"It was a captain named Matthews."

"I'll see to it personally you get a pass that will get you through the lines safely. I outrank Captain Matthews, so I can put a stop to his interference. I was promoted to Major just before the battle at Prairie Grove."

She looked at him, puzzled by his response. "Why would you help us?"

"Because of what you did for that dying boy over there . . .

and because it isn't fair the way your family has been treated. Besides, you're the most spirited and beautiful woman I have ever met. I would hate to think you didn't think well of me."

Cassandra smiled shyly, caught off guard by the handsome major. "After all we've been through on this journey we'd be grateful for any kindness you could show us." She moved closer to him. "How badly are you hurt?"

"If it heals all right, I'll live. I was shot through the shoulder. It seems to have missed any bone and exited my back cleanly."

"Let me see your bandage." She gently unbuttoned his shirt and pealed it back to expose the wrap covering the wound. She felt herself becoming aroused as she ran her fingers gently through the curly dark hair on his muscular chest. She tried to be casual as she unwrapped the bandage covering the wound.

Major Kenton Doyle winced with pain as she pulled the cloth free to expose the wound. It was clotted with a dark scab over the center of the hole. New blood oozed from the edge of the scab.

"It doesn't look too bad." She was relieved to see it look so clean. Many soldiers she had helped had wounds full of pus and smelling of decay. She pulled a bucket with clean water to her, dipped a soft cloth into the bucket, and bathed the wound. Then she wrapped it again with new cotton cloth. "There, that should feel better." She looked into his eyes and they locked for a second.

"Thank you, Cassandra, you have a very gentle touch." She was still sitting near him and he felt intoxicated by her perfume. He felt the softness of her body pressing against him and the warmth of her hand as it lingered on his chest. He felt the stiffening, throbbing arousal grow as if it had a mind of its own. He hesitated, then leaned forward and kissed her. She was shaken by the kiss and pulled away from him.

"I'm sorry, that was very forward of me. I didn't have any right to try and kiss you, Cassandra. I hope you'll forgive me."

Cassandra didn't know what to think. Here she was being

held against her will in this hospital and being forced to take care of the enemy. These people fought for the very same army that had killed her father, destroyed her home, and given her nothing but grief for months. She hated herself for being attracted to this man, yet she felt a powerful pull toward him. He was indeed handsome and, more important, he had been kind to her. Was she interested in him because he was forbidden, or simply because she had been away from male companionship for so long? She wasn't certain, she only felt the burning need to be loved, to feel again the heat of passion and desire as she had for Evan Stryker months before. She knew this wasn't the time or place to decide. She needed space to sort her feelings.

Cassandra leaned forward and returned his kiss passionately. As she pulled her face inches back from his, she said, "I forgive you. I guess I wanted you to kiss me, too."

"Wha hoo! Way to go there, Major. Ya think you could chase up a pretty nurse for me to kiss, too?" The comment came from the soldier lying on the cot next to Major Doyle.

Cassandra was startled by the yell. She pulled away from the major and rose to her feet. She looked about her and saw a room full of lonely, wounded soldiers staring back at her. Some were smiling, others just looked envious. All motion had stopped in the room and all eyes were on them. She looked back at Kenton. "I guess this isn't the proper time, is it?" She could see the regret on his face, knowing that for now it was impossible.

"I'm afraid we do have a bit too much of an audience. Get some paper and a pen from the doctor, and I'll write out a pass that will get you through our lines."

With all eyes on her, she felt embarrassed. She moved toward the church office. As she passed through the rooms she spotted Elizabeth. "Tell Kat I've got good news. Captain . . . I mean, Major Kenton Doyle is here, and he'll give us a pass through Union lines."

Elizabeth's eyes lit up with excitement. "I'll tell Kat!"

Cassandra found some military stationery in the doctor's

office, along with a pen and an ink well. She carried them swiftly to Major Doyle.

He took the pen and with his good arm wrote out the pass. When he finished he handed it to her. "I'm probably a fool for doing this. I'd like to keep you here just so I could spend even a little time with you. My conscience would never rest if I kept you here amidst this den of misery and death. Take it and leave here first thing in the morning." He paused. "Cassandra, do you know where I might find you? Would you give me an address?" His eyes pleaded with hers. "Perhaps, when this war is over, we could start afresh."

"I'll write out the address for Harlan Thomas in Lafayette County, Missouri, and the address we have for Andrew Covington's Plantation near Batesville, Arkansas. I'm afraid that is the best I can do. I don't really know what will happen or where we will live. Maybe, when the war is over, things will be different. I hope so."

He grabbed her by the wrist and pulled her to him. He ran his fingers through her hair and kissed her. "I hope you will remember me. Have a safe trip."

She stood, still holding his hand. "You take care of yourself, Major. I'll remember you. Thank you again for helping us."

"My pleasure," Kenton said softly. She could see the longing in his eyes. He didn't want her to go, but understood she must.

She turned and walked silently away.

41

Blizzard

Jessie squinted, straining to see through the swirling snow around him. The cold winter wind driving the soft flakes turned them from a thing of beauty to an instrument of pain. His eyes burned and watered, blurring his vision. The ground was completely covered, making the edge of the road harder to see. A blanket of snow was beginning to stick to the back of Star's Pride as he pulled the buckboard through the snow. Ross, lying on a pallet in the back of the small wagon, moaned.

"Jessie, you're about to bounce me to death back here. Can't you try to miss the larger holes?"

"Sorry, I'm doing the best I can, but the snow is starting to cover the holes and ruts. I can hardly see the road, so I don't know how you expect me to miss them."

"I think it's time we hunt a place to stop and try to build a fire. If we try to keep moving in this snowstorm we'll either get lost or freeze to death."

"My eyes are hurting something awful, and my hands are

so cold I can't feel the reins anymore. Soon as I can find us a grove of trees to block some of this wind we'll pull in."

It took less than half a mile to find a suitable spot, and Jessie stopped the rig. He unhooked Star's Pride from the harness and tethered him to the rear of the buckboard. They were out of hay, but he gave the horse a ration of grain. They had a few pieces of wood, brought from the previous camp that they had managed to keep fairly dry. Using it for a starter, they soon had a blaze burning not too far from the side of the buckboard.

Jessie crawled under the small wagon and scooped out the snow that had fallen on the ground beneath it. He then spread his bedroll out under the wagon. When he was done, he helped Ross from the buckboard and moved him underneath. But the buckboard was too small to cover them both. They could get their heads and parts of their bodies under the makeshift roof of the wagon bed. Their legs were exposed to the snow, except for the protection offered by the blankets. The heat of the fire helped warm them. Jessie took their worst blanket and tied it between the wagon wheels on the opposite side of the wagon from the fire. It helped block the wind and kept some of the snow from drifting under the wagon.

They had to make do with corn bread they had gotten from a kindly farmer's wife the previous night. It was dry, but they had water to wash it down. Anything that could take the edge off their hunger was welcome.

As he lay beside Ross, Jessie thought about how lucky they had been. The day after the doctor had worked on Ross's leg, Jessie found a farmer willing to sell his old buckboard and harness to Jessie. Jessie and Ross used twenty-dollar gold pieces their mother had sewed in the lining of their jackets at Briarwood so many months ago. Without the wagon, it would have been almost impossible for Jessie to transport his wounded brother.

They were lucky to have their bedrolls and regular field gear with them. From the captured Union wagons the brigade had taken, they had gotten extra socks, some extra blankets for Ross, new boots, a frying pan, and a coffee pot. They managed to get half a pound of coffee beans that they hoarded carefully. In the morning they would brew some up after melting snow in the pot.

The captured wagons had been filled with much-needed supplies for the Confederate army facing a hard winter. In the forty captured wagons they found boots, shoes, blankets, hats, arms, sugar, coffee, rice, flour, hams, tobacco, cigars, tents, and camp equipage. Ammunition in the wagon train had been minimal. If there had been more the army could have stayed and fought.

By the light of the fire Jessie examined Ross's leg. It was swollen and fiery red. The leg throbbed and kept Ross from rest until total exhaustion made it possible for him to sleep. So far, Jessie had been able to move him about, and Ross had maintained a clear head. Ross was still clear of fever, but Jessie couldn't tell if the wound was beginning to heal. He didn't like the looks of it and hoped it wasn't beginning to fester. He wrapped a fresh cotton bandage around Ross's thigh.

"How long do you think this snowstorm will last, Jess?"

"I don't know. If it keeps falling like this it'll be darn near impossible to make any distance tomorrow. We don't have enough food to stay here very long."

"Got any idea how far we have to travel yet? I sure have a hard time keeping track from the back of the buckboard."

"The way I figure it, we're about ten to fifteen miles east of Clinton. Three to four more good days of traveling ought to get us to Batesville. I don't know how much delay there will be with this weather though."

Ross pulled the blanket up tighter around his neck. He wasn't as cold as he had been earlier. The warmth of the fire had chased away the chill. He listened to the snowflakes sizzle in the fire. "I don't know what I would have done if you hadn't come along to take care of me, Jess. I guess I would have been at the mercy of the hospital corps or left to be captured by the Yankees."

"I know you'd have done the same for me, Ross."

"Just the same, I'm mighty grateful. This leg is so painful, I'm not good for much."

"Don't worry about it. I'm just glad we're both alive and have this time together. Now, try to rest. I don't know what problems we'll face by morning."

"Yes, you're right. I'll try."

Ross tried to fall asleep for more than an hour. The cold, harsh wind howled through the trees. He could hear the branches of the old oaks creaking and moaning under the strain of the stormlike banshees in the wind. The blankets tied to the wheels slapped and popped against the stronger winds. In the distance he heard the lonesome bark of a coyote. Snow sifted in around the blankets. He tried not to think of the storm. Instead he thought about Valissa Covington.

He had not seen her since the two days he had spent with her on the Lightfoot Plantation near Clarendon. She had made quite an impression on him, and since then he had received a few letters from her. Still, he had not known her long and had never met her parents. He was afraid of the reception he might receive after dropping in unannounced on people he didn't know. He felt it was presumptuous to expect Valissa to take care of him now that he was wounded, but where else could he go? To make matters worse he had sent his family there. That is, if they had received the letter.

He had mentioned his family's plight to Valissa in a letter, but there hadn't been time for a reply. He only hoped they would be willing to help his family find a place to stay. He had faith in his judgment of her. He was sure she was from strong Southern stock who would not turn them away in their time of need. At least, he hoped not. He hadn't said anything to Jessie, but he was plagued by doubt. Soon weariness overtook his tired body and he drifted off into a troubled sleep.

Jessie woke to a bitterly cold dawn. The snow had stopped, and the sun was already glaring off the blanket of white. The fire had burned through the night only because he would wake to add wood to the blaze. The snow falling on the blankets had melted from the heat of the fire. The top blankets were soaked, but he knew once they left the comfort of a fire they would quickly freeze. Steam drifted from the blankets into the crisp air.

Jessie rose and took out the coffee grounds from the previous morning. He filled the coffee pot with fresh snow and melted it over the fire, adding more snow as he felt necessary. Then he added the ground beans and let the pot warm on the fire. Soon it was ready; he poured coffee into two cups for Ross and himself. He dug out the last of the corn bread and each had a square of it to eat.

Ross looked up as Jessie handed him the cup and the bread. "Looks like we got four to five inches last night."

"Yes. It's deeper where the wind has drifted it. Still, it could be worse. I figure we can move on, but this will slow us down."

"Better to move on than to stay here and starve to death. I don't want to freeze into gigantic icicles," Ross said with a grim smile.

They packed up camp as quickly as possible, cleaned the snow off the top of the buckboard, and started the journey again.

Cassandra stood at the window watching the snowflakes swirl and float down to add to those already covering the ground. Frost formed in the corner of the window panes and, when she stood too close, her breath fogged the glass. She sighed heavily, disappointed in the storm that would delay their trip. She supposed it could have been worse. If Judge Bandenburg hadn't asked them to stay in his home they would still be on the road and caught in this snowstorm. She was grateful they were nearing their destination. Jasper was more than half-way to Batesville, but she knew the weather was not likely to get better with winter officially here.

Her mind drifted to thoughts of Kenton Doyle. She hated to admit it, but there was something about him that attracted her. Even though she didn't want to give in to those feelings, they lingered despite her best efforts. She guessed they would still be slaving away at the hospital and, perhaps, would have had their wagon stolen from them had it not been for the pass. The wonderful pass that freed them from the hospital, got them past Captain Matthews and his men and through all the Union picket lines they had encountered. She marveled at how easy it was once the soldiers saw the order written by Major Doyle. For that she was forever grateful. She laughed at how mad the arrogant Captain Matthews had been when he had seen the pass. The little banty rooster of a man didn't like being out-ranked and having his orders overridden.

The trip had been less than pleasant as they fought the frigid weather and the rigors of winter travel. Still, they made good time. It had taken them only a week to make Jasper, Arkansas, where they now found themselves. The judge had been most kind to offer them the hospitality of his home. She wasn't content though and wouldn't be happy until they reached the end of the journey. Once they reached Batesville, she wondered how they would be received or even if they would have a place to stay. All she knew, all any of them cared about, was that it was the end of the journey.

She leaned her head against the cold window pane. "Please, God, let the storm end so we may continue our trip. I just want this trip over."

42

End of the Journey

The old, slightly hunched black butler shuffled into the parlor to summon the daughter of his master. "Miss Valissa, there's a young soldier at the door askin' for you. Says he has a friend of yours in a wagon out front. The boy is mighty anxious to talk to you. He says they come far to see you."

"Thank you, Henry. Did he say what his name was?"

"Yes, ma'am, the one at the door says he's Jessie Kimbrough, an' the one in the wagon is Ross Kimbrough, Missy."

Valissa was stunned. She had received several letters from Ross, but she had not seen him for several months. She was caught off guard, for she hadn't been expecting him. "Did you say Ross Kimbrough is here?"

"Yes, ma'am, that's what the boy said. He says he got his brother out in the wagon and his name is Ross."

Valissa turned to her mother sitting in the large rocker next to her. "Mother, I know this is sudden, but it seems we may have guests. Do you remember the gentleman I told you about, the one I met at the Lightfoot Plantation?"

"Yes, Val. I'm not deaf. I heard perfectly well what Henry said. Isn't he the one you've been writing to who had you walking around in a daze for weeks after you came home?"

Valissa blushed as she looked at her mother excitedly. "Yes, Mother, he's the one. He was such a dashing gentleman. I know you'll be impressed with him."

"Then you had better see to bringing him in here before he freezes to death. Land sakes, it's been colder than blue blazes of late. Well, don't just stand there, Henry, like some no account field hand. Fetch the people in here. Val, you had better go and greet them, then bring them to me. I'm not getting any younger, and I'm anxious to see what had you mooning around here like some love-sick calf for nearly a month."

"Yes, Mother." Valissa moved quickly to the front door. Henry tried to hurry, but he was no match for Val who brushed by him. She saw a young man standing six feet tall with long, brown, wavy hair. He had gray eyes that showed intelligence and a smile that came easily. She thought the young man would be handsome after a bath and a shave. His uniform showed wear and was heavily soiled. The overcoat startled her at first because it was Union blue, but she found it reassuring his pants were Confederate gray with yellow cavalry stripes.

Valissa spoke first. "Welcome to Covington Manor Plantation. Our house-man said that you were Jessie Kimbrough. Your brother has told me about you in the letters he wrote."

"Yes, madam, I'm Jessie. I'm very pleased to meet you."

"I heard Ross is with you. Is there something wrong? Why isn't he in here with you?"

"Yes, he's out in the wagon. He got hurt at the battle of Prairie Grove almost two weeks ago. We got caught in a bad snow storm a few days back, and he started running a high fever. Ever since then he's been pretty sick. Sometimes he's out for quite a while, and sometimes he talks pretty crazy."

"We'd better get him into a room upstairs. Henry, see if

you can round up a couple of the hands to help Jessie carry him upstairs, quickly now!"

The gray-haired butler answered with speed, "Yes, Miss Valissa. I'll fetch some of the hands directly." He shuffled off in his peculiar small steps as fast as he could go.

"Henry has been with the family a long time. You'll have to forgive him. His arthritis has slowed him down as the years have passed."

"I'm mighty grateful for you taking us in like this. We didn't know where else to go when Ross got wounded—neither of us trust the hospitals. He's wanted a good excuse for a long while to come see you. You've been on his mind."

Valissa's smile showed she was a little embarrassed, but her face also showed her anxiety. "How badly is he hurt, Jessie?"

"He caught some fragments in his leg from a cannon shell. The blast killed his horse, and the same leg broke when the horse fell on him. A doctor at the field hospital wanted to take his leg off but Ross wouldn't let him. With a little persuasion, the doctor took the fragments out of his leg and set the bone. Ross was doing fine until the last few days. I suspect all this cold weather, with him injured and all, has been hard on him."

"You can trust us to take good care of him, and I hope you'll stay, too."

"That's very kind of you, ma'am. I hope you'll accept my apology for my rough appearance. In the army it is difficult to keep as clean as you would like." He looked about anxiously. "Do you think they'll be much longer? Ross has been pretty sick, and it's very cold out there."

"It shouldn't take very long. Please, Jessie, I'd feel much more comfortable if you would just call me Valissa or Val instead of ma'am. It makes me feel like you're talking to my mother."

"Yes, mad . . . I mean, Valissa."

She nodded her head approvingly. "That's better."

Henry hobbled into the hall. "I got four of the field hands comin' round front right now, Miss Valissa."

"Thank you, Henry. Would you please inform Mother that one of our guests is injured and the other one will need to clean up before he meets her. Also, ask Etta to come up to the guest room at the top of the stairs."

"Yes, Miss Valissa, I'll see to it right away."

Valissa moved quickly to follow Jessie through the front door. She had been hesitant to see Ross for it had been such a long time since they'd first met. What would he be like with an injury? She didn't know how she would respond to him.

When they reached the wagon, she realized she wouldn't have to worry about conversation. Ross was unconscious and lying in the back under a pile of blankets. She looked at the handsome face that made her heart pound with excitement just a few short months before. His thick blond hair, high cheek bones, and strong jaw line, covered now by a dark blond beard, made him every bit as ruggedly good looking as she remembered.

His skin looked pasty. She could tell he was fighting a fever, his body shook with a chill. Jessie directed the men to carry him upstairs into the guest room. Valissa followed them.

"Get those filthy blankets off him."

"Yes, ma'am," said one of the field hands as he gently unwrapped Ross. Then he carried them out as he and the rest of the field hands left the room.

A strong-looking, middle-aged black woman who reminded Jessie of Fanny walked in, but this woman was older than the cook from Briarwood Plantation. "Miss Val, Henry told me you wanted to see me right away."

"Yes, Etta, we have a guest that has been injured and is sick. I want you to clean him up and see what you can do with his wounds. He's been running a fever. This one is very special, so you take good care of him."

The black woman shot a look at her that said she should know better. "Now, Miss Val, you know I'm gonna do my best. That's why you called me up here, now ain't that right?"

"Yes, Etta, I know you're good at healing."

"Well, I'm gonna do better if'n you all scoot on out here and let me work. Go on now, give me some workin' room."

"I swear, Etta, sometimes you act like you own this plantation. I wish you would show more respect in front of our guests."

"Don't mean no disrespect, Miss Valissa. I just say what I have to say, that's all."

Jessie followed Valissa down the stairs. He tried not to stare at the swing of her hips, but he felt his eyes drawn there despite himself. Yes, indeed, Valissa Covington was every bit the beauty his brother had claimed she was—If anything, he had not given her full credit.

At the bottom of the stairs Valissa stopped to talk to him. "I'll see to it our people get you something to eat and prepare a hot bath for you. I hope you'll fit in some of my brother's clothes. You may wear them until your clothes are cleaned."

"Thank you, Valissa, a bath would feel wonderful, and food has been in short supply the last few days. Would you please let me know if there is any change in Ross?"

"Surely, I would be glad to." Valissa called for Henry, and after a time the old man appeared. She gave him his instructions and he led Jessie off to get cleaned.

Valissa needed some time to sort her feelings, and she didn't want to answer questions she had few answers for. She headed for the comfort of her room.

Valissa gazed off into space, letting her mind wander until a knock came at the door. The noise jarred her back to reality. Time had passed quickly, and she guessed she had left Jessie over two hours ago.

Etta was at the door. "There you are, child. I took care of that gentleman for ya. I got him outa those filthy clothes and all scrubbed up. I looked over his hurts some an' I'd say the break in his leg is healin' just fine. They done a good job of setting it." She kept watching Valissa while she talked and moving her hands to illustrate each point she made. "I took the bandages off his wound, an' that's why he's feelin' poorly. It was festered up some. I took that old leaky scab off, drained the pus out of it, and put one of my mustard poultices on it. I'll keep changin' it regular like and it'll suck the poison right out, given a few days." She looked worried. "But that boy don't have enough meat on his bones to carry him far with him bein' so sick."

"Do you think he'll make it, Etta?"

"Hard to say, Missy, he sure is a sick one he is. I figure he's gonna be laid up a good while, and he's gonna need plenty of care. If his spirit is strong, an' God is willin', he's got a chance. Could go either way, I'd say."

"I'll try to spend as much time with him as I can and help take care of him," Valissa said earnestly.

"If the boy can break his fever an' we can get the poison out of him he might make it. I guess I'd best get down to the kitchen and see what I can cook for the other one to eat. Ain't gonna be long before everybody gonna be yellin' for some vittles again. I declare, I ain't ever gonna catch up on all my chores." The housekeeper turned and hurried away. Valissa heard Etta grumbling to herself all the way down the hall.

43

Covington Manor Plantation

Valissa sat in a chair watching over Ross's troubled sleep. Under the influence of delirium she had heard him talking about his home and family, the war, and people she supposed were his friends. He often cried or yelled as if he was in pain. One night he called her name and smiled.

She found herself studying him for extended periods of time. She loved his thick blond hair and beard. The strong and dashing face fascinated her. She liked to see his dimples and his strong, straight white teeth when he smiled. She had bathed his forehead and chest with cool wet cloths, and she had admired his strong chest and broad shoulders. When no one was around, she enjoyed running her fingers through the coarse hairs on his chest. There was a powerful magnetism to his rugged good looks she could not deny.

Many times she had helped Etta change the bandage on his leg and replace the smelly poultices that seemed to heal his wound. He went in and out of consciousness, and during those brief periods when he was alert she got him to eat as much chicken soup and meat broth as she could. During those times, before he would drift off again, he talked and thanked her for her help. His genuine appreciation of her efforts made her feel warm and tender.

Meanwhile, Jessie had nearly recovered from his sore chest. The swelling and the bruise were gone, but he still felt pain when he tried to lift too much. He tried to be useful around the house, but it had been difficult for him these past two weeks as he helped keep vigil over his brother, Ross.

Valissa's father, Andrew, had returned from Little Rock. Although surprised, he had not objected to the unexpected house guests. His loyalty to the South was strong, and he was happy to offer his home as refuge to Southern soldiers wounded in battle.

For Ross, the days slid by easily, one into another. Through fever-blurred eyes he thought he saw an angel hovering over him, an angel with the eyes the color of new bluegrass. Those deep green eyes with just a hint of blue in them showed character and concern. Her abundant auburn hair caressed her head and shoulders like a lovely halo. Her enchanting face comforted and cared for him as he drifted in and out of consciousness. He felt her tender, soft hands stroking him with cooling cloths, bringing a measure of relief to his fevered body.

In the times he was conscious he talked to his brother Jessie, met Etta and thanked her, and enjoyed the loving attention of Valissa. She took the time to feed him soup or broth a spoonful at a time. She saw to it he got plenty of water to drink. He tried to be modest around her, but because of his illness he found it an impossibility. He knew he was seriously ill and was grateful for finding his way into such gentle care. If he were to die, he would have at least experienced the tender touch of a beautiful woman.

Many a night Valissa had fallen asleep sitting by Ross's bed and in the morning had awakened stiff and sore from sleeping in the chair. Her mother worried about her spending too much time with Ross, but in the end accepted the need for someone to take care of him.

This particular day followed what had been an unusually rough night. The morning found things little changed. Ross was delerious from a high fever and his bed was soaked with sweat. Valissa and Jessie were concerned, fearing he was taking a turn for the worse and worrying he might die.

Even Etta had been worried. She came back often to examine him to see if there was any change. "Child, you gotta keep that boy cooled down. He's runnin' a high fever and if it don't break soon he's gonna cook his brain. I think the time of reckoning is a comin'. I suppose the choice is up to him an' the Lord; we just gotta wait an' see which way it goes."

They stood vigil over him through another day and into the night. Valissa took the late-night shift and stayed with him through the early morning hours. She continued to bathe him often with the cooling cloths and spoon-fed him snow to help cool him. She changed the cloths on his forehead and neck often. Still, when she left him alone for a few moments, beads of sweat would pop out on his face and body. As the long hours wore on, she dozed off in the chair.

Valissa heard a far-off voice call to her. At first she couldn't understand, for she was in a deep sleep. Then it came again. This time it didn't seem so far away. Her mind began dragging her back to consciousness, and she felt something warm grasp her hand and squeeze it gently. She turned her head and with sleep-filled eyes looked at Ross Kimbrough. He looked different to her now.

"Good Morning, Valissa. It looks like you've spent another night in that chair."

Even through her sleep-clogged senses Valissa knew there had been a change. She quickly jumped up and put her hand on his forehead. "Ross, I think your fever has broken. How do you feel?"

"My head is clear for the first time in days. I don't feel hot or cold either. I don't think I'm ready to go dancing, but I feel better." He paused. "Say, do you suppose you could round up something for me to eat? I'm hungry as an old bear."

Valissa smiled brightly. "I'll see what I can find. I'm sure Etta can have something up here for you in no time." She dashed out of the room, yelling her delight to everyone in the house. "Ross is awake! Ross is awake! The fever has broken!"

Ross lay in the bed smiling and laughing as he heard her exuberance. He still felt mighty weak, but he knew the worst was over. He had thought for a time the doctor was right and should have taken the leg. Ross knew he had teetered at the edge of death, but he survived and he was whole. His leg was still sore to be sure, but it no longer felt like it had a hot chunk of burning coal lying on it. It would take a while for the bone to knit, and longer still for him to quit favoring it, but he would gladly pay the price of exercise to regain its full use. Shortly after Valissa left the room, Jessie rushed to his brother's side and gave him a big hug. "You liked to scared us to death, big brother. I was sure you were going to die on me. You're looking much better."

"I'm feeling better too. What have you got there?"

Jessie held up the crutch in his hand. "This? Just a big ole club. Thought you might need a good beating." He swung the crutch above the bed, an ornery smile on his face.

He paused and held it where Ross could admire it. "It's a crutch." He handed it to Ross. "I made this for you while I was waiting on you to recover. I think you're going to need it for a while, until that leg heals."

Ross looked at the stout crutch carved out of oak timber. The top was smoothed, polished to fit under his arm and support his weight when he walked. "Thanks, Jess, I'm planning to put it to good use really soon."

Etta stormed into the room, taking charge. "Not right away you ain't! Not till I says you can." She turned to Jessie and motioned for him to get out of the way. "Scoot now and let me in there so I can take a look at that leg."

She yanked the blankets back rapidly to expose the wounded leg. The sudden move startled Ross, and he found himself staring at his nude body beneath the sheets. He reacted instinctively and tried to cover his exposed, naked body by pulling the blankets back over him.

Etta looked up at him, puzzled, and again snatched the blankets back exposing his nakedness. She then shot an indignant look at him. "What's wrong with you? I been helpin' Miss Valissa take care of you for a long time. You ain't got a thang I ain't seen before and I ain't got time to be playin' no peek-a-boo games with you! Now hold still an' let me take a look at that leg of yours."

Ross felt the burn of embarrassment as his face flushed crimson. It had not occurred to him that Valissa and this demanding black woman had seen him naked. It was not the first time, to be sure, he had been seen nude by a woman, but those rare occasions had been by moonlight or firelight and in the heat of passion. He didn't know how he was going to face Valissa the next time he saw her.

Etta ignored his discomfort and continued to work on his leg. She unwrapped the bandages, then removed the poultice. She reached into the bucket of water sitting by the bed and bathed the wound.

"Yeah, I think my poultice done worked its magic. The pus seems drawn outa that hole in your leg. I reckon it's gonna heal nicely now. I think we'll wrap it lightly this time and see if we can't get a good scab to form over it to protect it while it finishes healin'."

To his embarrassment Valissa walked through the door and strolled over to peer at the unwrapped and cleaned wound. Instinctively, Ross quickly moved his hands and cupped them over his privates.

Valissa noticed the sudden movement and saw the crimson blush on Ross's face. She smiled mischievously. "Well, you're certainly looking better." She winked at him, then looked down at the wound on his thigh. "Etta, the leg looks much better. I swear that poultice of yours works wonders."

"Soon as I wrap this lightly, I'll go down an' bring up somethin' for this soldier to eat. You see that he eats it. Every little bite of it."

"I promise he'll eat it all if I have to feed it to him myself."

Etta finished her work then put the blankets back over Ross. Then she left to prepare the food. Valissa and Ross found themselves alone.

Valissa moved to the edge of the bed and sat beside him. "Etta will have your food up here soon." Her eyes softened as she looked into his face. She ran her fingers gently through his hair, smoothing the loose locks from his forehead. He looked into her eyes, then drew her close and softly kissed her. She didn't resist and returned his kiss eagerly. They finished with their foreheads together, their lips inches apart.

He felt the sudden flow of warm blood in his groin and the stiffness began to push up the blankets in his lap like a tent pole. She could feel the throb of it with each beat of his heart against her. She looked down at the rise in the blankets with amusement, her eyes twinkling with mischief. She drew back from him to look into his face. "Why, Ross Kimbrough, I do believe you *are* feeling better." She laughed lightly, a soft husky laugh. Ross blushed even brighter as he pulled her to him and kissed her again. They were still kissing when Etta walked through the open doorway.

"I guess he's feelin' better, the way you two are a carryin' on. Miss Valissa, you should be actin' more like a lady. Why, if you mother was to see this she'd skin your hide."

Valissa jerked away quickly and smoothed her dress. Then Etta set the tray of food down on a nightstand by the bed. "You best get your mind on eatin' and gettin' well—and off other things." She turned her back to Ross and faced Valissa. She winked and gave a quick smile to Val that Ross couldn't see. "You best see he eats this food now, Missy." Then she walked away from the room, smiling.

The next three days passed quickly and by the fourth Ross began moving around the house with the aid of the crutch. Ross was astonished that his illness had carried him through Christmas and past New Year's Eve. He had finally met Andrew and Mary Covington the day of his recovery.

On this fourth day after the fever had broken, Ross hobbled

into the family room. Andrew motioned for him to take a seat near the fire. "Care for some brandy?"

"Thank you very much, Mr. Covington. I'd enjoy a glass."

"Henry, get the lieutenant a glass of brandy."

"Yes, Massa Covington." The old black servant made his way to the brandy decanter, poured a glass of the brown liquid, then gave it to Ross.

"Thanks, Henry."

"Massa Covington, if there isn't anything else, I wonder if it be all right if I go on to bed. Arthritis surely is actin' up again."

"Yes, Henry, good night."

"Thank you, suh. I'll see you in the mornin'."

Andrew Covington puffed deeply on his large cigar. He leaned forward as he glanced away from the fire to look at Ross. "How's your leg?"

Ross had just finished his first sip of the brandy. As it slid down his throat it left a fiery path. His eyes watered a little as he spoke. "It's felt better, that's for sure. I think it's mending." He swirled the liquid in the glass.

"I suspect you're anxious to get back to your unit."

"Yes, I suppose in a way I am, but I also know I wouldn't be much of a scout the way I am now. I figure the war will still be there when I'm healed. Isn't any sense fighting it, just takes time to heal a would like this." He tipped the glass up for another sip. This one slid down easier than the first.

"Yes, I suppose you're right about the war. At times it seems there will be no end to it, that it will go on forever."

"It can't last forever. Sooner or later one side or the other will lose the ability or the will to fight. One side will prevail."

"It has to be our side. I'll be damned if I will live under the heel of the Northerners! They want to tell us how to live, force us to do things their way. By heaven I won't stand for it. If we lose this war I'd rather leave the country than admit defeat at their hands."

"The army is determined; I believe we have the will to win. Robert E. Lee has beaten them at every turn in the east."

Andrew took a puff on his cigar, then leaned forward on his chair. "I don't question the will of our fighting men—if only the government would just get out of the way. Seems at every turn they take our best fighting men out of Arkansas, Missouri, and Texas and ship them back east to fight. My son, Benjamin, is in the army of Tennessee with the bloody Seventh Arkansas Infantry. We lost our other son, Corey, at the battle of Shiloh in Tennessee. Still, it isn't enough for them. They stand around and scream for more. Don't those fools know how important the Trans-Mississippi region is to the Confederacy? Properly defended, with her own men and led by good commanders, we could win the war here in the west. Instead they send only the generals they want to get rid of to this area. Most are unfit for duty elsewhere."

Ross nodded in agreement. "I know when we lost the battle of Elkhorn Tavern they immediately took our entire army and shipped it to Tennessee to fight at Corinth. We should have gone to save Missouri! I didn't understand it then and I don't now. They just gave up on my state."

"It seems Missouri and even Arkansas is low on their list of priorities in Richmond." Andrew clamped down with his teeth on his cigar. "It's always seemed a strange thing to me. We left the Union for state's rights. Yet we are forced to endure the leadership of men in Richmond that give us little more say in our affairs than we had in the Union."

Ross quickly drank the remainder of the brandy in his glass, then set down the empty glass. "I believe we must fight together if we are to have any chance to survive, but I believe we can't abandon Missouri or Arkansas. If they would put Colonel Shelby in charge of the armies of the Trans-Mississippi and give him the power to mass his troops for an all-out attack on Missouri, the Yankees would be forced to forget their siege of Vicksburg. Problem is Richmond isn't aware of his ability to lead yet. I've ridden with him and I'll tell you this—his men would follow him to hell if he ordered it."

"We can only hope that some day someone in Richmond will wake up to the need for good leadership and decisive action in our region instead of abandoning us." Andrew sighed heavily. "All I know is that it's difficult just dealing with the problems of war in Arkansas when we meet in the state congress. God knows it keeps me busy enough."

"I believe General Hindman is a good general, and so are Marmaduke and Shelby. Problem is ole Granny Holmes is so old and afraid he won't let our field generals fight with a free hand. Just think what we could do if we had all the troops from Texas, Missouri, and Arkansas that are serving in Tennessee and Virginia back here to fight!"

"Yes, I've thought about it many times, but dreamin' won't make it so. We have to do the best with what we have. If we were just given a general the likes of Robert E. Lee or Stonewall Jackson things would be different."

Ross shifted in the chair as his wound began to throb. "I know we could drive the Yankees clean out of Missouri if we had that kind of leadership. I'm not saying Jo Shelby is as good a general as Lee and Jackson, but I'd match Colonel Shelby against any cavalry commander in the South."

Andrew looked doubtful. "Are you telling me you think Shelby is better than J. E. B. Stuart, Nathan Bedford Forrest, Joe Wheeler, or John Morgan?"

"Since I've never met or rode under any of those officers, it would be a tall claim to make. I honestly believe he is just as good as any of them and probably better than most. I think it is a hard thing to measure, but I know Jo knows how to use cavalry effectively. He knows when to dismount for a fight and when to ride fast and hard. I think he could surprise them all if he was turned loose in charge of a large cavalry command."

"He has won a solid reputation. Maybe someday he'll get his chance."

"Mr. Covington, I have enjoyed the conversation. I'm afraid though that this leg has sat in a chair long enough." Ross rose from the chair. "I think I'll turn in." He began walking with the aid of his crutch to the stairs. Over his shoulder he yelled, "Good night."

"Good night, Ross, I'll see you tomorrow."

44

Reunion

Jessie sat before the fireplace in the parlor. It was the most comfortable location in the house, and the place the family most often gathered at Covington Manor. Only the dining room—at meal time—was as popular. Jessie rested his feet on the footstool and felt the warmth of the fire as the heat soaked through the soles of his shoes. Next to him sat Andrew Covington in his comfortable, over-stuffed chair. His wife, Mary, rocked quietly next to him, working on some of her crocheting. Andrew was deeply involved with a book he held in his lap, lazing away the late afternoon on this winter day. Jessie didn't mind, for when Andrew was reading there was no need to keep up a conversation. Jessie could just enjoy the warmth of the fire and the comfort of his thoughts.

Jessie glanced up. Old Henry came shuffling into the room. "Massa Andrew, Massa Andrew, I have a young lady at the door, says she wants to talk to the massa of the house or Miss Valissa."

"Did she say what her name is, Henry?" Andrew asked.

"Yes, suh, she says her name is Cassandra Kimbrough. Should I show her in, suh?"

Jessie couldn't have been more stunned. He knew, as did Ross, the girls were heading south, but they hadn't heard a thing from them since they received the letters carried by Wash Mayes clear back at Cross Hollow's camp. Ross and Jessie had speculated that the girls probably would spend the winter in some town along the way. When the cold weather of December and January struck, both held little hope they would see the girls anytime soon.

Jessie sprung quickly to his feet. If Cassandra was here, then Katlin must be here too. He hurried toward the front door, not worrying or caring about waiting for Henry.

Over his shoulder he heard Andrew say to Henry, "Well, of course, show her in immediately. Oh . . . never mind, Henry. Looks like Jessie will see to it for you."

As he neared the door he spotted Cassandra. When he first entered the hall she had her back turned to him. She heard the sound of his steps and turned. Jessie watched with amusement as Cassie's jaw dropped in shock. Her face was quickly transformed by joy and tears came to her eyes. He rushed to her, sweeping his sister into his arms.

She held him close then said near his ear, "Jessie, my God, what are you doing here?" Not waiting for an answer she asked, "Are you all right?"

Jessie couldn't contain himself any longer as he began to turn her so he could look at the door. "Is Katlin with you? Is she all right?"

"Yes, she's out in the wagon. Lordy, is she going to be surprised when she sees you!"

"How is Mamma? Is she any better?"

Cassandra held him close. She hesitated, not knowing how to respond. Jessie sensed the words she could not bring herself to say. He pulled himself back to look into her eyes. "What's wrong with Mamma?"

A new host of tears came to Cassandra's eyes. "I'm sorry to have to be the one to tell you, Jess . . . Mamma is dead."

Jessie couldn't have been more stunned if he had been hit

in the face with a ten-pound sledge hammer. He spoke, not wanting to believe what he had heard. "She's dead? Mamma is dead? . . . What happened?"

"She was very sick with bronchial pneumonia, but she didn't die of it; well, not exactly. She got into one of her terrible coughing spells and passed out. She fell down a flight of stairs and broke her neck. She died quickly, she didn't suffer. The doctor didn't think she had much chance of recovering, Jessie. This was better for her, instead of dying slowly and in pain."

She grabbed him and pressed herself tightly against him again. She felt the sobs coming from deep within him as the pain of his loss came home. She let him have a few moments with his grief, then she said, "You didn't answer my question, Jessie. What are you doing here?"

She leaned away to see his face. She knew he would be unable to disguise his answer if she was looking in his eyes.

"I was slightly wounded during the battle of Prairie Grove. That was good in a way, because it allowed me to bring Ross here. Problem is, I need to return to my regiment now that I'm better."

"Ross is here?" She snapped out. "What's the matter with Ross?"

Jessie could see the fear in her eyes. "Nothing to worry about now. He was wounded in the thigh and the leg was broken, but the worst is over. He just needs a little more time to heal. He's upstairs resting."

Cassandra felt the need to reassure her brother. "Don't worry about making a speedy return to your regiment, Jessie. While we were staying at Judge Brandenburg's house in Jasper, Arkansas, we heard the news that General Marmaduke has taken his cavalry division to strike at Springfield in Missouri.

"We heard they intended to cut the supply lines of General Blunt so he can't stay in Arkansas. Colonel Shelby's brigade went with him. It will be some time before they return to Arkansas. It would be near impossible for a lone man to find his way to the brigade while they were operating in enemy territory. Just wait for them to return. No one would expect more of you."

"I guess you're right. Besides, I don't think there is any danger of the war ending before I fight some more." He strained to see out the window, but holding Cassandra made the task impossible. "Who do you have with you in the wagon?"

"I have Katlin, Elizabeth, Fanny, Jethro, and Becca with me."

"Becca—isn't that the girl that takes care of Katlin from Riverview Plantation?"

"That's the one."

More than anything else, Jesse wanted to see Katlin again. He pulled himself loose from Cassandra and rushed for the door. He yanked it open and hurried to the veranda. From there he could look down the steps to the wagon. He spotted her upturned face and was filled with joy. "Kat! Katlin," he yelled, racing down the stairs two at a time.

He could see the recognition on her face mixed with disbelief; then her expression changed to delight. Katlin screamed, "Jessie!" She jumped down from the wagon. She was delayed only a moment as her skirt caught on the seat. She tugged herself free and ran to him. She had only taken a couple of steps when Jessie reached her. She hopped into his arms and he swung her around once, carried by her momentum. His lips eagerly sought hers and they locked in a loving embrace.

Jessie pulled himself away to look at her. "I'd almost forgot how beautiful you are."

Katlin smiled, her eyes glistening with tears. "Oh Jessie, I've missed you so. I was so afraid I would never see you again."

"I wouldn't let anything happen, not when I have you waiting for me." He pulled the locket containing her picture from beneath his shirt. "I've worn this constantly since you gave it to me. I've had you with me every day, and whenever I've had the chance I've opened it to look at your picture. I know it must sound foolish, but I believe it protects me and brings me luck."

"It doesn't sound foolish. I gave it to you so you would remember me, and I prayed every day for God to watch over you." She paused and looked at him like she was trying to drink him into her soul. "I've wanted to be with you so much I was afraid to even hope you'd be here. I thought you'd be with the army." A look of puzzlement came across her face. "Why aren't you with the army, Jess?"

"Ross was wounded at the battle of Prairie Grove. I got permission to bring him here to heal."

A look of worry and concern appeared on her face. "How bad is it? Is he going to be all right?"

"He was extremely sick for a while. I thought we were going to lose him, but he's made it past the worst of it and just needs time to recover. He got shot in the thigh and had his leg broken when he was pinned under his horse."

"I'm anxious to see Ross." She looked hopeful. "Is Calvin here, too?"

"No, he's still with Colonel Shelby."

Elizabeth, Fanny, Jethro, and Becca had been watching the loving reunion of Jessie and Katlin. For Elizabeth it had been particularly hard to restrain herself from intruding on her brother. Now, as he began looking around at the others, she abandoned all restraint. "Jessie!"

Jessie turned toward his younger sister and waited with open arms and a broad smile as she ran to him. "Come here, Sis."

Liz buried her face into his chest as she gave her brother a big hug. "Oh, Jess, I've missed you so. The trip down here was so scary. I thought we would never get here."

"Well, you're here now. I can't believe how you've grown! I'll bet you're an inch taller than the last time I saw you, and you're starting to fill out. Like it or not, this trip has gone a long ways toward helping you grow up, if appearances mean anything."

Jessie let go of Elizabeth and stepped over to greet Fanny and Jethro, who stood smiling and waiting patiently.

"Fanny, I'm sure glad to see you. I've missed your cooking and those good ole hugs of yours."

Fanny grinned ear to ear. "Jessie, you ole sweet talker. You ain't changed one dang bit." She grabbed him and gave him a hug that nearly squeezed the air out of him. She let go after a few moments and stepped back to take a better look at him. "Land a Goshen, boy! If you ain't losin' weight. I 'spect what you need is some of Fanny's good cookin' to put some meat back on your bones. Ain't they feedin' you proper in the army?"

"They feed me when they can, Fanny, but they work most of it back off."

"I reckon they do at that." Fanny turned and motioned to Jethro. "Jessie, I want you to meet my husband, Jethro. After Cassie and your ma gave us our freedom we got married at Riverview."

"I know, Fanny, Cassie wrote and told me in a letter. I sure was happy to hear it." Jessie turned and gave Jethro a hardy handshake. "Jethro, I couldn't be happier. I was beginning to think you would never ask her."

Jethro smiled his shy smile. "Yessuh, Massa Jessie, I sure was glad she said yes."

"I can see married life has agreed with you." Jessie's look became more serious. "I want to thank you for seeing these ladies down here safely. You did a wonderful job and I'm proud of you." Jethro smiled and looked down at his feet.

Jessie could see that the big man was embarrassed by his comments, but he knew Jethro was touched deeply by his remarks.

"Thank you, suh, they didn't really need much help. This bunch of women can sure enough handle themselves. Every one of them done what had to be done when it came the time."

"Just the same, Jethro, thanks."

Fanny motioned to him. "This here is Becca, Jessie. She come along with Miss Katlin to help take care of her."

Jessie smiled at the girl. She was more reserved and shy than the girl he remembered. The Becca he knew was a vivacious young girl, high on life and anxious to experience it head-on. He remembered her at Riverview flirting with the young men as she tested her newfound charms. Harlan Thomas had always kept a watchful eye, and he had taken precautions that no one took advantage of her inexperience. He could tell there had been a change in her, but she still had those striking curves and good looks. "Hello, Becca, it's good to see you again." He paused. "You must have done an excellent job of taking care of Katlin for me."

Becca just nodded shyly. She leaned away from him and looked uncomfortable. He wondered if it was just him or if she was now shy around all men.

He pulled Katlin to him again and put his arm around her waist. "Come, I want to introduce you all to the Covingtons. I expect Ross will be anxious to see you. You'll probably have to visit him in his room. He tried to do too much yesterday and his wound started bleeding a little again. Valissa has confined him to bed for a few more days."

They all walked up the stairs and into the house where Andrew, Mary, and Valissa Covington waited for them in the parlor. Introductions went smoothly. Henry led Fanny, Jethro, and Becca to temporary quarters beyond the great house. For now, they would stay in the slave cabins.

It was apparent this group of visitors would severely overtax the accommodations at Covington Manor. Fortunately, Andrew Covington had a solution. "I suspect that since you will be in this area for an extended time you will feel more comfortable in a place of your own. A friend of mine, Joe Farnsworth, has a place not more than a mile up the road from here.

"He is involved in a shipping business. Before the war he owned a riverboat company that shipped cotton down the White River to the Mississippi, and all the way to New Orleans. When the war started he sold the riverboats and bought ships to carry cotton to England and Europe. I am a partner in Mister Farnsworth's shipping business and the last we heard Joe was living in England and involved with buying and equipping ships to run the blockade. When he left here, he asked me to look after his place until after the war. With this war going on and so many refugees and vagabonds swarming over the country it has been a constant fight to keep people from destroying his home.

"It's become more and more difficult to keep some of my people over there with so many of them running off to the Yankees. Half steal what they can before they go. I know Joseph Farnsworth would rather have someone of good character living there and looking after it for him. Would you consider moving in there and helping me take care of it?"

Cassandra was delighted. This was even better than she hoped, for she had been afraid they would be an imposition on the Covingtons. She didn't want to be a burden, especially not on strangers. Perhaps, in this way, they could even be of assistance. "It sounds absolutely delightful, Mr. Covington. Is it furnished?"

"Yes, it is. When Joseph left his home he took few items with him, other than his clothes. Traveling these days means you have to travel light. They need to load every bit of cotton they can get on board to sell in Europe, and I suppose he figured he'd need furniture in his home after the war."

"We would be pleased to accept your kind offer."

"Then it is done. I do have one request. Please call me Andrew. Mister Covington seems so formal."

Cassandra smiled. "It will be a pleasure, Andrew."

"It will take a few days for us to clean Farnsworth House. I hope you will stay with us for a few more days before you move in."

"We would be most grateful for your hospitality and the opportunity to get better acquainted with your family."

"Then it is settled. I have a neighbor that might have a good milk cow and some chickens for sale. With times getting as difficult as they are, you'll need them. It is nearly impossible to buy eggs and milk in town anymore," Andrew finished with disgust.

"Fresh eggs and milk would be a pleasure after this long journey, Andrew. We have the money we need to pay for them if he can spare the animals."

Etta walked into the parlor from the kitchen, and the conversation quieted. "Excuse me, Massa Andrew. How many people are we havin' for supper?"

Andrew paused to count the people present and those out of the room. "Seven at the dining table and Ross upstairs. You and Henry let Kimbrough's people eat with you in the kitchen."

"Yessuh." She turned and exited.

"Andrew, why don't you offer our guests a drink so they can relax," said Mary.

"Yes, of course, you're right, dear. Henry, please serve our guests."

Cassandra stood near the fireplace. "I'm sure the others would enjoy a drink." She motioned toward Katlin, Jessie, and Elizabeth. "I hope you won't think of me as being rude, but I haven't seen my brother, Ross, for a long time. I'm afraid there is some sad news he must know. If you'll excuse me?"

"I want to go too, Cassie," said Elizabeth.

"No, you wait here for a little bit. I have to tell him about Mother, then you can see him."

"Can I wait in the hall?"

"No, Liz, I promise I'll come get you after we talk. I just think it will be easier if I tell him first."

"I don't know why you always have to be in charge of everything," Elizabeth said belligerently.

"Because I'm older than you, that's why." Cassandra paused. "Please, Elizabeth, let's not argue in front of our hosts."

"Oh, all right, I'll wait," Elizabeth said more quietly.

Valissa got up from her chair. "I'll show you the way to Ross's room."

"Thank you very much, Valissa. I'm sure by now he's heard the commotion in the house and is wondering what is going on down here."

Valissa led the way as the two women made their way up the stairs. As much as Cassandra was anxious to see her brother again, she dreaded breaking the news to him of the death of their mother.

45

New Arrangements

Three days passed as Covington Manor adjusted to the strain of so many new houseguests. During those three days, work began on the final preparation of Farnsworth House for occupation by the Kimbroughs. Andrew took Jessie to purchase the milk cow and chickens.

Ross absorbed the shocking news of the death of his mother. He grieved hard for the first two days, but found solace in the reunion of his family. It was hard to stay too depressed with his attention distracted by his growing desire for Valissa.

Jessie also had to come to grips with his grief, but his was tempered by his passionate love for Katlin. The long separation and the uncertainty of war had made them desperate to cling to each other for whatever precious moments they might have. They spent long hours together, trying to find as much time alone as possible. Before the three days were over, Katlin and Jessie announced their plans for an immediate marriage as soon as the Kimbroughs could get settled in the Farnsworth House.

Etta stormed out of the kitchen on the third day and marched herself directly to Andrew Covington. Her face was twisted with anger, her forehead wrinkled. "Massa Andrew, I ain't much of one to complain, but you'se gotta do somethin' about that big ole nigger gal in my kitchen. She walked in here like she done owned the place. She's a sayin' how she does it this way and that when it comes to cookin'." Etta gestured wildly as she talked. "I told her this is my kitchen, and I ain't gonna let no nigger from Missouri walk in an' tell me how to cook. She can help with the washin' and the table settin' if she has a mind to, but I'm the cook around here! Can't you find somethin' else she could do?"

Andrew found it hard to stifle a growing desire to laugh. "I know this has been a difficult time for you, Etta. You've done a wonderful job running our kitchen and the house for years. I'm sure Fanny doesn't mean it as criticism when she offers her suggestions on cooking. I'm sure she just wants to help."

Etta looked puzzled at his comment. "What's this criticism mean, Massa Andrew?"

"It just means she wasn't finding anything wrong with the way you cook. She was just telling you other ways you can handle things. Some of them might even be better."

Anger flashed swift and sure in Etta's eyes. "That gal best not be sayin' I don't know how to cook. If I wanted to know anything from her, I'd ask."

Andrew began to loose patience with his slave's angry display of temper. What had been funny before was now becoming an irritation. He snapped back at her, "I expect you to control that temper of yours, Etta. She belongs to guests I have invited to stay in my home. She is a trusted cook and housekeeper for the Kimbroughs. I will not tolerate anymore outbursts on this matter, is that clear?"

"Yessuh." Etta was calmer now. The anger in her master overriding her own.

Andrew could see she wasn't happy about the circumstances, but she would keep it to herself. Andrew felt his anger soften. "I want you to treat them as you would want to be treated."

"Yessuh." She turned and moved to the kitchen sullenly.

Andrew could hear her muttering under her breath as she went. "Why, oh why, do I put up with her?" he asked himself. He knew the answer. For all her faults Etta ran a clean house, was one of the better cooks in the valley, and he respected her.

Epilogue

Cassandra strolled out onto Covington Manor's wide veranda and leaned her shoulder against a column. The sun felt warm against her skin and the brisk air of January gently caressed her. She gazed across the Arkansas landscape as she pondered the past and her future.

Her family had survived some horrible ordeals over the last year. Briarwood was gone, along with her mother and father, but they had survived against many odds on their journey south to Arkansas. They were enjoying a family reunion of sorts, and she knew they had much to be thankful for. Ross continued to recover from his wound. Jessie was already well, and he and Katlin were planning their wedding day. More good news arrived—they received a letter from Calvin and he was doing fine. So were Gilbert Thomas and Evan Stryker, the handsome Texan. She looked forward to seeing them all again.

Soon, the Kimbroughs would have a new place to live. A new place for a fresh start in an unfamiliar land. Hopefully, it would be a safe haven away from the fighting in Missouri.

Perhaps, when the war ended, they could return again to Missouri and rebuild Briarwood. She knew the war was far from over; there were many dangers on the horizon, and she feared what new tragedies might lie ahead. Still, Cassandra felt more confident than she had in a long time.

Cassandra's mood darkened, however, as she thought about the many wrongs of the past still left unsettled. She knew Major Benton Bartok, Captain Robert Anders, and their henchmen were continuing their reign of terror in Lafayette County. She worried about Harlan and Caroline Thomas, who had remained on their Riverview Plantation. She had many friends still at the mercy of the Yankees.

Already her brother Ross was contemplating revenge against the leaders of the Third Kansas Cavalry. She knew her family would never be at peace until the score was settled and Major Bartok was dead.

Her brothers had told her about William Clarke Quantrill's men and how fearsome the young boys were in battle. While Captain Quantrill was off to Richmond, Virginia, seeking a promotion, his men were honing their war skills under the tutelage of Colonel Jo Shelby's Iron Brigade. When spring arrived she felt confident Quantrill's bushwackers would head north to exact revenge against the Jayhawkers plundering and murdering across Missouri. Quantrill's men were fueled by a hatred born from murder and wrongdoings committed by the Kansas Jayhawkers and Red Legs, now riding under the banner of the United States army. From what she had heard, they would not rest until scores were settled.

Thoughts of Becca's rape and rescue came flooding back to her. The rape had made a profound impact on Becca. They were all changed since those carefree days at Riverview and Briarwood. She again marveled at how satisfying it had been to kill the leader of the Yankee deserters. She had an inner strength now, knowing she could kill again if need be to defend herself, her family, or her friends. The awareness of her ability to protect herself gave her a feeling of confidence.

Through it all, she was grateful for the companionship of Jethro and Fanny. Their marriage was one of the highlights that was buried among so much of the tragedy that had occurred over the last few months.

Cassandra's thoughts turned inward. She knew she was captivated by the young Texan, Captain Evan Stryker. Their romance had blossomed early and held promise. She was ready to fall hopelessly in love with him.

. She recalled with a blush of her cheeks the powerful attraction she had felt for Major Kenton Doyle of the Second Wisconsin Cavalry of the Union army. He had helped her despite her bitter attitude and guided her through Union lines, but she couldn't forget the color of his uniform. She must not forget he was fighting for the enemies who had done so much to her and her family. If not for the war, things might have been different for the two of them. She wondered if their paths would cross again in the future.

Cassandra sighed deeply. The future held danger. The dark clouds of war still swirled about them. But the future also held promise.

The Kimbrough family saga continues in Book Two, *Kansas, Bloody, Kansas*.

About the Author

When you talk to Randal L. Greenwood, his lifelong love for American history comes shining through. Since he was in the fifth grade he has been fascinated with the American Civil War and Western history. "My mother's family were Missouri Confederates and all my ancestors on my father's side were Union veterans. For some reason the Rebel in me has always ruled my heart."

Randy has lived most of his life in Hugoton, Kansas, in the southwest corner of the state. He received his B.S. in History from Kansas State University in 1972.

"I've been a full-time professional photographer since 1978. Photography offers a visual creativity to my life, while writing gives me other outlets to express myself. I feel photography helps me visualize." Randy is married to Rebecca Richmeier Greenwood and is the father of three children, Evan, Amber, and Ciara.

His interests include collecting Civil War, Western history, and World War II European theater air-war books and novels. "My favorite hobby is watching and following Winston Cup stock car racing. I collect the diecast and cards. These guys are my heroes, and I follow them like others track baseball or football teams." His other interests include playing paintball, and watching boxing, horse racing, and movies.